DOG PARK

DOG PARK

SOFI OKSANEN

Translated by Owen F. Witesman

ALFRED A. KNOPF NEW YORK 2021

THIS IS A BORZOI BOOK
PUBLISHED BY ALFRED A. KNOPF

English translation copyright © 2021 by Owen F. Witesman

All rights reserved. Published in the United States by Alfred A. Knopf,
a division of Penguin Random House LLC, New York, and distributed in Canada
by Penguin Random House Canada Limited, Toronto. Originally published in
Finland as *Koirapuisto* by Like Kustannus Oy Helsinki, in 2019. Copyright © 2019
by Sofi Oksanen. Published by arrangement with Salomonsson Agency.

www.aaknopf.com

Knopf, Borzoi Books, and the colophon are registered
trademarks of Penguin Random House LLC.

Library of Congress Cataloging-in-Publication Data
Names: Oksanen, Sofi, [date] author. | Witesman, Owen, translator.
Title: Dog park / Sofi Oksanen ; translated by Owen F. Witesman.
Other titles: Koirapuisto. English
Description: New York : Alfred A. Knopf, 2021.
Identifiers: LCCN 2021001350 (print) | LCCN 2021001351 (ebook) |
ISBN 9780525659471 (hardcover) | ISBN 9780525659488 (ebook)
Classification: LCC PH356.O37 K6513 2021 (print) | LCC PH356.O37 (ebook) |
DDC 894/.54134—dc23
LC record available at https://lccn.loc.gov/2021001350
LC ebook record available at https://lccn.loc.gov/2021001351

Jacket photograph by Alfonse Pagano / Getty Images
Jacket design by Jenny Carrow

Manufactured in the United States of America
First United States Edition

A glossary of terms is provided at the end
of the novel for the reader's reference.

DOG PARK

HELSINKI
2016

Perhaps everything would have gone differently if I'd recognized her immediately and known to flee. But I didn't; I didn't even turn my head when the stranger sat down at the end of the bench, a pained slowness to her movements. Hoping she would understand that I wasn't looking for conversation, I loudly rustled the pages of the book in my lap. I wasn't in this park looking for company.

The book belonged to the library just a stone's throw from the park and its fenced dog run. Carrying a bag bulging with novels made my stops at the park look natural. Whenever anyone happened to ask, I told them how much I liked animals and watching them play but that I couldn't keep a pet of my own because of allergies. The woman sitting next to me didn't have a dog either, I noticed, but otherwise my attention was focused on the street surrounding the park. Furtively I glanced at my watch, although I knew I was on time. I was afraid I'd come for nothing.

The woman extended her legs and stretched, as people often do when considering how to initiate conversation—a yawn, a straightening of a jacket, or a hand gesture laying the foundation for comments about the weather or other trivialities. However, there weren't any questions about my book or any platitudes about the temperature.

Sliding to the other end of the bench, I increased my distance from the interloper. Recently I'd begun paying a different sort of attention to the others idling in the park. The retirees and unemployed people strolling here just needed an excuse to get out. Perhaps someday I would be like that, after I no longer had any reason to visit the park or any kind of schedule to my life. Then I too would want my neighbors to hear the bang of my front door as a sign that I was busy and had friends to visit, and then I would come here to be part of the world by watching other people's lives.

A white miniature schnauzer approaching the dog park received admiring glances from passersby. My companion on the bench perked up. As she leaned forward slightly, I expected her to finally work up the courage to say something, maybe about the schnauzer's grooming or its exemplary obedience, but the woman remained silent.

I

Invisible

A VILLAGE,
MYKOLAIV OBLAST
2006

When I entered the bedroom for the first time since childhood, I recoiled at the sight I encountered. Framed pictures of me graced the table, the chest of drawers, and the wall. For the most part they were yellowed advertisements cut from newspapers, showing me using my curves to peddle everything from stain removers to car parts. I'd sent the pictures to my mother as proof of my modeling work, assuming they would end up in a scrapbook, but Mom had turned them into a full-room shrine with eye-catching splashes of color and mark-down percentages competing for attention. There was nothing in these pictures to celebrate, let alone remember with pride. They made me ill.

After removing the clippings from the walls, I swept the pictures on the chest of drawers into my arms and shoved the whole lot into the closet. On top of the pile lay a yarn ad featuring skeins that glowed with all the colors of a crackling fire.

By suppertime, the pictures were back in their places—even the chestnut puree ad, which I despised. My mother's swiftness astonished me. She had managed it while I was outside inspecting the garden with my aunt. When my aunt entered the bedroom, she put a hand on my back and whispered that I shouldn't deny a mother the right to be proud of her children. I couldn't tell her how wrong everything had gone. My aunt looked at me and gave me a squeeze.

"We're expanding the plantings, and Ivan is helping, so we're fine," she said. "I'm so glad we have you home again, Olenka."

My aunt had aged, as had my mother. The dog standing guard in the yard was new. Otherwise nothing had changed since I left. A stork's nest still sat on top of the electric pole, though the birds had already flown south, and there were still dead men's jackets hanging next to the front door. One was my father's, and the other belonged to his sister's deceased husband. According to my aunt, it was good for visitors to think we had men in the house. We'd moved in with her after my father's funeral, and now I had returned to this house of lonely widows where we gave each other flowers on Women's Day. That thought made me ask my aunt whether Boris was still making his *horilka*. As she fetched a bottle, I finally changed my shoes for galoshes. They were new and lightweight, maybe silicone. Bought for me, presumably.

The next morning, I walked to the bus stop and looked to see what was visible through the cracks in the garden fence and over it from farther down the road. There was nothing to attract attention, and no one would come to inspect this plot of land by chance. The situation might be different once the flowers were blazing red. But my aunt was right, we would need more poppies. I was an extra mouth to feed, and the previous evening I had already ordered us some thirty-liter canisters of drinking water. Abroad I'd become accustomed to drinking water constantly and had completely forgotten the state of the wells here. I didn't know how I would pay for my order. I would have to abandon the way we models keep our weight in check. A thicker waist was the least of my worries.

I didn't want my aunt to seize on Ivan's suggestions—to borrow money from him and not to increase the size of the poppy fields— even though I trusted him and his desire to help. A tall field of corn could conceal even a large flower planting, and our hired hand, Boris, could handle the expansion. He was Ivan's brother and like a son to my aunt. Still, I didn't want us any more dependent on the gang

Ivan worked for and to whom he delivered the compote derived from the poppies. I hadn't planned a future like this for us. We wouldn't even be talking about poppies if my face had paid off. We would have closed the compote kitchen, and I would have built my aunt a new house in place of the old one or bought an apartment in the city. They never would have needed to worry about every sign of instability that might affect their already insufficient pension payments.

I'd claimed that homesickness had brought me back. I don't know who believed that, though. I hadn't been able to send money for years. I had to fix this situation. I had to find work.

I began to visit the city to look for job postings. Often a bevy of girls brimming with hope and emitting clouds of perfume rode the same bus to the Palace, where bride shows were held for foreign bachelors in the conference rooms. As their destination approached, the girls with short hair would add more hairspray, and the girls with longer locks would grab their brushes, whose strokes fell in time with the rhythmic clinking of lipstick tubes, powder cases, and pocket mirrors. I'd spent years in back rooms full of similar dreams of bright futures; only the scent cloud on this bus also contained the stench of rancid rouge. The girl sitting behind me was powdering her cheeks with a puff that hadn't been washed in years, and many of the girls' dresses featured patterns familiar from the pelts of wild cats. I listened to their conversations and wondered whether I'd have to try my luck the same way, even though I knew none of us was any more likely to find Prince Charming abroad than here. These girls didn't know that yet, though, and their excited voices reminded me of my own escape to Paris. I'd been nervous, too, and afraid that I might do something wrong. I'd also wanted more than my home could offer. I knew this road.

Once we arrived, the flock of girls fluttered out, leaving the smell of old cosmetics and young hair as they click-clacked arm in arm toward the hotel. Business was clearly booming, and that made me think of something that might help.

· · ·

On the way to the Internet café, I stopped to inspect the weathered flyers attached to the electric poles, trying to pick out any companies that seemed like bride agencies. If I couldn't find the solicitations I was looking for on the poles, power boxes, or phone booth walls—or online—I would have to waste money on newspapers and go through their help-wanted pages.

But I was in luck.

The agencies weren't looking only for brides, they also needed multilingual women to work as interpreters. I tore off all the phone number flaps fluttering at the bottom of one flyer. Then, after a moment's consideration, I removed the entire leaflet from the pole, as well as a couple of others, to reduce my competition. I decided to begin my calls that day. I couldn't fail. I was more than qualified. Hope bloomed like a flower, the brushes of its petals on my cheeks restoring the self-confidence I'd lost.

I landed an interview the next day, but I didn't get the job. Instead of giving up, I simply swung my hair and arranged another. The mood of the girls racing to the city on the bus was infectious, and there was no shortage of bride agencies. There were three on Lenin Prospekt alone, as well as on Sovetskaya and Moskovskaya. I would get to know the industry, save what I could, and maybe someday manage to set up my own business—perhaps one that would offer tips for winning the hearts of Ukrainian women, helping to choose personal gifts for one's ladylove. We would remind men that a gentleman should bring flowers, offer his arm, open doors, and help his date out of the car. Or maybe I could search for faces suitable for Western magazines and open a modeling school in one of the many million-plus cities of Siberia, where nationalities had blended in unique combinations because of the camps. I always used to lose out to those girls, with blood from every corner of the Soviet Union—Eastern Europe, the Baltics, Asia, many of the indigenous peoples. However, a plan like this required capital, and that I did not yet have. Soon I would, though.

I was on my way to the bus station when a vaguely familiar girl ran after me. Greeting me, she said she'd seen me in the queues at the bride agencies. She had also been trying her luck there. Today she'd applied as a bride at the same agency where she'd also applied for a secretarial position.

"At least it doesn't cost anything," she said. "You should do it, too."

"I don't know."

I dug out of my bag the ads I'd been collecting, to ask her for tips about the different companies, but before I could ask my questions, she shook her head.

"Don't bother."

"What do you mean?"

Then I listed the languages that I spoke at least passably. I knew English, French, Russian, Ukrainian, Estonian, German, and even a little Finnish. Foreign words had always stuck in my head easily. I was probably the most linguistically talented woman in the whole oblast, where there was even a shortage of English speakers.

"You'll find a husband in no time."

"I don't want to get married. I want to be an interpreter. Or maybe a visa agent."

The girl laughed and pulled her boots up toward her thighs. Her skirt was short. I realized I had dressed wrong for today. I should have been showing off my other assets.

"My cousin's friend is an assistant at a company that was just looking for an interpreter. She told me who got the job," the girl said. "Some girl who's dating the boss's son."

Looking up at the tangled web of trolleybus wires, I wished for a drink. Nothing ever changed in this country.

"And yet you keep going to interviews."

"You have to try everything. Maybe the owner's son will drop by the office while I'm there and fall in love with me. That's how my cousin's friend got her job, too."

The girl fluffed her hair and gave me a wink. Pulling a pack of slim cigarettes out of my bag, I offered one to her. I was anxious at the thought of returning to that room contaminated by all those ads with my picture in them. I suspected I'd have to live there longer than anticipated. My aunt had called all her acquaintances, as had my mother and Ivan. Everyone promised to tell us immediately if they heard about a suitable job. No one had gotten back to us yet, though.

"You can make a good living in travel documents. You could set up your own visa agency," the girl said, "but for that you need connections and a fat wallet. I have a better idea."

"Okay, spill it."

"They need pretty faces at protests. You get paid right then, and they take everyone who wants to do it."

I vaguely remembered my mother mentioning this. After the Orange Revolution, ads had begun appearing on the electric poles seeking participants for demonstrations. The nature of the events always remained unclear. But the pay was the most important piece of bait, and they always mentioned that.

"My brother makes a little in the screamers."

I frowned.

"You haven't heard of them? The work is almost the same as marching in protests but louder, and they have to rehearse. Actually, it's more for men. You have a boyfriend, don't you?"

I shook my head.

"Then come with me to carry banners. Sometimes the bus rides are long, and I could use the company. Call me if you're interested."

The girl rummaged in her pocket for a ripped ad, wrote her phone number on the back, and handed it to me. My throat tightened. I would have liked to invite her for coffee and cognac, but she was in a hurry to pick up her child from day care, and her *marshrutka* was around the corner and would leave as soon as the seats in the van were full.

At home a mood of panic greeted me. Boris sat rocking in the corner, his hands covering his head. My mother and aunt were still in their funeral clothes, which they'd put on that morning to travel to the burial of a distant relative. I thought something must have happened at the funeral, until I found out what was wrong. The compote kitchen was empty. Even the television was gone. We'd been robbed. The house had been left unguarded for just a moment before Boris came to work, and that had been a mistake.

I wasn't worried about the thieves. Ivan would track them down and make sure they understood they had touched the wrong people, knocked out the wrong people's dog. That wouldn't bring the compote back, though. I remembered the love with which Boris had watched over the poppies' darkening pods, how well he'd cared for them and his kitchen. The robbers had taken the best stuff in the oblast. Nothing remained.

The ad on the electric pole wasn't the only weathered notice seeking beautiful girls, but it was the first one that said directly it was not an escort service, a bar, or a bride agency. It also expressed a warm welcome to young mothers, as well as married women. That caught my attention. I realized it could be just another way of luring in fresh meat. However, I was getting desperate and was sick of all the headlines asking, "Why should a beautiful girl be poor?" The job interviews had not borne fruit. My aunt had already talked to Ivan about the lost compote and the possibility of a loan. But I didn't want to go down that road. My family's plight was a result of my failed career. It was my fault, and I had to fix it.

The ad hinted at significant lump-sum payments, and only one phone number tab remained at the bottom of the paper.

The woman who answered the phone became excited when I told her about my years as a model. In the background, I could hear the tapping of a keyboard as she searched my name. I hoped the browser would take her to my old agency's site. My pictures were still there. I'd looked at them a couple of times on the computer at the café. I didn't know why. It was as if I wanted to torment myself or needed courage to present myself more confidently in the interviews.

"When can you come visit us?"

"Wait a moment, I'll check my calendar."

I was standing on Lenin Prospekt, outside a bride agency called Royal Relationship. Next up, on Moskovskaya, Arrows of Amor and, next to Hotel Metallurg, the Slavess. Also, disintegrating in my bag was the phone number of the girl who worked as a protester. Quite a lineup. I started walking back to the bus stop and tossed the girl's contact information into the street. The office was located in Dnipropetrovsk, so the journey would take time. Still, I was ready to jump on a train at a moment's notice.

"It would be nice if you could bring a picture of yourself, and maybe also of your family—parents, grandparents, aunts, uncles, cousins," the woman said. "The more, the better. We want to know our employees, who you really are and what your strengths are."

"What kinds of pictures?"

"Anything. A picture is worth a thousand words," the woman said with a laugh. "The director is coming from Kyiv next Monday on the evening flight and will have to return on Wednesday."

I banged my toe on a raised paving stone. Was this company doing so well that its director flew between Kyiv and Dnipro? Only ministers of parliament and top businessmen did that—people with money to burn. Was I really going to have a face-to-face meeting with such a person? Or was this woman trying to make an impression on me, make it clear they were a boutique operation? My hand instinctively went to my hair. My roots were showing. At my aunt's house, we only had a summer shower. Washing out hair dye under it was difficult, so I'd have to go to a hairdresser.

"The director's schedule next week is very busy in Kyiv but more relaxed here. So, will meeting on our premises work for you? If you send your account number, we'll transfer money for a train ticket. Will an SW-class carriage be acceptable?"

I managed to reply in the affirmative and hoped that the interruptions in my breathing weren't audible on the other side of the line. The stink of coal in trains nauseated me, so a ticket in a two-person cabin was a pleasant surprise. But something didn't add up. I'd found this ad on an electric pole, not in the newspaper or online or even in a marshrutka. I'd found it in a place they didn't have to pay for, not where successful companies advertised. How did the director of a company like that have the money to fly between Dnipro and Kyiv, and how did a company like that have the resources to buy a job applicant an expensive train ticket simply for an interview? I didn't understand the rush any more than the scope of the request for photographs, let alone what the job actually was. The woman's enthusiasm made me suspect organ donation, though I didn't get what that had to do with my family photos. But what did it matter? The pay was the thing. The woman continued chattering, saying something about the gift of life, and then returned to the travel arrangements. I decided that I could give up one kidney. One was enough to get by. And half a liver. They would pay even more for that.

I didn't share my suspicions with anyone. The excuse I came up with for my trip to Dnipro was an interpreting job, and that lit a spark in my mother's eyes. She began to stride back and forth in the kitchen, her back straight and her cheeks shining like the side of a brand-new bus, as if wanting to tell everyone the good news, even though the audience was only my aunt. I didn't want to worry them. They wouldn't know so much as my job description until I'd been promoted to coordinator.

HELSINKI
2016

My heart leaped in my chest when the father followed the mother and the dog into the park. Both children were also with them. The boy, who trailed the others, looked animated as he rooted in his quickly dwindling bag of raisins; I nodded almost unconsciously at the family's healthy snack habits. Last week I hadn't seen the children and blamed a bout of the stomach flu that had been going around. Now all of them appeared healthy. To look at her, you wouldn't have believed the woman had been sitting up nights at her children's bedsides, and she'd even managed to go shopping: her new sandy-brown trench coat would have looked good on me, too, and the girl had a scarf I hadn't seen before. When his phone rang, the man answered it and smiled at his wife as if apologizing. The woman brushed his arm and pressed her head against his shoulder for a moment. Even the mad dash of their schnauzer when they let it free was a flawless performance. Its rare white coloration attracted attention; at dog shows, it always won. For a moment, I admired the dog as it ran and the watchful posture it adopted when it stopped after noticing something interesting in the distance. The boy hung back at the gate. After shaking the final raisins from the bag, instead of throwing it on the ground, he placed it in a trash can. He'd been raised well and had the same good manners I would have taught a child.

The clank of a lighter interrupted my observations. The woman who had sat down next to me lit a cigarette. Glancing at her irritably, I just had time to recognize the familiar floral pattern on her slim cigarette pack before I returned my focus to the family disappearing behind the rocky hill. My companion was not Finnish—Glamour cigarettes were not a local taste.

"In America they called us angels. Is that where you learned it?"

I wasn't sure if I'd heard correctly or if my mind was playing tricks on me. My gaze was still focused on the family, my chin raised. I didn't dare turn my head and confirm what I'd heard. The woman continued, and the longer she went on, the surer I became that this wasn't a hallucination. I knew her, and she knew me, and we were both sitting on this bench in this Helsinki park as if the years hadn't passed between us. Word by word she dislodged one stone after another of the foundation I'd carefully built for my life. I had never imagined that it would happen this way. That it would begin with these dulcet descriptors she tossed into the air like Lomonosov porcelain teacups, watching whether I'd remember what she was talking about. Whether I'd remember that, years ago, I'd been the one to use words like these to lure girls to work for us and that I'd also used them on her. But of course I remembered. I remembered every trip wire in every saccharine adjective, and each of them bent my shoulders lower, as if that might help me disappear from this bench. Syllable by syllable, I felt myself shrinking.

"But you always managed to find the girls who no one ever praised. They were exactly what you were looking for."

"You weren't like that."

"Many were."

She smacked her lips and stretched out her arms like a ballerina.

"How did it go?" she asked. "*Swan Lake.* My arms reminded you of *Swan Lake.* Was that it?"

"They still do."

She laughed, her windbreaker rustling, and I saw that familiar wing motion. I was fond of her controlled way of moving. With each step, her foot met the ground as if an auditorium full of people was looking on.

When we took the pictures for this woman's portfolio—she was just a girl at the time—she had done splits in the dress I chose. Even though she was only warming up for the actual photo shoot, there was something unforgettably intimate in the combination: the floral swing dress, the rehearsal room, the flexible ankles. It was as if she had forgotten the photographer. The makeup artist had spent an hour with her brushes on the girl's face, but you never would have guessed. When I saw the finished folder, I'd known that Daria would become my star and that she would make me a star.

Daria stood up and started walking toward the gate of the dog enclosure. I'd recovered from my shock enough to realize what this meant. Meter by meter she was approaching the family, and meter by meter images began to pop into my mind of what would happen when the father recognized her. First, he would be shocked, and then he would take out his phone. The mother would start to scream, the dog would go wild, the girl would burst into tears, and the boy would stare at us, wondering at the cause of the mayhem, and when the mother dragged her children to safety as the police sirens approached, the boy would look back, and the sight of the ragged women who had sent his parents out of their minds would be burned forever into his memory.

The family had split up during our conversation, and Daria stopped for a moment as if considering which one to approach first. The father held the little girl by the hand, and they were going after the dog, which was out of sight, while the mother's attention had been captured by a golden retriever puppy, whose owner was chatting with her. The boy was hanging around by the street. Daria tilted her head, made her decision, and opened the dog gate. Only ten meters of rocky ground remained between her and the mother. I would be exposed in an instant; I would lose everything I had succeeded in building over the past six years. I would lose my entire new life in Helsinki. My future would be numbered in days, perhaps in hours.

I turned my eyes skyward. My mother believed in God and the saints, but I did not. Still, I raised my scarf to cover my head as if I were in a church and muttered something that could have been a prayer, and it was that simple movement of covering my head that woke me up to the fact that I still had two functional legs. I had to stop Daria.

The schnauzer shot out from behind the hill with a terrier on its heels, and the pets' wild play captured the family's attention. They didn't see my swaying steps or how I nearly tripped on my scarf and people moved to avoid me as if I were drunk. Daria was only a few meters away from the woman and was already opening her mouth.

"Do you want money? Is that what this is about?"

I'd made it in time after all. The corners of Daria's mouth curved into a smile. The mother's back receded. The dogs were back under control. Leash hooks snapped shut around collar rings.

For a moment I thought Daria would laugh and say something about my clothes and how little my appearance bespoke affluence, but instead she froze in place and didn't try to pull out of my grip.

"How much would you give me?"

I followed her gaze. The family was preparing to leave the park. The mother adjusted the girl's coat, and then her daughter threw her arms around her mother's neck. Daria flinched as if she'd been hit. I felt a tremor in her bony arm. What if she wasn't in the park to blackmail me or this family? But everything about her argued for the assumption that she needed money. She'd lost weight, and her clothes hung off her. They were rags, the faux leather of her boots flaking and her shoulder bag gaping open to reveal tears in the lining that had been repaired with tape. Daria had made good money. Where had she squandered her earnings? Had someone taken her savings, or had she gotten tangled up with the wrong man? Had she used it to help her family? Had she used everything to get them out of eastern Ukraine and away from the war? Hadn't the money been enough to build a new life? Or had she wasted it earlier and now had to get her hands on more cash to help the family members she'd left behind? According to my mother, the Donetsk People's Republic had taken some people's homes while offering others a path to riches because the refugees had left behind so much wealth. Some joined the separatist forces voluntarily, while others were press-ganged, and deserters were shot. Some joined because otherwise their homes and possessions would be confiscated, and their loved ones would be left destitute. Could Daria's arrival be related to that? What if the separatists had forced one of Daria's two brothers into their ranks and he wanted to get off the front? Or what if one of her relatives had been kidnapped? Daria watched the park until the family disappeared from view, and her gaze went dark like a candle burning out. I took a deep breath. I'd received a reprieve.

"You won't get a penny from me if we're recognized."

"Did they recognize you?" Mockery flickered on Daria's mouth, and she licked away a drop of blood that had appeared. Her lips were dry and cracked.

"Yeah," Daria snorted. "They don't remember you any more than me. You're just as unique to them as I was to you."

I had called Daria unique. The most unique. I had praised her bone structure and her language skills, her IQ and her gymnastics background. Her smile had been as cloudless as the Texas sky and her chin like a shining mother-of-pearl caviar spoon.

"I was convinced you wouldn't remember me even if I said my name when I sat down next to you that first time," Daria said. "You weren't expecting me to find you before anyone else, were you?"

I remembered how once as a child I'd been separated from my father in a tunnel. Dad had found me within seconds, but I'd already had time to worry that I would never see him again and that something unimaginable would attack me from under the wall formed by the crowd's dark winter coats. Now I felt that again. Except that no one would save me. No one but me. I would have to try to figure out myself what was going on.

"Can we at least talk about this somewhere else?" I asked and looked at my hands. The blood had left my fingertips.

DNIPROPETROVSK

2006

The director of the company spread out on the table the stack of family photographs I'd brought. I hadn't prepared, and never would have suspected that I'd have to review the photos in the actual job interview. I hadn't seen any pictures of my father in years.

"Are you all right?" the woman asked, which was when I realized that I'd covered my mouth with my hand.

"I just miss him," I said, taking the proffered handkerchief. This sentimentality surprised even me. I was embarrassed. Why hadn't I prepared for this better? I'd made my mother collect the photos, claiming that when I was abroad, I'd wished I'd had a family album. Mom probably thought I was planning to move. She tried to ask me about it, but I quickly shoved the photographs in my bag and slipped out. I trusted that my mother wouldn't choose anything that would distress her daughter. Like funeral pictures. At least I didn't see any of those in front of me.

"Your father died in some sort of accident . . . was that it?"

The director spent another moment inspecting the photographs like a bad hand of cards, then she went to a cupboard to retrieve a bottle and two glasses, along with a box of chocolates. Focusing on the weight of the crystal in my hand and the cognac burning away the tightness that had formed in my throat, I ordered myself to get it together. I'd screwed up: I hadn't given a thought to how my father would look to a stranger's eyes. When he died, I was fourteen, and it felt like I was fourteen again, at the mine where my dad had taken me. In the topmost shot, a group of men who had just finished their shift were smoking, bright sparks burning in their black fingers. In the background was the old bathtub used to hoist them out of the hole. Someone sat unwrapping his toe-rags and grinning with a row of shining teeth. They all looked the same under a layer of coal dust, except for my father, his face gleaming clean in the center like a full moon—he was the only one lacking the third eye of a headlamp.

There was another photo from the same time. In it, my father stood next to a man I didn't recognize, who wore a leather jacket. The smiles of a deal well done caressed their cheeks. Behind them stood two vans, Bukhankas, and amid all the gray, black, and brown gleamed a chaffinch egg–blue ZiL truck.

In the most recent photo, my father had a couple of days of stubble and wore only a sleeveless undershirt. Its yellowed piping hung slack. In his fingers lolled a cigarette in a holder, and his elbows rested on the kitchen table. On the windowsill, tomato seedlings in need of thinning grew wild, the sticks holding them up bent and helpless. Between an open bottle of pickles and an enamel bowl filled to overflowing with boiled potatoes stood an unlabeled vodka bottle. The mood was despondent, the heavy glass ashtray barely visible under the mound of ashes, the matchbox empty. There were three glasses but no sign of visitors. I recognized the waxed tablecloth and the wall of our house, its canned pea–green color. I couldn't figure out who had taken the picture or why. Where was the father I remembered with the manner of an owner and the nonchalance of a moneymaker? The man in this picture was tired, sties and life weighing down his gaze. No sign of his youthful good looks remained, not even a hint.

The director pushed the pictures back.

"Your mother is good proof that being photogenic is something you inherit, as was your father when he was younger. What happened after that? And what about Snizhne!"

"We didn't actually live there."

"Your résumé says that you went to school there."

"Only for a little while."

"But your father was from Snizhne, as were his parents. Why on earth did you move there? From Tallinn, in the nineties no less?"

The director shook her head. This clearly made her doubt the intellectual gifts of my family, as it did me. It had been stupid then, and I was still paying for it. Leaving my aunt's house no longer seemed likely. I hadn't been able to prepare mentally for the job I was applying for because I didn't know what it entailed. However, as the interview progressed, I began to understand what was going on and why Snizhne mattered.

"Your chest X-rays," the director said. "What do they show?"

I frowned in confusion, though I already sensed what she meant. My father stared back at me from the table. He had developed the early pictures of himself, and their edges curled like birch bark. Some of the shots had triangular brackets still stuck to them from where my mother had removed them from her own photo album.

"Once we had a client who was a Ukrainian-American environmental researcher who wanted a donor from her family's home region in Donbas, Stakhanov, right next door to Snizhne," the director said. "In the end he changed his mind and chose a girl from the least polluted oblast in the Soviet Union—not in Ukraine. He wanted to avoid risky material. Some Western clients are extremely environmentally conscious. If they start doing searches about Snizhne, the results won't be good. Want to try it yourself?"

The display of the desktop computer rotated toward me.

"Look."

The director typed in a few words, and the screen flooded with views that would startle anyone. Just like those final photos of my dad.

"Our office specializes in serving foreigners, and images like this don't give a good first impression. They arouse suspicions that our girls are motivated by money rather than the calling. Snizhne comes across as a poor, desperate city."

I was already halfway out of my chair when the director started to talk about the agency's future prospects. Apparently, the interview wasn't over yet. She had just wanted to put me in my place by making clear the factors that reduced my market value. Now, instead of presenting more harsh realities, it was time for a relaxed account of how the director had begun her business in the great cities of the

Soviet Union, Dnipropetrovsk and Kharkiv, where she had found skilled workers eager for jobs because the collapse of the empire also meant a crash in specialist employment. Her plans had been received with joy, delighting even the ordinary person on the street—because of her, the entire medical profession had not vanished into the West. Listening to her, my interest in the job began to grow beyond the pay. I was fascinated by this woman, by her talent, which it was impossible not to admire, and by her ability to seize the opportunities she encountered. It was in that moment that my faith in her was born. I wanted to be like her.

"Did you know that the first test-tube baby in the CIS was born in Kharkiv? Our medical staff and researchers are world class. But do you think that's enough for Western clients? Of course not. So, we have to change the way we work," she said. "They ask about groundwater, pollution, problems from the mines and their hereditary impacts. On the other hand, we don't have to build bomb shelters for the nitrogen tanks, like we did for the Russians. In our Kyiv office we don't need anything like that, because there our new clientele is made up mainly of Westerners, and they're our primary target group."

I considered how I could improve my position.

"You would probably get pretty good image search results for Dnipro," I suggested cautiously. "This is a great city and always has been."

I was still afraid that my years in Snizhne might show in any blood tests, chest X-rays, or other tests I knew nothing about, and this job might remain a dream. There was no rational basis for this fear—I just didn't have time to think the matter through. The coordinator I'd spoken with on the phone had gushed about my pictures. I'd thought I might be paid immediately and would return to the countryside in triumph, just to tell my mother that they wouldn't need a loan from Ivan. My options were limited. I could look for a man with an open wallet, but that would take time, and I'd already had enough of Western jackasses during my years as a model. Then I remembered dimly that I might know something that could increase my value. Something that would make this woman understand that I was a good fit for this profession.

"I received my vaccinations properly. Back in Tallinn."

"What do you mean?"

"The prequalification form didn't ask about it, and no one has requested my vaccination certificate. But they should have. It means I'm a suitable surrogate if not a donor."

The woman's eyes blinked a few extra times. This hadn't occurred to her. Maybe I still had a chance. If not here, I would search for another agency, knowing now what kinds of applicants they preferred. I would avoid anything related to Snizhne and would wipe that from my personal history. Or I could find a less exclusive agency. They had to exist.

"If you haven't had any problems with vaccinations, you're lucky," I said and nodded at my father's picture. "His friend was involved in the vaccine business. Donbas girls aren't risky material because of the pollution but because the locals are skeptical of vaccinations, and half of the children in the area don't receive them. And then there are others who get the same stick too many times because the schools got into the business, too. What could be the consequences of receiving the rubella vaccine every school year? Or what if an unvaccinated donor comes down with a disease in the middle of the process? You probably know how poorly rubella mixes with pregnancy."

The director pursed her lips and looked at me with new eyes.

"You're a smart girl," she said, and I caught a glimpse of one of her canine teeth with a beauty mark–sized smudge of lipstick on it. She smiled at me and at the possibilities, and I prayed in my mind to the Holy Mother of God. This had to work.

"We'll have to come up with a way to handle your dad. And Snizhne. That needs to disappear. We'll have to find another home for your father's parents. You went to Paris from Tallinn, right? Just like Carmen Kass?"

I didn't understand what she was getting at. I knew who Kass was, of course. An agent from Milan had found her in the Kaubamaja department store in Tallinn. She had been luckier in her modeling career than I was. Or smarter.

We went through everything that was good to share. If clients asked about Chornobyl, I should mention that I lived with my family in Tallinn at the time of the accident. From there, my parents had later moved to Mykolaiv, nearer to my father's sister since she wasn't up to caring for their elderly parents alone. Because I couldn't show the more recent pictures of my father, we moved his death to a year when he still looked presentable. My cousin who died in the Afghan War was left in the family tree but not the fact that my aunt had gone crazy after receiving her son in a zinc coffin with worms slithering out of the gaps in the seal. Clients were interested in three successive generations, and so it was best if there were no unnatural deaths, or any diseases that could be seen as genetic, either physical or mental.

"If any of your relatives are in prison, you should tell me now."

"But imprisonment isn't hereditary."

"Aggressiveness is. And you shouldn't tell that joke to any clients."

I knew what she meant. Around here, the honest people are in prison, and the liars are in parliament.

When I asked if this meant a new family tree had to be pulled out of a hat for every Ukrainian, I received a bright shower of laughter in return, accompanied by a clicking of fingernails on the tabletop that sounded like summer rain.

"Westerners don't know how to think that way. A donor's father has to have a legal job. I won't even ask what your father's accident was or where it happened. Our *kopankas* don't fit into their world-view. That was where your father worked, right, at an illegal mine?"

"I didn't say that."

"And prison? What about that?"

"My dad managed to die before he ended up behind bars."

"You aren't the first miner's daughter to come talk to me, nor the first whose family's livelihood comes from kopankas."

I understood very well that my father's story was ill suited for my portfolio if I wanted well-paying clients. There was no room here for drunkenness, for suicides, assisted or genuine, let alone for illegal coal mining or poppy plantations.

"Let's forget all that and concentrate on finding the right education for you. A couple of years of comprehensive school isn't enough, so what if you left modeling to study and graduated from the Kyiv National Linguistic University?"

I had passed the test. I was approved. My new boss called me a window-dressing girl and wanted me to move to Kyiv, where we could serve Western clients better, and she even promised me an advance.

I could give my mother money, and I would get my own apartment, my own bathroom, running water again, and a new phone to replace the one I had, which was on its last legs. I could look forward to restaurant food, espresso, and the life of an adult instead of a failure to launch. The boss arranged papers that said I taught English and French, which was completely believable given the language skills I'd picked up out in the world, and according to my payroll statements, I taught private evening language lessons. An account statement purchased from a bank was necessary for the visas. The balance shown on it made me laugh in disbelief. I was beginning to look perfect, and so was my father. His records were changed to depict a construction worker who had died in an accident on a job site, and his final employer became a contracting company in Mykolaiv. According to my boss, the company was a reliable partner in situations where girls' personal information needed a little aesthetic enhancement. So Snizhne was erased from my family history as if none of us had ever even visited.

I'd been ready for anything, but now I rejoiced: I was able to keep my liver and kidneys and didn't have to knock on the doors of any more bride agencies. Compared to that, donating a few eggs was ridiculously effortless.

I didn't tell anyone about the donations. And no one asked later how I'd ended up in the industry. My boss sometimes said she'd snapped me up in an instant once she realized how sharp, cosmopolitan, and skilled at languages I was, and everyone immediately assumed I'd started out in the office as a coordinator. My donations were irrelevant and, as I progressed in my career, I came to believe that telling anyone about them would have knocked me down to the same level as the girls. I would lose my position of authority.

I didn't lie to you deliberately. I considered these embellishments to be harmless cosmetic corrections of the sort everyone made.

HELSINKI

2016

"You don't have a man," Daria commented at the bar. "It shows. Do you have anything else? A *dacha*, a house, even a car?"

Pretending not to hear her questions, I ordered us both coffee and cognac. It was only when I took out my wallet that I released my grip on Daria's arm. The precaution had been pointless, though: she left the park with me without resistance, which surprised me. I still didn't fully comprehend that I was no longer the one with power over her. Daria didn't need to escape me.

"At least you have a job, don't you?"

I carried the drinks to an empty booth. The bar was like any watering hole on these streets, and we were like any other customers looking for a drink except that we didn't order beer. There weren't many people, as was appropriate for early on a Monday night, so only a few extra pairs of eyes saw us together. Two exits, still without doormen.

"I work for a translation company," I lied.

"You were always so good at languages."

I tried not to betray my relief. Daria didn't know where I got my money and maybe not where I lived either. That was something, though it didn't answer the most important questions: how she had found me, and why now?

"Well, spill it. Did he leave you?"

Daria took a handful of nuts from a bowl that had been left on the table and settled into the bench as if anticipating a good movie. I remained silent. I didn't intend to correct her assumptions. I would let her think that I'd had someone.

"Were you married?"

My fingers curling around my glass did not deceive Daria. She grabbed my wrist, and after opening my fist, she read my entire life from my hand. My inflamed cuticles made her click her tongue. The watch that appeared from beneath my sleeve had belonged to my mother, and Daria giggled at it. I knew how my ringless hands looked.

"No wonder he left you. Children?"

"No."

"You wouldn't have made a good mother anyway."

Daria couldn't know how deep that cut me, and I couldn't let her see. I bit my tongue and allowed her gaze to appraise my stretched collar, my cleaner's hands, and my colorless lashes without any extensions. The light of the bar was more compassionate than the spring reveling outside, but that didn't help. Nothing about me suggested success. Daria cast a significant glance at my backpack, and her expression seemed to say, "So that's what you've come to?" My downhill slide clearly caused her pleasure.

"You can't afford to pay me," she said as she savored the cognac, knowing why I didn't take to my own glass so eagerly: bar prices were high, and I didn't believe Daria would offer to pay. I had always covered everything when we went out together.

"I'll find a way. Just name your price."

"And then what? What do you think you'll get for that money?"

"You know."

"To friendship," she said, raising her glass and laughing.

Daria's teeth were still white, and only her canines showed even the slightest hint of tobacco stains. Still, she couldn't afford to look down on my state of decline. Didn't she realize how she looked? Before, her cuticles had been healthy, her nails her own, without any ridges, their surface as flawless as a newborn's. Her fingers were easy to imagine on the strings of a violin. Now there were mourning bands on her nails, her knuckles were chapped, and her previously enviable skin looked as thin as a hotel registration card. Her hair was in better shape; however, her blond, waist-length locks were a thing of the past, and in their place she sported a dark A-line bob. Something had happened to her, but what? It couldn't be the war or what was happening with her family. I knew those things. Ending up like this took years.

"You were probably hoping that someone other than me would have caught up with you first."

Daria leaned over the table to look at my face, took me by the cheek, and pinched. For a moment, I thought she would put her finger in my mouth to check the condition of my teeth. I pulled back, though I should have shown that I wasn't afraid and simply stared back at her. I knew how difficult girls were kept in line; I just hadn't been forced to do it myself.

"How do you sleep at night? Do you even dare to close your eyes? No wonder you look like this."

Daria pulled her phone out of her pocket, turned it over in her fingers for a moment as if considering whom to call, then lifted it in front of her. The flash fired. Instinctively, I covered my face with my hand, but too late.

"Those bags under your eyes." Daria giggled and magnified the picture on the screen glowing in her hand. "What do you think? What would they pay for you?"

For a second I thought she was assessing my value as a donor. Then I realized what she was referring to. She was waving in front of my eyes fresh evidence that she had met me, that I was here, in Helsinki. She could extort money from me, the agency, her old clients, you, everyone. Did she want to sell me to my old boss? Would that be her final revenge? Or had she ended up as a bounty hunter because she was broke? But if she had come after me, why did she want to expose us to the family in the dog park? Was that just teasing? Was that what she had become, my Daria?

"The world doesn't revolve around you," she said. "I didn't come because of you."

I lifted my gaze, stopping at Daria's jaw, the tip of which had become sharper. "Or for money."

I snorted and turned to look outside.

"Even though I know that's an impossible idea for you," Daria continued.

"What the hell are you doing here then?"

"I wanted to see the family. That's all."

"See the family? Do you intend to blackmail them?"

"I wanted to see what the girl has grown up to be like."

Daria let her phone thump on the table. I couldn't imagine any reason for her to lie, and I remembered the hunger in her eyes as she watched the children in the dog park. If she had come because of them, she wasn't trying to get revenge on me. At least that was something.

"It's forbidden. You signed the papers. We don't do that."

" 'We,' " Daria repeated, and one eyebrow went up.

It had just slipped out. There was no "we" anymore. No boss, no office, no personal desk. No credit cards. No errand boys. No one to order to handle unpleasant tasks. I had never talked to Daria this way, without any trump cards. I didn't know how to act or what to say. For a moment I wondered if I should finally tell her about my own donations. Would that change her attitude toward me? I wouldn't just be her ex-boss, I would be one of the girls, an equal. I rejected this idea. At least for now.

"Shall we have another?"

Daria pushed away her empty cognac glass and waited for me to go to the bar. She was in no hurry. She didn't glance at her watch or the door or the window. She didn't lower her voice, and, unlike me, she let her hands wander and tap at her phone, her glass, and the bowl of nuts, and it wasn't because she was nervous. She just didn't care what I thought about her behavior.

"The same?" I asked, but I didn't wait to listen to what was likely to be a more expensive request. The four-centimeter shots disappeared all too fast. I decided to switch the drink to a more affordable Jaloviina cut brandy. I would present the mixture of cognac and spirits to Daria as a Finnish specialty that was worth a taste. At the counter, I glanced back.

Daria sat in her seat like a mushroom, her back toward one of the doors. If I did get out without her noticing, in no time she would realize I had fled, and all she would need to do was make one call and send my picture, and everything would be over. My body would be thrown from the roof of an apartment building or wrapped in plastic or a rug and dumped at a construction site or into the sea. No one would do that to a friend. We had been friends, but we weren't anymore.

Daria sniffed her drink. I waited for her to hold her nose at the Jaloviina and tell me to get her something else. However, her nod of acceptance showed that my trick had worked.

"To the dog park family," she said and raised her glass. "Tell me everything."

"I don't know them."

"Don't even try."

Daria slowly said the children's names. In her pronunciation I could hear how long she had practiced this, even though the Finnish letters were still uncomfortable in her mouth. Girls weren't supposed to know anything about their clients' offspring, especially none of the kids' names. Under the table, I clenched my hands into fists.

"Did you come to Helsinki for the children?" she asked.

"Of course not. I didn't even remember that the family lived here."

"And then it suddenly came back to you?"

"Exactly."

I touched the glass to my lips. The old watch slipped from under my sleeve again. Daria's eyes swept back over my wrist and my nails, and smile lines traced the sides of her mouth. She loved this situation, her dominance. Had I enjoyed that in the same way? Had I derived pleasure from the fact that I could sit a candidate down on the couch in my office and interrogate them about things they didn't want to tell? I hadn't invented those questions, though. I had just repeated the words printed on the stack of papers and written down the answers. And Daria hadn't been embarrassed by them, let alone upset. She had wanted the job and understood what it required.

Daria prodded me with a coaster.

"I ran into them by chance on a business trip," I lied.

"And then you started to follow them? Do you intend to blackmail them?"

"Me?"

"You. You look like you could use some extra income. Why else would you keep an eye on them? I've seen you in that park at least three times. Isn't that a bit too dangerous for you?"

"I go to the dog park when I miss you."

"Come off it."

"It's true, really. The daughter has your smile."

Daria's chin trembled; I had finally hit on something.

The door of the bar opened, and the draft cooled my skin under the shirt plastered to my back. I wiped my upper lip. My options were limited. I could send an anonymous message to one of the agency's employees that Daria had been seen spying on her old clients, but I rejected that idea out of hand: Daria would only have to show the picture she had taken of me and the game would be up. The best thing would be for me to run away. Right now. I could grab Daria's phone off the table, head out that door, and take a bus to the airport or the harbor. And after that? Escaping was expensive and living underground even more so.

I let the water run until it was ice cold and then rinsed my face before checking to see if anyone had tried to call me. I touched the screen: no messages, no unanswered calls. No reason to fear that everything wasn't fine at home, and yet the woman who stared back at me from the ladies' room mirror was panic-stricken as I selected my mother's number, and the beep sounded in my ear like a foghorn, for far too long. Had something happened already? Why hadn't I tried to reach her right away from the park? I hadn't wanted to arouse Daria's interest or reveal to her that I had anyone in Helsinki. That might have been a mistake.

"Is anything the matter?" Mom asked.

She had answered. She was home. She was fine. She was making dinner like any other day. In the background I could hear the clatter of a steel pot, and Promin FM was playing the news from Ukraine. The relief made me lean on the tiled wall for support.

"What took so long to answer?"

My voice hadn't had time to recover. It was still as thin as an emergency whistle and put my mother on alert. She shut down the computer, and the radio fell silent.

"You sound strange."

"I'll be just a little longer. An unexpected work thing came up."

"Really?"

My mother could always tell when something was wrong. I had made calls like this before, if for other reasons. Sometimes I had wanted a moment of peace. Other times I'd just needed quiet. Mom understood that. She understood that I preferred to cry alone, although sometimes she seemed to wonder whether I would do something to myself, and then I wanted to slap away the solicitous hand she would place on my shoulder. This time she was on the right track, though.

"Should I be worried? Or pack?"

"Don't be dramatic. I'll see you later."

A slovenly woman who was slightly tipsy tottered in, banging the door. Turning the water on again, I waited for it to get cold and wiped my neck with a wet paper towel. I drank water straight from the tap to clear my head. I couldn't get drunk, not now. I didn't know how I would end the evening. If Daria was staying at a hotel, would I escort her there? And what if she didn't have a place to sleep and forced herself on me? I didn't want to show Daria where I lived. On the other hand, how did I know she hadn't followed me home from the dog park before? But if that was the case, why would she reveal herself to me only now?

My fingers began scrolling through phone numbers again. There weren't many. Only contact information for people whose floors I mopped and the number for my boss at the cleaning company. I didn't have friends anymore, no one to ask for help except my mother, and this time she couldn't. Then the longing hit me again at the wrong moment. I missed you.

I carried more Jaloviina to the table and hoped that the onion rings I'd ordered would arrive soon. I'd thought Daria didn't like alcohol. I'd been wrong. She raised her glass.

"To women? To all the mothers? How about that?"

Raising my glass, I noticed that Daria's phone had disappeared from the table. That was enough to make me flinch when the front door banged, and I couldn't help but glance behind me. How long had Daria been following me, and how many pictures of me had she taken? Days, weeks, months, or even longer? And what if she had already sent photos to the hyenas chasing me? I didn't know who would come after me first: my old boss, you, your errand boy—or would you all come at once?

The onion rings didn't arrive, so I went to complain to the server bustling around behind the bar while I also ordered another drink for Daria. She was starting to become intoxicated. I tried to rectify the situation by setting a pint of water in front of her along with her glass of liquor, as was the local custom. Daria raised her eyebrows as she took it, sticking her finger in the water and then flicking it in my face.

"What am I supposed to do with this?"

"Drink it."

"When did you start drinking water with cognac? Tap water?"

Daria shook her head like the waitresses in Ukraine when a diner was leaning toward a dish they couldn't recommend. The gesture was always subtly confidential and the gaze direct. Daria looked at me in exactly that same way and surprisingly clearly even though her eyes glistened with inebriation. It was as if she knew more about me than she should. Turning my face to the window, I concentrated on watching the two retirees who had stopped to chat on the street. Both of them seemed so spry. I could almost hear them talking about their vacations and their many hobbies, and imagining the new potatoes they would buy at the market.

Daria shrugged and suggested another toast. "To Helsinki, the city of unexpected meetings?"

She knocked her empty glass on the table. It was small, and the Jaloviina was dwindling far too fast. I shuddered to think of the bill.

"Why on earth did you come here?" Daria asked and cast a significant glance around. "Helsinki isn't Paris or London or Vienna."

"Helsinki is a perfectly nice city."

"Answer my question," Daria snapped.

I swallowed for a moment. I didn't know this person anymore. What was she capable of, and what did she want? The dog park family would be sure to shell out a pretty penny to prevent us from messing up their perfect life, and my ex-boss would pay even more for me. That had to be tempting, no matter what Daria claimed. The bag of cash you would offer I didn't even dare to guess. Daria would be a millionaire, in dollars.

"I happened to get a Finnish passport," I said tentatively.

She nodded, accepting my answer. A passport from this country was a stroke of luck for anyone. However, I made the mistake of instinctively pulling my backpack closer to me on the bench, and Daria noticed it.

"Show me."

I bit my lip. I couldn't claim to have left my passport at home. A person in my position could never be sure when she would have to leave, and Daria knew it. She snatched the passport from my reluctant fingers and, bending its red cover with a professional touch, found it to be genuine.

"A Finnish citizen, Ruslana Toivonen," she said, trying out the name. "Who is Ruslana Toivonen?"

"I don't know. A Ukrainian married to a Finn. She moved to Sweden and sold her papers because she was broke."

"You can get legitimate work with this," Daria said. "It's excellent. Even though she is younger than you."

I put out my hand. I wanted my passport back.

"I could hold on to this for safekeeping," Daria said. "Just like you kept my papers."

Pulling back against the backrest of the bench, I nearly squeezed my backpack again, but I managed to control the urge. Daria didn't need to attach any more attention to it than she already had. She didn't know that I also carried Ruslana Toivonen's driver's license and health insurance card. They had been included in the thick packet of documents that had even included a passport for a woman who could pass as Ruslana Toivonen's mother. Unfortunately, the collection didn't have any other travel documents suitable for a woman my age. I wouldn't be able to flee under anyone else's papers. However, Daria didn't really know anything about my new identity. So how on earth had she managed to track me down? Had she monitored my mother's trips to Finland? That seemed doubtful. My mother's precautions had always been thorough, and no one else had managed to find me through her. Not my former boss. Not you. Was it really as simple as Daria looking for the dog park family and happening to run into me? Could it really be coincidence?

"Are the biometric identifiers yours or this Ruslana Toivonen's?" Daria asked.

"You can get through the Helsinki airport without those."

"You must not have had time to wait for a perfect passport. You took what you got and trusted in luck. Do you know that sometimes I imagined what your escape was like?"

Daria mimicked horror and crushed my passport against her chest as if in the throes of a heart attack, until she burst out laughing. I was never going to get such a good package again anywhere, so I had to let Daria play with my precious document, let her take pictures of it, let her pretend to rip it, let her treat it as if it meant nothing, so she wouldn't realize how important this passport was to me.

"Do you remember the time when we fell into the clutches of that customs officer at the airport? First, he took his time looking at our passports, and then he ripped out some pages and said we'd never get anywhere with damaged documents. The boss was furious. I'd never seen her so mad before."

The basket of onion rings arrived.

"After your stunt, she went even more berserk than then. All of the girls were questioned, especially me. Everyone was sure I knew something."

"But you didn't tell them anything."

"What would I have told?"

Daria threw the passport at me, and it hit me in the chest.

"Get more drinks."

Gradually a glass wall was growing between us, and Daria was starting to slur her speech. I didn't know what she would be like in a deeper state of drunkenness. Would she continue mocking me, get violent, or go sentimental and start confiding in me? I hoped for the latter but in vain. A sudden nausea drove Daria to the ladies' room. In the meantime, I drained a pint of water as if in secret. Pulling a small, round tin of Golden Star balm out of my pocket, I breathed in its scent of camphor and menthol. I still had things to fight for.

The ladies' room door swung open, and Daria staggered back, aiming her steps at the exit. Gathering my belongings, I hurried after her and offered to take her to wherever she was staying. Figuring that out took some time, but finally, I managed to wring the name of the hotel out of her. That was a relief. She didn't refuse the ride I offered her, although she resisted the seat belt that I tried to pull over her chest when we got into the taxi. I let her be, clicking in my own and remembering Aleksey's expression when I suggested he should dig out the seat belts buried between the cushions of the back seats in all of the office cars. *Seriously?* Aleksey's expression had said. Are these Westerners crazy? I'd held the line, and Aleksey had also replaced the broken seat belts with new ones. Those were the little insights that earned me my boss's trust; I knew what Westerners wanted.

As the taxi set off, Daria squeezed my hand and muttered something I couldn't make out, until I realized that she'd said, "We'll always be friends, won't we?"

Daria's eyes were closed, and I couldn't tell whether she even meant me. The murmuring continued in a disjointed jumble of words that made no sense. Something about bad parents, something about bad company a girl grew up in, something about how a girl had a bad brother, a bad mother, and the wrong life. I didn't understand whom she was talking about. When I tried to clarify, I received no response. I turned my head to the window.

We had been in cars like this before, squeezing each other's hands, and though Aleksey had always driven carefully, the bumps in the road had made Daria whimper. The trip through Dnipro to the clinic wasn't long, and yet it had felt endless. I'd assured her I wouldn't leave her alone. Despite our furs, our hands were cold. Daria's face had swollen, and her rings got stuck on her fingers. But she didn't complain. She never complained. If everything went well, I would become the office manager. The boss would move on and hand over the whole country to me to handle so she could focus on directing operations in the rest of Europe. Everything had been possible then. Now all I could hope for was survival.

Every now and again, the Helsinki taxi driver glanced into the back seat. Daria's drunken groans put a serious look on his face and made me think about the extra cost of this already expensive taxi ride if she vomited. I forced a plastic bag on her that I'd found in my pocket, but it would be too small. My sympathy was with the driver. Before, it wouldn't have been. Before, I wouldn't have thought about who would have to clean up. My new way of thinking was that of a cleaner—I detested it.

My Good Things List had fallen out of my pocket while I rummaged for the plastic bag, and I only noticed it after stepping on it for a while in the footwell. Picking the paper up, I wiped my shoe prints off it. On top was my latest addition. I had made the entry only a few hours ago, because I'd been feeling exceptionally good. I had actually hummed on my way to my final apartment to clean for the day, and when I noticed, I laughed at myself. I was alive. Spring would soon be in bloom. Perhaps not the chestnuts of Kyiv or its acacias or poplars, but trees would still blossom. This fit of good cheer led me to a decision: the sixth summer of this new life could be a good one. I could stop being nervous. The memories could fade, the bruises could heal. Maybe I could even be happy.

That decision had made me pull out my list, which I'd been keeping for some time, of all the positive aspects of my new life. The first letter wavered as if written by a child, and the pen shaking in my hand pierced the paper. But still I managed to write "hometown." I had a place to call home and streets to hum on. The wobbly word did not disappear from the paper even when I closed my eyes and opened them again. Maybe it was true.

Daria had fallen asleep and was snoring with her head against the taxi window. I looked at my list, intended for moments of despair just like this. Its purpose was to remind me that a lot of things were good and getting better all the time. The people I served were all more pleasant that any of the ones I'd fussed over in my previous life, and that was why the words "my clientele" stood near the top of the list. At the very top was "the dog park."

Many items that once felt like significant achievements suddenly seemed childish, despite the fact that I still clearly remembered the first time I slept through the night without waking. In the morning I'd thought my feeling of lightness was an illness, until I realized what it was and immediately recorded it on my list. Soon I'd added how I could wait for the bus, right next to the street, without a care. I no longer feared that someone would push me into traffic, and my heart didn't race like a stampeding horse whenever a car with tinted windows pulled past. The metro had earned its own entry in my Good Things List, too. Before officially recording it, I'd practiced walking on the bright orange platform in the relaxed way the locals did. The existence of the list constantly encouraged me to find new things to add. I was in love with the subway in my new hometown. It ran so close to the surface of the earth—it was so open, so bright, so perfectly suited to the way this country lived. But now I realized it had never been for me. I'd just assumed it was. How had I ever even imagined that this city could become something as permanent as a home?

DNIPROPETROVSK
2007–2008

I took in the view from the windows of my newly renovated office. An old woman with a stooped back swept the street, her broom scraping the cracked asphalt like chalk on a chalkboard. I stopped up my free ear with a finger in order to hear my aunt on the other end of the line.

"Are you listening? Your mother just wants to chat," she said.

I could guess what this was about. If my mom wouldn't bring it up herself, there was only one explanation. At regular intervals, a friend of a friend of a friend appeared at her door in the hope that I could help her daughter become a model. These starlings were rarely good for anything, although after I was promoted, I took on a few as donors. I'd also sent a few to talk to the coordinator who handled surrogates, and I'd referred others to reliable bride agencies for a commission. But I wanted to get free of the whole thing, so after I got off the phone with my aunt, I immediately called my mother.

"Just listen for a second. This Daria, she's a good girl," my mother said. "She's completely different from the others."

"You've said that before."

In my mind I could already see the bleach-burned hair and the tiger-striped shirt—one more starling I could never introduce to my boss. I pressed the tip of my fountain pen to my calendar. If my next client hadn't been waiting, I would have assuaged my irritation with a hundred grams of cognac. I didn't like beggars.

The elderly woman sweeping the leaves had reached the corner of the building. The floral scarf that covered her head seemed familiar. My mother had owned a coatdress made of the same fabric. In Snizhne we'd eventually cut it into floor rags.

"Maybe you don't remember her? Daria was so small then."

"When?"

I already knew whom she was talking about, but I still asked. Blond hair, braided with bows the size of peonies, under her short skirt the scabby knees of a child. She had stared at me from the other side of the road with the shy curiosity younger kids have for their older peers. I remembered one day when I was standing in front of our new house in Snizhne, chewing three-day-old gum as I cursed my life and mulled over my plans for getting out of the pigsty my parents had dragged me to. My dad was drumming the steering wheel as he waited for a man I recognized as the girl's father to finish talking to an older boy. After the discussion ended, the man noticed his daughter hiding behind the electric pole and shouted at her to hoof it home and fast. Startled, the girl ran off. The man jumped into the car, and my father's Zhiguli left a trail of black smoke as it accelerated along the bumpy road toward something that would result in my father not coming home that night and my mother waiting up, pacing in a circle that shrank and shrank until she stood still.

I didn't want to see Daria.

I pointed out how busy I was and ended the call in the middle of my mother's sentence. After tapping the desk for a few seconds, I opened the window to cool my head. A rain shower had filled the street with umbrellas, the women's colorful and the men's black. The phone rang again. Mom, of course. This irritated me. I didn't owe something to every hard-luck case my mother happened to know. On the other hand, if I accepted her request, I could itemize the reasons why this silly girl from Donetsk was useless, and that might smother my mother's passion for forcing more hussies like her on me.

Measuring Daria's body with my gaze, I paused at her shins. The new couch she was sitting on was Scandinavian style, and she fit as perfectly with the aristocratic green of the background as a glove purchased from a Viennese glove shop. But I still continued my assessment. I snorted, huffed, and disabused misguided notions. I didn't want her to imagine she was in some special position just because my mother had known her parents. But inside I was surprised. Nothing about her reminded me of Snizhne. Rather, I saw myself in her—visiting a Paris modeling agency for the first time, struck dumb by the elegance of the people who walked down the corridor as I waited my turn. I'd been sure that I wouldn't be good enough. That someone had made a mistake and that I would be placed on a flight home at any moment.

Pushing my chair back, I inspected the girl's feet, which were visible behind the coffee table. Like most of these slim young things, she wore flat sandals with a centimeter of heel hanging over the sole, which were entirely unsuited to the autumn weather. Just like I had worn. Just like all of us who didn't have the means to buy new shoes, like all of us who were too shy to remind our mothers how fast our feet grew and so we continued wearing our sandals, last year's sandals, years-old sandals, after we'd stopped growing taller or the weather turned too cold for summer shoes. But this demonstrated that she had the character for this work. Daria endured my gaze and did not appear surprised when she realized what business I was in. Instead, she seemed delighted our office didn't specialize in girls looking for sponsors. Presumably that was what Daria had suspected at first, and she had come even so.

I was used to how our clinical questions about sex partners and sexually transmitted diseases made girls' ears redden. I could guess their unspoken thoughts: the girls took the inquiries personally and hesitated when I began to quiz them. But Daria was in a class by herself. She never lost her composure as I asked whether she'd been tested for this, that, and the other disease, or whether she'd ever had sex with someone who had been tested for a venereal complaint. After moving on to the section about drug use, I pressed to know whether she had engaged in intimate relations in exchange for drugs or money in the past six months, and Daria still didn't flinch, stammer, or blush. Her forehead remained unfurrowed, and her hands remained still, folded like a napkin in the shape of a swan. The prequalification form was written to satisfy the demanding criteria of our American customers, but for me it was something else: an excellent test of a candidate's character. Daria passed brilliantly.

"I'm not in any hurry. But would you be able to tell me when I might . . ."

Daria's gaze dropped to her lap, and she began to pick nonexistent crumbs from her skirt. I perked up. A moment ago, Daria had been as elegant as a table setting at a five-star restaurant, but her question had instantly shattered that harmony.

"It is customary to pay only after a client has been found and committed to the project," I replied. "Before then we have to do all the tests, wait for results, and see if we can get you on the list."

I had sat in that same place myself and over the course of my job become accustomed to the performances some girls put on, up to and including glycerin tears, but the sudden change in Daria still surprised me. I too had thought I'd get paid immediately and would have been willing to go a long way to feel a stack of bills in my hand. Daria looked ready to do anything right then and there. She seemed even more desperate than I'd been, which meant this wasn't just the usual student problem of her stipend not covering her living costs. I tried to come up with a suitable plan of action. If I turned her away, she would run to one of our competitors, only to receive the same answer. She clearly didn't have the patience to wait for the next busload of bachelors and the chance of salvation they offered, so if things went badly enough, she would find another way to get her money today. But then I would have no use for her: I couldn't do anything with a girl who had hepatitis or HIV or only one remaining kidney. I couldn't let her pawn her body. I couldn't let her go down that road.

After flipping through Daria's passport, I tossed it on the table like so much rubbish.

"You don't even have an international passport. You haven't traveled to a single one of the countries where we do business. Do you know how long a process it is to get your first visa?" I asked. "It isn't cheap. And you aren't married either. Do you have any concept of how difficult it is for a single Ukrainian girl to get into a place like the United States? Do you maybe have family there, something we could use to justify your trip across the Atlantic? Do you really think our girls are welcomed with open arms everywhere just like that, with a snap of our fingers?"

I pushed my chair back as if I was tired of explaining obvious things to idiots and then walked to the window in a show of calming down. Rubbing my temples, I pretended to think. I heard Daria swallowing. I allowed some time to pass and let in some fresh air to dispel the scent of lily of the valley emanating from Daria. Actually, getting visas was a pushover if you knew what to do and whom to contact, and if you could pay.

"What if I only served clients in Russia? My internal passport would be enough, and I wouldn't need a visa—"

"Are you simple? Our business strategy focuses on Western countries."

I returned to the table.

"You clearly don't realize what your biggest problem is. It's Snizhne."

Watching how my words affected Daria, I tried to remember what my mother had said. She hadn't mentioned Daria's acute need for cash, so I didn't know the cause for her desperation. I never listened when my mother gossiped about news of people from Snizhne. But I could still guess at the kinds of trouble anyone from the area would be facing. Daria's brother was probably mixed up in some shady business like her father or had tried to steal from someone. And yet I didn't offer Daria any words of comfort or return to the question of payment. Instead I pushed that aside as if it were a minor issue and focused on explaining to her what a difficult case she was. A risk, hard to sell. Her photos were great, but that didn't mean anything, and finding her first client could take time. Browsing through the prequalification forms, I pointed them out to Daria. In the stack was an entire section devoted to substances that were harmful to donors: asbestos, smoke, pesticides, radiation, lead, and a whole host of other poisons.

"I didn't even bother to ask about these."

I pushed the pile in front of her.

"Why didn't you tell me up front that I'm not good enough?"

Daria couldn't hold back her weeping anymore. The tears that stuck to her long lashes made her look like a rosy-cheeked doll, and the swelling of her lids gave her eyes an Asian exoticism. She even looked good wearing desperation.

"All problems have solutions," I said. "If they remain between us. Just us. Do you understand?"

Daria looked up at me from under downcast eyebrows and pushed a napkin across the table. I picked it up and waved it like a white flag between us. That was the decisive moment. I let time pass. I didn't pick up the pen she tried to offer me, and I didn't write down the amount of the bribe I would accept, as Daria expected me to do. I did make some calculations, but only in my head and only to myself. Even though arranging the papers was cheap, my boss was strict about expenditures. That was her way of ensuring that no one would dare steal too much, and the standard also applied to me. I couldn't risk trying my luck and slipping something into my own pocket—this job was too good. However, with Daria I was willing to take a risk. The more I turned the numbers over in my mind, the surer I was that I could keep costs under control. We didn't have to remake everything about Daria's background. Her parents looked presentable enough in their younger pictures. For her age, the mother was still relatively wrinkle-free, and the father's athletic background was genuine, as were Daria's years of gymnastics training in Donetsk, where she had been coached by a famous Soviet Olympic medalist.

A name like that would make excellent reading in Daria's biography. Too bad Donetsk didn't look any better than Snizhne. On the other hand, I could find an equally well-known coach in Dnipro and arrange things with her. Then we could say that the family moved to Dnipro before the children were born. Daria's father had died, but if I bought him an engineering diploma and created a job for him in one of the construction companies in Dnipro, we could chalk his death up to a support cable failure on a job site. The story began to take on a coherent shape in my head. The only challenge was that Daria didn't want to reveal the real nature of her work to her family, so she couldn't bring any of them to show off. Clients would have to content themselves with photographic evidence. Someday Daria might change her mind, though, and then she could take on clients who had paid to meet their donor's relatives. I would put up her mother and brothers in the cozy apartment I'd rented in the center of Dnipro for such meetings. I would just change out the photos in the picture frames. Daria had two handsome brothers, the younger still in high school, the older officially unemployed. Both of them were useable, though the older brother's work situation needed to change. I deduced that he worked in the illegal mines. The younger brother probably did, too. Both of them likely earned about sixty dollars a month. If I got them real jobs, not just papers, the whole family would be mine. I screwed my eyes shut and thought. Daria's brothers. If they were anything like their father, I could guess who was to blame for Daria's anxiety. It turned out I was right. A question about her older brother set off a flood of tears, and, sputtering, she explained that Pavel might not ever be able to work again. The family needed money for a new surgery, and he couldn't earn any money. Pavel had a young wife and a small baby. I knew what this meant. At the illegal mines, everyone was responsible for their own health. The family wouldn't be able to provide Daria with any support at school beyond a few jars of jam, and she was afraid she would have to drop out.

Without writing anything on it, I ripped the napkin in half. In that moment, I could have made Daria work for me without pay for the rest of her life. But I didn't demand that. Not even though Daria was prepared to sell herself for any price. I wanted something more significant: her loyalty, her gratitude, and her trust.

"No, not this way," I said. "I don't want you to be in debt to anyone, ever. Not even to me. But that perfume you will not wear when you meet with clients."

Pushing the back door of the office open, I fished a cigarette out of my pocket. One matchstick after another broke before I got the tip burning and cast the matchbox to the ground. The conversation had gone perfectly until a wave of vertigo hit me so hard that I was afraid I might pass out. The blood had leaked from my fingertips, making them sting as I held my pen. I'd left Daria on my couch and stumbled into the hallway muttering something about an urgent telephone call. I didn't understand what was going on with my head. Was it Daria and the memories that flooded the room when she was there? Or that I didn't know whether she represented the opportunities I'd lost or the ones I could get? Or neither? The guard dog at the neighboring building began to yap, and I noticed that the cigarette in my fingers was steadier now. The color was returning to my hands despite the cold. I had made my choice when I tore that napkin in two, and I did not intend to turn aside from it.

After emptying the trunk of the car, Aleksey came and offered me a handkerchief. I took it and blew my nose.

"Couldn't you find something for that girl?" Aleksey asked. "I saw her in the waiting room. Anyone would want a daughter who looks like that."

"She has a lot of potential, but where did she come for help? Here."

"This is a good starting point for other plans."

"My mother knew her parents."

"Everything will work out," Aleksey said. "Usually it does."

"Not in Cyprus."

"There's no use dwelling on that anymore."

A few months earlier, one of the girls from our Cyprus clinic had escaped to seek help for complications that our doctors had ignored. She died after getting to a hospital, and Aleksey was sent to clean up the mess. I was supposed to find a replacement for the deceased donor. The situation was difficult. The girl had been unique, a Tatar graduate of the Kyiv Conservatory, and the client was an American Tatar. I failed at my assignment, unable to find an ethnically suitable donor. I was afraid of having to return to my old job, but our boss tempered justice with mercy. I vowed that from now on, we would always take girls to the doctor if there was any reason to suspect ovarian hyperstimulation or internal bleeding. The boss suspected that the clinic director had bought his medical degree and made me rerun background checks on all of our specialists. We were forced to dismiss a few of them.

Aleksey gave a deep sigh.

"Did you hear me? You handle everything better than that fuckup in Cyprus did."

Aleksey was right. Daria would not share the Tatar girl's fate. Even though any donation was a risk, girls around the world were donating constantly, many of them over and over again. Few experienced complications, and almost no one died. Letting a desperate, penniless girl slip through my hands would be a gamble, too—I wouldn't have any way to get her back. Someone else would snatch her up, permanently.

I sucked on the filter of my cigarette so hard that the burning tip moved, crackling halfway along the paper. I kicked a nearby trash can, and it didn't even budge. It was a solid Soviet piece, made of concrete, from a time when futuristic forms were meant to manifest the story of our successful conquest of space. Aleksey stepped back. I waved to indicate that everything was fine. I took another cigarette out of the pack and kicked the trash can again. I should have gotten rid of this honeycomb monstrosity long ago. But it was always here, like many other things in the backyard, which needed new asphalt or flagstones on the ground and new plaster on the walls. A coil of electrical wires rested on the door frame like a cat on an oven mantel. Everything else was crumbled, decayed, cracked, and peeled, except this trash can. It brought to mind a beetle struggling in a concrete pit, unable to see over the edges to the world beyond. But I could see. I saw the future that Daria could have.

. . .

I took a deep breath and walked back inside. In my office, Daria was staring at the shreds of the napkin. She barely dared to breathe. Without a glance at her, I spent a moment arranging my things and then pulled out a letter of intent and an envelope of money, even though I had yet to talk to my boss about this new girl. I gave Daria a down payment immediately after she had signed for the money and executed the contract. She could use that to pay for clean sheets for her brother in the hospital and many other things besides. Tomorrow Pavel would get all the medication he needed, and the doctor wouldn't miss him on his rounds. He would probably be seen first.

I had Daria on my hook, now and forever. I would never have to resort to extreme measures with her as I did with the girls who thought they could blackmail clients, embezzle, or act as private entrepreneurs. Daria would be mine because I had done her the favor she needed right now.

I talked with Aleksey about the way forward. If Pavel could get a legal job and better pay after recovering, the younger brother could abandon the kopankas and focus on high school. Daria's new job would mean traveling a lot, and she wouldn't be at home much, so I wanted Pavel working close to his parents. Still, some distance from his old circle wouldn't be the worst thing. I suggested the Karl Marx mine in Yenakiieve, but Aleksey shook his head.

"You might regret that."

"How so?"

"It's one of the mines that's been shut down because of hazardous working conditions."

"Isn't anyone digging there anymore?"

"Of course they are."

"Where are the working conditions good, then?"

"Nowhere." Aleksey laughed. "You must not follow the news."

Aleksey was right. I always changed the channel when I heard someone mention coal. There were too many accidents and too many miners' protests, and the coal smelled too much on the trains, near the tracks, and in the train stations. But of course Daria's family would keep abreast of things like that.

"Well, give me some suggestions."

"How about one of the quarries in Kryvyi Rih? It is farther away, though."

"Are the working conditions better there? How expensive would it be?"

"A thousand dollars should cover it."

A short while after our conversation, a methane gas explosion occurred at the Zasyadko mine in Donetsk, killing more than a hundred workers. They were buried beside the mine. The incident was big enough that I couldn't shut my eyes to it. The pages of the newspapers were filled with mourning relatives, red carnations like drops of blood, and brightly colored handkerchiefs crushed by the hands of weeping women; and as I looked at these photographs, I found myself squeezing my hands into fists as well. After that, I entirely gave up tracking the news. I still heard about the accident at the Karl Marx mine, though. I recommended Aleksey for a significant pay raise, and the boss didn't object, because she reasoned that the girls' mental states needed protecting. A relative trapped underground for weeks on end, whether alive or dead, would be distressing enough that the entire process could be ruined.

After arranging things with Daria, I called her mother to tell her about Pavel's new job. In the background I could hear the clatter of bottles and the clicking of an abacus. Valentina Sokolova was still working in the shop, the same one she was supposed to quit after I visited. Or maybe the shop was different, but the work and the abacus were the same. I thought of the years of wear on its wooden frame and looked at my fashionable office: the clean electrical sockets that I'd ordered fixed first thing, the walls from which I had removed the flaking Soviet-era paint. I had made it after all, farther than any of the Sokolovs, and I would go even farther.

Valentina Sokolova's voice was the same as I remembered, just more worn, like last year's calendar. To my relief, she didn't treat me like the daughter of her old friend, the child to whom she had sold clumps of sticky candies, but rather like her daughter's employer, with respect. She laughed with relief, though she was still anxious about pensions.

"It may seem far off to you young ones," she said. "But I've seen so many times how people get stuck in the kopankas without even realizing. They give you your money every week, unlike at the state mines, but you pay for it later. Hoping for a pension is pointless."

Worried that she might start reminiscing about the past, I instinctively stood up, as if that would help anything. But she was a wise woman—she understood what not to say and continued chattering about retirement. Maybe her concern was genuine. Sitting back down, I continued drawing a spiral on my calendar. The circles were already filling the second page. I promised myself that I would end the call before I made it to the next spread and started to talk about the first steps of Daria's career. I wanted to find out what this mother knew about her daughter's job. Daria and I had decided that there was no need to tell anyone about her actual job description and that her family could think she was working as a model, as Valentina Sokolova had hoped and seemed to believe based on what she said. Then she returned to her sons.

"We agreed they would always call home at the end of each shift."

I didn't understand what she was implying and waited for her to get to the point. The abacus had gone silent, and I couldn't hear any customers. She was alone and could speak freely now. I hadn't asked after the condition of the brother in the hospital. I suspected that was where we were going next. I'd assigned Aleksey to learn the general outlines of Pavel's accident. According to the *militsiya*, the coal pit in the backyard of Pavel's grandparents' house had collapsed while the brothers were working down below. This news had made my eyebrows go up—pulling shifts in a larger kopanka hadn't been enough for the Sokolovs. The militsiya officer had snorted that accidents like this happened constantly, and that was the reward for getting greedy and digging too much. In his opinion, the family should be thankful: both boys had lived, and the whole house hadn't collapsed. I snapped an Analgin tablet out of the blister pack I kept in the drawer, swallowed it, and continued my spiral on the calendar page. I could cut the call short and then send an apologetic text message about my battery running out. Valentina Sokolova sighed and took a deep breath.

"Once my boy took a double shift and didn't let us know. My daughter-in-law ran to me crying that she hadn't heard from Pavel after work, and I was sure that I had lost my son. We gave him such a telling-off that he never made that mistake again. No mother should have to experience such things. Nor any wife."

The secretary came and peeked through the door. Our visa agent had been waiting his turn for a while now.

"I just mean that I wouldn't want Daria to find a coal miner for a husband," Valentina Sokolova said. "And I don't want her to come back here. Daria has the chance for something more. She's at the university, after all."

I let go of the pen. Now I understood. This mother didn't want her own life for her daughter.

I didn't dare tell my boss about Daria before she came to visit our office in Dnipro. My investment in Daria would be pure loss if she had an allergic reaction to the injections or couldn't produce enough eggs, and my boss hated losses. I hoped I could explain better face-to-face why I had taken the risk.

"We don't give advances," she said, frowning severely. "There's a reason for that. And how much did this brother's job cost?"

I pointed at the numbers in the folder I'd organized for this meeting. The director was sitting in my chair, behind my desk, as she rubbed her teeth with her finger to remove some red lipstick, which then became pink fingerprints on the white surface of the desk. Was she wondering whether giving me responsibility over the Dnipro office hadn't been a good idea after all? Had I stepped out of bounds? I had taken serious liberties with Daria, and my boss hadn't forgotten the Cyprus scandal. That had called my competence into question, and my initiatives seemed to fail time and time again. I didn't have any more room for mistakes.

"Sometimes I've put my money on the wrong trotting horse, too," she said and began to browse through the papers, muttering something about learning from mistakes.

I hadn't tampered with Daria's health results. There was no need for fabrication. She had no hereditary diseases. We had run a chromosome analysis, and her blood tests and ultrasound were in order. Her IQ was brilliant, and her studies in mining engineering at the Dnipro National Mining University were real. I'd also tested her language skills. Her German was just as good as she had claimed, and she had also dutifully enrolled in a course to improve her English. Clients who could not speak more than one language would consider her a genius.

"A muscle test?" the boss said, perking up.

"Athleticism is an important attribute for many clients. Daria's muscle cells are perfect, and her ACE gene indicates excellent potential as a runner."

"Did you come up with this?"

"I happened to read an article that talked about ACE genotypes."

Of course I wouldn't have added the results to her file if they hadn't been excellent, but because I'd invested such a significant sum in Daria before we knew whether she would actually work as a donor, I was counting on this new way of making money to earn me mercy in my boss's eyes. I was right. She didn't even glance at the expense total. That didn't matter anymore.

"You're a real wizard," she said as she closed the file, and an entire sky full of stars sparkled in the diamonds on the face of her wristwatch. "What do you think, would this girl be a fit for that Helsinki couple? You remember them, right?"

I nodded. I knew the Finns from before, and they had just made contact about expanding their family again. The woman had been a competitive gymnast when she was younger, and the man's running career had ended with a knee injury. For them, physical talent was a priority worth paying for.

The nails this client had pressed into my gums were indelibly etched into my mind, as was the industrial taste of her hand lotion. Still, I didn't want any softer a start for Daria. This meeting was a test.

"Do you have makeup remover?" the woman asked me after she finished checking Daria's teeth.

"Of course."

I had already set out a bottle on the side table in the conference room. The woman was rough as she scoured Daria's skin like a frying pan with a scrubbing pad. She was acting exactly as I remembered, lobbing questions about the donor over her head to the coordinator but never saying a word to the donor herself, not even a greeting. And yet she always wanted to meet them personally and inspect them with her own hands. After scrubbing Daria's face and stretching her skin, the woman moved on to examining her scalp and testing the quality of her hair, even though I had already checked it—no micro rings, no weaves. Her hair was her own. Finally, she let go of Daria's hair, which she had been twirling like the belt of her camel-hair coat a moment ago, and gave a sigh of satisfaction.

"Tell her to undress."

I guessed that this part was the reason her husband had been sent into the city with the guide. When I was their donor, he'd learned about the city's tsarist history, but this time it was Soviet modernism, whose iconic buildings dotted Dnipro from the glory days of the rocket programs. I had promised to take the woman to the Poplavok Café, which was shaped like a spaceship, where her husband's tour would end, and then I could take a picture of them to send to their friends as evidence of the nature of their visit: architectural tourism.

Daria obeyed, folding her clothes on the couch and then, after warming up for a moment, doing the splits. I had never been able to do that. My ankles didn't bend like a Bolshoi ballerina's, and my posture wasn't nearly as regal as hers. The woman measured Daria with her gaze and then began to squeeze her muscles. Only a slightly quicker swallow revealed anything of Daria's feelings, and the veneer that appeared in her eyes. I was proud of her. Despite her inexperience, she behaved like a well-trained horse.

"I loved Nadia Comăneci. The gymnast," the woman said. "I wanted to be just like her. You have so many gifted athletes over here."

I held back my retort by biting my lip. I didn't point out that Comăneci was not from Ukraine but rather Ceaușescu's Romania, where this woman never would have wanted to live. She wouldn't have wanted to be like the invincible Nadia, the perfect-ten girl, who had been placed under a travel ban because of the danger of her defecting. Daria and I could laugh about it later. After snapping pictures of our clients on the shore of the Dnieper, I would take Daria for coffee and pastries and remind her of how much money she was making. This woman was an exception anyway. Usually they worshiped the donors. And how a client behaved during the process never told the truth about what kind of parent they would metamorphose into.

"Daria would have become an Olympic athlete if she hadn't sprained her ankle so badly," I reminded her.

"She's taller than most gymnasts. And most Ukrainians."

"The sport only attracts shorter girls because athletic opportunities are so limited for short people. But Daria had a passion for gymnastics, and she's also an exceptional choice considering your husband's height."

My explanations were pointless, since she had already made her decision. I could feel it in the warmth of her body and her dreamy stare as she gazed approvingly at the shape of Daria's shoulders, her body structure, the size of her feet, and the shape of her arms. Her skin would do. Her hair would do. Her teeth and eyebrows would do. No glasses, no blood transfusions, no transplants, no excessive exposure to X-rays, no travel to risky countries, all of which would have required separate notations on a form. No physical diseases, no mental illnesses, no medication. Not for her, her mother, her father, either of her parents' parents, her siblings, her aunts, her uncles, or her cousins. Daria didn't even have cavities in her teeth, and her tooth enamel was so white that you would have assumed it had been bleached. Daria was perfect, and this woman wanted a perfect daughter.

I understood her infatuation. I had experienced something similar when I first saw Daria sitting on the couch in my office. My former modeling agent's voice had begun playing in my ears, promising this girl a career that would take off like a rocket, and things began bubbling up in my mind that I hadn't known I'd missed. I could taste the flavor of success on my tongue and feel in my breast how the cameras had loved me, and I knew that I would make them worship Daria. She was still an unripe plum hanging on the tree, but she wouldn't be for long.

The plan had developed in my head in seconds. First, we needed a healthy child to prove Daria's suitability as a donor. After the baby was born, Daria would get more important clients, better fees, and enough savings built up in her sock to back away in time. She would donate a few times, no more than that, definitely no more than that. In the meantime, I would raise capital and gradually we could begin to think about Daria's entry into the modeling world. We would shoot for the catwalk and settle for nothing less.

At the same time, I was following Natalia Vodianova's dizzying race from one *Vogue* cover to another. I remembered all too well how quickly Soviet features had gone out of style, even though only a little earlier all the big movie roles had been going to faces with precisely those features. The change could happen faster than you guessed. But Eastern models hadn't yet lost their luster this time around, and Daria had something of the "Supernova" Vodianova in her. Daria could be the next hot name. In order to succeed she would need me, and that wasn't just because a little encouragement would work wonders for her self-esteem, as it had for mine. Without me, Daria was sure to make the same mistakes that I'd made and end up worrying about where to find her next meal or how she would pay her rent if shoots didn't start appearing immediately.

I decided to get Daria her own apartment in Paris, or we could share one. She wouldn't have to experience the life I'd faced in the agencies' dormitories, in their bunk beds. Of course, there had been more Russians than anyone else, and one of them had been astonished when I'd spoken Ukrainian with another girl from here. Ours was a superfluous language, apparently. Life was sometimes straight out of the Soviet army. One of the girls poisoned her rivals with castor oil in order to get into a test shoot while the rest of us lay moaning in our beds. We were all enemies. The old hands didn't want to share what they'd learned with us less experienced girls. Some of the girls couldn't take the competition or the hunger and went home before they even got started. Some of them did escort gigs at the same time, while others moved or were moved over to that industry altogether. That wouldn't happen to Daria. I would protect her from everything.

Daria's relationship with the camera was in a league of its own even in her amateur shots, and both my review of her prequalification form and her first client meeting had shown she was compatible with modeling work. Because of her years of gymnastics, she was accustomed to using her body as an instrument, a tool that had to withstand the gazes, talk, and endless criticism of others. Her relationship with her own body was professional. And this wouldn't be her first time in the West, as it had been for me. The shelves of food at a regular supermarket wouldn't seem extravagant to her. She wouldn't stop to marvel that every block had a butcher, a fishmonger, and a pastry shop with sagging counters. She wouldn't walk the streets of Paris with drool hanging from the corner of her mouth and wouldn't be shocked by the bloody meat. Instead, she would know how to answer properly when waiters asked her how she wanted her steak. I had made mistakes like that. She wouldn't be like me. She would be much better. And I wouldn't cheat her. I wouldn't skim her pay any more than was good manners, and I intended to give her the gift of a magnetic nickname. Maybe the Rocket. That sounded even better than Supernova.

I would become Daria's agent, and when we'd walk from show to show I would pretend not to know the people we encountered. They would say hello and hurry over to chat, indicating that we were old friends, and I would frown a bit as if trying to remember whether we'd really met. I would smile in regret, supposedly not recalling them. Not the photographer who always told me to take off my shirt regardless of the nature of the photo shoot. Not the man who had mocked us as pigs after surprising us wolfing down croissants because we were so hungry. Not the countless hands that were careless with pins or scissors during fittings. Not the hair stylist who cut off my ponytail without asking permission, thereby robbing me for months of the opportunity to participate in shoots that required long hair. Not the woman who had drawn lines on my hips with a marker to indicate excessive fat as if I were a diagram of cuts of meat. I wouldn't remember any of them, and I would charge double for anyone who had implied that I'd better spread my legs if I wanted work.

The more I thought about it, the more I was prepared to be flexible about certain things. Daria didn't know that my boss had stopped embellishing girls' backgrounds, but adjusting a birthplace wasn't a big deal in itself. There were always risks involved in the process, and some of the girls ended up as our clients later. Anything could happen. If I'd had a daughter considering donating, I would have encouraged her to try it only after having her own children, if then. Personally, I had quit as soon as I became a coordinator. I couldn't imagine that Daria would continue if there were other prospects available to her, which there were.

Daria was naturally gifted, and when she began treatments, she lit up like a Christmas tree. Still, I wanted to see with my own eyes how she would cope with having bedroom games, alcohol, and so many other things declared out of bounds. So every day I took her out to walk or to eat or to shop. But nothing seemed to cause her any problems. Once when I suspected she was experiencing some foot swelling, I took us shoe shopping and encouraged her to choose a pair of boots and a couple pairs of shoes one size too large, all on the office. When we came out carrying the shoeboxes, she laughed, and there were tears in her eyes.

"Now I understand so much better women who cry in movies. I've never been like that," she sniffed as she hooked her arm in mine. "It's like I'm someone completely different. Like I have someone else's soul, someone else's emotional life. You should try this, too. It's amazing."

I remembered how I'd felt after my eggs were collected, the constant vomiting, the tender abdomen, the hot water bottles. Even though Daria approached the mood swings brought on by the hormones as an exciting adventure that would make her a wiser person, I wanted to lead the conversation elsewhere. Next to the shoe store was a fur shop. Pointing it out to Daria, I promised her a bonus if the retrieval results were good. A fur vest, fox or wolf. This promise made her eyebrows arch like a bow, and then she sniffed again.

A moment later, the café's honey cake put her in a cheerful mood, and she tapped her finger as if accompanying the clattering of the abacus at the cash counter.

"How are your studies with all of this going on?" I asked. "If the retrieval day and your tests happen to overlap, just tell me. We can pay a doctor to prescribe you sick leave."

This didn't seem to worry Daria.

"I'm doing better than ever," she exclaimed. "And you can't guess how happy this swelling has made my mom. She was afraid I would starve to death as a model."

The first retrieval yielded about forty healthy, active egg cells. Daria refused to rest more than one night before going out on the town to celebrate her success, and she seemed perfectly at ease as she tried on the fox vest I had promised. After shopping, we went to eat, and even though Daria had to keep her jacket open because of the aching in her stomach, as we stopped at a traffic light she looked more like a deer pausing on a ridge than a girl from Donbas balancing in the joint of an articulated bus.

As we sat down at our table, I casually asked how her love life was going. Daria looked down. I covered the irritation in my expression with my champagne glass. We had to put a stop to this.

"It's good to have fun in life, but men don't deal well with women who have their own careers," I said. "And you do now."

Daria clearly hadn't thought about this. She still considered herself a student, for whom lunching in the university cafeteria was a luxury. When I encouraged her to try the salmon, her eyes went wide at the price. I focused on reading the menu as if it were more important to me than our topic of conversation. She needed to believe that this was her own decision.

"I like my freedom," Daria said spiritedly after a moment.

"Of course, you can see whomever you want, dear. Have you decided what you're ordering?"

Peering over the other tables, I pretended to search for the server.

"Traveling is probably less complicated without men."

"If you only knew." I laughed. "After the initial infatuation wears off, every suitor becomes a millstone around your neck. If he isn't demanding clean shirts, he's chaining you to the stove. Or are you already dreaming of having your own children?"

Daria seemed shocked.

"If you want a traveling companion, you can take your mother with you. Or your brother and his family."

"We aren't supposed to reveal the purpose of the trip to them, though, are we?"

"We can say it's for a photo shoot. We can take them along to an event where you're just getting to know your clients. Of course, we would arrange all the passports, visas, and such," I said. "Don't you want to give your mother a vacation to Spain or America?"

Daria smiled.

"Listen, there will be plenty more beaus in your future."

I was sure the guy who'd been courting Daria was handled now. She was a clever girl, and I intended to take her out into the world without the burden that a lover usually became. Few men understood that a donor's condition as the retrieval approached was anything but appropriate for lovemaking. Sometimes a man's sympathies had to be secured with a new phone or some other gift. If the boyfriend was already aware of his girlfriend's job, he might intrude on a trip, assuming we would also pay for him and that it would be one long vacation in the sun. If a girl had been concealing her livelihood, its exposure usually led to the man demanding that she quit. I wouldn't take any risks like that with Daria.

Once we had an appropriate trip scheduled to a city where I knew a good photographer, we would start putting together a modeling portfolio, and Daria could tell her parents about real photo shoots, real commissions, and real cover pictures. Nothing could go wrong.

HELSINKI
2016

After paying for the taxi, I escorted Daria to the hotel lobby, nodding in passing to the receptionist and pulling Daria after me into the elevator. After getting to the room, she tumbled onto the bedspread, which was stretched so tightly around the mattress that there was no question of her crawling under the covers in her state without help. Assuming she would fall asleep almost instantly, I moved quickly. Pushing the laptop I had found on the table at her, I asked her to put on something catchy for us to listen to, like Svetlana Laboda, and poured her a cognac from the minibar. Amazingly, Daria managed to pound her password into the keyboard before she passed out, and then I had a fully open computer in my lap. After Daria's breathing slowed, I stopped the music. I sat down on the edge of the bed and looked around. The Radisson Royal wouldn't have impressed me at the peak of my career, but it had been a long time since I'd sat in a hotel room where someone besides me was responsible for the cleaning, and I remembered the Kyiv Radisson. After starting work at the agency, my boss had pointed to the building as if it were a lighthouse we were navigating toward. Before the arrival of Radisson, she mostly despaired at the accommodation situation in the Ukrainian capital. The stagnant heat of our summers released a smell from wallpaper that foreigners didn't treat with the same compassion that I did. To them it smelled musty, not like childhood. They wondered at the hotel registration cards, jingled the room keys in their hands as if they'd forgotten the time before key cards, and hefted the key fobs as if they were dubious artifacts. They were shocked when they saw how we cooled rooms even in ten-story buildings by opening the windows, which they peered from with gulps of terror. These observations made them doubt the quality and safety of our services. *Safety* was the word they always repeated. My boss was sick of it.

The Kyiv Radisson eliminated most of the office's accommodation problems, and my boss had reason to rejoice. Other chains followed and soon covered the whole country. Confidence in Ukraine was high after the Orange Revolution. That would speed up operations in Dnipro, Kharkiv, and Odesa, and the country would become even more attractive due to the visa-free travel offered to EU citizens. Over the years, faith in the speed of development flagged, as always, but before my transfer to the Dnipro office, I'd met clients in that Radisson. No one had complained about the apathetic staff or the lumpy pillows whose constant dampness brought to mind a cellar. Once they stepped into the lobby, clients believed that they were almost in Europe, and I felt the same way. Or even better. Everything had been like one long birthday party. I had just gotten my life back, left my mother's house, fallen in love with the Kyiv spring, and sung Vopli Vidopliassova as I drove my own car, the first of its kind.

Daria didn't wake up, even though I took my pinky finger and nudged her cheek, which had lost its fertile elasticity. The grooves that ran from beneath her nose were like slits in paper, her chin was a rough crust of bread, and her skin was the pallid brown of a fading autumn, as if she were already decomposing. That association made me take a step back and wipe my fingers on the blanket. I didn't want to touch her, but I would have to if I intended to get my hands on the phone that was under her back. I had forgotten that. For a moment, I considered whether to turn her on her side. Instead, I slid my hand under her. Daria didn't wake up. Her eyelids didn't even flutter when I pressed her thumb to the display to open the lock. It worked effortlessly. Still, I was nervous.

My first job was to remove the photos of my passport, then my face. The recent calls list came as a surprise: there weren't any. The results from Daria's laptop were equally negligible—her browser's search history was empty. However, there were plenty of photos of the dog park family and of me. With clumsy fingers, I attached her phone to the computer and then inserted the swag memory stick from my cleaning company that had been bouncing around at the bottom of my bag in order to copy the pictures. I saw my back, my outstretched leg, my boot with the zipper undone to ease the aching of a long day's work. The worn tip of the boot looked like the end of an old dog's muzzle. I glanced at Daria. She was still asleep, snuffling peacefully without any regret for having watched my private moments and recorded them along with my poor posture, my boot top hanging open, the family's daughter, the pussy willow buds she held in her hand, and her brother. I'd never had the nerve to photograph them. The way Daria had watched the children in the park scared me as much as the fact that she'd found me. The brazenness with which she'd photographed them made my skin tingle. Did she remember how my father had looked? Had she recognized my features or my father's in the boy?

I zoomed in on the phone screen. The boy squinted in the sun. He would be a charmer, that was clear to see, as clear as my own downward slide, and the feeling of shame that washed over me was crushing. My hair was a mess. My roots were obvious. My clothes were ragged. This was how these children saw me. How this boy saw me.

The moment with the pussy willows, immortalized on the camera roll, was from an evening preceding Holy Week when I'd heard the mother talking about Palm Sunday trick-or-treating with another dog walker. Inspired by the conversation, I decided to buy chocolate eggs and wait for an appropriate moment. I would give them to the girl for the twig she had decorated herself and then also offer some to the boy, who wouldn't mind a sweet, even though he was already too old for Easter crafts. We would talk. We would converse.

However, that didn't happen. The chocolate melted into the lining of my coat, or maybe it was because of my damp hand, which returned to my pocket again and again for nothing. I realized that my plan was crazy. Any parent would consider an adult approaching their children to offer candy suspicious. I still couldn't stop the feeling of disappointment, though, and it must have dulled my attentiveness. Nothing else could explain why I hadn't noticed Daria visiting the park at the same time. But why hadn't I spotted her before? Was I so enraptured by the family that I had become blind to my environment? Daria had watched me, trained her camera on me, maybe even sat on the same bench with me, and yet I was alive. She had had time to report my whereabouts to my ex-boss or to you. Or to arrange an accident for me. But she hadn't done that. She wasn't after me. She didn't want revenge. Our meeting was nothing but a chance occurrence occasioned by my weakness, and I could only blame myself for it. Over the past months, Daria had taken more pictures of the dog park family's children than of me. The image files had no record of my front door, my commute, or my mother. However, there was frame after frame of the family, including the door to their building and their windows. Daria had heard the children's names when the parents had called out to them. She was here because of this family, not because of me. She was telling the truth. Was this family so important to her, just as important as they were to me?

I remember how hard it was for me to settle into life in Helsinki. The feeling of relief after my successful escape passed in a heartbeat, and the winter became one long, dark, sleepless night. In the end, I didn't know why I'd bothered to flee or why I dragged myself to work only to return to an apartment echoing with longing, where the coffee cups were always in exactly the same place I'd left them in the morning and where there were never anyone else's smells, never anyone's messes but mine. I hadn't known I could miss such things.

My old passion for studying languages had disappeared, and reading required too much concentration, but something of my former self still remained. My ears worked like before and automatically picked out new words from passersby. And that's how I remembered the dog park family. I was on the tram, and a couple sitting behind me was talking about luxury properties in the city. One word rang in my ear like a spoon in a teacup: Siltasaari. I recognized the name of that neighborhood. My old clients had been from Siltasaari. I pressed my finger into the side of the bench. By the time the family returned to our office for their second child, I was already a coordinator, and as I handled their paperwork, I finally learned their name and address. The Internet told me the rest. The man was a successful engineer, and the woman was the marketing director of a large company. Their life seemed perfect even then. I had studied a map of Siltasaari, admiring pictures of Töölö Bay without guessing that one day I would be here, too, and that they would live barely a stone's throw from my own tiny apartment. After the couple had rounded out their family with our help, I decided to forget them, and my decision had stuck.

But now I could run into them at any moment. The thought made my mouth go dry.

I got off at the next stop, shivering uncontrollably as if I'd just climbed out of a frozen lake. I had a Finnish passport and a new life in a city that smelled of the sea, but my carefully constructed ice castle was in danger of melting. I could already feel it cracking. I called information despite the cost and hoped that the family had moved. My hope was in vain, however, and my fragile peace was gone. I couldn't go out without wondering whether I would run into them, whether I would end up in the same checkout line, whether we might arrive at the post office or the tram stop or the corner store at the same moment. Would I even recognize them? Would the parents remember me, and if they did, what would happen then? Was the woman the kind of mother she had made us believe? Was she still blond? Did she still wear the same kinds of camel-hair coats? Was she home with the children or did she work in an office? Did the siblings run or do gymnastics as their mother had hoped? I had to see what they looked like.

Once the thought had taken root in my mind, it burned like a mustard poultice left too long on the skin. I knew the burning would only go away when I tracked down the family. As I investigated their social media, I convinced myself that I was only concerned with my safety. I had to recognize the children so I could avoid any pitfalls. Ceaselessly I reviewed possible ways we could meet, and my imagination knew no bounds. I understood that it would be wise to move farther away. However, people like me were in a weak position in the housing market—the rent for my two-room apartment was cheap because it was in such poor condition, and my current neighborhood served my needs: it was anonymous and populated by immigrants. I would have trouble finding a similar situation.

I spied on the family online without discovering anything about their life beyond a taste of what they wanted everyone else to see: updates on the boy's hockey team, the girl's riding lessons and gymnastics classes, pictures of a dog in a park, pictures of a dog on a training field, pictures of a dog at dog shows and the rose bouquets won at said shows, Easter grass and the Scandinavian-style pale interior decoration of a home. Lots of birch, rag rugs scattered like summer clouds, windows without drapes—the family loved natural light. I went walking in Siltasaari and looked at the upper floors of their building, but the lack of curtains in their home didn't help: the family lived on the top floor, and all I could see was the light that flooded from their windows. That made my hunger worse.

Still, I didn't dare move forward and had to content myself with tracking their movements online. I even created a fake social media profile to try my luck at getting just a little closer. The family's social life seemed lively. I guessed that they wouldn't pay much attention to a friend request from a woman they didn't seem to know, that instead they'd approve it out of hand, and I was right. Without attracting any notice, I disappeared into their crowded friend list and gained access to pictures of their children's faces, which hadn't been public. I also learned their names: Väinö and Aino. I told myself that this had to be enough. I had gotten what I'd come to get. I would recognize all of them, and I could avoid them. I now knew that the boy was fine and just as he appeared. To my surprise, he resembled my father more than me: the shape of his eyebrows, how his nose sloped, his dark hair.

Afterward it was difficult to understand why an airplane exploding in the sky spurred me into motion to approach the family. The Russians shot down a Malaysian airliner in July 2014, and this event led me to begin recklessly visiting the dog park. These things should have had no connection. I was in Helsinki; the plane went down in Russian-occupied eastern Ukraine, and no one I knew was on board. But its wreckage dropped in an area I remembered all too well.

When I heard the news, I was washing the kitchen counter in the home of a certain retired gentleman. I noticed the sound of the TV increase, and at the same time my phone began to buzz in my pocket. I glanced at it. Mom. I didn't answer. As I picked out individual words from the news reader's dry narrative, they pulled me forcibly toward the living room. The old man stood up from the couch, looking back and forth between me and the television, and then asked if I was from Ukraine. Returning to the kitchen, I downed a glass of water and then watched the water flow from the faucet. I turned the tap to the right and to the left, from cold to hot, and focused my thoughts on the fact that here we drank water straight from the faucet without any complicated water purification system. Here you wouldn't find a gas hot-water heater in the bathroom. Children who grew up here didn't even know what that was. If they visited Ukraine, they wouldn't recognize a water kiosk. They would think that the purified water vending machines that appeared on the sides of buildings were selling soft drinks and would drink the tap water out of old habit and then be surprised at the expressions of the locals if they were seen doing so. I focused my attention on the drop of water clinging to the side of my glass as if nothing else mattered, even though the monotone voice of the news anchor bored into my head with the insistence of a drill and my phone buzzed in my pocket. I didn't want to know anything about the people who lived in eastern Ukraine. I didn't want to hear about anyone who had bodies or body parts, heads or hands, rain down on their yards. I didn't want to hear about anyone who had a burned Dutchman fall through her roof. I didn't want to hear about the people who would have to move into their cellars and whose children would have to walk to school past pieces of airline seats, and I didn't want to know how it would affect the course of the war. The Russians blamed the Ukrainians, and the Ukrainians blamed the Russians. No one seemed to know what had really happened.

The world had never heard anything about the hamlet of Hrabove before that Malaysian airplane exploded over it. Suddenly every country who'd had citizens on board—283 passengers and 15 crew members—was involved. For a moment I thought that this would stop the war, that outside forces would immediately put an end to it. But the moment passed quickly as I swallowed this childish fantasy with another glass of water and understood that none of this would matter in the slightest. The war would continue. There would be more corpses, headless or burned or blasted into nothing, and maybe more airplanes falling out of the sky, and no one would ever be held accountable.

The old man crept into the kitchen, keeping one eye on the television screen. I shifted my weight from one foot to the other. I took a deep breath. Squeezing the glass, I stared at the water droplet as it struggled against its surface tension. Soon the old man would start to ask what was going on and whether Putin had gone crazy, and he wouldn't stop his pestering until he received an answer that he couldn't get from the news. He wanted something more genuine, something that he could pass on to his children.

. . .

The headlines about revolutionaries gathered in the Maidan changed the atmosphere at work, or perhaps it was the escalation of the situation. After President Yanukovych sent his troops against the citizens assembled in Independence Square, people woke up, the newspapers took notice, the reporters came out of their stupor, and every Finn I met started to look at me with new eyes, as if it had just dawned on them that their cleaner was from a country where things happened. Where an uprising was taking place. Where new revelations were appearing daily about the president. Where the president was a Moscow puppet, a certified asshole. Before that, they'd probably thought I was Russian, and that was why everyone lamenting the news first wanted to make sure of where I was from. I told them I was from Kyiv, not eastern Ukraine, and after hearing that, the Finns would breathe a sigh of relief and express their regrets. If I had been invisible to them before, the revolution made me all too visible, and soon the war being waged turned me into a sort of exclamation point for them.

At first this frightened me, until I understood that it was just a question of sympathy. I remember how one time I had a falling-out with a Russian cleaner from whom I used to buy Analgin and Corvalol from over the border because she traveled to Russia more often than my mother did to Finland. Over the years, we had become a good working team. I'd even attended her birthday party. The war changed things, though. The elderly man whose windows we were washing came to watch our work and finally asked about the situation in Ukraine. My companion flew into a rage, accusing the Ukrainians of being bloodthirsty fascists, and I threw my bottle of cleaning fluid at her. The incident ended up reaching our boss's ears. I thought I would be fired. However, the Finns mounted their own sort of protest, and many informed the company that they didn't want any Russians in their homes. That resulted in me being given the Russians' shifts, along with a warning that there was no reason to talk about Putin during work hours. No one wanted their homes or strawberry fields or any other workplaces turned into political battlefields when their staffs were made up of Ukrainians, Russians, and representatives of other nationalities that were involved in one way or another. Apparently, the same agreement was made elsewhere. In the press, they called it the Strawberry Peace.

Finns asked me for advice about the safest way to send aid to the revolutionaries. Some began reminiscing about the Winter War, and a year after the fighting began, the older people began to wonder if the war would eventually spread here. As a result of the economic sanctions imposed on Russia, cheese meant for the eastern market was sold in Finland for a song, and people started calling it Putin cheese. They bought it by the cartful, and they joked about it all the time. It was a real hit. People gave it to me as a gift when I went to clean their homes, and we laughed about it together.

After the plane went down, I didn't want to listen to the radio, watch television, or read the news online. My mother was visiting me just then, and she wanted to go home. I didn't let her. The war might spread. The border might close. Anything could happen. At the end of my workday, I was greeted by an apartment that had become a Babel of news channels. My mother tracked events in Ukrainian, Russian, English, and Finnish, even though she only understood two of those languages. I turned off all of them, once even interrupting a broadcast during the Ukrainian national anthem. But my mother would sneakily turn them back on. We continued this for weeks. I held my tongue when Mom said that the pain was always worse for those who were away. Unlike my mother, I no longer thought about the airplane, the body parts falling from the sky, the Donetsk refugees who had filled Dnipropetrovsk, the businessmen who had transferred their money from Donetsk to Dnipro, or how rushed you must have been. I thought about the family living in Siltasaari and how close to them I dared to sneak. My mother's talk and the voices of the news reporters were like rain falling against the window, which I saw but which didn't touch me. It was as if I didn't understand what the water pattering on the glass was, where it came from or why.

Maybe the change came because the airplane blew up right over Snizhne, just a few kilometers from the house where my father's parents had lived. But the same feeling hadn't been caused by the Russian troops taking control of Snizhne, nor by the flags of the Donetsk People's Republic now waving above the area, nor by the stream of war refugees from Donbas, nor by any other war news. Nor by any of the bodies. Nor by the missing, the imprisoned, or the lines of wounded. Nor by the pictures of the lines of trucks loaded with weapons driving into Donbas from Russia, whose Russian drivers claimed they were delivering humanitarian aid. Nor by the pictures of the bombing of Snizhne and its aftermath, of the people who had moved into their cellars, of the bodies wrapped in carpets, of the bundles along the roads, of the ambulances, which were the same ones we used to call *tabletkas* because they looked like pills with round headlights for eyes. Nor by the videos where an old local accused the Ukrainian army of being fascists who were killing their own citizens and begged Putin for help, nor by the fact that the same woman could be seen in other videos playing a local from somewhere else, whether it was a mother of small children from Odesa, the mother of a soldier from Kyiv, or an anti-Maidan protester from Kharkiv. Russian television devoted generous interview time to this hireling. Once she spoke in front of a collapsed house in Snizhne, sounding like a political commissar and waving pieces of shrapnel in her hand. Behind her, the entrails of the house spilled into the yard. According to the Ukrainian army, its planes hadn't been flying during the time of the bombing, and Russia was accused of trying to use the attack to make Ukraine look guilty. There were plenty of eyewitnesses to the Russian tanks. None of these news reports surprised me, and I also wasn't surprised when it later turned out that the Russian crew who transported the missile that brought down the Malaysian aircraft had driven their vehicles through Snizhne in broad daylight, even stopping to rest next to the Furšet supermarket. Maybe they'd been hungry. Maybe they had bought a bag of sunflower seeds as a snack or maybe something more filling like chicken wrapped in lavash bread. I thought of Lenin Prospekt, where the shop stood covered in daffodil-yellow corrugated metal, and of the men standing holding shawarma wraps, drinking beer from two-liter bottles with sweat on their foreheads. Or maybe they wanted ice cream and water. July was so hot in Snizhne. Maybe the men had cooled themselves with the same *plombir* ice cream I had, holding a softening waffle cone in my hand and wondering how to get out of this backwater. That market with the yellow sides hadn't existed then, but maybe the soldiers thought the same thing, cursing their mission to this remote district and dreaming of their next leave. Then they wiped their mouths, threw their trash on the ground, flashed a V-sign at any passersby, and went to blow up an airplane.

My father's parents' house had been very pretty and well kept. Maybe now a separatist family lived there, and maybe that family was digging our coal. Representatives of the new authorities had taken over the kopankas and were making money on them. My mom thanked the Holy Mother of God that my grandparents weren't around to see the destruction, the greed, and the looting. It galled her but not me. I had thought the place was getting what it deserved. As far as I was concerned, every inclined shaft and pit mine could explode, every blast furnace could be snuffed out, and every building could collapse, but now I felt ashamed of having had those thoughts. Just a stone's throw from our former home there could have been hundreds of thousands of Russian soldiers. Seventy-five percent of Russian citizens were in favor of war against Ukraine. The size of that percentage and the number of boots on the ground hit my consciousness with a force that made my ears ring. I couldn't ignore it by shrugging or calling the opposition *vatnikes*, idiots who slavishly followed Putin. They really and truly wanted to kill us.

I had always hated Snizhne, the whole area, but suddenly that felt wrong. Just as wrong as having left the city that could have become my home. I found myself wondering what would have happened if we'd stayed in the house Dad got for us and I'd never run off to Paris. Would I be just as happy as I had been in Kyiv after finally getting control of my life? Or would I have been eager to build the family business? Would I have joined my father's enterprise, would I too have belted Vopli Vidopliassova in my car in Snizhne, or would I have sung something else? Would I have fallen in love with a local guy, married, and taken my children to the family graves with a basket of *paska* Easter bread? And would that all have fallen apart because of the war, and would burnt pieces of bodies have flopped down on my

dinner table? Would my sons have collected shell casings and shrapnel as they played, and would my husband or father have negotiated
with the separatists about the mines, the kopankas, and coal deliv-
eries? Would my mother have resisted and my resourceful father
adapted? Maybe he would have gotten along with the new overlords.
Maybe he would have grown rich.

Or maybe he would have received a bullet to the brain, and in
any case we would have fled either to my aunt's in Mykolaiv or with
the other refugees to Dnipro or Zaporizhia, making our home in a
shipping container, and I would have prayed every night that the new
residents of my grandmother's home would meet a bullet or a land
mine or a pack of dogs, and relished the thought of how hungry the
dogs left behind by the refugees would be, because they would be
completely wild, even wilder than the wild dogs of Chornobyl.

But we had left Snizhne long ago, and I hadn't participated in
the revolutions, not any of them, on any side. I hadn't joined the
separatists or the Ukrainian army, which also allowed women into
its ranks, or any of the other things I might have done if I was still in
Ukraine. Instead, I watched the progress of the war from a city where
such things were merely headlines in the newspaper, and for some
reason my mind returned to the lines of Yevgeny Yevtushenko. They
repeated in my mind as if I had just now understood what they said.

> I am
> each old man
> here shot dead.
> I am
> every child
> here shot dead.
> Nothing in me
> shall ever forget!

The words pounded in my head like an uninvited guest who
refuses to go home. I woke up to them at night. I found myself writing them down even though I intended to write my shopping list,
and I caught myself muttering them aloud while sweeping floors.
They left me in peace, though, when I built up the courage to venture

to the dog park. The park bench became a soft movie theater seat I could sink into and empty my mind. There I could watch the family live their life like a story that could have been mine if everything had gone differently.

The first time, I ventured into the dog park under the merciful cover of darkness. Creeping along, I approached the bench where one family member often sat. I sat down cautiously, as if the slats were glass, and then took in the landscape, their landscape, imagining what their life must be like in a country where dogs had their own parks, better maintained than the public spaces in Ukraine. I circled the park tree by tree and traced the fence of the dog enclosure, counting how many steps it would take to get to the street if I was caught. I practiced until I was out of breath. No one appeared other than a head I glimpsed once in the distance, which probably belonged to a homeless person. No one came wondering what I was up to. In daylight, the situation would be different. Still, I decided to try. The next time I would come during the time the family walked their dog. I would disappear if anything suggested I'd been recognized, even a lingering glance. Then I would never return. I would dye my hair, find an apartment somewhere else, maybe in another city, and look for a new job. The family would just think they had been mistaken. For a while they would be more watchful of their surroundings, but soon they would forget the whole thing and conclude that their imaginations had been playing tricks on them. If that didn't happen, the agency would be able to calm them down. My former employer was used to dealing with paranoid clients who called after thinking they'd seen their children's features in a stranger. No one in the office would take them seriously.

After gathering my courage for a week, I went to the park in broad daylight. On the way, I checked how I looked in my hand mirror. My jacket had a hood, whose drawstrings I tightened and loosened repeatedly. Sweat made my sunglasses slide down my nose, and my library books weighed on me. I'd thought to grab them after realizing that I couldn't afford to appear idle. Poisoned dog treats had been found in the park and its vicinity, and people were on the alert. I had prepared well, and yet the feeling still ate at me that I wasn't good enough to enter this family's sphere, not even the park they frequented. The collapse of my standard of living had made me the embodiment of my new profession. Nothing in me resembled the person I had been. My skin was becoming leathery, the pores gaping open. I had traded lipstick for Vaseline, hundred-euro pantyhose for thrift-store rags. I carried a backpack just like the locals here, and it hadn't felt at all ridiculous. Nothing remained of my previous self, and that was precisely as it should be. They wouldn't recognize me. Even so, I was embarrassed to appear in public like this. I feared seeing contempt in the boy's eyes for this undesirable if he happened to glance at me. Did my fears stop me? Of course not. I couldn't stop, not anymore.

When I finally saw the family in real life in front of me, I clung to the armrest of the bench, sure that their dog would sense my intentions. It was so sharp, so alert to its surroundings that it could not fail to understand the danger I represented. When the schnauzer charged at me, the mother would run over. She would shout and defend her pet, which never behaved this way, and then she would recognize me.

The dog didn't stop to sniff me, though, let alone wag its tail.

The woman watched the girl romping with it.

The man focused on his call.

The boy stood by the gate and didn't seem to notice what was happening around him.

He was concentrating on his phone.

Slowly I stood up and walked toward the boy, sure that soon the woman would shriek and rush at me, scratching me with her manicure-hardened nails, tearing at my hair and dragging me away without the man attempting to stop her. Someone else would call the police. The man would hurry away with the children and call my old boss.

I stopped for a moment a couple of meters from the boy. He didn't look up from his phone; his fingers continued tapping. He didn't see me. The dog running in the enclosure didn't interrupt its play to stiffen and growl at me. The boy's nose was still my father's, but the sheen of his skin was mine.

I realized that my fear of recognition was my own vanity, a remnant of my previous self, who had been awfully sure of her own irreplaceability. I should have known better. The family wouldn't know me even if I still visited a hairdresser regularly and the leather of my handbags was as high-quality as before. People like us were invisible. The memory of our faces melted like snow from their minds because none of our clients wanted to remember our existence.

One frigid day, something unexpected happened: the woman approached me herself. Reading on a park bench wasn't plausible in the winter, so I had adopted a new habit of circling the area as if out on a walk. I saw the woman open the gate of the dog enclosure. Speeding up, I began to cross the street before she could reach me. However, she remained standing by the fence, and when she noticed me slip between two cars across the street, she set off after me, seeming to try to catch up. I was sure I'd been caught. She had remembered. I stopped. What if I just let it all happen? I closed my eyes, waiting to be struck. But no. The woman said hello, apologizing for the interruption and assuring me she wouldn't keep me long. At first, I didn't understand what she was saying. Then I caught on. She was hoping I would take a picture she could use to make a Christmas card for her relatives, and there was no one in the park she could ask to help. The day was so remarkably beautiful that she didn't want to miss its waning light and the untouched surface of the snow.

I captured the winter landscape and their moment of radiant family bliss in a way that only a person who lacks such a dream can do.

After this episode, the woman nodded to me when she passed. The rest of the family followed suit. A smile, a nod, a greeting. The dog wagged its tail and let itself be petted. The girl made more lively contact, the boy less or none at all. He didn't even look at me, let alone smile, as the girl did, eagerly following her mother's example. Still, I was hopeful and began carrying treats in my pocket. I would sneak them to their pet, and that would make us friends. I trusted in the dog's memory and convinced myself that the situation was

sure to repeat. The woman would need the help of a passerby when
the weather was perfect or a cloud pattern or sunset was unusually
photogenic. Gradually the brief nod would deepen into chatting, then
into more genuine conversation, and with the treats on its mind, the
dog wouldn't want to stop playing with me, and then the boy would
stop and say hello as well.

That never happened, though.

The slight nods ceased.

The dog wagged its tail at other people but not at me.

I was surprised at how seriously I took it, how much a small nod had
meant, how much I'd expected the situation to develop in a different
direction. In the evening, I emptied the bottle of horilka Boris had
distilled and Mom had brought, and assured myself that I'd found
what I'd gone looking for: the certainty that the family didn't recognize me and evidence of the parents' good qualities. The woman
was the mother she had claimed to be. The man was the father I had
imagined him to be. I was only visible in the boy as whispers in his
features. I'd succeeded in stealing a slice of their life at a moment
when they were still spending quality time together as a whole family,
and that would have to be enough. Within a few years, the boy would
stop coming to the park, and the woman would long for the days
when he still sucked the ice that had soaked into his mittens. In the
blink of an eye, the boy would be going to high school and later perhaps to university, and if he did, he would receive decent financial aid
instead of living on sacks of potatoes his parents mailed. If he served
in the army, he was unlikely ever to fight. He wouldn't crawl into a
kopanka after school to dig coal tainted with ash and sulfur, and he
wouldn't turn his hockey sticks into weapons by pounding nails into
them. He wouldn't learn to make Molotov cocktails out of light bulbs.
A war wouldn't divide his family any more than a revolution would.
His car wouldn't be set on fire. His phone calls wouldn't be listened
to. He wouldn't buy a dashboard camera in case a police officer who
pulled him over tried to shake him down or someone claimed he
was guilty of an invented accident. No one would wrap him in plastic
and dump him in a landfill. He would be able to open his door to

strangers without worrying. After graduating, the boy would buy an apartment where he wouldn't need burglar alarms, and he wouldn't hoard electric space heaters in case Russia shut off the country's gas lines. He wouldn't know anything about social orphans like Boris, who had never been allowed into school and who would be forgotten in institutions for the rest of their lives unless a relative like Ivan happened to rescue them. If the boy ever visited Ukraine, it would be on holiday, and he would act like all the other Western tourists. He would take photographs of the air conditioners hanging from the exterior walls of the apartment buildings and laugh at them but fall in love with the old women who sold flowers on the roadside, adding carrots with bushy green tops to their selection during harvest season and becoming berry sellers as the summer came to an end. The boy would find something authentic and genuine in the stooped grandmothers. There was a word for that, poverty, but he wouldn't recognize it. He wouldn't cry to the same songs as my mother and I did. He wouldn't laugh at the same jokes. He wouldn't speak the same language. He wouldn't learn the same customs. He wouldn't offer his hand to his girlfriend as she climbed out of the car, and he wouldn't take her gently by the elbow on the stairs. He wouldn't long for watermelons, apricots, chestnut flowers, or murals on the walls of buildings. He wouldn't feel a vague homesickness, because he would have a home to return to. I imagined all the unpleasant things he would avoid because his home was here, repeating them in my mind so I wouldn't think about all the good things he would miss, the ones I was missing.

I drank all night because the decisions I made were the right ones, despite the fact that you and I and our son could have been like the dog park family and spent all our free time together. I would have had a new trench coat every spring, with my hair blown out at the salon, and on idle mornings you would have woken up to a breakfast tray laid out by our son's sticky hands and in your pockets found building blocks, rocks, and the maple leaves he carried around in the fall.

All that would have been possible if I'd told you about Snizhne and Daria as soon as we met. Then maybe nothing would have gone wrong. You would have forgiven me for the minor embellishment.

Someone else would have received my promotion and advanced in her career, but I wouldn't have been forced to leave you or run away.

I also should have shared with you the news about our son, Olezhko, and I should have done it without delay when I realized I was carrying our child. I intended to. I thought, if everything went wrong, you would believe your child's mother above the others. And if you didn't, you would still help for your son's sake.

Daria tossed and turned, muttering in her sleep, but I couldn't make out the words. Setting down the pillow I'd been squeezing, I stretched my fingers, which were stiff from clenching them. I had to keep going. There were thousands of pictures on Daria's phone, the earliest from three years ago. I didn't find any more of me, but that didn't make me feel better. She had documented other women. She had watched mothers and children. She had secretly photographed people I desperately did not want to find in Daria's phone, and the situation was worse than I could have imagined, because in that group of former clients, I found the most important one. The pictures of Lada Kravets and her children were recent, taken from astonishingly close up, and there were a lot. That signified a danger I needed to focus on. However, my heart told me to do otherwise—as soon as I had found the Kravets family, I began to search for you. You were there somewhere. I wanted to see your face. Your hands. Your neck. Your car. Your shadow. That terrace at Mimino you liked so much, or that café in Vienna. A picture taken from a distance of a dinner table, maybe with Lada Kravets adjusting her lace scarf and you sitting next to some woman who would clearly belong to you. Even just a glimpse of the places that were your places, the Kravetses' places, which would tell me the photograph had recorded your breath if nothing else. But if there was no sign of you, my fears might have come true. You wouldn't be coming after me. Someone else would. Maybe that would be easier.

I recognized you instantly, even though only half of your back appeared on the screen: your right shoulder was still just a little higher than the left, the position of your head familiar. I enlarged the recently taken photo. Lada happened to be looking straight into the camera and appeared so hale and happy, so everything I'd never seen in her before—and completely unaware of the person spying on her children. Lada's son held his mother by the hand, and a strange woman pushed a stroller with a girl sitting in it. The woman, who I assumed was a nanny, did not have her hair blown out, and a home-made skirt covered the uneven bumps of her hips. Next to them scampered a toy poodle dressed in a Burberry jacket. Based on the buildings visible through the trees, at the time the picture was taken they were in London, in Belgravia. How did you not notice the danger stalking you? Was Daria so skilled that she evaded even your gaze? I'd have thought that after what I did, you would be more alert than ever.

I didn't know what to think. Of course, I'd considered that, in the end, you might have been blamed for everything. I just didn't really believe it. You were a survivor, or you had redeemed yourself, that much was now clear. Otherwise you wouldn't have been in a photo-graph so close to your boss's daughter-in-law and her grandchildren. That told me everything important: you were still part of the Kra-vets family. There you were, of all people. You were older, but you were the same, and you were alive. But for how long if the Kravetses learned that Daria had been spying on them under your care?

I should have dashed straight out of that hotel room. I should already have been on the run. But instead, I searched for more signs of you, greedily scrolling through the camera roll, until I spotted some shots taken of old newspaper photographs. In one of them, Lada Kravets was holding her baby. The blue of the Party of Regions flag glimmered in the background. I remembered well the event from six years ago, and the scene on the phone dragged me back to that room where we stood side-by-side listening to the guest speeches. We leaned against the wall, avoiding the camera lenses. Closing my eyes, I felt your breath on my neck, the warmth of your body at my side, smelled your scent in my sweat. Heat clawed furrows in my back, and my new boots squeezed my feet, even though I'd stretched them for a week with vodka. The day had been full of toasts, speeches, and international speakers. Our country's aim was to repair the disaster of the previous year when we had been forced to return swine flu vaccines from the United States. Too many people thought their real purpose was to sterilize the poor, that it was pure eugenics. Rumors of American plots spread like wildfire, as did a measles epidemic, again, and the same politicians and businessmen who had spun up the rumor mill were now dripping honey words into the ears of the guests about reviving domestic vaccine production. Lada Kravets and her babies made a good impression at such events, and because I represented several foundations that promoted children's health, my task was the same: to burnish the tarnished reputation of our country. In order to start production, we had to pry more support from the German delegation. You whispered in my ear that the German guests were irritated about the equipment they had already donated, which had been intended to launch the very production for which we now needed funding. Ten years had passed, and the equipment hadn't been put to use—there wasn't even information about its physical location. Feeling themselves cheated, the Germans were angry, and their desire to help was sapped. They simply didn't trust the new government's vaccination program.

"You could do something," you whispered.

"Like what?" I asked.

"Like smile," you suggested. "At least."

My job was to convince the delegation that new political winds would change everything, and that President Yanukovych was the man for the job.

At dinner, I was placed next to one of the Germans. I told him that, before we added new girls to our lists, we vaccinated all of them just to be safe, and only with vaccines certified by our own doctors. But I couldn't choke down a single bite of the food and instead pushed it around so it would look eaten, and only drank the wine that had also been poured for the Germans. Then I told my companion that it would be better to give up. Let it go. Our government ministers preferred to gild their dachas with the grants they received. The Germans should personally visit the tuberculosis sanitoriums on which their countrymen's money had also been squandered, and I was willing to bet they would find neither hide nor hair of any patients.

I only stopped my uninterrupted litany when I noticed your long glance from the other table. The Germans were frozen, watching me. I was in trouble, I already knew that, so what did it matter? I would lose you either way. What significance did anything I let out of my mouth have?

The next morning you told me that the delegation was suddenly on its way to the Crimean Peninsula. They wanted to visit the facilities they had been supporting, and you asked whether I had something to do with that. I pulled my jaw behind my fox-fur vest and assured you that I had done my best. In Crimea, the travelers would be greeted by a pile of rocks and an overgrown statue of Lenin in the yard where the miners under treatment at the once magnificent sanatorium had spent their time.

But my behavior toward the Germans was the exception. Their visit happened to coincide with one of the days when my nerves were on the verge of snapping. Still, I managed to keep my head above water and behave normally except for a few scenes, one of which you witnessed then. You still imagined that what we had could endure, and I did my best to make that happen. You held my hand because we were lovers, and I held yours because I was drowning.

Last year my mother heard a rumor that Lada Kravets had moved with her family to Vienna. Mom told me about it in passing, and I pretended it was completely irrelevant to me, even though I soon found myself browsing pictures of Vienna online, wondering what you were doing at that precise moment, whether you still lived in the house I remembered so well. I'd chosen its chandeliers from an antique shop your boss's wife, Maria Kirillovna, recommended when she still thought we were building a home together. If the family was in Vienna, so were you. Maybe at that very second you were in a restaurant on the banks of the Danube eating *tafelspitz;* I could taste the applesauce and horseradish so strongly that my nose burned. Or no, it was January, dancing season. You were preparing for an evening in the company of a lady, and that woman would turn her back to you, lift the curls that had fallen from her bun, and ask you to do up the zipper buried tightly in the fabric of her evening gown. I could hear the rustling of the dress and see your fingers on it. That woman could have been me. I could have been dancing the waltz with you that January evening if I hadn't been forced to flee because our world was not going to change despite the war and the new government. For you the dances are the same, the villas in Nice are the same, the boarding schools your children attend are the same, and the cost of the cars you drive is the same. Perhaps you have a new partner, or one you've lost, new business relationships in place of old, but nothing is worse. Perhaps quite the opposite. Perhaps you're doing better. Perhaps the war has become a lucrative business for you, and you have more money and power than before. Perhaps the emergency laws brought by the conflict have opened up entirely new angles, and why wouldn't they? The newspapers reported that your boss was funding the Dnipro Battalion to fight against the separatists and that his private army formed an essential part of the volunteer forces. I didn't believe this was only about patriotism and securing his investments, though that must have been part of it. The criminal investigations launched as part of the Maidan revolution had revealed tangled networks of corruption, causing a wave of suicides by high-profile figures. Never for a moment, though, had I imagined anything like that could touch you.

I'd tracked the progress of the revolution from afar and sometimes was sure that Russian tanks would roll into Dnipro. After the occupation of Crimea, I watched the latest Russian news broadcasts on my computer to see if overnight not just Crimea but all of Ukraine had been added to the Russian map used for weather forecasts. I wasn't the only one.

When I saw that pictures of the Ukrainian trident had appeared on the wall of the abandoned Parus Hotel, I wanted to be there painting blue and yellow on the street. My head would have borne a wreath of flowers, and our son would have been so excited. We would have hung the Ukrainian flag in the office and sung the national anthem at concerts. Together we would have watched as Dnipropetrovsk began to show its colors—how the statue of Grigory Petrovsky, who gave his name to the city at the beginning of the Soviet era, fell—and heard how Dnipro's very own Brezhnevian anthem stopped playing in the trains and at city council meetings, ceasing to welcome comrades and workers or cause people to stand. I would have liked to experience even a moment of faith in change, in a new world, a new future, even if it meant being disappointed like so many others. Young men return from the front knowing how to fight. What do you think these veterans will think about the slow pace of change, about how while they watched their friends die, nothing in your life has changed?

During the revolution, I often thought about my boss and imagined how she might vacillate between the Ukrainian flag and Putin's picture, pacing her office hanging first one and then the other on the wall, finally shoving them both in the closet. The office's website now says that Russian donors are no longer accepted, but I'm sure Putin's beautifully framed portrait is still in storage somewhere just in case.

I let Daria's phone rest in my lap and massaged my face. I was in a hotel room where I shouldn't be, and I was looking at a woman I shouldn't be with, as she slept on top of the covers. I was remembering things best left forgotten, and that slowed me down, as feelings often do. I straightened my numb legs and stood up to listen to Daria's breathing, wondering whether her sleep was as deep as before and whether she would invent some way to end me if she didn't see me when she awoke. If she assumed I'd fled, would she snap? I decided to throw more sleep sand in her eyes. Thinking I could make out the familiar scent of valerian root, I navigated to the bathroom. And there it was, a bottle of Corvalol. After mixing a generous amount of the barbiturate into a glass of water, I lifted Daria's head and spooned the liquid into her mouth. Mumbling, she spluttered and swallowed. On the bedside table I wrote a note in which I promised to return for breakfast, then removed the memory stick from her laptop and returned the phone to its place under her back. Covering my head with my scarf, I slipped past the reception desk in the lobby. Every step I took was shaken by the throbbing in my chest and the fear boring into it, and yet with each step I longed to be able to take your arm. Every footfall ordered me to head to the harbor or the airport. But I didn't do that. Too many questions about Daria still hung open, too many lives were in danger. And I couldn't disappear without saying goodbye to my mother—she would be sure that I'd been killed.

At home I pulled the suitcase I had brought with me from Dnipropetrovsk out of the attic. I didn't allow my mother's long look to trouble me: I claimed I was just making space in the storage room for my winter clothes. She didn't say anything, not even about the strange time of night for housekeeping, but I waited for her to go to bed before opening the suitcase.

The scent of Tobacco Vanille still clinging to the clothes filled the entryway like a box of winter apples fetched from the cellar, and I held my breath for a moment. I didn't know whether Karl Marx still had his prospekt in Dnipro or whether Leonid Brezhnev's portrait and commemorative plaque had already disappeared from his birthplace. Since the revolution, there were hundreds of cities and tens of thousands of streets that needed renaming in Ukraine, along with all the Lenins and other statues to be toppled. But while the Lenin Prospekts and Gagarin Prospekts had already or would soon experience this fate, the contents of my bag hadn't changed since my escape.

Pulling out a wrinkled dress that should have been folded in tissue paper, I wondered what I'd been thinking when I packed it. It might have gone perfectly with my snakeskin pumps, but in Helsinki it was useless. Had I thought I would continue my life the way it had been? Was that why I had brought it? Or was it because of you? My boss had given me the dress for a philanthropy gala, one of the endless events we used to attend to build relationships. Charity had become fashionable once the moneymen in Ukraine realized what a good way it was to buy honorary Cambridge doctorates and attract the brightest Hollywood stars to headline their soirees. It laundered money, it provided legitimacy, and it could make any face respectable. This was the dress I wore to the party in Zaporizhia, where we sneaked out during intermission, you and I. I was afraid of what my boss's reaction would be if she noticed my disappearance, and yet I followed you into the shadows of the theater's pillars all the same. I had begun to wheeze within an hour of arriving in the city, and after listening to my breathing for a moment you told me a story about the teachers who had warned girls all over the country about boys from Zaporizhia. Marrying one of them meant, as part of the deal, getting Zaporizhia as a home. You winked and remarked that you'd moved away from here ages ago. My heart skipped a beat, and you suggested a little walk; we would have a better view of the theater's handsome façade from the small park on the other side of the Lenin Prospekt that ran in front of it. I would be able to see the entire pediment atop which stood a statue carrying both a harp and a hammer and sickle. There was something in the position of the female figure that reminded me of my boss. At the statue's feet, two Komsomols held a banner, and for a moment I wondered if you were teasing me, suggesting that I was like an adoring young zealot with my boss. When I heard the bell signaling the end of intermission, I started for the door, but you took my arm. Under your smoldering gaze, I suddenly felt an irresistible urge to get drunk and forget everything.

I'd received the shoes from you later, as well as the ankle boots, which I had packed in their shoeboxes with shoe trees shoved in them as if I had endless space in my luggage.

Acacia petals had stuck to the bottoms of the pumps from our last walk together. I picked them off and held them in my palm. It had been May, and the park was as white as winter as we waded through the acacia drifts and poplar fluff, which fell on us like snow, and you told me about receiving a beating when you lit the cottony fuzz on fire at your babushka's house. It had burned well.

I threw the shoes back into the suitcase. I hadn't used either pair here once. The life of a person without a car in this Nordic country contained too many grates, too many rubber mats full of treacherous holes, and altogether too much slush for heels. Or maybe I'd wanted to save them because I didn't have a man anymore to give me expensive gifts. Pressing my nails into my palms, I tried to change the direction of my thoughts. But I couldn't. The moment when you surprised me on my way into the Passage Mall was too vivid in my mind. Daria and I had already moved to the Silverleaf dacha for the process, and I had come to downtown Dnipro to buy boots. When I heard someone shouting my name, I stopped and was surprised to see that you had been waiting for me at the carousel next to the shopping center. You had roses, and they were for me. You suggested a walk, and even though I wanted to go with you, I hesitated. My job was to monitor Daria's injections personally, and I didn't want to betray my boss's confidence. It wasn't enough for her that the nurse responsible for the injections lived in the dacha. So I decided to head back as soon as I'd finished my shopping. You followed me into the mall, and afterward we stopped at the carousel. I looked away from you, toward the Palace of Culture and the statue of Lenin. Marshrut-kas whizzed by as yellow as traffic lights. You continued your coaxing. Just a little walk. Just one drink if not dinner. Just a moment if not the whole evening. I glanced at the clock on my phone. And even as I did, my feet began to move as if of their own accord, and I let you take me past the circus to the banks of the Dnieper. There were no fire artists or jugglers, and the weather was too much even for the fishermen. I turned my face into the stiff breeze, which carried the pleasant scent of halva from the sunflower oil factories, and snatched up a bouquet of roses abandoned on the iron rail of the promenade, making it dance before dragging it away. I had no thought for my responsibilities, only for the girl for whom those flowers had been meant and who had not come to her rendezvous, and how any bouquet I ever saw left anywhere always made me so sad.

I shoved the ankle boots I'd purchased at Passage back into the box, which lay atop a bottle of hair dye, some false eyelashes, and a pair of sunglasses that had cost an arm and a leg. Tickling the side of the shoebox was a fox-fur vest that did suit this northern weather. However, only Russians wore furs in Finland. I hadn't given up the vest, though, unlike my wolf fur. I touched the soft garment. I would only get pennies for it, not enough for a new escape. My head began to hurt, and I suspected it was due to the perfume, which I hadn't used in ages. After moving to Helsinki, I'd bought some imitation fragrances, but I'd had to give them up after receiving some complaints, which taught me a lesson about how we do things here in Finland. The personnel manager at the cleaning company where I worked had sized me up from head to toe as she lectured me. Looking at her, I felt like I was seeing my former self. I, too, had kept an eye on my little birds' perfume usage whenever we had a client coming from the Nordic countries. Scandinavian noses were sensitive:

they always complained about the cleaning products in the hotels and the smell of chlorine in the water.

Once I noticed a bottle of Tobacco Vanille on the shelf of a home I was mopping. There was a film of dust on top of the cork, so the freshness of the scent surprised me. I was alone, and after completing the cleaning, I sprayed some perfume on the pulsing veins of my wrists. That night I awoke to your breath on my neck, but when I reached out, the bed was empty.

I crammed the evening dress back into the suitcase. I didn't want to know how ridiculous I would look in it or if the zipper would even close. I pulled out a silk blouse. Among my belongings were also items that stirred some optimism, like pencil skirts and a couple of jackets. If they fit me, I could spend my final days wearing clothing that felt like my own and gave me some semblance of dignity. I could try to be the woman with whom you had thought you would share your life. At the bottom of the suitcase I found an unopened package of pantyhose, shoe polish, and a clothes brush.

I looked around for anything else to bring and hesitated over the empty cardamom tube I'd bought for our son. I'd seen Finns storing their children's baby teeth in them and thought that could be Olezhko's first step toward becoming one of them. Now I would leave everything that reminded me of him. I had tried and failed, failed at everything.

I woke up to throbbing in my chest and raised my head. I didn't understand how I could have fallen asleep at the kitchen table given my situation. Pressing my fist to my heart, I attempted to calm its racing. My laptop screen was dark. I'd been searching Daria's pictures, which I'd transferred from the flash drive to my computer. When the throbbing threatened to spread to my temples, I stumbled off to search for my Analgin. As I filled a glass with water, I noticed the crows that had gathered in the tree outside the window. It was as if my distress had called them forth to watch for the moment when their prey would succumb. I tugged the curtains closed. The sound pounding inside of me was so loud that you had to be able to hear it. It couldn't help but call you. It wouldn't stop. It would expose me, leading you along my trail. It made me want to run. And I did run, to the entryway to grab the handle of the suitcase waiting there. It was ready, just as ready as it had been when I fled Dnipropetrovsk, and I began to drag it toward the door. Stopping to put on my coat, I pulled on the fingerless gloves my mother had made for me. My gaze paused at my hands, at my short nails, which six years earlier had been hard and sure. Then my escape had been successful. I had my furs, my styled hair, and my lash extensions. I looked like I flew constantly, like I could afford to do so, and still I'd been a bundle of nerves at the Kyiv airport. How on earth did I think I could get away now?

I sat down on the floor next to my mother's shoes. I still wondered how I'd played the part so effectively then, how I'd managed to look the part of a determined businesswoman at the border. The security guards had been busy going through all the glass jars clinking down the X-ray belt, and I mentally thanked those grandmothers and the constant problems they caused. The babushkas didn't understand why they couldn't carry breakable jars of pickles in their hand luggage, and usually they were allowed through with their gifts. No one had the time to notice the tremor in my hands, the pools of sweat under my arms, or the socks sliding down in my boots, and my Finnish passport barely rated a glance. Nonetheless, I expected to feel your hand on my arm at any moment, to hear your whisper in my ear asking me where I thought I was going. Sometimes I think that maybe you let me go, that you gave me time to escape. Would you do that now, too? How could I get you to believe that I had already suffered enough? The airport staff didn't allow bottles of pickles in hand luggage anymore—my mom hadn't been able to bring to Finland a single jar from her full cellar at home, and she bemoaned nothing more. Maybe you wouldn't let me go again. If you even did then. Maybe I was just trying to convince myself.

Often, I wonder what the people I left in my past imagine happened to me. Some probably thought I was dead, that my body had been wrapped in a rug and dumped in a landfill. Others maybe thought I was living on a paradise island sipping champagne. No one would suspect that any middle-class lady in Helsinki could afford my services now. Wasn't that a heavy enough punishment for me? That my life was like this, an exile of sorting strangers' laundry and tidying up after other people's kids? Would you let me keep this insignificant life of mine if I explained why I had done what I did?

The sun rose, and the street sweeping machines began their work, but I hadn't found a solution during the night, as I had hoped. I twiddled with the key card I'd taken from Daria's hotel room as if it were a crystal ball, even though it didn't offer me a window into her head. I was still browsing through the photos on my laptop. Hours of searching hadn't given me any more answers. I was still amazed at the number of families in the pictures and all the children with Daria's dimples—most of them were new to me. I'd tried to save Daria, but the coordinators who stepped into my shoes had not. I didn't understand why Daria had agreed to this and why the office hadn't looked after its investment. Had a flood of customers into the country taken them by surprise? Was it because Thailand had finally grown tired of its reputation as a baby factory and banned surrogacy for foreigners? That had definitely made the country seem unreliable in the eyes of the client base. If India followed suit, Ukraine would be the new king of the industry. International developments in the business were constantly guiding couples toward Ukraine. I calculated how much Daria must have earned. If she had developed a taste for the good life, perhaps she got greedy. Maybe a car or a fur coat hadn't been enough. She had decided to want everything and to keep donating as long as they kept paying her properly.

But Daria hadn't earned anything lately. I was sure of that. I wouldn't have dared ask the girl whom I'd left sleeping on that hotel bed to spot me any more than ten dollars, if that. I would have been embarrassed to introduce her to anyone.

To help me think, I went to the refrigerator for some of the *salo* Mom had brought and poured myself a glass of the birch sap horilka Boris had made. I had to concentrate. I had to review our past cases of girls who had turned problematic. Daria was just one of them, nothing more. Usually the issues arose when a donor became useless to us after the process was over—that was a hard blow for most, as was the loss of perks like an apartment. Some girls looked for new ways of making money to maintain their standard of living. Sometimes they tried blackmail. But Daria could get more money from you than from any of her former clients, and all at once. Still, she hadn't sold me out, not yet. I repeatedly came back to the same conclusion: it couldn't be the money. There had to be something else behind this. Maybe Daria couldn't stand that no one from her old life understood her calling as a giver of life. Income, gifts, and travel were not the only attractions of the job; the feeling of purpose could also be addictive. Almost no one donated only once, and Daria was no exception. Could she be one of those girls who didn't know how to live without being worshiped as a saint anymore? Or one of those who, because of the hormone fluctuations, ended up in such deep waters that life lost all meaning? Or one of those who couldn't find relief for her agony even from God? Sometimes girls simply fell apart. Any of these explanations could apply to Daria. Or could she be one of the girls whose perceptions of their work changed once they became mothers themselves: someone else had given birth to real children from their eggs. But Daria didn't seem like a mother. Her lifestyle and the pace of work these pictures revealed wouldn't have allowed it. However, this group of girls could develop an obsessive desire to contact their previous clients. Usually they claimed they had vital information about a child's health and that they would provide more details as soon as the family called.

We never forwarded those messages. All they caused was trouble, trouble like Daria passed out in her hotel room.

I found myself counting the numbers of girls and boys in the pictures as if they were a bouquet of flowers. If I saw an odd number of children, they would be like a funeral arrangement, maybe for me. If it was even, I still had hope of survival. But what if there was an odd number of girls and an even number of boys? I rubbed my forehead. The horilka hadn't cleared my mind. None of my past problem cases were comparable to Daria. This wasn't a nut I knew how to crack. And I didn't want to repeat the mistake I'd already made once, dismissing Daria as one more ordinary girl in the crowd of donors.

"What are you doing sitting in the dark?"

My mother, who had appeared in the bedroom doorway, went to

pull the curtains open and then began to change the sheets. The light hurt my eyes, and I turned my back to the window. Mom had been with me for only a week and had already ironed all the linens, even though here all anyone usually did was pull tight, fold, and stack vertically. No one expected any more from me at work. However, Finnish customs did not change my mother's ways.

My eyes scanned the room, saying farewell as I paused in turn at each object my mother had put so much effort into bringing here. I would have to leave everything from the tablecloths embroidered with poppies to the *vyshyvanka* shirts. I would finally be able to get rid of the pillowcase my mother was shaking in her hand. It was made from the same fabric that we had hoarded during the final days of the ruble in Tallinn and that had traveled with us to Snizhne. After discovering how deficient my store of bedding was, Mom had dragged to Finland sheets made out of it. My financial situation hadn't allowed me to object. Mom dropped the dirty laundry into the basket and stopped next to me, smelling of marigold cream.

"Do you plan to tell me what's going on? Something's bothering you."

Silently I stared at our feet. At my mother's slippers, her perpetual slippers. Her varicose veins. My bare toes and their chipped nails. I thought of the guest slippers Mom had brought from Ukraine that no one ever used. She still placed them next to my bed regardless of the fact that slippers weren't a part of Finnish life any more than energy crises or clicking electric heaters were, and I'd told her that I intended to live like the locals. I no longer needed to worry about whether the war in Ukraine would affect the price of heating gas—changes like these were mentioned on my Good Things List, my now utterly useless list. This spring would not be the spring of my life. This spring would not be anything. I could just as well roll up in my blanket in bed and lie there until you came and put a bullet in my forehead.

"Tell me what's wrong," Mom said.

Shaking her hand off, I went to lean on the headboard with both hands and squeezed it to keep myself from closing the curtains. It was a normal Tuesday morning, and I was supposed to let the light in, but it made me feel like a target even if no one could peek through a sixth-story window. I didn't understand why I was still home. One of the families I cleaned for was on vacation. I could get the keys from the cleaning company without anyone noticing. Why hadn't I sent Mom there or back to my aunt's house? How could I get her out of here? What could I invent so she wouldn't be afraid for me?

"Isn't Auntie missing you yet?"

"In the country?" Mom asked in confusion.

I watched as her gaze swept over my pathetic wardrobe and rejected the possibility of a lover who might want a Ukrainian bride but not her relatives. She remembered what I looked like when I had someone: being with you had made me change my sheets all the time. I never had overnight guests anymore, and I slept in the same linens for weeks. I looked like a woman who would never have a man again. No man would pay for my company, and my bed stood in empty mockery. I would never have a real home. I would always be on the run.

"Auntie is getting old," I said. "How is she getting along out in the country on her own?"

"Boris helps."

"Boris? He's a grown man who doesn't know how to read!"

"Boris is reading fine now," my mother said. "And he's getting better all the time. What's going on with you?"

My mother looked hurt. If she got angry, I was ready to leave and slam the door behind me. I glanced at the clock. Soon Daria would wake up and start to wonder what to do with her information about my whereabouts. Or maybe she already knew what she would do and was savoring the idea like breakfast in bed. I had to get Mom and Olezhko to safety. I would push them away by force if necessary.

"How do you think Auntie will handle everything? The spring planting, the aster beds, the tomato seedlings? Is the outhouse roof still leaking? And what about the greenhouse?"

"Boris will help, and so will Ivan if need be."

"Ivan keeps his brother busy with his own businesses. What on earth were you thinking coming here at this time of year? Auntie isn't getting any younger."

I found myself shouting these last words. My mother crossed herself. She waited for me to continue, but I didn't.

"Olenka, my plane tickets were the cheapest I could get," she said in a conciliatory tone and reminded me how expensive it would be to change them.

"I'll arrange everything," I said.

"Isn't it another week until your payday? Are you in trouble?" she asked. "If you need money, I can ask Ivan for an advance. He pays us well for the poppies."

"Didn't we already talk about this? Weren't you just worrying that Ivan isn't content with compote anymore? Weren't you complaining that Boris has been practicing milking poppy pods? That the compote cook is becoming a heroin chemist? Why do you think Ivan was so enthusiastic about getting Boris his own bank account? Don't you understand anything?"

Mom stared at her hands in her lap. I had already guessed that Ivan was moving up in his career. Mom just hadn't wanted to worry me, limiting herself to vague mutterings about Ivan considering development opportunities for his business. Compote was the cheapest opiate product available, only good enough for the poorest and most desperate. If compote was sugar wine, real heroin was cognac, and that scene would bring with it completely new dangers.

"Why the hell are you still here?" I shouted. "Didn't you say yourself that drug raids had increased since the revolution? Didn't you say you knew about an eighty-year-old babushka who was just arrested? What will Boris do without you? He needs more support than I do. I'll get you the money for your ticket!"

My own voice startled me. I had just promised something I wasn't sure I could follow through on. Numerous ways of making money raced through my mind, but I wasn't capable of any of them anymore. Why hadn't I taken other opportunities? Why hadn't I saved more diligently? Why had I quarreled with my coworker who had been bringing me medications from Russia practically for free? Before our falling-out, she had suggested that I join her in receiving packages for Russians from abroad and taking them to St. Petersburg. The unreliability of the Russian postal system would have provided a way for me to make extra money, but I'd rejected it because I couldn't contemplate getting a visa from the Russian embassy. She probably had other ideas, though. I was weak, stupid, and frightened, and that's why I was broke.

"For God's sake, tell me what's going on," my mother said.

Invoking Boris clearly wasn't enough. Neither was pointing out that my aunt would have to do all the spring jobs on her own. I had to raise the stakes. My chest pounded. I couldn't think of anything else. Or, I could. Still, I didn't want to say it aloud. But I had to. I pressed my fingernails into my palms.

"You could take Olezhko home."

My mother's sigh sounded like a balloon emptying. The pet name had slipped out by accident. My mother didn't like that I called Oleh Olezhko. It made her doubt my sanity, and I felt that instantly.

"So, this strange behavior is just because of Oleh, not something else?"

"Haven't you been waiting for when I'd be ready for you to take Oleh with you?" I'd refused the first time she'd suggested it.

"I can't leave you alone in this state."

"You have to leave before I change my mind."

My mother rose from the bed and walked toward me, but I retreated. Her compassion was disturbing my concentration. I went to the wardrobe and pulled her empty roller bag off the top shelf. I had to get Mom and Oleh on a plane. I was on the verge of telling her I was sorry, but I didn't want her hand stroking my cheek, so I kept quiet. I had to stay functional. Having my mother in my home was a mistake, and Olezhko was a mistake. Mistakes were wounds. Wounds bleed and leave a trail, and trails can be tracked. If you can be tracked, you will be caught, always.

"Oleh is dead," Mom said. "Nothing will bring him back."

The urn was on the bedside table. Mom picked it up and brought it to me. She ordered me to look at it. I couldn't, not today, not now.

"I'm not leaving until I'm sure that you won't deteriorate again. Then I will. Then I'll take Oleh home and hold a proper funeral. Do you still hear him crying?"

During my first winter in Helsinki, when I realized that the snowsuit I'd purchased for Oleh would remain untouched on the shelf, I considered buying sleeping pills on the street. But I didn't dare. I knew I would take all the pills at once, greedily, like sugar wafers when I was a child. At night I lay awake with the phone next to me, hoping it would ring. Either you or my mother should have sensed my distress. Either you or my mother should have known to call me at that moment when I needed you most, and I was disappointed when you didn't. The phone lay mute like a stone at the bottom of the sea. I hated it. I couldn't talk about the situation with anyone. I couldn't tell a soul because of the strange twilight state I was living in, where one day what had happened felt real and the next it didn't.

I don't know how I would have survived if the neighbor who rang my doorbell in the middle of the night hadn't unwittingly intervened. The noise startled me, and I staggered into the entryway not daring to open the door. At that particular moment, I wasn't afraid that the predators tracking me had finally caught the scent. I was afraid of something else: the shadows lurking under my bed, the forms flicking just out of sight, the lure of the stairwell. I was sure that the only thing waiting outside would be a railing whispering my name.

The mail slot rattled. I recognized my neighbor's voice.

"Is everything okay in there?"

Nothing was okay, but why was my neighbor asking? My twilit mind assumed that she must have been woken by the baby's crying, and I opened the door. As the startled neighbor looked me up and down in my bathrobe, I began thinking of child protection, the police, social services, and all the other officials who could take Olezhko away from me. I forced a smile.

"Just a little crying," I said. "I'm so sorry."

"But if you need any help . . ."

The woman sucked in the end of the sentence with an intake of breath, as Finns do, especially women. So the acute danger had passed. Finns didn't talk that way if they intended to take action. I gave the widest smile I could and wished her good night. After getting rid of the neighbor, I paced in the entryway for a moment, wondering what to do. The woman would return if she heard any bawling or screaming again. Or her husband would. They would talk about me—maybe they had already done so—and they would call social services. My identity would be discovered. Even more frightening was the thought of losing Olezhko.

I couldn't delay anymore.

With trembling fingers, I typed out a message to my mother. With a whooshing sound, it flew off to the secret phone I had left for her, which Ivan had hidden in my mother's chest of drawers under my father's funeral photos. I hadn't exchanged a single word with my mother since my escape. We had parted on bad terms. That was why I doubted she'd respond, and the ring tone surprised me. I expected to get an earful, but my mother's voice was as soft and warm as milk. That gave me the courage to tell her about Olezhko, and as soon as I had, our past arguments were forgotten. Mom promised to begin making travel arrangements in the morning. That immediately brought her closer. Soon she would be here, and everything would work out, or at least part of it, at least a small part of it. I didn't want to end our conversation, afraid that its calming effect would also stop. So I continued asking for news, surprised at how calmly I took it when my mother told me that you had come to visit them after my escape. I hadn't talked about you with anyone for ages, and I thought the crying would overwhelm me again. However, Mom made everything sound ordinary, as if we were discussing whether there should be more dill in the cucumber salad. As if my mother and I chatted every day about Olezhko and you. As if it was normal that I was living under an assumed name in Helsinki. As if your visit to my mother's house had been like any potential son-in-law dropping in on his future family. It wasn't, though. Mom and I were just playing along. Mom claimed that, despite the situation, your behavior had been polite, your search superficial, and that made me feel like you were also pretending with us in this strange game. Apparently, you had come to the countryside alone, apologizing for the disturbance as you asked whether my mother knew what I'd done. Mom had shaken her head, as had my aunt. After pausing briefly, you told them what had happened, searched the house, and checked their phones. Finally, you left your number and told them to be in touch if I gave any sign that I was still alive. I didn't know whether Mom was telling me an embellished version or the truth. I wanted to believe the latter.

"Do you think he knows everything?" I asked.

"Everything everything? Hard to say."

I would have liked to ask more, to quiz her about whether you'd seemed more angry or disappointed, whether you were hurt or vindictive, or whether it looked like I had left only a paper cut on your heart that no one would ever notice and you would recover from without any trouble despite the aching. My throat began to constrict, so I decided to change the subject and return to travel arrangements.

"Does Auntie know about the situation?"

"She knows enough. She can help me invent an excuse for my trip. Otherwise the people in the village will wonder."

"What if Auntie says that you're traveling to Tallinn to watch your brother's grandchildren?"

"That's a good explanation. No one would think twice about me being gone," she said. "Not that anyone is watching us anymore."

"Who was watching you?" I asked, startled.

"It lasted a few months. There was this expensive black SUV parked outside all day, every day."

My mother ended the discussion by asking whether I was remembering to take my vitamins and rest enough, and I found myself saying yes to everything.

. . .

Only after Mother arrived did I realize that I must not have told her something important, because she brought gifts—children's clothing—and I couldn't immediately remember what I had forgotten to report. But she instantly realized what was going on, and that night I fell asleep in her arms, content that she was with me even though I'd only asked her here because I couldn't trust myself. Two months had passed since I'd lost my reason for building a life in Finland. One day, I'd been observing local mothers as I cleaned their homes, inspecting their pantries and changing tables, trying to understand their custom of putting their babies to sleep outside in the freezing cold. Everything had been good. But in the morning, everything was different. I found blood on the sheets. The pain didn't come until later.

But this wasn't the right moment to reminisce about Oleh. I had new reasons to save my life in Helsinki. I wasn't on my way to the airport or the harbor because I wanted to see the dog park boy grow up. I had nothing else left. I wouldn't let Daria take that away from me.

Daria was still sleeping when I slipped back into her hotel room. The heaviness of the intoxication had vanished from her breath, and her sleep seemed more superficial. I wiped my fingerprints off the key card, Daria's phone, the door handles, and the tap in the bathroom. I picked up a pillow. It was soft down. I looked at Daria with her protruding collarbones and visible ribs. She wouldn't put up a fight. I knew there was no reason to hesitate if I wanted to solve this problem, and yet I expected to feel something, some yearning for lost friendship or pity for what I saw: the extinguishing of our agency's brightest star.

But I didn't feel anything.

I set down the pillow. The hotel security cameras had recorded me. I couldn't end this yet.

I opened the minibar but then closed it just as fast. I had to stay alert. You were getting closer. I could feel it in the air like the changing of the seasons.

I didn't know whether you'd believe my version of how and why everything went wrong. I didn't know whether you'd believe a word I said even if I told the truth. I would never have intentionally done anything that could lead to losing you, Olezhko, or our future.

But you have to believe that I didn't kill Viktor.

II

The Road to That Newborn Baby Smell

DNIPROPETROVSK

2008

I was standing behind sheer curtains watching a strange man in the street. He was smoking a cigarette in short pulls, holding it protected in a cupped hand as he turned his head toward each car that drove by as if waiting for someone. I didn't know who he thought he was fooling or who any of our clients who acted this way thought they were kidding. Sometimes couples walked past our office several times before venturing inside. Some never built up the courage, and others took years. Foreigners usually arranged meetings in advance, though there were always a few who pretended they were on a regular holiday and walked past our agency as if simply seeing the sights, not realizing every Western tourist in this town was a sight herself.

But this smoking man was easy to identify as a local just from the color of his suit. I had noticed this only after my years abroad. Ukrainian businessmen loved a particular shade of blue. I shouted to the secretary that if a well-heeled man in a suit came in, she should send him straight to me, as I had a couple of hours open in my schedule.

"I don't really know how this works," the man said at the door. "I've never . . ." He trailed off. He hadn't introduced himself. There wasn't anything strange about that, though. I assumed it was due to his job or position. He was a little over forty, his leather shoes were well polished, and from under his cuff peeked a watch that I guessed cost as much as my annual salary. A driver was probably waiting on a nearby street.

"We can arrange everything," I said with a smile and indicated that he should sit.

I noticed the stubborn mustache of sweat on his upper lip. I expected him to begin by delivering a made-up excuse for his spouse's absence or by playing the part of a man who wanted an introduction to our operation at his wife's request. With local couples, the woman always made contact first. However, my guest didn't mention his wife, and I didn't ask. He could clearly afford our services, and that meant we would proceed on his terms.

His trip to the sofa took a while. With every step he seemed to be searching for an excuse to talk about anything other than the reason for his visit. He stopped to flip through the stack of magazines on the side table and to inspect the display cabinet—but once he realized it contained pictures of clients and their children, he cringed and turned, again looking for some other topic of conversation, until he spotted the Mariage Frères tea tin on my desk. He asked whether I had been to Paris recently. I replied that I had lived there for a long time. I left out that during those years I didn't have money for tea like that and frequently went hungry. When I visited Paris for work later, I bought Ladurée macarons and Mariage Frères tea as soon as I arrived in the city just because I could finally afford them. He wanted to know how I had ended up in Paris. Unconsciously I took a step backward.

"You don't want to talk about it," he said. "Excuse me. I didn't mean to pry."

He still hadn't sat down, and now he seemed to have forgotten the sofa entirely.

"It's nothing. I worked as a model there."

The man looked at me with new eyes. I guessed he was considering whether or not I was using modeling as a euphemism for working as a paid escort, so I told him about the beauty contest announcement I'd seen in the paper. I was tall for my age and decided to participate. And I won. After the collapse of the Soviet Union, the modeling market had opened up to the East, and Eastern girls represented a new exoticism. I was fifteen at the time.

"It's been a while since those days," the man said. "My father was just starting his business then. Like so many others."

I looked at his watch. My new client's father had clearly succeeded in his business, unlike my own. That increased my curiosity. My boss loved rags-to-riches stories, and American guides to success were a favorite. She was constantly underlining tips in these biographies and urging us to search them for the factors that had led to the millionaires' breakthroughs. But now I was starting to think that I might be able to offer my boss a new kind of guidance even if she thought she already knew the local success stories. I was also thinking that the door might be opening to a new public relations network. Something all my own. I needed that because of the Cyprus scandal. And because of Kryvyi Rih.

I'd been promoted to coordinator early the previous year, and I was searching for something I could use to prove I was worthy of the position. The city of Kryvyi Rih caught my attention on a map one evening when I was marking the places that the most of our girls came from. We'd never had anyone from Kryvyi Rih. Why not? The others had already left the office for the day, so in order to help along the plan forming in my head, I cracked open a bottle of Transcarpathian cognac that one of our donors had brought in and opened the window to the spring evening. As I rolled the silky surface of a thin cigarette in my fingers, I knew I had already made my decision and raised a glass to myself. Like Dnipropetrovsk, Kryvyi Rih was home to a highly educated populace, a remnant of the peak years of Soviet industrial production, and I would find an endless supply of scientists, genuine diplomas, and self-written dissertations waiting for me. I saw the offspring of these great thinkers and chess masters as an opportunity to create something unique in the agency's service offerings: guaranteed quality at an affordable price. Even though the income level in the Balkans was a far cry from Western Europe, the middle class was growing, and traditional values were respected. For a woman, childlessness was typically seen as a great catastrophe, so the area was full of potential clients, and geographic proximity would be an asset to us and to them.

I made some calculations and read some research, and the more I learned, the more convinced I was of the profitability of my strategy.

In Kryvyi Rih, we could get a donor for a hundred dollars, and I could easily march her whole family out to talk to clients about nuclear physics. Most of the girls who brought us fake diplomas didn't understand that I couldn't take a risk like that—a client who was a mathematician would notice immediately if a donor or her relatives didn't know anything beyond their multiplication tables. Kryvyi Rih girls wouldn't have problems like that.

I decided to present my idea to Aleksey first and waited for the right moment. One day as we were going to the railway station to meet a new girl, it seemed that my moment had arrived. But the donor was nowhere to be seen. After standing on the platform for a while, we peeked into the empty car, which had its door left open, presumably because of the heat. The conductor looked at us with regret and apologized for the technical issue. Whenever long-distance trains approached the station, the loudspeakers played a welcome hymn in honor of Dnipropetrovsk and the workers, but now the comrade singing was stuck on repeat. I began to suspect that this was going to take longer than we had thought. We asked the conductor about our girl and showed him her picture. He shook his head. Aleksey and I glanced at each other. Either the girl had failed to come or the secretary had given us the wrong time again. Or the wrong train. We returned to the car.

"What do we do?" Aleksey asked as he drummed the steering wheel. "What if she decided she didn't need the job and went to get some sun?"

"I'll call the secretary."

My call went to voice mail. The girl didn't answer her phone either. Aleksey adjusted the air conditioner and glanced anxiously at the bare stems of the roses spread out on the back seat. He still bought his wife flowers every week and was looking forward to the end of the workday so he could get back to his family. I considered whether I still dared to suggest my plan. We had only worked together for a little while, and I was still shy around him. I was nervous.

"This is the third time. Why hasn't this secretary been fired yet?" I asked. "Is she related to the boss, or does the boss owe someone a favor?"

"One or the other. You're right. We need to get rid of that birdbrain."

I continued trying to get hold of the secretary and worked on my opening salvo to capture Aleksey's interest. Finally, I reached her. In the background I could hear cackling. Someone's husband was getting a tongue lashing. It sounded like she was drinking champagne with her girlfriends. Nevertheless, I managed to work out that the right train would arrive an hour and a half later, maybe. We decided to wait in the car, and then I plucked up my courage. Pulling my papers out, I handed them to Aleksey.

"Kryvyi Rih? Seriously?" he said. "Have you ever been there?"

"I know, I know. The pollution is a problem, but . . ."

"That city hasn't ever even seen a blue river, let alone white snow."

"Don't exaggerate. The situation is much better now."

"When I'm there, I always feel like I've been sniffing glue," Aleksey said.

"Just listen."

And I talked for an hour. I described the customer segment. The couples would travel straight to Kyiv or Dnipro without ever catching a glimpse of the smog in Kryvyi Rih. Or we could send them to Cyprus. We had a clinic on the island, travel there was easy, and expenses would remain low. There was no need to worry about the health problems the girls and their relatives might have, because we could blame the strain on their kidneys and lungs on where they lived, not hereditary factors. And besides, the client group I was targeting would be more interested in price, beauty, and easily documented intellectual background. They wouldn't be like Americans.

"These girls deserve a chance."

Aleksey browsed through the photos of my candidates. I had already instructed my little birds to staple advertisements to the electric poles in Kryvyi Rih and on the bulletin boards at the universities and dance schools. The number of responses had surprised me, as had their quality. No one complained about the one-hundred-dollar commission, and everyone was overjoyed at the possibility of a free trip to a lovely Mediterranean island. I saw that Aleksey was beginning to warm to the idea, and he finally nodded that yes, this made sense, and yes, the boss might be interested.

And so she was.

But the Tatar girl who died in Cyprus ruined everything, and my boss decided we had to sell the island clinic that had tarnished our reputation. I didn't find a new Tatar girl fast enough to replace the donor who had died, and the client decided to switch agencies. I was punished, losing control of the office we'd established for handling the Balkan area, which was given to one of my former subordinates, who made the situation even worse. She accepted payments from girls to put them in the donor catalog without any care for background checks. Some of them were minors, which became apparent when one girl's grandmother began calling, wanting to know who had been giving her fifteen-year-old grandchild money and who was offering her free vacations. Then the news media caught the scent, so we shut down the entire Balkan program. My little birds collected all of our ads from Kryvyi Rih.

The girls on the list who knew me called. Their mothers called. Their fathers called. I stopped answering. I threw the flowers they sent in the trash. The bottles of cognac and boxes of chocolates left at the reception desk in my name I distributed to the old ladies who swept the streets or sold flowers on the side of the road.

My boss noticed my downcast mood and told me to forget about the Kryvyi Rih girls. They would find miners who earned good money in their own city, fall in love, and have children who would follow in their fathers' footsteps. They would be content with their lives because they wouldn't know anything else. And because of that, they wouldn't know to miss the things that I might, my boss reasoned, casting me an unnerving glance. It was like she was wondering whether she'd made a mistake in trusting me.

. . .

The new owner of the Cyprus clinic kept the old staff and even hired the coordinator we had fired, the one who handled the Balkan strategy after me. Soon, rumors began to circulate about their methods. Some customers paid cash for fresh embryo transfers, undergoing the same procedure multiple times before beginning to wonder if any transfers had even been done. One case later went all the way to court: tests showed that a child born using in vitro fertilization wasn't the client's, even though there had been no discussion of using donors. My boss sent me a news article about the scam, as a reminder of my lack of judgment. She included a calculation of when the child in the lawsuit had been conceived: the clinic had only just changed ownership. She thought we were lucky that the Tatar girl had died when she did, since it woke us up to how the place was being managed. Otherwise the mess in the news would have come crashing down on us.

My setbacks didn't end there. The opportunist who became my boss's right hand in Kyiv after my misfortune came to audit the Dnipro office and have a look at the books. She brought her own men with her and sat in my office as if it were her own while everyone else did the work. I couldn't complain, because the Balkan program was my brainchild and the people who had managed it had been recruited by me. I had been duped as much as anyone. However, responsibility for launching operations in the area was undeniably mine, and it had dropped me from pet to pariah. I suspected someone was already dreaming about how to redecorate my apartment. My home was located in one of Dnipro's dazzling twin towers, and anyone would have killed for the view. When I watched the sunset through those windows, it felt as if the whole city was mine. I never wanted to lose that view or that feeling.

I met Viktor Kravets at just the right time, because he was such a significant client for my boss. With his help, I could recover the status I'd lost in her eyes. I never would have raised a hand against Viktor.

I recognized Viktor's uncertain walk from a distance—he looked just as uneasy as he had in the street outside the office—and moved my bag on the bench to make space for him. I'd chosen Globa Park as our meeting place. The Pioneer train with its little station, the zoo, the bounce castle, and the ice cream stands made for a perfect sunny day surrounded by the noise of children, and I watched in satisfaction as one little boy who had been feeding the birds bumped into Viktor and made him freeze in place. The boy's mother scooped him up and seemed to apologize. Viktor set off again so fast he looked like he was running away. I called his name, and he scanned the area for me until he saw me waving. The meeting was the third of its kind. We hadn't gotten very far. In fact we hadn't made any progress at all.

"Am I late?" Viktor asked after sitting down next to me. "I apologize."

"It's nothing," I said with a smile and pointed at the Ferris wheel with its teacup seats. Lying, I said that it was my goddaughter's favorite and mine as well. As expected, my words caused a reaction, although a surprising one: tears filled Viktor's eyes.

"I'm sorry," he said. "I haven't been here in a while. There are so many—"

Viktor's voice broke. I looked at the clamshell roof of the outdoor theater as if it was extremely interesting and prepared to finally hear something about his wife. Globa Park never failed me. I always brought clients here when their budgets began to falter after numerous unsuccessful attempts, and this place without exception brought their emotions to the surface. After our visit to the park, clients were usually prepared to mortgage their homes to continue with us. I didn't see any reason why the same method wouldn't work on Viktor.

"I was just asked to be a godfather," Viktor said.

"But that's wonderful," I said.

"Not for me. I think my friend is taking pity on me. All of them already have children, so being a godfather is just a handout."

Still nothing. Not a word about the wife.

"I don't think I can do it."

Viktor searched for something in his pocket. Sunglasses. I couldn't see his gaze anymore, only his red nose. Dilated blood vessels moved on his skin in time with his sniffling like worms in newly turned earth. He was pitiful, raw, and I would help him. At that moment I didn't need anything else to be happy.

"We can solve this," I said comfortingly. "We have the best experts."

Standing up, I took a few steps and then looked over my shoulder to see if Viktor would follow. Laboriously he set off after me like an old man and was startled when a kid munching on a quark cheese–filled chocolate bar happened to cross his path. I stayed a discreet distance ahead and gave him a moment alone. Perhaps he was imagining himself at the baptism where he would hold his friend's child in his arms. Perhaps he could hear the murmur of the guests and feel their eyes on his skin, filled with compassion or schadenfreude, depending on what kind of relationship he had with the onlooker, and perhaps he was afraid of strangers' questions about his own little ones, unintentional or conscious jabs. I was sure he would concoct a dispute that would end the friendship and allow him to avoid the event. He wouldn't be anyone's godfather, not before I completed my task.

Finally, Viktor caught up with me, and I hoped that the moment had come. We had reached the Pioneer train. Thanks to me, someday he would bring his own children to ride on it, and he would bear his paternal love like a badge of honor won in battle, a pride worthy of wearing on his chest.

"Tomorrow I'm going to speak at the opening of an orphanage," he said.

Still nothing. We wouldn't deal with the issue today either.

"My father has a foundation that supports orphanages, and he wants me to take more responsibility for it. At this point in my life, that feels just as impossible as writing a speech about children."

He pulled out a piece of paper whose folds had already begun to wear. In his other hand he fumbled with a tissue as if not knowing where to put it. Discreetly taking it from him, I threw it in the garbage.

"My secretary made some notes, but I can't read them."

I took the speech and looked over the text. It was boring and predictable. The sort of thing a secretary would scribble if she was afraid of being fired.

"You don't think it's good," he said.

"We could go through it together," I offered.

"If it isn't too much trouble."

"Of course not. Orphanages are close to our heart."

Viktor cleared his throat.

"And what if you gave the speech?" he said.

As soon as Viktor had made his proposal, relief washed over his face. I didn't reject the idea. Our job was to go at the client's pace, and this client could really pay off. I had a colleague who used to work arranging international adoptions, and her warm relationships with the ministry and the judiciary were the reason she was hired. Why couldn't I form my own network, including with these orphanages? The men my boss had sent who were auditing our books were still skulking around the office. Even though there was nothing wrong with our bookkeeping, I suspected someone had their eye on my job, and slipping something problematic into our receipts would be child's play. I needed something that would make me as valuable as my counterpart with the ministerial contacts.

Viktor was the answer to my problems, and I couldn't wait to give the speech. I already knew which dress I would wear. The light wheat-colored one. It would go well with the Party of Regions blue I expected to see at the event. I still didn't understand how important the client I was dealing with was, though. Whatever anyone has told you, I really didn't know who Viktor was. All I knew was that he would be sufficiently important in my boss's eyes. That was enough for me.

On the podium, the speakers changed, showers of applause came and went, and cameras flashed. One of the photographers crammed into the room had pulled a curtain over the windows that shone light onto the rostrum. Mentally I thanked him for making the light more flattering despite it being midday. Tomorrow the main picture in the newspaper would show some minister of parliament cutting the ribbon like always, but readers' eyes would stick to the shot of me like flypaper.

I stood against the wall of the hall. The seats had filled up quickly, and I was annoyed that I had lingered outside; the air still had the foul odor of the factories, and the crowd would only increase the temperature. I didn't want to ruin my elegance by sweating. However, I didn't regret my dawdling for long. I had a good vantage point, and there was time before my speech, which I used to my advantage to size up the ripening harvest of the orphanage. The choir waiting with bows in their hair brought to mind a bed of peonies. These girls, who had ended up here because of their parents' history of prison or hard living, would be perfect for my budget-conscious clients. All that concerned them were beauty and passable health. The girls whose pasts were too difficult to be donors would be surrogates, happily accepting a roof over their heads and food on the table in payment. My best finds would come from the girls who had ended up here after their parents left the country in search of work. All of them needed pocket money, so there would be no lack of motivation. We just had to reach them first and snatch up the ones we wanted before someone else decided to come wait for them to turn eighteen and walk out the door of the orphanage. Since the Orange Revolution, competition had accelerated in all areas of business, and I had no intention of being trampled.

The choir conductor began to bustle performers toward the stage, which was decorated in the party colors as expected. I picked out Viktor's profile in the front row. As his head turned back, I stood on my toes and he recognized me, smiling and whispering something to his companion, who left her place and began to make her way back; she was coming to fetch me. I was surprised that Viktor Kravets wanted to make our acquaintance so public. Then I realized why. The family's foundation and our agency's common interests provided a good excuse for our meetings.

Even though the choir was already singing, one by one the audience's eyes snapped to me, and the crowd parted with some clattering of chairs. The girls I passed simpered at me. They assumed that I was someone who mattered and hoped that I would notice them, buy them, and pluck them out of this place. In some of their eyes I saw expressions that were too adult, in their gestures a languid seduction learned in the saunas and a willingness to do anything to get high, but there were also unsullied buds among these wilting flowers. I would pay the director to keep my buds as buds and not let them run away or allow some petty thug to start them shooting up and ruin them before they were of age. On my way to the platform, I thought about our country's underage orphans. Sixty-five thousand of them lived in institutions.

The applause for the choir could just as easily have been for me, since I was taking the podium at the same time. The jovial conversation I'd had with the director of the orphanage in the morning gave me confidence, and the hungry gazes of these sycophants gave my figure an extra heel's worth of height. All of the orphanages supported by the foundation would soon be mine. As I waited for silence to fall, I heard the rasping of the ribbons in a girl's hair who was standing a little farther off when she rubbed their ends together. I began by smiling at the cameras in that way I knew, and I said in my mind the same words I always said when the demanding eye of a camera lens turned toward my face: love me. It worked without exception, including this time on you. I didn't know you were there. Later you said that I had looked like the goddess of victory and that you had wanted me from that second on.

My speech at the orphanage was the first of my successes. I went from one industry event to another, accepting every invitation related to child welfare that I received, flitting to conferences and parties where prominent philanthropists gathered. The international guests liked me. UNICEF liked me. Everyone liked me because I specialized in speaking in a way that used appeals for sympathy to loosen purse strings.

After the speech I gave at that orphanage, my boss flew to our office without warning and burst into the kitchen just as I was reviewing the donor options I'd assembled for Viktor. The secretary's frightened face flashed behind her. Immediately I guessed that this had to do with my client. I had checked what the Internet said about Viktor, and there were as many pictures of the man as of Putin's daughters—none at all, or at least so blurry that the person in them was impossible to identify. Still, I was sure that Viktor had more status, power, and money than all my other clients combined.

"You know who Viktor Vitalyevich Kravets is, don't you? Whose son he is? Whose only child? And whose godson? And whose best friend his godfather is?"

I stood up. My boss was gasping. I'd never seen her so agitated. I turned off my computer, then cleared away dirty cups to make space on the table. Since the intruders had taken over my office, I'd been forced to work in the kitchen and could only use my own space when I had client meetings.

"Viktor Vitalyevich's godfather's closest friend is Gennady Vekselberg. Does that name mean anything to you? Vekselberg is a member of the Privat Group troika, and Vitalyevich himself sits on numerous boards of Privat Group companies."

I accidentally swallowed the candy I'd been sucking on. This was beyond anything I'd been able to anticipate. There was no escaping the Privat Group in this city. Its logos adorned everything from the iron railings on the riverside promenade to the massive side of the Parus Hotel, and customers frequently mistook the group's colors to be a reference to the Ukrainian flag. This error wasn't far from the truth, though, since the Privat Group was practically a state within a state. The world would be ours if we kept Viktor happy, and nothing would undercut my position ever again. I bit my lip so I wouldn't laugh out loud. The scum that had infested my office would be gone by morning.

"Bring me our A-list candidates."

I had already selected our best girls. My boss grabbed the stack of files from me as if we were fighting against time. And in a way she was right. We had to be a step ahead no matter how unsure Viktor was. Endless waiting could lead to the client slipping off the hook.

"Couldn't Aleksey do any better?" she asked, agonized.

"He did his best."

Aleksey had managed to acquire some pictures of Viktor and his wife, whose beauty was said to be extraordinary. Based on the poor-quality photographs, it was hard to say. My conversations with Viktor had not yet resulted in him sending me his information or proper photos. The boss shook her head, comparing the couple to the candidates and beginning to toss portfolios on the floor. Occasionally she muttered something about eyes that were too far apart, a head that was too small, hips that were too wide, a slutty expression, parents who were too wrinkled or fat, or a Buratino nose. Her forehead glistened, the number of lipstick streaks on her teeth grew, and her nails galloped purposefully on the table. Lunchtime came and went, and my stomach began to rumble as I hoped that I had guessed right. Now and then her muttering would stop, and she would wave her watch hand like a scepter, throw one of the pictures in front of me, and ask why the hell we had old maids like this on our lists.

"Not all clients are beauty queens," I pointed out.

"No one wants an ugly baby. Especially not an ugly woman."

The secretary peeked in again through the open kitchen door. No one had dared come inside. My boss didn't even seem to notice that we were dodging messy dishes as we scanned the files, even though she could have emptied my office of the men working there, and we could have held our conversation on proper chairs. Surreptitiously I swept away a candy wrapper that had been crinkling irritatingly under some file folders and secretly crossed my fingers under the table. Finally, my boss started crossing out the names of disqualified candidates with a black marker.

"These. One of these," she said, tapping the thin stack to her right with her fingernail. "Oh, and do you know who recommended us?"

I shook my head. Still, I wasn't surprised that they had settled on our agency. As much as the elite preferred to address their health concerns abroad, our laws were unique in respect to assisted childbirth: only the future parents enjoyed any legal protections, and the donors or surrogates had no rights whatsoever. Viktor Kravets would not receive better service outside Ukraine, and there was no one better than us in the industry, because our company was run by a woman whose instincts were without compare and from whom I was constantly learning new things. Years ago, she had come up with the idea of buying a fertility clinic, but due to the structure of the transaction, no one knew that the owner was the same as the agency that brokered donors and surrogates. It was a stroke of genius. The clinic doctors could never be accused of eugenics, because only the agency staff talked with clients about what qualities the child would have. Our façade was impeccable, and we were always ahead of everyone. We had added psychological testing of the girls to our offerings before anyone else and established a seemingly independent office with a psychologist who had made a name for himself in London. For my part, I had come up with the idea of beginning a service specializing in document authentication. Every step in this development strengthened our reputation, which spread like wildfire. To prepare for an increased flow of clients, we stepped up our search for girls, because the future was clear: anonymous donation would not be possible forever elsewhere, but here it would be. The change in the law in Great Britain alone had exponentially increased the number of clients arriving from that island nation. With us, clients could choose the child's sex, the name of the surrogate never appeared on the birth certificate, clients were never bothered with background checks, and we had an endless stream of Caucasian beauties to act as donors.

That was why I had been prepared to endure humiliation and mistrust to fight for my position. It had been worth it, because I was becoming the confidant of an individual close to the Privat Group, and not even the sky was the limit for friends of Privat.

The boss ordered me to clear the top girls' calendars, just in case. Clients such as these would not wait. One of the girls the boss had approved was Daria, who had already helped two women become pregnant. Her ability to produce viable eggs was phenomenal, and her facial features had something in common with Viktor's wife. They even both had dimples. That would be enough if Viktor was going to father the child himself.

"Which one has the problem, the wife or the husband?"

"He hasn't said a word about his wife yet."

The boss rubbed her teeth with her finger. The lipstick streaks disappeared.

"They're always more willing to deal with the problem if it's the woman," I said. "Is anything known about her?"

"Lada Kravets has been focused on Jesus for the past few years," the boss said and suddenly sat up. "Why on earth are we in the kitchen?"

When the boss returned to Kyiv after our private dinner, I walked toward my office with determination, relishing the thought of throwing the vermin skulking there into the street, but the room was empty. All that was left of the men was the pungent scent of aftershave. I opened the window onto the backyard and took a deep breath of the early summer that flooded in. Aleksey was leaving. He pointed to the old barberry shrub. I nodded back. The candy bush had finally blossomed.

The terminal at Dnipropetrovsk International Airport looked like an abandoned warehouse with a sign on the roof that read аеропорт in an old-fashioned font that was barely legible. Some of the letters were still lit. More of the streetlamps had given up, and despite the twilight, only one of them was burning. We were waiting for the flight from the United States, which was late, in Aleksey's car, which was a considerably more comfortable place than the terminal. One of our formerly most trusted girls was returning from a gig, where she'd tried to blackmail some clients. It had cost us. We'd been forced to give the couple a discount and waste a tremendous amount of work time calming them down. Girls like this made me look like a fool who could be led around by the nose.

I turned the air-conditioning up as if it could blow away not only the girl but the terminal and Viktor's wife, who was vexing me before I had even met her. Aleksey knew this and that about her, and the more he told me, the more I wanted to let someone else deal with her. I would have preferred not to think about her at all. Still we spent our time making up things that Lada Kravets had enjoyed as a child that we did not.

"They probably had a car."

"No doubt," Aleksey agreed.

"Real coffee, smoked sausage, and marzipan."

"A pocket calculator. Japanese."

"And jeans."

"Sneakers."

"A whole row of winter boots, all the right size."

"But none of that could help her get pregnant."

"No. It couldn't."

But this didn't give me any pleasure either. Lada Kravets and I were from the same generation but the offspring of entirely different realities. She was a native of Dnipro and had grown up with the countless delights of the closed city and the perquisites of the *nomenklatura*. Her parents had belonged to the leadership of a missile production facility known as the juicer factory, and the Soviet Union had shown its best side to her family. That shouldn't have been a problem for me. I was able to provide first-class service to clients with whom I never would have spent my free time. However, in the case of Lada Kravets, something was different.

"You can be sure the boys in that family didn't have to worry about hazing in the army. Or anything, really," Aleksey said. "They could have drowned the officers in cognac."

It had been ages since I'd thought about my cousin, whose portrait hung framed at my aunt's house surrounded by my advertisements. Now I did. Estonian women had kept their sons away from bad places during their military service using Vana Tallinn liqueur. That was why it was so hard to get. Of course, Dad managed to arrange things, and when my aunt came to Tallinn to visit, she was supposed to take bottles back to the officers. We took her to the railway station and helped her get her baggage and the liqueur bottles onto the train.

But she didn't make it in time.

I lit a cigarette and opened the window, then threw the matchstick out. Viktor's family's wealth didn't bother me in the same way as Lada's.

According to Aleksey, Viktor had attended the Dnipro Institute of Metallurgy, which seemed to churn out millionaires constantly, but his family had worked with their hands. Viktor said that his grandfather had been a miner, just like mine. Those men had dug nearly all of the coal for the Soviet Union. In the meantime, little Lada and her parents and grandparents had been relaxing at their dacha nibbling on smoked sausages, without ever learning how to stand in line, and when the Soviet Union collapsed, they had a head start on everyone else in arranging things as they saw fit, and so the missile stockpiles, the aircraft stockpiles, the mines, and the quarries all went to them at bargain-basement prices. That gang had held on to their privileged position for decades, from one revolution and administration to the next, and now I would be providing them an heir to send to Oxford to study as the family companies continued to suck metal and coal from our ground until nothing was left. It was wrong, and it rubbed like a stone in my shoe. I realized I even liked the American princesses more than her. Giving in to their demands was easy, because it was easy to laugh at them. When they noticed that people smoked in all the cafés here, they would demand that their donor not visit any of them, and we would agree and gush about how healthy the donor's diet was, showing them the homegrown cucumbers and tomatoes the old ladies sold in the square and reminding them that all Ukrainians ate produce from their home gardens, which was all organic, of course. Silently we could snicker. Lada Kravets didn't amuse me. But her husband's family represented opportunities that no American could offer me. A couple of years from now, I wouldn't have to worry about any of this anymore. Other people would pick up the girls from the airport, and other people would go around to orphanages and search for donors in apartment blocks where people carried their water from a well. Still, this thought brought me little joy. I didn't understand what was wrong with me.

The plane finally seemed to be landing. We climbed out of the car and went to meet our girl.

"You don't have to come with us all the way into the morgue," Aleksey said.

"I can't believe how stupid she was."

"We can also drive to the kennel."

"The morgue is fine," I said. "And thanks, but I'll come along. I have to learn to control my nerves."

"You get used to it, even the smell. In a couple of years, you won't even think about it," Aleksey said. "Smoking helps. My babushka still smokes three packs a day. As a young girl she helped put casts on the wounded, and worms would eat the flesh under the casts. It was impossible not to faint. They were ordered to smoke."

Aleksey pulled a round tin of Golden Star ointment out of his pocket. It also helped if you put camphor balm up your nose. That was his own tip. I put the tin in my bag and decided to follow his advice. An image flashed in my mind of our previous visit, when the forensic pathologist had just been dealing with a body whose face had been beaten beyond recognition. I'd had to run out.

Pulling my belt tighter around my jacket, I followed Aleksey toward the terminal. In addition to our car, there were three other automobiles in the parking lot. Drivers were dozing in two of them, and in one sat a woman who was obviously a madam from an escort service, who cast me a cross glare and then rushed ahead of us into the arrivals hall as if I intended to steal her client or employee.

We waited behind the madam, next to the two-meter-long luggage belt. The bags tumbled off the end of it onto the floor and began building into a tottering mountain. This luggage belt was ridiculous for a city of a million people, a depressing sight just like the whole Soviet-era terminal, which echoed with the same sounds as every railway station, airport terminal, and hall built by the empire. I closed my eyes for a moment. Was my melancholy due to the acoustics, the floor tiles, the building materials, the wooden railings, or what? In Kyiv I had faced fewer challenges but had a more meager bank account. However, I'd always been in a great mood. At the Dnipro office, my responsibilities had grown and so had my income and my worries. Was I not up to this?

I snapped my eyes open and told Aleksey I was going to the ladies' room. My mascara had made a small anthracite-black arrow in the corner of my eye. After wiping it away, as I left, I threw a couple of coins in the saucer for the woman who watched the restroom. She didn't even glance at me, let alone thank me. Even so, I returned to drop a bill on the saucer as well. A hundred grams of cognac was what I needed to relax my nerves, but I couldn't have it, not now. I blamed my depression on the Kravets woman and the girl we were here to pick up.

The clot of ten people that had exited the plane had finally reached the terminal. A few businessmen, a few American bachelors, a few escorts returning home, and a blond sashaying arm in arm with her sponsor. Our girl was hanging back at the tail end of the group, her gaze scanning the room as the other travelers began to rush to save their bags from the mound. She was probably looking for her fiancé. We suspected he had been responsible for her stunt, but only we were waiting for her. The guilt was visible on her face even from a distance, and she tried to hide behind her hair. As much as she might attempt to shrink, there was no escape.

"The boss knows she isn't one of yours," Aleksey said.

"Does it matter?"

"Think of Daria. She was your find and would never pull a stunt like that little idiot."

Soon the girl would understand her options: either donate for us without compensation until the loss incurred by the agency had been paid back with interest or have a tag tied around her own toe.

In a couple of years, I would never have to take anyone to the morgue again. Someone else would do it, not me. That was why I would endure the Kravets prima donna.

Of course, the aversion I felt toward Lada Kravets was alleviated by what Viktor could offer. I won't deny that. When I arranged this meeting at Viktor's office, I'd thought the formal surroundings would help move my agenda forward. But I forgot my mission as soon as Viktor handed me a piece of marble to inspect.

"Beautiful, right?"

I touched the surface of the stone. I nearly kissed it, it was so lovely. The apple of Gennady Vekselberg's eye, the Menorah Center, had been Viktor's favorite subject for weeks, and this marble showed how dazzling it would be. International conference facilities, a five-star hotel, a Holocaust museum. A timeline that would tell of the city's great and tragic history but also of its triumphant future. In a few years, the Menorah would be the world's largest Jewish cultural and business center. If Dnipro had long been a major trading hub, now things would move to a new level. I had the honor to be among the first to see the latest plans.

"I received these from my godfather today and I couldn't wait to show them to you right away," Viktor said, smoothing out the drawings resting on his desk. "My father hasn't even had a chance to review these yet."

I too had something to show Viktor, something that made me nervous. I had arranged this meeting after finally receiving a semen analysis from our clinic, which revealed that the endometriosis reported by the wife's doctor wasn't our only challenge—Viktor's sperm were C-grade at best. Such a sensitive issue was impossible to bring up before I'd received a sign from Viktor that he was ready to deal with the problem, though. Talking about the Menorah was another way to avoid the actual subject.

"I know Vekselberg well," Viktor said, as if in passing. "Gosha is a great man, my godfather's business partner."

Viktor used Gennady Vekselberg's nickname and did it with a warmth that told of time spent in each other's company, a friendship as solid as old money. I swallowed, wishing that the analysis papers would disappear from my bag or that their results would magically improve.

"You could have an office here, too," Viktor said and tapped the Menorah drawings. "I'm sure Gosha would be interested."

The piece of marble had grown warm in my hand. I was passing through doors that had been shut to me. That they weren't anymore gave me a tingling sensation. It felt like the future I deserved. The depression that had followed me from the airport had vanished, and that was enough for me. The details about how Viktor Kravets had achieved his position didn't interest me. I was so biddable I could be seduced by a piece of marble.

"I didn't know that Vekselberg had any interest in our industry."

"Orthodox Jews rarely dare to speak about these issues, even though many of them experience the same challenges."

I wouldn't have guessed that Viktor was aware of how religious purity requirements complicated childbearing. Some of the Orthodox preferred to resort to our clinic's services rather than engage in sexual relations on days forbidden by their religion even though that was when they were fertile. My boss would be ecstatic. The city was full of wealthy Jewish families, and this new center would attract even more.

"Take the pictures with you. You can show the plans to your boss." Opening my bag, I placed the pictures in it, careful not to wrinkle them. The moment wasn't right. But what if the right moment never came? I decided that Aleksey or an anonymous courier could deliver the results to Viktor later, so he could digest the news in peace. Then I would try again.

Viktor's desk didn't hold a single photograph of his wife. There was nothing in the entire office that indicated he was married. He wasn't even wearing a ring.

Friendship quickly sneaked up on us in the course of these prob-
ing conversations, as I came to know Viktor, and he came to know
me. We strolled on the riverside promenade and often ended up on
Monastyrskyi Island. Once, as we approached the monastery, Viktor
nodded to a wilting rose bouquet on a rock and called it a memorial
to a romantic encounter gone wrong. I blushed as if caught shop-
lifting. Viktor had noticed that my gaze often paused on abandoned
flowers. Suddenly I was hit with a realization. A divorcée. I looked
like a divorcée. But what was it that gave that impression? Was it that
my eyes lingered on left-behind flowers and love locks? How long
had he been observing this in me?

"I'm sorry," he said. "Breakups are always hard."

"It isn't that, Vitya. Or it hasn't been for a long time," I replied
too quickly, so quickly that I unintentionally confirmed his assumption. My blush deepened. Compassion was running between us in
the wrong direction. I was supposed to offer it to him, not he to me,
and yet I began to tell him about the American boyfriend I'd been
living with, who had demanded that I pay half the rent to prove to
him that I wasn't just with him for money. Finally, I'd returned to the
same apartment packed with dozens of other models that I'd left to
live with him. After that, I'd started dating another American. Eastern girls had been in his blood, and he kept a secret diary where he

listed the sexiness percentages of girls from different countries. The last of my Western lovers was a guy who had a strange fantasy about the purity of exotic Eastern girls and so refused to use condoms. I didn't mention that to Viktor, but I could have. Our relationship had become that close. I told him things that I'd never spoken to anyone about, because he did the same.

"You're home now," Viktor said. "You don't need to worry about those Western pricks anymore."

I tried to laugh. Despite the cold wind, the island and the promenade were full of couples walking hand in hand. The same way women with baby fever saw strollers everywhere, I seemed to be constantly bumping into newlyweds with their photographers. This walk was no exception. I turned my head away from a bride in her white dress. I'd been alone too long and too long a vessel for other people's sorrows.

Viktor dutifully filled the silence by telling a story about some friends in Odesa who had made a sport of stopping a random romance tourist, forcing him to take off his clothes, and throwing them in the sea. Then they took pictures as the naked man fled the scene. I think I smiled at the image. Viktor knew how to lift my glum mood, and he recognized the yearning in me, just as I did in him, even though we yearned for different things to make us whole. That made Viktor special to me, and it made other clients feel like puppies hanging from my teats, their eyes not yet open and thus incapable of seeing me. The pups only smelled the milk, and to them I was only someone who could offer them a path to the scent of a newborn baby.

"And once . . ." Viktor began, this time admitting he'd been part of a group of friends when they ran into some Turks who were surrounding some women on the beach. The girls had scampered off after noticing them, leaving the Turkish Casanovas at their mercy. Viktor and friends had given them a dunking simply for the fun of it. "I don't think they'll ever come back to Odesa."

Next, I expected him to ask whom I wanted thrashed.

"You'll meet someone," Viktor said suddenly. "You can't not."

"Vitya, of course I can."

I expected him to retort by saying something about how a beautiful woman like me couldn't end up alone, but then I realized he was precisely the person who wouldn't say anything of the sort. A perfectly constructed life didn't ensure that you would get what you wanted. If anyone knew that, Viktor did. As much as I wanted to hate him and everything he represented, I couldn't, and it wasn't just because of the Menorah marble I'd put on my desk and which I held daily in my hands—Viktor cared. Maybe I'd been alone for so long that anyone's sincere sympathy was welcome. I wasn't planning to hurt him, let alone kill him. I wasn't on the path to vengeance, and I didn't become his friend so I could get close to the object of my hatred, because Viktor was not my enemy. He was my friend, and I was his.

Still, I should have listened to my heart and let the revulsion I felt for Lada Kravets win. But I didn't. Viktor's trust and our mysteriously deepening connection were more important, and besides, would you and I ever have met otherwise? How could I regret what we were? Or how could I have resisted the allure of Silverleaf?

The guard checked my name and Aleksey's on his list, as well as the car's license plate, before waving us through. The boom lifted, and our car glided into the Silverleaf villas, which I'd heard about but never visited. I pressed my face against the windshield. The road was deserted, the asphalt new and black and as smooth as a skating rink. As the headlights swept through the dark forest, the amber trunks of pine trees sprang into view. Among the trees we caught glimpses of swings and jungle gyms with colors so bright that they seemed more appropriate for a cartoon than the edge of a forest. The lack of fences astonished me: some residents had contented themselves with hedges, and no one had a high brick wall. The yard of each home was exposed and barer than I had expected. Only the occasional barking of a guard dog reminded me that we weren't abroad. I guessed from a distance which dacha belonged to the Kravets family. Unlike the others, it looked inhabited. Or at least the brighter lighting made me believe so. Once Viktor left, it would become the same sort of empty clothes hanger as the rest of the houses with dim lights shining from within like illuminated wardrobes.

When we climbed out of the car, I felt like I'd landed on another planet. It was so quiet . . . and the air—Daria would fall in love with it. Aleksey whistled quietly. Even he hadn't known there were this many rich people in Dnipro. The number of castle-like buildings was a surprise.

How could we have known? Silverleaf was protected from the eyes of the common folk.

The tour of the house took a long time. Viktor wanted to show off every ornate dimmer switch and birdcage; apparently the building was a replica of some villa on the Dinard coast that often appeared in Hollywood movies. I didn't try to keep up with the narrative, instead focusing on watching his gestures and tone. I concluded that they had housed donors here before. Otherwise Viktor wouldn't have mentioned the marbled bathroom, which was equipped with products deemed safe for donors. The refrigerator would be filled according to the same instructions, and a chef would handle meal preparation. Viktor had given the same tour numerous times. How many times, with whom, and how had their collaboration ended? But at least my slow softening was bearing fruit, since we were finally getting to the point. Viktor had needed time, which had also been necessary for building trust. The boss would be thrilled with this news, and Silverleaf would offer a comfortable setting for Daria during the process. I would get the Kravetses to choose Daria, I had no doubt. I wanted her to get this job, because she was a girl from Snizhne. Her family was still there. Then she could quit.

I felt proud spreading out the candidates' pictures on the glass of the living room table. But Viktor retreated toward the backrest of the sofa, and the way his gaze groped in the darkness beyond the windows was not what I'd hoped for. I glanced at the assortment of girls again. I had placed the beach shots on top. Those always worked, regardless of whom I was trying to impress. Except for now.

"I can leave all of the materials here if you'd like to review them in private," I suggested. In one of the pictures, Daria stared into the camera in a red bikini. I had chosen her a swimsuit that covered more than most. The bikini had been too large for Daria, though, so we had adjusted it in the back with safety pins and tape. The result had a chaste appeal. Maybe the scantily clad girls bothered Viktor because he thought it was somehow inappropriate to look at donors that way. I hadn't run into a problem like this before. His gaze didn't move to the bounty on the table, to Daria. He kept his eyes on the shadows outside.

"I don't know how to suggest to her that we try again."

Immediately I realized who he was talking about. His wife didn't even know that he was arranging a new round of treatment. No wonder I hadn't met her. But what if she wasn't willing to go along with it again?

"I can speak to your wife," I said.

"Would you?"

Viktor came to life. Moving to sit next to me, he took my hands and squeezed them firmly. A doubt flashed through my mind that I was facing something I wouldn't be able to fix.

"Are you sure she's ready to do this?" I asked.

"I am, of course. The previous attempt just ended so badly," he said.

"Recovery takes time," I said.

"It wasn't her fault," Viktor said. "I've tried to convince her that she shouldn't blame herself. But I've repeated it so many times in the past few years that I'm not sure I mean it anymore."

Viktor seemed startled at what he'd said. His fingers shook, but his grip did not slacken.

"So many times that it doesn't sound believable anymore?"

He looked into my eyes.

"You know what I mean. Someone else has to say it to her."

I forced myself to remain still, ignoring the heat emanating from Viktor, which made me sweat. This was a test. He wanted to know whether I'd react the same way his wife did, shrinking away from being close to him. I had never seen them together, but I was sure. Maybe his wife wasn't the only one who couldn't look at him. Maybe Viktor's parents didn't know what to say and avoided the subject. Maybe Viktor used lewd humor with his friends regardless of the fact that every double entendre was a jab at himself, and even if the others didn't think so, he did.

"I try to remember how in love we were when we met. We started studying at the same time, but she dropped out. The looks people gave her were too much. Everyone was sure that we got married so fast because she was expecting. Doesn't anyone ever have a wedding in this country for any other reason?"

Viktor took his glass from the table and drained it in one swig.

"We haven't slept in the same bed for years, and we've become strangers to each other. She avoids looking at me and spends her time searching for help from energy fields and stars. She's tried to blame our situation on everything from our diet to the seat heaters in our cars. An endless stream of healers and priests is forever traipsing through our doors. I'm sorry that I haven't talked about this before."

To give Viktor time, I examined the savory snacks on the table. I'd barely touched the vodka. I understood his loneliness and wasn't surprised when he revealed that he had also tried to recapture his lost manhood outside of his marriage. The confessional tone deepened. He was now in my hands. I had been aiming for this moment, and still I was too nervous to rejoice in my victory. The way he hadn't touched the food worried me. Viktor had been drinking from his bar cabinet before we arrived. I didn't want our meeting ruined by excessive alcohol consumption, so I pushed a slice of bread with caviar into his hand. He accepted it.

"I tried my luck with quite a few other women. Those were wasted years; I see that now."

"And did you go to specialists for advice?"

"How often do men go to the doctors first?" Viktor said and laughed.

He had been mulling this over for a long time, which was apparent from his relaxed tone. The use of donated sperm wouldn't upset him anymore. Perhaps he would be satisfied for his wife to be visibly pregnant and give birth, and no one else would ever know the background. I was relieved that the situation was progressing at such a rapid rate.

"I met a girl on a business trip." He sighed. "At home things were already difficult, and the pretty company cheered me up. After a couple of months, she announced she was pregnant. I proclaimed the joyful news to my friends, and we all celebrated it together. When the baby was born, I was the happiest man in the universe. I even talked about the baby at home, and my wife expressed her willingness to adopt it."

Viktor's cheek began to twitch. He didn't even realize he had mentioned his spouse, whom he had avoided talking about for so long.

"The child wasn't mine. The bastard was someone else's. Finally, I had to look the truth in the eyes and admit to myself that there was something wrong with me, too."

"A paternity test?"

"My father demanded it. He was right to suspect the slut was a fortune hunter. That's why his lawyers are handling the legal issues with your office and a clause was added to the contract about a DNA test for any baby that's born. My father borders on paranoia about this."

I wondered whether rumors had reached their ears about couples who had come for fertility treatments and been cheated. My boss had been visibly agitated after reading a news story about some Italian parents who had been swindled at a Russian clinic. Because she wasn't easily frightened, I suspected that similar cases might exist in our agency's history. Maybe at the beginning of her career she had tried to save on expenses. Maybe I'd also sometimes given our doctors the impression that it would be best to exchange the customer's useless cells for ones that would actually develop into living children, and I'd received praise for my results. But we didn't operate like that anymore. Over the long run, that sort of thing was too risky. With this couple, it would have been crazy. Viktor misinterpreted my silence.

"I apologize. I don't mean to express any lack of confidence in you. My father thinks I'm naïve, and he isn't entirely wrong. In a situation like this, it's easy to end up grasping at straws and chasing pretty smiles."

Viktor stared at his watch. He rotated it on his wrist. He was as shy as a schoolboy.

"My life got pretty dark after that whore betrayed me. Day and night, I thought about how she must have made fun of me to her friends, and every woman I met seemed to be laughing at me. This probably sounds silly."

His tone was tentative again. I limited myself to a shake of the head, even though I should have said, "Not at all." I did that many times during our discussion, tamping down my sympathy, until I felt the need to go to the restroom to shake out my cheek muscles to relax them like models did during shoots so their expression would seem more present again. Instead I resorted to another trick, secretly pinching my hands. The pain pumped adrenaline into my veins and kept my gaze clear. At the same time, I tried to restack the pictures of my laughing girls.

I didn't manage it in time, though. Viktor reached for the folder. I could hardly breathe. All of the photographs catered to American tastes, full of pearly-toothed smiles, but they weren't right for this client. The same went for their introduction videos. If I could have gotten Viktor to open up earlier, I would have had new materials made. I had blundered again.

Viktor dropped the folder back on the table. His eyes had come to rest on the autumn night outside. On top of the cavalcade stood Daria, looking flirty in her best shot, which we'd taken at the end of a long day of shooting when the photographer noticed a flowering guelder rose tree and told Daria to stand in front of it. I noticed the long face she pulled at this suggestion and quickly began to tell her how the other models and I were once ordered to laugh as loud as we could. I got Daria to bark with laughter by describing the stunts we'd resorted to in order to keep that up for hours on end. What I left unsaid was what kind of article the pictures were taken for. The piece dealt with women's and men's experiences of fear, and the title came from interviews conducted by a famous author on the subject. I remembered it well: Men are afraid that women will laugh at them. Women are afraid that men will kill them.

"How do people usually decide? How do they know who will be a good fit?"

Viktor's face was still turned toward the garden. Furtively I reached out my hand and closed the binder.

"Usually customers have specific criteria they don't want to give up."

"Such as?"

"Everyone wants good hair for their child. This is especially important for women."

Viktor straightened up and emptied his glass. Something in his gestures told me he was close to tackling the binder seriously. I picked it up and placed it in my lap.

"We can return to the candidates later. We don't have to do everything at once."

"There's no point putting it off."

Viktor reached out his hand, and I began picking photos at random from the portfolios. Each one caused some sort of reaction, a
cringe or a wrinkling of his mouth. I didn't show him Daria. The old
beach shot of Daria had made her previous client sigh and declare
that finally they had found the one. For that woman, it had looked
like Daria was running toward her and her alone. I kept that photograph held tightly between the covers of the binder and the binder
in my lap.

"Some claim that finding the right donor feels like you always
knew how your child would look."

"And what if that feeling doesn't come?" Viktor asked.

"Then we start with the criteria. What is important to you?"

"Discretion. Anonymity."

"And the child? Do you want a girl or a boy?"

"Boy. Maybe a girl later. First a boy."

I slowly placed my hand on Viktor's sleeve. Finally, a clear answer.

"Usually the right one seems to speak straight to you from the
picture," I said. "Like she's calling to you. Some describe it as an experience of recognition."

Viktor tossed the pictures I'd given him on the floor and went
to pour another drink. The evening had started out promisingly, but
now it was going in the wrong direction.

Viktor's suit had a proud cut, but it didn't keep him upright as
he leaned into the bar cabinet, presumably trying not to cry given the
way his head was trembling. I couldn't even feel envy for everything
he had, because he didn't have what he wanted most.

I packed the folders into my bag. I would have new pictures taken
and send them to Viktor and his wife, whose wishes I knew nothing about. That made planning the photo shoot difficult. In the early
stages of the process, clients acted as if anyone would be acceptable
as long as the child was healthy. Exploring the thick catalog seemed
almost more unpleasant than browsing a dating website or the
selection at a mail-order bride agency. But, without exception, clients experienced a mental shift as they worked through the catalog.
The situation gave them power, the ability to decide, to complain,

and to choose. At first, the image of a child's slender nose was just a flicker of a thought, but soon their imaginations would gallop off toward shampoo commercial hair, women's magazine skin, and trophies held aloft at school sports competitions, and they would forget all about their original budget. Then they would begin dropping the uglier or less talented candidates as if by accident, the choices intoxicating them like a sudden windfall. Some of them began to guard their donor like an investment, and the way this dacha was outfitted revealed that the Kravetses fell into this category. I expected that before long I would receive a list of banned substances for their donor, and I expected comprehensive camera surveillance to be part of the dacha's security system. That was what little Maria Kirillovna Kravets could do to guard against the donor accidentally putting on lipstick, dying her hair, or spraying herself with something that they imagined would affect the girl's hormone balance. I calculated the bonuses. Daria would do well. Because they wanted the donor to live under monitored conditions during the process, the base fee would be double. The project was proceeding significantly more slowly than normal, so we would be able to charge more for that as well. Daria's family would be able to survive for a long time on the money from this job, and I would start preparing her to change careers. I didn't intend to make the leap until I had enough capital to fund the first steps of Daria's modeling career and ensure that both of us could get through any doldrums. That was why I would continue working at the agency until I could get the international fashion designers interested in Daria. The Kravetses would be Daria's final clients, though. I was sure of that.

"We've already done this so many times," Viktor finally said and returned to the table with the glass in his hand. "I can't anymore."

The sides of his nose were red, and his eyes were swollen.

"The first time we framed the donor's picture and hung it with our icons. Not here, but . . . Father Arseni blessed the picture and prayed constantly. We gave money to the church. Everything was perfect. Or it should have been."

I understood now what Viktor had meant when he'd brushed the kitchen countertop and said that it was spectrolite, which was supposed to provide protection, reduce anxiety, and increase self-confidence. As he said it, his voice had faltered in a familiar way. The spectrolite must have been procured for the dacha at his wife's request, along with the red carnelian, polished pebbles of which had been placed here and there in bowls. Just as I realized this, Viktor picked up one of these dishes from the coffee table and dashed it on the floor. I was startled more by the sound, like a wall collapsing, than the act itself.

"She thought that specific donor had spoken to her. The one whose picture we put up on the icon wall."

I assumed Viktor meant his wife.

"But everything went wrong," Viktor cried. "We were so stupid that we tried to get the baby to be born on a day when the stars would be aligned perfectly, so that his horoscope . . ."

The sentence trailed off again. Viktor emptied his glass and poured more Khortytsa. I decided to call my boss as soon as I got home. She could get in touch with Viktor's father and confirm the wife's consent.

"I can't choose anything anymore. My choice will just be wrong, cursed, doomed to failure. You choose."

As my boss and I made our way to Viktor's father's office to sign the documents for the process, I didn't know that my life was about to change, and that it wouldn't be a result of the contracts being finalized but because of you. I was about to see you. I wasn't at my best. All my fretting had left a pimple on my cheek, and my boss was just as tense. In the elevator she slapped my arms, ordering me to keep them straight. We didn't need crossed arms or any other hostile body language in this meeting. Neither of us had met Vitali "Veles" Kravets before. He had a reputation, though. Aleksey told me that Veles's nickname had come from a long-ago fistfight: his defeat had seemed certain, and he lay on the ground looking dead. That made his opponent careless, and, while he basked in his glory, Vitali hit his enemy with a broken bottle. Because of the mess his opponent had made of his forehead, people started calling him Veles, the horned Slavic god, the lord of the underworld who had risen from the dead.

However, our fears were unfounded. The success of our agency had clearly made an impression on Veles, who casually discussed the business landscape with my boss as our lawyers finalized details that had already been reviewed multiple times. There was no sign of Viktor or his wife. If I hadn't seen evidence of her existence—her signature and Aleksey's photographs—I might have suspected Lada Kravets was a ghost. Despite the phone messages I'd left for her, she had never called me back. According to my boss, Lada was aware of our progress, and that had to be enough. It was enough for my boss, at least.

The release of tension made my head fall. I tried to stay awake by counting the dead animals that covered the huge office walls. Lion. Wolf. Bear. Exposed predator teeth. Moose antlers. On the back wall an entire crocodile. I had noticed the stick-on label next to it when I entered, the crosses on it telling me that the room had been blessed. A stuffed carp was submerged in the golden tassels of the curtain. The air-conditioning hummed, and the gilded grandfather clock ticked like a somnolent metronome. Occasionally its rhythm was interrupted by chirping from the birdcage, and then a crack would break it entirely. Crunch, like a chestnut smashed under a shoe. Or the shell of a snail. The irregular crunching coming from the corner of the room continued. I was sure I hadn't heard it before. Out of the corner of my eye, I spotted a man sitting in an armchair watching us. Above your head hung another bear trophy and a stuffed bird with a long beak. You were sitting at a small marble table. On the table was a crystal bowl full of nuts. As you smashed them with a nutcracker, you dropped the shells on the floor. Suddenly I was perfectly awake.

"Viktor Vitalyevich won't leave his wife."

Sitting in the back of the car, at first I didn't notice the words coming from the front seat. I was focused on fixing my makeup, and it took a moment before I realized that it was inappropriate for the driver to be speaking to me in this tone. The aftershave could have been more discreet, too. So someone new was behind the wheel. Quickly I identified you as the man I'd seen at Veles Kravets's office. I remembered your insolence, dropping the nut shells on the floor, and gradually I realized what you had said. Lifting my hand to my hair to conceal my expression, I pretended to adjust my coiffure. A divorcée. I looked like a divorced woman to you, too, even though I hadn't split with anyone for years. What else could you have meant by that? Or was I overanalyzing?

I decided to ignore your comment. During the drive, I concentrated on my papers and the challenge ahead. Lada Kravets was finally meeting with me at her dacha. Viktor had conveyed the message and said he thought it was best for him to keep out from under foot.

"You could have waited inside," you said. "Then you wouldn't have gotten your feet wet." I decided that the car was being driven by a man who always made ill-timed comments. The downpour had turned the front of our office into one big pond, but that stretch of street was far behind us now as we passed the suicide apartment blocks. Everyone who wanted to end their lives in this city climbed onto the roofs of those buildings. Despite the fact that I always tried to turn my head away, they attracted my gaze like a magnet.

I remained silent. We hadn't been introduced, and I didn't know who you were. Therefore, I had no reason to talk to you about anything, and your words struck me as very strange conversation starters.

The weather had cleared and the asphalt was glittering as you parked at the gas station. I was still browsing through my folders as if I hadn't noticed that we'd stopped or that you were circling the car to open the door for me.

"There's more space up front," you said.

I didn't budge. The parrot cage you'd picked up from the veterinarian along the way was taking up the seat next to me. But I was slender enough to pretend that it didn't bother me. I didn't want to sit next to you in the front. I had a sense that for one reason or another you didn't like me. Maybe it was because of the way you'd been watching me. I felt like I was being evaluated. The sound of your lighter made me want a cigarette. I continued reviewing my files, and moments later I heard your steps receding toward the gas station. Once your back had disappeared from sight, I climbed out of the back seat. Clearly no one smoked in the car, so I assumed it must be for the wife's use. The bird also must have belonged to her. You didn't seem like a man who was into parrots. A stray dog that had ambled up to me pushed his muzzle toward the back seat, searching for scraps. Shooing it away, I stubbed out my cigarette and lifted the hood covering the cage. The feathers were the colors of the Ukrainian flag, brash and bright yet as deep as in an old painting. Quickly flexing toes clicked on the edge of the cage.

"Her name is Ostankino."

I lowered the hood. My legs were outside, since I'd only leaned into the car to lift the covering. That was a mistake. I had no choice but to straighten up and turn toward you. I looked past your shoulder for somewhere to fix my gaze but failed. I blushed.

"Nice to meet you," you said as if we'd just encountered each other for the first time. "I'm Roman."

I didn't reply. For a stranger, you were standing too close. Dior Fahrenheit. That's what you smelled like. I noticed a car a little farther off being filled with natural gas, and I focused on that. This car ran on gasoline. It hadn't been outfitted with a natural gas tank, and it wouldn't be, because this car transported people who had the money not to, no matter how expensive fuel was. The people who used this car were driving toward a good future, and I had to deal with whatever came along on that road.

"It would be much more comfortable to sit in front."

You opened the front door, and I didn't want to seem impolite, so I allowed you to guide me to the passenger seat. I stared at my hands and wondered whether I'd be able to reach my things in the back seat and whether that would be interpreted as rudeness, as if I was refusing conversation. I decided to let the papers be. The car set off.

"What do you know about Lada Pavlovna?" you asked. "Has Viktor told you anything about her?"

I didn't know how to answer. I didn't know whose friend you were, whether you thought I was Viktor's mistress or aspiring to that role. Why else would you have said he wouldn't leave his wife? Or was it that you were evaluating my thinking as a coordinator, who might suppose changing spouses would make this all easier to solve? These deductions made me tug down the hem of my skirt. Infertility led to divorces. However, our employees did not venture into forbidden territory.

"You must know something."

"Only what I've read from her medical files."

That was the first sentence I spoke to you, and the last word trailed off because I realized that I'd interlocked my fingers. It felt like a bad omen, like watching an airplane seatmate begin praying just before takeoff. You didn't notice, though, just like you didn't notice my gaze floundering like a lost insect flitting from one corner of the windshield to another. My mouth was dry. You couldn't know my true thoughts about Viktor's wife. I forced my hands to relax.

"Lada Pavlovna may ask why you're in the industry."

"People often do."

"My job is to make sure that the project runs as it should and that they trust you."

"Why wouldn't they trust me?"

"Either way, I have to make sure everything proceeds as desired," you continued. "Your agency isn't the first one they've been through the whole process with. It took time for Lada Pavlovna to work up the courage to hope for a positive outcome after so many failures." I rolled down the window. Outside it was drizzling again. An office in the Menorah Center. Marble floors. My Balkan strategy and Kryvyi Rih had already failed. This project wouldn't. This would work. I could do this even if Viktor's wife no longer sounded merely like a pampered child. Still, what if I answered the princess's questions wrong? But how could I? We operated in the most intimate areas of human existence, so we were used to everything. Clients never asked anything personal except for details about our family lives. That always interested them. Because clients couldn't be allowed to think we were in the industry for money, the official story was that my boss's two children had started out in a petri dish because of severe endometriosis, which had attracted her to this line of work. No one doubted her story or mine. I told you that one of my childhood friends had been in an accident and was saved by a blood donor. That had changed my view on life, and when I was older, I wanted to do something just as significant. I thought it was unfair that every woman of childbearing age was constantly producing eggs that could change someone else's life. I'd borrowed this story from one of our donors. It was believable, moving, and true. I could deliver it perfectly, and it didn't sound at all like our girls were motivated by guilt, as was often the case if the reason wasn't simply poverty. If women encountered childbearing difficulties or life mistreated them, sometimes they searched for excuses for their abortions and thought that the problem would go away if they made amends by coming to work for us. For a moment, I worried that you'd found out about my own abortion. That had been a long time ago. You couldn't know about it. I hadn't told anyone, not even my boss.

"What is your friend's name? The one who was saved by the blood donor?"

You stopped the car on the shoulder and turned to look at me. Your gaze was a lie detector. Snizhne, was that what this grilling was about? In addition to my education and my father's fate, that was the only thing my boss and I had conspired to change about my life history. You'd already researched my background. You'd found witnesses, people who knew me or my family, someone who knew that my father hadn't worked for any construction company in Mykolaiv. You'd found a mistake. A lie.

"If Lada Pavlovna asks about this, she might call your friend."

"Let her call."

"Please."

Then you handed me a piece of paper with the name Lyudmilla Kornilova on it under an Estonian phone number.

"Save it on your phone."

I didn't understand anymore what was going on. Maybe I shouldn't have been surprised that you had conducted a background check on me, but did Viktor know? And what about his wife? Why were you helping me make my little white lies watertight? And what about Snizhne—did you know about that, too? Should I bring it up? Would that seem more honest? Expunging the city from Daria's past and from my own was just cosmetics, a small correction for Western customers' eyes. You wouldn't care about Snizhne, and neither would Viktor. But you would care about the deception. Because what else could we be lying about?

"Is this going to be a problem?" you asked. "I assume your friend should live in Tallinn, since that's where the accident supposedly happened."

"Who is this Lyudmilla?"

"Someone who will answer if anyone calls and tell the same story as you."

"How much?"

"What do you mean how much?"

"How much do you want for this service?"

"From you? Nothing."

Opening the windows, you lit a cigarette and held it outside the car. Regaining some of my courage, I followed your example. Lyudmilla's number glowed on the display of my phone.

"Who knows about this? Who do you work for?"

"Only Veles. He wants the project to go smoothly and isn't interested in the details. This has been a burden on the family for far too long. Soon everyone will go crazy. Business is suffering, and Viktor should have already entered politics. We have to draw the line somewhere. Do you really think I would spend my days doing things like this otherwise?"

I had passed your test and thanked my lucky stars that you had focused on the story you'd just made more credible. I decided to keep quiet about Snizhne. It wouldn't matter unless it came out. If exposing my blood donor fairy tale had been the test, then maybe you didn't know everything, you just wanted me to think you did. We smoked in silence, looking at the roadside stalls where the vendors had to use plastic sheets to create some protection for themselves and their potato sacks. Occasionally a passing car obscured them. There was little traffic, and no one was stopping, so the sellers were shivering on the roadside for nothing. I couldn't lose this client. I had to hold on to Viktor's wife no matter the little princess's whims, and I needed to make friends with you.

"Lada Pavlovna always asks everyone involved in the donation process how they ended up in the industry," you said. "It's best to be prepared."

"Shouldn't these issues have been properly addressed before they signed the contract? Or couldn't we have waited to begin synchronizing the cycles of the donor and the mother-to-be?"

I'd never run a process in which I hadn't met the woman who wanted the baby before things had progressed to this point. The situation was exceptional in every way. That was why I had made clear to the doctor that failure was not an option. Go ahead and raise everyone's dosages. This time. Just this once, so we can get through all of this as quickly as possible.

"We tried," you said. "Sometimes things have to be allowed to move at their own speed."

"Why do I get the feeling that the mother-to-be will be more challenging that Viktor Vitalyevich in this case? Am I right?"

"I don't know. Maybe. No. It doesn't matter. Viktor won't leave his wife. The church, elections, and divorces are a difficult combination. Not to mention the business's various ownership issues. Everything will go fine as long as you remember your story. Your candidate looks great."

"Daria is definitely the best," I said and realized that none of the principals had commented on my choice of donor. Veles hadn't even touched our folders in his office. If he found browsing the girls' pictures as embarrassing as his son did, had the same fear of their faces his son seemed to, perhaps approval of the choice had been foisted on you. If you'd done a background check on Daria, too, I hoped that you'd used the same spot-check method on her as on me.

"Is there anything else it would be good to know?" I asked.

"No, probably not. Lada Pavlovna hates abortion. I doubt that's a surprise, but you don't have girls like that, do you?"

I glanced at you. Your expression was inscrutable. Maybe you were serious, or maybe it was a joke. Naturally there was a column for this on our pre-qualification form. None of our donors had admitted to terminating a pregnancy. They were at least that smart. Officially, there were no women on our list whose halo would be tarnished by such an act, and if clients asked, I reminded them that statistically the country was moving at a brisk pace toward Western abortion figures, though I didn't mention the growing gulf between eastern and western Ukraine. Too much had been made of this issue in the West. If previous generations had been used to having the right number of children to move forward on the waiting lists for apartments and then handling their subsequent family planning mainly through abortion, why would the next generation be different? Why should it be? Lada Kravets had to know the situation in her home country.

Suddenly I realized that my silence might seem suspicious, and I tried to come up with something related to the topic to say, until I noticed a faint smile on your lips. Whether you admitted it or not, you were offering me an invitation to embellish the truth in whatever way the situation demanded.

The priest had been sitting on the couch for more than an hour reviewing my files. I was beginning to think this was another test, and the mother-to-be wouldn't arrive for our arranged meeting. Even so, I attempted to remain calm, and after spending some time watching the peacocks prance on the lawn, I moved on to inspect the impressive bookcase. Rows of gold-embossed, leather-bound books stretched to the ceiling. Then I did a double take. Between the covers there was only blank space. The pages were missing.

"Metropolitan Peter Mohyla's *Trebnik* from 1646," Father Arseni said and pointed to the display case behind me. "Go ahead and have a look. You may pick it up."

I expected to feel the lightness of an imitation book, but the *Trebnik* was genuine. I didn't ask why this national treasure wasn't in a museum. Placing the book back on its stand with tingling fingertips, I moved on to take in the white grand piano. In its lacquered surface I saw a smudged ink mark, probably the signature of some person of note. Then I heard the leather-backed files slap down onto the table. My boss had forbidden me to use plastic. Everything had to have style, as well as content.

"We're trying to work differently this time than before," Father Arseni said. "There have been so many disappointments. Lada Pavlovna doesn't want to know anything about the donor, preferring to place her trust in the opinions of the rest of us. She doesn't dare to imagine the child beforehand."

I returned to the table. In order to have something to do with my hands, I stirred my cold tea with a spoon. It wasn't gilded, it was gold, because it had the weight of gold. I felt like bending the handle to try its authenticity, even though I should have been focused on listening to Father Arseni. I felt uneasy and was surprised when I realized why. It was you. I missed you. As soon as we'd arrived, you left to deliver the parrot to its mistress. I stared at the vortex generated in the teacup. I didn't even know you. This feeling made no sense. Or maybe it did. During our drive, you'd become my ally—we had the same goal, and you'd already helped me. Without you, I wouldn't have known how important the priest was. Still, I believed I had survived the first steps: I'd requested a blessing, behaving in every way like a true believer, and then there was the cross around my neck that you supposedly had with you just by chance. I was beginning to think that you had an intense desire to be rid of this project.

"Of course, I've been discussing the situation with our physicians daily," Father Arseni continued, thereby making clear his position as the man who had decision-making authority in these matters.

For a moment I was afraid there was something wrong with Daria. I was about to be fired. I would lose Daria, my car, and the view from my apartment. I would be forced to move back in with my aunt. I'd dreamed of building a new house for my family with a water pump and a bathroom. But that wouldn't happen now. We would have to expand the poppy field. Boris would have to teach me to cook compote. Considering my future clientele momentarily made my vision blur. I was going to be a cheap drug dealer.

"I'm very satisfied with Daria."

Father Arseni let each word drop casually. One by one. Like pearls.

Even though the dacha looked like a log cabin from the outside, inside it smelled and felt like a church, and Lada Kravets looked like she was always on her way to worship. A calla lily–white lace scarf covered her head and shoulders. Her hand was a bird wing that periodically lifted the cross around her neck to her lips. Her nails were short, unvarnished, and as androgynous as a small child's. She did not match the image I'd created of her or what I'd envisioned based on what you'd told me during our drive.

I couldn't believe that such a slight woman had beaten a donor. I'd met any number of clients whose hearts had been hollowed out by their unjust fate, and sometimes the rage that bubbled up was as explosive as mine gas. It infuriated them that alcoholics and junkies could have children without thinking about it and that some women churned out abortions like they were visiting the corner store. By the same token, I'd met countless donor candidates who couldn't accept rejection, and some of them made me glance over my shoulder in dark alleyways. Lada Kravets gave no sign of that. All I saw in her were sadness and fear as she greeted me and sat next to Father Arseni. I decided to treat her like a first-timer and reviewed the process from start to finish, even though the cycle synchronization phase had already begun. I talked about estrogen and progesterone and their effects, and about the egg recipient's and donor's schedules, repeating the medical vocabulary and looking at her each time I used a foreign-language term, and she listened as if she had never heard any of it before, repeating words like *blastocyst phase, retrieval,* and *fresh transfer.* Discreetly I checked her hands. Those were the hands that had assaulted a healthy young woman; you'd shown me pictures on your phone after seeing that I doubted what you were telling me. The break in Lada's fertility treatments was due to this episode. After that, you and your boss thought it was better to focus on recovery for a while. It was easy to believe that the woman sitting in front of me had blamed her donor for her miscarriage, but not that she took a car, drove herself to the girl's house, and put her in the hospital by beating her with nail scissors. Now I understood why the Kravetses had chosen our office. It wasn't just because of our spotless reputation. They couldn't get such dedicated service anywhere else—whatever happened, we would handle the situation. But could that episode recur? Did I need to be afraid for Daria? What if we created another pregnancy that failed, or what if the child wasn't welcome for some other reason? And how were the hormone treatments affecting Maria Kirillovna Kravets? Did she experience uncontrollable outbursts like some did?

Lada Kravets was adorable. I hadn't expected that.

. . .

Before my departure, Father Arseni suggested a little walk in the park. He wanted to show off the new prayer chapel. After we stopped in front of it, I placed a scarf over my head, and after we entered, I bowed, crossing myself and kissing the feet of Christ Pantocrator and hoping that Father Arseni wouldn't notice my inexperience with the belt-low bow. I couldn't even remember the last time I'd attended church. However, Father Arseni was anxious to present the icons he had imported from Moscow. Apparently, the chapel had been blessed by the Patriarch of Moscow himself. In the most recent acquisition, Christ of the Fiery Eye, I recognized familiar features: the patriarch had sat as the model. I stood in front of the icon, and Father Arseni clearly expected something. At the last moment I realized what and quickly bowed, made the sign of the cross, and pressed my lips to the feet of the patriarch immortalized in the holy image, and then bowed again. Cold shivers ran down my spine, and stiffness began to spread into my fingers. Why did Father Arseni want to show me the chapel Lada Kravets had built, and why this icon in particular? In order to show me what I would be up against if we failed, tried to cheat them, or broke our contract in any other way? Not just Viktor and his wife, but the church, the patriarch, and God.

You were waiting by the car and opened the door for me. A jar waited on the front seat. I placed it in my lap, and the car started rolling to the gate.

"Was it that bad?"

I forced a smile, since the meeting had been a success. Father Arseni hadn't had anything bad to say about Daria, the schedule, or anything else. Nor had the intended mother. As per your tip, they had asked me why I was in the industry, and I got through it by mentioning the name, Lyudmilla, that you'd given me. My first encounter with Father Arseni and his beloved "Sister" Lada had been successful, and my report about the meeting would please my boss. But despite the obvious cause for celebration, I didn't feel like champagne. That night I would buy the latest fashion magazine and check the hottest photographers for Daria's modeling portfolio. I would begin to prepare Daria emotionally for her change in profession as soon as the retrieval was complete. The glass jar felt cold.

"That oil isn't for salad," you said. "It's for Daria."

What looked like a jam jar had a glass top with a rubber seal, and the contents were white like lard. I opened the lid. It was skin cream.

"Do you remember Allan Chumak? The healer who appeared on television during perestroika?"

"The hypnotherapist?" My giggle was involuntary and genuine. With his hand gestures and muttering, the white-haired Chumak had taken control of the airwaves every morning at seven-fifteen. His remote healing placed the entire Soviet Union in a trance. When the energy transfer was in progress, there was no sound from the television sets. "Don't tell me the mother-to-be has been watching Chumak's old recordings and holding this jar of cream in front of the TV screen. Isn't she a little young for that?"

"Faith is not a matter of age. And what about the other one, Anatoly Kashpirovsky, do you remember him? There are DVDs in the glovebox. Those are for Daria, too."

Opening the glovebox, I took out the cases. From between them fell a photograph in which Kashpirovsky, looking like an aging porn star, stared at me intently with his familiar Mr. Spock hairstyle. The black leather jacket was the same as before. I rubbed my lips. The scent of roses and beeswax that had clung to them after kissing Father Arseni's hands had transferred to the tea as well. Now it had dissipated. I wasn't cold anymore either. I realized that you had turned up the heat without me noticing.

"An acquaintance of my aunt visited Kashpirovsky's private clinic in Kyiv. The psychotherapy clinic he founded right after perestroika started," I said.

The broadcast equipment on Ostankino Tower later launched him into the skies of the entire Soviet Union, at which point my aunt called her friend to learn: her friend had been cured of cancer and thanked God that she'd been able to get treatment before Kashpirovsky's meteoric rise. As I remembered, the miracle monger's show was canceled because there were claims it caused heart attacks and nervous breakdowns in viewers. I turned the picture over.

"Kashpirovsky's second coming is underway," you said. "I've heard rumors that our miracle man may be returning to the screen. He's very popular in Moscow."

"Seriously?"

"I'll send your aunt some tickets."

"Don't. I won't be able to handle it if that starts again."

You laughed out loud. It was so surprising that I jumped. Not because I hadn't seen you laugh before, but because something told me that you could be good company when you weren't at work. I don't know what I based that on. The image of you having fun with a woman. I pinched myself. A divorcée. A divorcée would think that. A desperate woman who dwells on others' halcyon love lives even when there are no signs that they exist. It just feels so certain that everyone else is happy, but I never will be.

"Kashpirovsky has been touring for a long time in countries where former Soviet citizens live, and he came and gave Lada Pavlovna some private sessions. Kashpirovsky is an old friend of the family, and the treatments helped Lada Pavlovna find peace after her last miscarriage," you said. "Each session was recorded and watched many times."

The gate to the dacha was already far behind us, but the scarf was still on my head. After removing it, I shoved it into my bag and stole a glance at my pocket mirror. My face had a rose-hip flush, and I realized that I was planning to take a look at the recordings before giving them to Daria. Why on earth? Because when I was a child, I drank water that we'd placed in front of the TV during that guy's broadcasts? Because I felt indecisive? Or was I worried that my vague longing and empty heart were beginning to hamper my work? That it was becoming too visible? Or did I intend to watch the séances because I'd lived too long in Ukraine, and the country's state of confusion had begun to look normal to me again? Once, one of our donors told a client that Ukraine was like a real-life Grimm fairy tale. The interpreter had wisely left that untranslated.

"My grandfather didn't want to be cured of his alcoholism, so he always left when the broadcast began," you said.

It took a moment before I realized how personal that comment was, and how surprising. It was like a confession. My head instantly emptied. I opened my mouth, intending to express a thought that was just forming, but then I saw the vendor stalls along the road. If I made a mistake, next year my mother would be shivering in a booth like that with sacks of carrots. The moment passed. The moment when I could have told you about my father and everything that had happened in Snizhne, and why I'd lied about that place. I could have changed the direction of my fate, and everything would have gone differently. I just didn't dare. And later I didn't dare because I'd kept silent before. How could I have explained it?

In my hand, I hefted the last package of napoleon pastries available at the counter. Two of them were smashed. I couldn't decide whether to buy Viktor's favorite in crumbs or a cake decorated with flawless royal icing and buttercream. People came and went, but no decision materialized. Since my meeting with Lada Kravets, even the smallest decisions had become difficult, and every one of them felt like a sign that I should be able to interpret correctly or else I would turn down the wrong path. A girl giggling into her phone swept out of the staff door. She jostled me and didn't apologize, instead continuing her flirty babbling about a wedding, and I remembered my cousin's wedding picture with the newlyweds posing in a similar shop. The heavily pregnant bride leaned against the sausage counter, and a fluorescent lamp hung over her veil as people dressed in winter clothes made their purchases around the couple. Access to the registration office was through the shop, behind the staff door. This shot was the bride's favorite, because she thought she was at her most beautiful.

"Get both."

I jumped. I hadn't noticed you.

"I saw you come in."

Placing the cake and the pastries in my shopping basket, I pulled my fox vest tighter, as if it could conceal the pounding in my breast. In the chest pocket of the vest was a roll of dollars for sudden departures. Ever since returning from the dacha, I'd begun preparing for that eventuality almost without realizing it.

"Lada Pavlovna sent you tickets for the Kashpirovsky sessions," you said and handed me an envelope.

"You could have mailed them."

I wanted to get rid of you, so I took the tickets and put them in my handbag. Did I really have to use them? Did I have to attend with Daria? Did you ask Lada that? There would be disabled people there, of course. But there would also be hordes of women wanting to heal their heartbreaks or infertility. There would be men who thought they'd find the secret to wealth. There would be parents with dreams of the great therapist magically making their children healthy, restoring their sight, giving them back their hearing, or ending their drinking. The gaze of every person in line to enter would glitter with hope, including the ones who were infatuated with the hypnotherapist. If I gave the tickets to my mother, she would head straight for the night train in hope that Kashpirovsky might say something about her dead husband. I didn't remember what Dad had done when we set water glasses out to receive the remote emanations of the hypnotherapist. Or was it Dad who put the glasses out? Had I drunk out of them with him? I struggled to remember but couldn't. I couldn't even recall my father's face.

"You don't actually have to go see the miracle man," you said with a grin. "I'll tell Lada Pavlovna you were delighted with her gift."

Heading toward the checkout, I hoped that you would disappear. You had read my thoughts all too well, and it bothered me. I decided to give the envelope with the tickets to my boss. She would be excited. Any acquaintances of the Kravets family would be sure to be able to get into the back room, which would be bulging with potential clients, and Kashpirovsky would have useful contacts as well. As I began loading groceries onto the belt, you watched me as if we were shopping together. As she rattled off the total, the cashier addressed you, and I found myself being annoyed. I had my own money.

"I'll also tell Lada Pavlovna that the recordings of the Kashpirovsky sessions have been given to Daria, and that she's using the marigold cream daily."

I fumbled for my credit card with sweaty palms. You couldn't know that the jar was still at my apartment. I'd tried it after a bath and had such normal dreams that night that I didn't remember them in the morning. Nothing had changed. Except that when I woke up, the first thing I'd thought about was you. I decided to take everything I'd left in my living room to Daria tomorrow.

The girl at the cash register wished us an affected good evening. I felt like slapping her for never having said that to me before. I barely managed to control myself and stopped at the door of the shop. Your car was parked in front, and I expected to finally be rid of you, but then you took my shopping bag to carry it for me.

"Viktor will be at the office soon," I said.

"I know. I'll escort you there."

"It's only a few meters away."

"Your street is in really bad shape."

I couldn't argue with that. The puddles in the road outside the shop were treacherous. You offered your arm, and I didn't know how I could refuse. I blamed it on the cashier staring after us. I'd been visiting that shop for a long time, at every time of day, sometimes with girls, sometimes our secretary, sometimes my boss, often clients, but never a man who didn't belong to any of these groups. The cashier had always addressed the total due to me, and the irritation I'd experienced by the conveyor belt had changed to a strange desire to prove myself. I didn't care what the cashier thought. Still, I wanted to seize the moment and at least for a few steps make myself look like something other than a divorcée. And lonely. I focused on the road. The chestnuts that had fallen on the ground crunched under our feet, and there were so many that no asphalt was visible under them. The lights of the Planet Grocery receded. Only one of the streetlamps was burning. I should have been focused on my upcoming meeting, but I would think about that in a moment. Once you were on your way to wherever you would be going, to whatever woman you would be sleeping next to. To someone who wouldn't be me.

When my boss was planning to open an office in Dnipropetrovsk, this location had clearly stood out for the milieu of its charming tsarist-era street, which offered all the most important services: a twenty-four-hour Planet Grocery and the city's only accommodations preferred by Westerners, the Park Hotel. Four stars and a good restaurant that was open late. The area was quiet, our parking lot in the back had a fence, and the security guard who sat in the booth was reliable. However, today the street looked worse than usual. That was because of the piece of Menorah marble resting on my desk, which I had stroked earlier in the day, and the arm I was on.

"Do you have any doubts about this project?" you asked. "Do you want to quit?"

Your question returned me to reality. I didn't answer. I wondered if it was so obvious. Was I such a bad actor? A loose paving stone made me stumble, and your hand flew to grab me, and for a moment it felt like an embrace, one that didn't fit that street or that conversation, like something that belonged to an entirely different scene. You let me go. The light shining from the windows of the office illuminated the steps and reflected from the puddles in front of them. Like the moon shining on a lake, forming a bridge of light.

"Viktor likes you. That's a good thing," you said.

"And what if everything goes wrong?" I asked.

"You can always call me. Whatever happens. Whenever you need me. Whether it's Lada or Viktor."

"Viktor?"

The image that flashed through my mind was the face of the donor Lada Kravets had assaulted with nail scissors, not Viktor. I don't know why you only showed me the pictures of the results of Lada's fit of rage. Maybe you thought I could believe anything of Viktor but not of his wife. She was a woman, after all, a mother-to-be. Another chestnut crunched under my shoe. Or under yours. Or under both of ours.

"You no longer have the option of backing out. That wouldn't look good," you said. "I'm sorry."

I subtly turned down the heat on the office radiators. The patches of sweat under my armpits were threatening to spread, and Viktor's watchful gaze was making my movements stiff. Was he trying to see if any bruises had appeared on my face since my meeting with Lada? Hadn't he cast an appraising glance at my long-sleeved shirt as if guessing what it might conceal? Removing my scarf, I rolled my sleeves up to my elbows.

"The mother-to-be is taking a very active approach to the process," I assured him. "Our meeting was a big success."

The pictures of the mangled donor flickered in my mind like a broken fluorescent tube. She'd been paid for her silence, and nothing more had come of it. Nothing ever came of things like that, not for these people. Viktor came over next to me, took hold of my arm, and squeezed it insistently.

"Don't lie. Not to me, please."

After swearing that our encounter had been as warm as could be, Viktor let me go, shrugged, and returned to the couch, adopting his familiar position. Back straight, off the cushions, one arm resting on a pillow and the other in his lap. At Lada Kravets's dacha, I had seen a portrait of Viktor posing the same way with his father. Both of their heads were wreathed with golden laurels, and they were placed in a Roman villa. There were no other traces of the father-to-be in the dacha.

We didn't continue our conversation about his wife, although Viktor still checked my reactions to what he said. If previously I'd wanted to convince myself he didn't know about the surprises his wife had arranged, I no longer had any doubt. Looking for something to do with my hands, I remembered the napoleon pastries and began to load them onto plates, wondering whether I dared to go turn the temperature back up after all. I didn't.

"Both our sets of parents expect grandchildren, and I'm not sure whether they're more concerned about the future of their legacies or the way people talk," Viktor said. "You've heard what they call me."

He glanced at me. I shook my head.

"Limp-dick."

Another glance.

"It's hard to get respect here if a man isn't a man. And a man isn't a man if he's shooting blanks."

"Have you considered moving somewhere else, starting fresh in another country?"

"You can't change the land you love. Believe me, I've tried."

I attempted to respond to Viktor's look with sincerity, like before, but something between us had changed. I remembered the way Viktor had gained my sympathy by telling me how a slut with a deceitful laugh had haunted his dreams, leaving him unable to go out for fear of running into someone who would congratulate him on becoming a father. Now I kept offering him more snacks so I wouldn't have to sit next to him. Then I grabbed the sugar bowl I'd left on the side table. Then the spoons and more napkins, until I couldn't come up with anything else to arrange and I had to go sit on the same couch as Viktor, who had left his pastry half eaten. I held the cup in my hand and cursed the moment when I'd made the decision to sit so close that I felt the heat radiating from him. Why couldn't I act like I did with other people and stay in my own chair opposite the client? I swirled my spoon in my tea to keep my fingers busy. If Viktor took my hands again, he would notice their clamminess and the chalky color of my fingertips. He would see how I'd try to move farther away and would look for that shudder of disgust that he'd sought before without finding it. If Viktor's wife was capable of that kind of destruction with a pair of nail scissors, what could her husband do? And what kind of child would these people raise?

"I got the doctor fired who told me my sperm was weak. The news knocked my feet from under me, and I accused him of lying. And for wanting more money, supposedly for additional tests. It's been a while since then," Viktor said. "I felt completely useless." I was still stirring the sugar into my tea, since it didn't seem to be dissolving, the crystals just swirling around the edges of the porcelain. No one was in the building except for us, since the secretary had gone home. I didn't want to be alone with Viktor. I didn't want to be unique in this way. I didn't want to hear these things, and the intimate moment made my chest constrict. I was already making mental plans in case I had to leave the country suddenly. I would have to renew my fully stamped international passport posthaste. I tried to remember whether I knew anyone at the passport office, anyone reliable. I needed someone who could expedite the process, and I didn't want to ask any of our own staff for help. On the other hand, it was always easy to get to Russia, and my visa for France was still valid. Viktor was fumbling for words, and the rasping of his voice was like an old record player that occasionally faded to the point that I had to read the words from his lips.

"My father has agreed to act as my donor."

Instantly I forgot my passport worries and placed my teacup on the table. Were we really this far along?

"Have you already talked to him about it?"

"He suggested it himself."

Viktor spread his hands. At first, he had opposed the idea. But then he agreed. He didn't have any other options.

"We've tried micro-injection enough times in previous rounds. Or do you disagree?"

I shook my head. I was speechless. Was Viktor really ready for this?

"My parents want to do everything they can to help us. They will be phenomenal grandparents."

Viktor wasn't lying.

Lada became pregnant.

But I had chosen a rotten apple from my basket.

Daria ran away. I'm sure you can imagine my state of mind when the situation dawned on me. I couldn't tell anyone that Daria was missing, and I couldn't ask for help from anyone without revealing my own lies. I had deleted Daria's real hometown from her information, so I couldn't even suggest where we should really look for her. No one at work knew we were from the same place. Not even you.

I contacted her school friends. I tried to reach her relatives. I got hold of neighbors and friends of friends, and with every possible source of information I had to pretend to be running into them by accident and spin a story that allowed me to ask about Daria. I made an appointment with her hairdresser only to find that the last time Daria had seen her had been weeks before her flight. No one had heard anything from her. Daria had vanished like smoke on the wind.

Giving birth to a healthy child emboldened Lada Kravets.
    She ordered an icon.
    You may remember whom the icon looked like.
    But the model remained missing.

. . .

I received the promotion I had wanted.

We celebrated at the agency.

You may remember that I wasn't in a celebratory mood.

Daria was still out on her own.

My boss began to wonder about our star girl's dedication to her studies.

That was how I'd explained Daria's absence.

Around the office, people were wondering whether her apartment should be given to another girl until Daria came back to work.

No one had lived there for ages.

Gradually I disposed of Daria's belongings without anyone noticing.

I was afraid of the consequences of the Kravetses' happiness.

The moment when they would begin to hope for siblings for their little one.

The moment when they would become so reckless that they would want to meet their donor.

Would anyone else ever be good enough for them?

Of course not.

What would I say to them?

That I had lost their saint?

For a long time, I kept alive a hope that I would find Daria myself, by my own devices. I couldn't admit to anyone why I'd chosen a girl whose emotional state couldn't withstand the problems the process brought along with it. It was never only about the opportunities I saw that Daria could offer me.

I chose her because I had caused her family's decline long before all of this.

III

The Little Sun

HELSINKI
2016

Over the years you've probably heard every possible explanation, supplication, and lie that people can invent to try to keep themselves alive. Tears would be an old joke to you. If I had time for three words, I would tell you that I was expecting your child. Would that help? Would that make you hesitate, even for a moment? Would it make you believe that I never would have endangered our future by moving against your boss's son?

I've tried to force myself to contact you so many times over the past six years. Every morning I remember how we always used to call each other after we woke up if we had slept at different addresses. I couldn't get out of bed without your voice. I wanted to tell you everything. The thought that you would never know how things had really happened was unbearable. But all I could do was stare at the straight grout lines in my kitchen and the table with only my coffee cup. I couldn't dial your number.

Last night I woke up feeling a familiar nibble at my lower lip. The way you used to when you were pampering me or waking me up. I was sure that you had already come. My racing pulse raged in my ears, and I could still feel your bite on my lip as I sneaked into the hallway to listen to the sounds of the stairwell, sure that if you weren't outside the door, I would find you in my kitchen, and the flowers on my kimono would stick to my thighs, and the candles would flicker, and outside my bedroom window I would see plane trees, their trunks shiny, oily from the rain.

I pressed the switch. The lights turned on. The electricity was working. The stairway was empty. There were no coils of wire hanging from the low ceilings, the top of it was not decorated with rosettes, there were no decorative motifs along the walls, and it wasn't the staircase of a tsarist palace. The squeaking coming from the bedroom wasn't coming from you but instead from my mother sleeping in the guest bed. I didn't find you in the kitchen or in the bathroom, and I didn't know whether I'd feared or hoped to hear your breathing in the dark and the creak of the parquet under your feet like that night in Odesa, the first of our nights, after which I began to understand the true cost of my innocent arrangements.

Daria woke up groaning. She didn't seem surprised to see me in her hotel room, where I'd been waiting for a while by then. Maybe she remembered that I'd brought her here and imagined that I'd spent the night.

"Give me some painkillers."

From my pocket I took a package of Analgin and threw it onto the bed.

"Bring me water."

Curbing my anger at these commands, I went into the bathroom. The air-conditioning was effective, but not so effective that it could eliminate the stench that Daria had managed to create in there: a potpourri of pharmacy, Ukraine, and stomach acid. I held my breath to try to prevent the past from being absorbed into my system. It didn't help that the lights burned steadily, that the tile grout was clean, that the plugs were installed in the walls with Scandinavian precision or that there wasn't any filth on them, unlike the items Daria had hung here and there, which I'd inspected while she slept, without finding anything useful. For a moment I leaned my head against the cool tile wall and felt for the phone in my pocket. Ivan would have known what to do. Before, I'd always trusted in his help in difficult situations. But I didn't have Ivan's number anymore. I hadn't talked to him since I left, and he didn't know that my mother visited me or where I was. My stomach lurched. I couldn't think of Mom, not now. Or of Olezhko. Or of them in my unprotected home. I had to concentrate.

"Where are you?" Daria shouted.

After washing a glass with soap, I filled it and drank first before refilling it for Daria. At the bathroom door I remembered to remove the Zarya watch from my wrist and slipped it into my pocket. I couldn't deal with Daria's mockery.

"What are we doing today?"

"I need to go to work."

"And after that? Let's go to the dog park together."

"That's not a good idea."

"Yes, it is. I want to see the girl."

This thought reinvigorated Daria enough that she sat up, repeating the girl's name, Aino, savoring it as if she were sucking on honeycomb. All around her mouth there was dried drool, which crumbled in flakes to the bedspread as she spoke. The room needed cleaning as badly as Daria did, but I had put out the "Do Not Disturb" sign. The mess was such that the cleaners would notice it. I would have to handle it myself.

"What time do you get off work?"

"Late."

"You're going to leave early enough that we can get to the dog park," Daria said. "We should have gone out more often together before."

Despite her hangover, Daria seemed pleased with our cut brandy–soaked evening. I hoped that tonight wouldn't require the same outlay of cash. A knock came at the door, and I went to accept the breakfast I'd ordered from room service. After signing for the order with Daria's name, I closed the door in the boy's face. As I arranged the plates and poured the coffee, I tried to build up my courage. I hadn't been able to think of any way to get Daria under control, other than to remind her of her own family, though I truly didn't want to talk about the Sokolovs.

"How are things at home? Is your mother still in Snizhne?"

Daria slowly placed her fingers on the handle of the coffee cup and kept them there in a stiff position like a tin soldier's hand on the stock of a rifle. I had to keep going. This was working. That morning I'd tried to ask my mother whether she knew anything about the Sokolovs. My inquiry had puzzled her. We hadn't talked about the Sokolovs for years. I responded to her confusion by taking offense. I could handle things that I hadn't been able to talk about before. Wasn't that evidence that I was doing better? Couldn't she support my progress by taking Oleh's urn with her, by taking him to the country, preferably right away? I put emphasis on the word "urn." I could say it out loud. But my mother wasn't any help. It had been years since she'd heard anything about the Sokolovs. She didn't know whether Daria's brothers were at the front, and if they were, on which side, and so I had to proceed with caution. I didn't want to further complicate my relationship with Daria by arguing about Russia.

"And your brother, Pavel?" I asked.

"Working."

"Of course. How is Pavel's family? Didn't he have a child?"

I set the napkin, damp from my palms, on the table. I didn't have an amount I could write on it so that, after handing the paper to Daria, the problem would be solved. I couldn't comprehend how I had been so stupid that I hadn't skimmed anything back in the day. Everyone did it, except me, and now I was sitting here next to Daria, at her mercy. And now Mom and Olezhko were in danger. And now the idyllic life the boy from the dog park lived was in danger of being shattered. I glanced at Daria. A familiar enamel sheen had appeared in her eyes.

"And your little brother? Did he finish high school?"

Daria did not reply. I would have to continue grilling her, even though here I wouldn't be able to get her onto the hotel roof, and I couldn't remind her of the money she would lose. I didn't have any bonuses to offer her or any free vacations. I didn't have any means of intimidation. No Ivan. No Aleksey. No you. I didn't have relationships I could use to cause problems for the Sokolovs, not with the tax office, not with the police, not with the state security service, not with the people in power. But it had been family trouble that had brought

Daria into my stable. She wouldn't do anything to cause them harm. At least not the Daria I'd known. Didn't she understand that through her actions she was also putting her loved ones at risk?

Daria's breathing interrupted my reverie.

"Mom is in Dnipro. The agency gave us an apartment after you left. They thought it was better if I had company."

"So that happened at a good time. Before the war."

"Pavel and his family moved in with us. He developed kidney problems in Kryvyi Rih."

I'd expected Daria to express more emotion on this subject. I remembered her calling her mother every day and the way she'd showed me pictures of her niece. Now she didn't pull out photographs of anyone. She didn't even have any with her, as I'd seen when I searched her things. I realized that the woman sitting next to me was speaking about her relatives distantly, as if they were only a memory. I shivered. Our conversation wasn't reminding her why she had applied for work with the agency: to benefit her family. When I left the hotel, I would call my mother and emphasize how essential it was that she take Olezhko home as soon as possible. That every evening and night with Olezhko would make my healing more difficult, and that I might change my mind at any moment. I pressed my nails into my palms. I had to focus on Daria's family, not my own.

"Have you spoken with your mother recently? Is she well?" I asked.

"Why wouldn't she be?"

"Does she know where you are?"

"On a job."

As blind as mothers were about their children, there was no way I could believe that Valentina Sokolova still thought her daughter was capable of working. But I didn't object.

"And Pavel, when did you last hear from him?"

"Why all this sudden interest in my family?"

"If the dog park family recognizes you, they'll notify the agency immediately. Have you forgotten what happened to the girls who didn't follow their contracts? Or to their families? What if something has already happened to your mother? Or to your brothers? Or to your niece?"

Daria snorted and threw her crumbled roll at me. It fell on the floor. She was hungry, and what she wanted was wine, not a boring hotel breakfast, and she ordered me to bring her more to drink. This could all end right here, today. Squeezing the corkscrew in my hand, I reminded myself about the hotel security cameras. Sweat had made my shirt damp, and I had a hard time getting a grip on the wine bottle.

"It's almost like you care about my family."

I swallowed. I'd been afraid of this.

"Every time we visited my father's grave, we cursed the day you people came to Snizhne. Why couldn't you have stayed where you came from?"

After placing the bottle and the cork on the nightstand, I began to leave. Daria was provoking me, and I wasn't going to rise to it. Not today. I didn't make it to the door. Darting in front of me, Daria poked me in the chest. I stepped back. Daria followed. I let her hiss. I let her words whish past me without hearing them, and I thought of my Good Things List until she said, "You didn't come to my father's funeral."

Daria had only been a child then. She couldn't remember a detail like that. Maybe her mother did. Were these the kinds of things they'd been brooding over together?

"I had a fever."

"You didn't the day before."

That was when I'd buried my own father.

"You didn't bother to show up even though we paid our respects at your father's passing. We brought wreaths, we walked in the procession, and I placed carnations on your dad's coffin. Our fathers were friends. Our families were friends," Daria said. "But that doesn't mean anything to you."

Our parents' relationship hadn't been recorded in my memory exactly that way. But arguing was useless.

"You are toxic. Everything you touch turns poisonous, and I hope a mortar hits your father's grave," Daria hissed. "Although it already looks that way."

I ran out of the room.

. . .

I hadn't once brought my father flowers since the funeral, unlike my mother. Once my aunt mentioned my mother traveling on the night train to Snizhne with a basket full of Easter bread blessed by a priest and eggs dyed with red onion. I was working as a model then, and Mom didn't tell me about it. When the war came, the graveyard ended up on the wrong side of the front line, and we no longer had any relatives in the area who could care for our family graves. I wasn't sorry. Even so, Daria's words hurt, since criticizing my father's grave was none of her business.

My mother had chosen a picture for the grave marker that she wanted to see when she visited but which my father never would have approved. The stone was small, only what we could afford, and the portrait immortalized on it was no larger than my palm, with the shirt and collar only just distinguishable. The etching was based on an old passport photo, and in the end, Dad looked like he could have been anyone: a man with no car, a man with no honor, a man with no power, a man who had died in his own bed, under his own blanket, in a house where the wallpaper had been the same for decades.

But that wasn't what happened to my father.

DNIPROPETROVSK

2009

I told you about my father on my birthday. That evening I'd received a bouquet of flowers, which I threw in the trash as soon as the guests had left. A colleague had brought me red carnations with lace fern foliage, not knowing they reminded me of my father, who had bought similar bouquets for my mother on her birthday, because sometimes that was all that was available. Popular during the Soviet era, this flower arrangement was everywhere, even on postcards, and it could have taken me back to the happiest moments of my childhood. But it only reminded me of everything I'd lost. Of my father.

After cramming the bouquet into the trash can, I realized that my behavior demanded an explanation.

"My dad didn't like lace fern," I said, and I wasn't even lying. "He thought it looked like a weed."

Your compassionate gaze invited me to share more about my father, but of course you were thinking of the construction accident that had supposedly put him in an early grave. I could have told the truth that night. But the words that lingered on my tongue came out different than I hoped, and I found myself telling funny stories about him. In selected vignettes, I described him as an energetic man, and that wasn't a lie either, though I didn't mention how that exact characteristic helped him get out of his hometown when his compulsory military service offered the opportunity. My father had waited for the army like a child hoping for Jack Frost to appear. He wanted to go somewhere it would be good to live and from where he wouldn't return in a zinc coffin, and finally he managed to wheedle an assignment in the Estonian Soviet Socialist Republic. Acquaintances had sent him postcards from the capital raving about the shopping opportunities. Tallinn was exactly what he'd wanted. I told you he was from there.

It was a lie. My father was born in Snizhne, and that was why we moved there. We moved from Tallinn to my father's childhood home, into his parents' house, and later I realized he must have yearned for his hometown all those years he had lived elsewhere.

I couldn't at all understand why we left Tallinn after Dad had gone to so much trouble getting there. He often reminisced about his heroic-sounding adventures, how he'd raced to register his passport in Tallinn after he left the army. The deadline had been approaching, and he didn't have an apartment. Things worked out, though, when he hit on the idea of getting a job at a construction site where workers were lodged in a dormitory. That would give him the permanent address required for a residency stamp. He was able to register his passport, and he became a genuine Tallinner as if by a stroke of magic, again because of his ingenuity. The city offered him opportunities not to be found in Snizhne. Dad was particularly taken with the women in Tallinn. One of the most beautiful, a typist as sweet as bird's milk chocolates, became my mother.

Though my father's later life was a series of failures, in Tallinn everything was different. My father's energy was only a benefit, and his business ventures were successful. There was no hint that any of his ideas could lead to anything but happiness. If Dad shook a matchbox in his hand and asked me to guess what he had invented, I immediately knew something fun was coming, whether it was sausage he'd gotten from the back door of the factory or a way to test the ripeness of watermelons by knocking on their rinds. I believed he would always succeed at everything.

One of my father's earliest inventions was something we could feel proud to talk about, and it had to do with Finnish television, which was only available in the Soviet Union along the northern coast of Estonia. Of course, attempts were made to close that window onto the West by scrambling the signal coming from Finland, but Dad worked up an adapter that made it so we could see the shows. Other people wanted the device, too, and soon Dad didn't care one bit that his salary at the factory was lower than it would have been in the mines of Snizhne. The story of my father's first proper business idea being responsible for Tallinn's Western breeze was even appropriate for your ears, because I had to tell you something about my father, and this invention rooted our family so firmly to Tallinn that I could speak without worry about the scheme and even my mother's role in it. She worked in the office at the factory, so she had access to a typewriter, and at my father's suggestion she began to write up Finnish television program information, which she got from a Finnish acquaintance and had translated by one of her Estonian girl-friends. This was then distributed not only to factory staff but also to management and the informers. At the operation's height, Mom was copying hundreds of program listings each week, and Dad was spending most of his time at work assembling adapters. Gradually we collected a complete Lomonosov tea set, a mocha set, and a line of crystal glasses for champagne and cognac. Dad arranged a certificate of pregnancy with twins for Mom, and we were given a bigger apartment. But this was all I could tell you if I wanted to hew to the truth.

I couldn't foresee my parents' desire to move, even though there were signs of it as soon as the Soviet Union collapsed. How could I? I'd never visited my relatives in the Ukrainian SSR: everyone had always come to us because they wanted to shop in Tallinn, the Soviet Union's Little Paris. No one ever suggested we go to Donbas or Myko-laiv. When my Ukrainian cousins came to visit, I told them what the Finnish TV programs were about, and they got into *Dallas* and *Knight Rider*. They didn't have anything to tell that interested me.

When the borders opened, Estonians started leaving for Finland, Russians for Russia, and one day I realized that two of our neighboring apartments were empty. In one of them lived an old lady who fed me *okroshka* in the summer. The door was open, and the furniture was gone along with the babushka. Only the dog, a gray *bolonka*, had been left behind. The Finnish man who had bought the apartments talked with my father. Acting as the interpreter was a Russian chick in Western clothing who immediately captivated me. My mom was still spraying her hair with furniture lacquer, but this girl was clearly using something else, something that smelled good, like Finnish deodorant, and she had Walkman headphones hanging from the shoulder strap of her handbag. I'd seen them before on Finnish TV. Mom interrupted my observations with a cake box in her hand and ordered me to come help. I secretly stuck my finger into the buttercream covering the cake while I was arranging the crystal on the tablecloth. These were clearly important people visiting us. Otherwise we wouldn't have had Stolichny potato salad smothered in mayonnaise on the table. The guests had brought real coffee with them, and for that we brought out the tiny mocha cups we used on holidays. I was amazed at the table, which usually only looked like this on New Year's, and I sneaked slices of sausage, picking out their fingertip-sized eyes of fat, and my mother never noticed because she was following the conversation so intently. I really wanted to try the fashionable girl's headphones, and if Dad meant to start selling them, I intended to get my own. The girl noticed my glances and slid the plastic box into my hand with a wink. When I snapped the cover open, she whispered that it was a gift. I had never received anything like it, and I became completely immersed in the unfamiliar songs. I studied the device. It recorded. It had a radio. I could hear the Finnish stations.

I remember being sorry not to have had the device when all the boys still had to go into the Soviet army. I could have created my own little business selling cassettes recorded from Finnish radio stations, and maybe could have even saved my cousin. I knew that others had sent the officers recordings of music from Western bands they wanted to hear. Sending them through the mail might have worked better than bottles of Vana Tallinn. I may have been a little infatuated with my cousin, whom I'd met when his mother came to Tallinn to shop. After I finished thinking about this, I looked up and saw that Grandma had already pulled the suitcases out in the bedroom.

We left a couple of days after those special visitors came. I didn't understand the finality of the situation: I thought we'd just take my babusya to visit relatives in Vinnytsia and then, after stopping by my dad's parents' house in Snizhne, we would return to Tallinn in time to see the final episodes of *Dynasty*. It never occurred to me that any of us would want to live in a backwater covered in coal dust while the whole world was opening up, least of all my father. Mom and Babusya had just been laughing at the Lenin statues toppling in Estonia. But now we were moving to a place where they were still standing.

Dad stole a truck from the factory and went to buy fuel from the Red Army troops still in Estonia. Then he came to fetch us. I dragged my feet and kicked the suitcases buttoned into white sheet fabric bags to protect their cardboard sides. They were full of purchases from the time when we'd worried the ruble would lose its value and any goods were preferable, whether they were rationed or freely available. Dad told us to leave at least part of the load, like the pillowcases we had packed full. We would have everything we needed when we got there. Mom didn't believe him. She remembered full well her one and only trip to Ukraine. Then people had been forced to hitch rides in the beds of trucks into the city in search of bread, because in the country they didn't even have that. Dad snorted and rattled his matchbox as if that would get us moving. He thought Snizhne would be completely different now. Moscow wouldn't be allowed to suck Ukraine dry anymore. Those times were different.

I listened to their bickering and continued kicking the luggage until my foot went through the cardboard side of a suitcase, but that didn't delay our departure any more than my parents' war of words. Dad gave in to Mom, and all of the unused towels and bolts of sheet cloth bought during the last moments of the ruble era traveled with us to Ukraine like a wedding trousseau.

Babusya cried the whole way, although for different reasons than me. She was going home and would now be buried in the soil of her homeland. As I listened to her whispering in the cramped cab of the truck, I felt like a stranger in my own family. Memories had wriggled out like saplings from the gaps in the asphalt, and everyone else but me felt them in the soles of their feet.

· · ·

I don't remember when my grandmother started describing Ukraine as home. I'd thought she meant our apartment in Tallinn, and when I finally realized that wasn't the case, I thought she was just going senile. But I did understand Babusya's homesickness: she had been born near Vinnytsia before she was taken to Siberia, and she had always spoken Ukrainian to us. However, my mother's fate was different, since she had been born in exile. She spoke Russian with my father but had built her life in Estonia, and she had a brother who had no intention of leaving Tallinn. My uncle spoke Ukrainian to my mother, Russian to my father, and Estonian to the Estonians, haltingly, but at least he tried, and he had invited my parents to come work at his *shashlik* restaurant, which he had set up along the highway as soon as it was possible. So why on earth did the yearning my grandmother suffered from infect my mother? Why did she go along with my father's insanity? Had she really felt like a foreigner in Tallinn and longed to go to Ukraine, or was it all simply the fear of change?

Or was our departure accelerated by the fact that our moving truck also contained a briefcase full of American dollars?

Everything seemed to have started with Maxim Sokolov's call, which I answered. On the other side of the crackling line was a man who introduced himself as Maxim and asked for my father. I called Dad to the phone and went into the kitchen. I asked my mother who Max was. My mother set down on the table the half-full jar of sauerkraut soup she was holding. After taking a moment to choose her words, she responded that Maxim Sokolov was my father's best friend. When they were young, they had belonged to the same sports club, and Max, who still lived with his family in Snizhne, had even visited us before their daughter Daria was born. I had been small enough that I didn't remember the visit, though Mom said we had a lot of black-and-white photos of the two men. Those I remembered. In the pictures, Dad was always on some adventure with Max, fishing or competing at sports.

In the hall, Dad was stretching the phone cord and twisting it into a corkscrew. I expected my mother to get upset about that. But no. Her head inclined with intense focus in the direction of the vague sound of my father's voice, and her bare heel separated with a squelch from her slipper whenever she shifted position, the bottom of the slipper brushing the floor. The soup bubbled as the blue gas flame puffed at the bottom of the pot. The wooden spoon banged on the aluminum, continuing to circle aimlessly until my mother couldn't restrain herself from approaching the hall. By the time my father set the receiver back in its cradle, smoke was rising from the stovetop. Neither of them noticed. I rushed to close the gas bottle valve and switch off the burner. The living room door clicked shut. I sneaked behind it, unsuccessfully trying to hear what my parents were saying, but all I could make out were murmuring and the faint rhythm of a matchbox, which this time resembled maracas—my father was excited.

Once the conversation was over, my parents came into the kitchen, where I'd already set out the plates. Mom started lifting into the cupboard the dishes she had stacked in an enamel basin to dry, and Dad stood tapping ashes into the ashtray from his cigarette. I bent an aluminum spoon, and Mom didn't even tell me not to. Neither of them sat at the table.

"How do you like red caviar?" Dad asked.

Mom shushed him, but I nodded. Of course I liked it. Who wouldn't?

"And what if you could have black caviar? What would you say to that?"

I liked caviar, although I didn't understand that it meant Donbas.

The next year, Estonia's new parliament declared us foreigners. I didn't understand what that meant—probably endless sitting in various government offices, applying for work and residence permits, something like that, typically boring bureaucracy. My mother wondered in passing whether my Estonian grandfather, who was born during the first Republic of Estonia, granted us citizenship without language tests. I didn't understand why she was so worried about it. I was sure that Dad would manage to arrange things. He always did. Maybe it was around that time that they started talking more about Ukraine, and Babusya began reminiscing about the Carpathian Mountains, her homeland near Vinnytsia. Suddenly everyone wanted Ukrainian pears, Ukrainian apricots, and Ukrainian watermelons, as if we'd been starving for the past few years.

Just like all the other Ukrainians in Tallinn, we existed in a sort of borderland: to the Russians, we were some sort of inferior cousins from a vassal state, and the Estonians thought we were just normal Russians. Sometimes I would catch my mother looking at her Soviet passport the same way she looked at rubles before Estonia adopted its own currency. Like she didn't know what to do with them or like they were strange objects that had fallen from outer space.

I also hadn't noticed that my father didn't sit next to me to watch Finnish TV anymore, which was how I'd learned Finnish, just like the Estonians. My dad hadn't, though, so business opportunities with Finns always went to Tallinners with better language skills while my dad was left empty-handed. Maybe that was what made my dad contact his old friend and ask what was going on back home. Maybe that was why Maxim Sokolov called. Maybe that call was what got my dad talking about the nest egg he had for new ventures and how he wanted to seize the moment. That he wanted black caviar.

SNIZHNE
1992–1996

When we finally arrived in Snizhne after an exhausting drive, I immediately realized something was wrong—very wrong. I wasn't even sure whether my father's mother, whom I hadn't seen in ages, was even happy we were there or whether Babushka Galina's strange expression was disbelief. Gray metal teeth flashed without a smile, sending a shiver through me as I saw my own future. Dad left us in the middle of his mother's kitchen and went to meet his business partners. The truck was still parked in the street with all of our things. We had dropped Babusya Vilina with relatives along the way, and I thought we should have stayed with them, too. The reception at Vinnytsia had been more cordial and the city parks pretty and green. And now came this.

"Long trip," Babushka Galina said. "All this way."

My mother shifted her weight from one foot to the other. Babushka Galina continued gnawing on her bee glue and complaining about her tooth. Finally, she wiped her hands on the hem of her coatdress and took up her cane. I thought she was going to come hug us, but instead she took a drink from a water ladle and went to snuff out the wick of the vigil lamp.

Out of the corner of my eye I saw her crossing herself, and the way she brushed nonexistent dust off a portrait of her deceased husband posing with the medals of the Great Patriotic War on his chest as if ready for a Victory Day parade. Mom turned to look outside, even though there was nothing to see except for a dog on a chain yapping. I didn't know what had happened to the companion dog my grandmother had before. It had been a bolonka, a dog often pictured on calendars and cards, like the birthday cards Babushka Galina sent me.

"Maybe you should go to the store," Mom finally suggested.

She wanted me out of the way so she could talk to her mother-in-law in peace. Then they shoved some scraps of paper into my hand, and I realized what Dad had been muttering about before. They didn't have their own currency here. They paid for things with coupons called *karbovantsi*.

At the counter the abacus tinkled the same way it had in Tallinn, but the shelves were even emptier. The shopkeeper cut coupons from a piece of paper handed to him by the shop's only other customer and then skewered them on a thick needle in front of him. The woman seemed to be buying salt. I didn't know what I would have bought with my play money, so I left the shop and went for a walk. The apartment blocks smelled just as much like cat piss as at home, and their walls were of the same gray-white brick. Grass grew in the carcasses of unfinished buildings. Most of the few cars I saw were Russian, but there were a few Ukrainian models; Dad had told jokes about them on our drive, how the engine in a Zaporozhets was in the back and the trunk was under the front hood. There were none of the Western cars Dad liked.

The strange mountain standing guard on the horizon was new to me, and more walking revealed it wasn't the only one. Mine towers of every description pierced holes in the sky like the monument to Yuri Gagarin we had passed. The coal trucks were also new, as well as the bushes my father called caramel trees.

I passed a door with a latch that seemed to lead to a children's café. But the curtains looked new. On the wall outside was a mosaic of a familiar cartoon wolf and hare. *Nu, Pogodi!* was the name of the show. *Well, just you wait!* Well, just you wait, and we'll be back home before school starts. I simply couldn't imagine any other possibility. I lingered outside kicking gravel, then I sat down on the swing, which had peeling paint, and when I'd picked up some speed, I kicked the dog turds on the ground as far as I could. I was putting off returning to Babushka's house because I sensed that Dad hadn't returned and that the mood wouldn't have shifted meanwhile into one of joyful reunification while I was away.

I was right. When I walked in, Mom didn't even seem to see me. She and my grandmother moved into the bedroom to continue their conversation. The door was closed, the television was switched on, and the volume was turned up. The theme music echoing into the kitchen was *Vremya* from Channel One Russia, which meant it was time for the nine-o'clock news in Moscow. A plate of *syrnyky* pancakes and a jar of jam had been left on the table for me. The waxed tablecloth had gray knife cuts in it. I turned off the central radio. I didn't remember anyone in Tallinn listening to the programs broadcast through the central radio plug, even when the Soviet loudspeaker we called a cowbell was present on the wall. Instead I looked around. There was no sign of an antenna radio. Some loud bangs came from far away. Later I realized that they were gunshots, which we were never supposed to pay any attention to.

I didn't see my dad for a week. Keeping my headphones on, sometimes even without music, I crept around the house. I tried to intercept words I wasn't meant to hear, ones that might somehow explain the situation. I deduced that Dad had gone to Russia or Donetsk with Maxim Sokolov.

When Dad finally returned, he asked me to come out with him. Apparently, a walk would do me good. Dad walked in the middle of the road, while I skulked along the edge. I smelled liquor, but at least he was here. I noticed he'd adopted a new style of walking, with deliberately slow, slightly wobbly steps. Like he had all the time in the world and all this space was his.

"Don't you like any of them?"

I didn't understand what he was talking about.

"The houses," he said. "We don't have all day." As a coal truck approached, Dad barely got out of the way. Casually he waved at the driver. As if they were friends. As if he were giving the truck permission to pass.

"There goes the future."

I looked after the truck, which was leaving eddies of dust in its wake.

Dad smiled at me. I didn't see any reason to smile.

"There isn't anthracite anywhere like we have here in Donbas," he said. "So, have you decided? Which is the most beautiful house around?"

In a panic I pointed at a house with a mosaic on the gable end and shutters painted the color of finch eggs.

Then Dad walked in the direction I was pointing, kicked the gate open, and went to pound on the door. I ran after him. Chickens clucked, and a dog pulled at its chain. The woman who appeared in the doorway looked alarmed.

"How much do you want for this house?"

Dad pulled out a bunch of dollars.

"It isn't for sale."

"Now it is."

The woman tried to pull the handle. Dad shoved his foot in the door and pushed his way inside. I saw the woman's mouth gape open and her eyebrows arch like sickles. Her floral scarf disappeared into the shadows. I backed up to the gate and wondered whether I should go tell my mother what was happening. I didn't have time, though. Dad came out with the key in hand. Tossing it to me, he said we could start unloading the truck. He needed it for work.

The woman had left everything except her photographs. She'd left the chickens, the barking dog, the furniture, her late husband's medals, a mixed collection of Communist Party papers, a wardrobe of chintz dresses and long-legged cotton undergarments, a box of worn men's, women's, and children's handkerchiefs, each ironed and folded with sharp corners in its own pile, and a Slava alarm clock, which ticked with exactly the same sound as the one at our house in Tallinn and the one at Babushka's house. Dad was in a hurry, so he left us standing in this stranger's kitchen. Mom sat down on a chair. The previous resident's teacup was on the table, still half full, and on the stove an aluminum pot of green borscht was growing cold. We looked at each other. Glass crunched under my sandal. Mom picked up the coupons that had been left on the corner of the cupboard, fingering them for a moment before replacing them.

"Well, now," Mom said. "Should we start carrying the suitcases in?"

I didn't budge.

"There's really no rush. Just so long as we do it before Babusya Vilina arrives."

"What do you mean 'arrives'? Here?"

"Well, she can't very well live with other people forever."

"But why on earth would she want to come here? Wasn't she dreaming about Vinnytsia?"

"Don't tell Babusya about this house if you write her. Or about Svetlana."

I hadn't met Svetlana, but I knew the story. Babushka Galina's friend had lived on a nice plot of land until some bald Gopniks started coming by demanding the house or else. Eventually Svetlana sold her home for two hundred dollars and moved to Russia. Mom didn't need to specify why it was better to keep quiet about that. Babusya Vilina had been forced to leave everything, too, once, and she would never forget, especially what had happened to their animals. We wouldn't tell her how we had come by our new house, that much was clear. Still I didn't believe that Babusya would agree to move here. This world was completely different from the one to which she'd been longing to return.

"We'll let your father find what he wanted to come to Snizhne so badly for."

"And then we'll leave? Why can't we leave now? Or why can't we leave, just the two of us?" I demanded. "Let Dad come later."

"If we leave your father here now, we won't ever see him again," my mother said, her jaw quivering.

I went to test whether the television I'd found in the bedroom worked. The only station I could get was Channel One Russia. Everything else was just snow.

At least the new house we were calling home had running water, albeit only cold. After the summer months, the sun no longer warmed the water tank for the shower in the yard, and I began to remind Dad about it every time I saw him, not caring if I sounded like a snob. I missed our proper bathroom in our home in Tallinn, and I didn't understand my mother's indifference. Mom didn't even seem to notice the strange sediment at the bottom of the pot when she boiled water, or she just didn't dare seem difficult by complaining to Dad. I did dare, though it didn't help. After growing tired of my nagging, Dad suggested that I look for a better-equipped place for us to live. I didn't want a new house, though. I wanted to go home.

The smell of the previous resident lingered in the house for a long time. It clung to my clothes and my mother's dresses and her hair. I jumped when she tried to stroke my arm. She smelled like a stranger, and I smelled like a stranger, though we mopped the floors with chlorine, scrubbed the pots with ash and salt, dusted away the cobwebs, and scoured the doors especially carefully around the handles. We even sprayed the wallpaper with a bottle of real French perfume from a box Dad brought home one night. None of that got rid of the woman's odor. The dog didn't get used to us, and Dad started to get tired of its barking. I secretly let it go before my dad could do something like hit it or kill it. He didn't seem to notice that the whole house smelled like Yves Saint Laurent Opium and a strange old woman, a remarkable combination of impending death and luxury.

The news of Babusya Vilina's death didn't make me cry. I didn't cry on the trip to Vinnytsia, which took forever, or at the funeral, which was swarming with strange faces. I didn't cry even though as I buried my babusya, I was also burying my secret hopes of visiting her and staying permanently. I refused to internalize it and didn't understand why my mother started getting ready to go back to Snizhne as soon as the memorial was done. Why was she in such a rush to get on the night train, which would be as hot as a sauna? Mom didn't enjoy the scenery in Donbas any more than I did, and I wanted to stay, at least for a little while.

"We don't know what your dad will come up with in the meantime," she explained. "We'd better go look after him."

At the station, it was already so oppressive in the train that the thought of a night on one of its bunks made me sick to my stomach. I shouted to Mom that I was going to get something to eat and joined the press in the narrow passageway until I could get out, though my mother was shouting something about having enough food already. A woman was blocking the corridor behind me with her luggage, so Mom couldn't catch me before I jumped into the crowd on the platform. Maybe there would be a train going somewhere far away, I thought. Maybe there would be a train for Tallinn. Maybe there would be a train that could take me anywhere other than toward Donetsk

Oblast. I happened upon a conductor in a garrison cap, who was taking parcels for delivery in exchange for money. Would he hide me in his cabin or somewhere else? Could I shake off my mother completely? But the train wasn't going to Tallinn. Some other train would be. Some other train would have to. Some other train I could slip onto. I hurried forward as if this were my last chance to get home and then stopped when I heard someone talking about Moscow. Moscow? Why not? Better than Snizhne. The woman standing next to the train was taking something to sell in the Moscow markets in her big sacks. Someone else was hauling a bunch of carts to the same destination, *kravchuchkas*, which would make carrying the woman's goods more convenient, and the cart man immediately began trying to make a deal. I didn't have kravchuchkas to sell, let alone any currency, only the icon of the Holy Mother of God Babusya had left me, which I clutched in my pocket. Babusya had bought it from a Tallinn street vendor outside the Nevsky Cathedral, and it wouldn't get me very far. I didn't have anything to haggle over, to get money from, to escape with. My mother's voice called after me. Pretending not to hear, I pushed aside the long coats and the luggage, and charged headlong without any destination, until the crowd began to board the nearest train and the crush bore me along, giving me no option to turn back amid the determined travelers. I found myself on a local train, which tried in vain to close its automatic doors. A few of the windows were open. Through them more bags were quickly loaded, along with a screaming baby. I grabbed one of the benches and noticed that the faux leather seat covers had been torn off. Someone had sold those, too. I heard my name again. Mom had managed to squeeze in and dragged me onto the platform just as the train set off. She shoved a damp handkerchief into my hand and whispered that there were clean ones in the suitcase. I didn't understand why she did that. Then I realized I was sniffling. I hadn't shed a single tear at Babusya Vilina's funeral, so why now? I wiped my nose. The handkerchief was Babusya's. I recognized its silken, worn, light blue lines and began to cry harder. I would never move in with Babusya. I was going back to that hateful city, where everyone scowled at us, and to the school where I didn't have any friends. Babushka Galina had urged us not to talk about Vinnytsia or about our relatives who lived so far west. People in the east didn't like them and vice versa.

In my bunk on the night train, I pretended to sleep and tried to remember *Dynasty*. I'd missed the last episodes of the series, and no one had written to me about what happened. Before our move, my friend Evelin had been leaving to see her relatives in Sweden, and Marina and her mother were going to Finland to pick strawberries. They weren't interested in how I was doing, and why would they be? I doubted I even existed for them anymore.

A surprise was waiting for us in Snizhne. Dad had gotten a new TV and spent the evening tuning it. It was probably his way of apologizing for his absence from the funeral, and he boasted that I would finally be able to watch the Ukrainian channels. That didn't make Babushka Galina happy, and she banged the bottom part of the sideboard with her cane several times. I'd noticed her defiant cane use before, though I didn't understand the reason for it. She always did it when Dad came home. I'd checked the contents of the sideboard: a stack of face soap. Once some buckwheat appeared in there. Mom noticed my glances and told me what it was about. Babushka didn't like new trends and didn't believe in Dad's business plans. She didn't think pieces of paper like stocks had any value, since salaries and pensions were either paid in cans of fish, cotton wool, or pieces of soap, which we could make gravy out of for the potatoes next winter if we didn't have anything else. As Mom told me about the situation, it occurred to me that at least we could seal the windows for the fall; Babushka always shoved paper or fabric rubbed with soap between the frames. As I thought about this, I felt some satisfaction that at least one thing would be right. It was as if I had surrendered to the fact that we would stay in Snizhne. It was as if I was just as sure as my grandmother that my father's business activities wouldn't produce a real livelihood, even though the directors of the factories and mines were getting rich. They were all setting up their own business, trading coal for all manner of things, and some of Dad's old acquaintances were also involved, one of whom lived in the city of Donetsk and had even bigger plans than Dad and Maxim Sokolov. Dad never took us to his meetings. And no one ever talked about the briefcase of dollars he'd brought to Snizhne. I began to suspect that I had dreamed it all, Dad hiding the briefcase behind our couch in Tallinn and me checking what was inside during the night. Maybe I had been asleep when I saw the same briefcase in the footwell of the truck, too.

The new TV channels didn't bring me any comfort. All of the dubbing and interpreting of the scant foreign program offerings was handled by one man, and he sounded like he had a clothespin on his nose. His nasal translations were awful, and I began to fear that I would forget everything I'd learned from television in Tallinn, my meager English and Finnish. I heard that some people got a channel that broadcast American cartoons without dubbing, but we weren't that lucky. And Mom wasn't speaking to me in Ukrainian anymore. The language just disappeared. One night she called me Alyonka in Russian, not Olenka, and she didn't even notice.

I didn't understand what was happening to us. In Tallinn I had trusted my father to know how to arrange everything for the best. Now my faith in his business skills was gone. Sometimes I happened to see him from a distance in the city as he led a bunch of thugs with shaved heads somewhere or explained something excitedly to some boys dressed in sweatpants and leather jackets squatting against the wall of a building.

Once, on the kitchen table, I found a rerun request written by Babushka to Central Television. Mom had already signed Babushka's request that they replay *The Slave Isaura*, about a Brazilian slave girl's journey to freedom. The form demanded my name, too. As I dropped the envelope into the mailbox bound for Moscow, I realized how insane it was. Just like everyone else, I found myself anxiously looking forward to the telenovela *The Rich Also Cry* and other old programs that had been dubbed into the wrong language, and that always had women with narrower shoulders than on *Dynasty*.

Maybe that was when I started planning to run away, as I stood in front of that mailbox. Or at least it occurred to me that I needed dollars and papers. Though I was registered in Tallinn, I suspected that soon my Soviet passport would be useless. I wasn't sure whether I was a citizen of any country at all, whether I'd be able to get anywhere but Russia with my *propiska,* or whether we might even need a visa to stay in Ukraine. This didn't concern my mother the same way it used to. She waved her hand—Dad would handle everything. There was no point worrying my head about such things.

No one else in our family would be leaving that backwater.

One night I woke up to voices in the kitchen. It sounded like the conversation was about someone's fingers getting smashed in a car door. I recognized my dad's footsteps and his way of knocking the water scoop against the enamel side of the bucket. Mom never made any noise if I was asleep.

"That boy's mother came to visit me," Babushka said. "She told me what happened."

"Well, why didn't he sell his shares?" Dad said, and Maxim Sokolov backed him up. "The idiot wanted more dollars."

I remembered what Dad had said. I already understood enough about privatization and the dismantling of the Soviet system to know that the workers were all being given a number of shares relative to how many years they had been at their factories, and Dad and his friends were buying them up for someone, maybe that man from Donetsk.

"He'll sell. Everyone sells. Babushka Galina told the boy's mother he'll get fired otherwise, right? Where else does the idiot think he'll get work?" Maxim said.

Cigarette smoke snaked through the crack in the door. Maxim's tone was respectful, though there was something else in it, too, something that stung your nose like the smell of a damp pouch of chlorine powder.

"It would be more pleasant all around if Babushka Galina could explain the situation to her friend. Stupidity doesn't pay."

Dad accompanied Maxim's words with short, emphatic interjections: absolutely, of course, definitely.

"Why do I have to get involved in the messes you young men make?" my grandmother said.

Mom didn't say anything. She didn't even move. She was so quiet that my grandmother seemed like she was alone in the room with her son and Maxim. I made out the sound of a pot moving; Babushka had stood up to rearrange the containers meant for the seedlings, along with the glasses and newspapers, occasionally banging her cane as she did so, as if wanting to shake off mud that had stuck to it.

"That's enough," Babushka said. "Don't bring your business under my roof anymore."

The door slammed as Dad and his friend went on their way again, and Mom snapped back to reality, too, her slippered feet shuffling to the stove and the cupboard. I stretched my neck to see the alarm clock. It wasn't even midnight yet. Dad never explained where he was going. He was always in a hurry, and we rarely saw him. If we did, he was lying in bed nursing a hangover by drinking pickle juice from the jar, and after he recovered, he left. We were still staying with Babushka Galina, even though our belongings had been moved to the house that was supposed to be our new home.

"Privatization means opportunities," Mom said carefully.

"All it means is the president's family buying factories for chicken feed." Babushka sighed. "For the rest of us, privatization means threats and broken fingers. Or worse."

I wasn't sure whether I heard shushing. Some hissing sound.

"You'll still talk to your friends about those shares, won't you, Babushka?"

My mother repeated words she'd learned from my father as if she were speaking a foreign language, one she didn't really know but had to practice. In her mouth, the words didn't have the same self-confidence or emphasis as when my father said them. I don't believe my mother understood anything she was saying. But this time, she was missing the slightly contemptuous note that used to appear in her voice for the Western words gradually sneaking into colloquial language. I was amazed: she was parroting my father, parroting Maxim Sokolov.

I'd managed to learn a few things from Maxim Sokolov. He seemed to be just as resourceful as my dad, and he wasn't disappointed that his gifts as a boxer hadn't been sufficient to earn him a spot in the international ring. After that, he'd become a coach but was left without a salary after the fall of the Soviet Union, like so many others. However, he still had a stable of broke young men without jobs or futures. Maxim Sokolov had no intention of sitting in his gym chewing sunflower seeds. He would put his boys to work and accept the alternatives that were available to men like him. There was always work in the mines and the security industry. He chose both, and he brought my father on board—a business partner who not only shared his plans but mimicked his mannerisms. On the rare occasions Dad was home, he sat more ostentatiously, pulling the chair away from the table, almost to the middle of the room. At first, I didn't realize where he'd gotten that from. But when I saw him walking beside Maxim Sokolov, I saw his new walk had come from the same place as the bombastic way he sat.

The next time Dad came home to change his shirt, I slipped into the bedroom after him and offered him some cherry *mors*.

"I made it myself," I said and hoped he would stay at least long enough to empty the glass.

Dad didn't turn, continuing to rummage in the closet, knocking clothing off hangers and messing up Mom's neat, folded piles. I set the mors jug on the table and picked up a dress from the floor as I told Dad I would find him something to wear, keeping my voice as soft as semolina porridge. Dad moved farther away, and now he took the glass I was holding out, even thanking me. I noticed that the Slava watch on his wrist had disappeared. Instead he wore a plastic one, the dial replaced by digital numbers.

"This won't take long," I said. I found Dad's shirt almost immediately but still continued looking. "I think it would be fun to go driving, too, sometime."

I didn't dare look at him to see what effect my words had.

"Look at you now, girl."

I heard Dad pouring more mors, and his haste seemed to fade somehow.

"Did your mom tell you to ask?"

Handing him the shirt, I shook my head. Mom was at the store with Babushka and wouldn't hear anything about our conversation, let alone my suggestions. Dad cast me a measuring glance.

"Soon we'll go for a drive in a real Western car. What do you say to that, my little sunshine?"

I tried to look enthusiastic. On the street, a Volga was waiting for my father with a driver who opened the door for him. Just the week before, his transportation had been an orange Zhiguli with a rug over the back seat. In the footwell, I'd found a foam plastic animal, Gena the Crocodile's friend Cheburashka. That had been Dad's first car.

"For a Western car, you need those shares," I said.

"You're quite right, my little sun."

"Do you believe Babushka will convince her friends to sell them?"

"You clearly don't."

"I can handle it. For dollars."

Dad started to laugh. He didn't point out that I'd been listening in on their conversations.

"That's my kid," Dad said, nodding. "But this business isn't appropriate for little girls. We'll find something else for you. Something all your own."

As he left, he called me his little sun one more time and slipped an American ten-dollar bill into my hand, which I hid in my sleeve under my watchband.

That evening I went out in the backyard. The mouth of the kopanka was covered with a piece of sheet metal. I was forbidden to go anywhere near it because of the risk of collapse, but I still went secretly, if I was crying, if I felt anxious, or if my throat was too constricted. It was my own secret place. Now it also became the hiding place for the wooden pencil box that held my nest egg for getting out of there. I checked the bill, smoothing out the wrinkles. It looked the same as the dollars in my dad's briefcase, or the briefcase from my dream. I sniffed it. It did not smell any different from rubles. I would need many more of these for my plan, but this was at least a start. If Dad came home drunk, I could sneak more from his pocket.

Originally, Maxim Sokolov and his men dug the pit. I gradually began to understand a few of the rules they were playing by and how they laundered the coal. Everything that came out of these holes was taken for refining along with the state mine coal. State subsidies were paid according to tonnage. Dad and Maxim talked about subsidies in the same tone of voice as factory shares, and they were equally interested in trucks, lines of which were always driving to destinations where officially they weren't supposed to go. There was plenty to do for everyone who wanted to do it. I didn't know that these businesses were still in their infancy back then, that there would be even greater traffic jams at the coal piers, that the kopankas would become a threat to the legal mines, that they would cause the main streets of the city to crumble, that bodies would fall out of the graveyard into the pit dug next to it. That children would work in the pit and others like it for a dollar a day. Or that this was already happening and I just didn't realize it yet. I had no way to know how high my dad and his friends were reaching, that they wanted to touch the sky, to punch through it toward the sun. Like Gagarin.

Dad didn't forget my request, and occasionally he began taking me on his drives. On one trip, he suddenly stopped the car on the side of the road, so excited about the thing he was pointing at that he didn't even notice I'd nearly hit my head on the dashboard. Despite straining my eyes, I didn't see anything in the direction he was pointing other than the gloomy silhouettes of the coal spoil tips. Before, we'd gone together to the zoo and once to the Moscow Circus, but now it was only mines. I dug in my pocket for a handkerchief, and when I didn't find one, I secretly wiped my nose with the back of my hand, leaving black snot on it.

"Do you see those boys?" Dad asked. "Can you guess what they're doing?"

By following my father's finger, I finally made out a pack of young boys. I heard laughter and screams. They were having fun. Dad rolled the window down and waited for them to get closer.

"What did you find?" he yelled to them.

The gang of urchins stopped and eyed us. The shortest one lifted up something that looked like a chunk of rock.

"Can I try it?" Dad asked and climbed out of the car.

The kids gathered around him and presented their stones, and Dad gave them something that set off a ripple of enthusiasm. Maybe it was dollars, or gum, or Western cigarettes. I looked at his back as he lifted the rocks admiringly toward the sky.

The three stones that fell into my lap made me jump.

"Fossils," Dad said and slammed the car door.

Squeezing the side of the bench, I stared out. Behind the retreating pack of boys, I spotted a stooped old lady, who was loading her bags with pieces of coal that she deemed satisfactory, stopping to lean on her cane from time to time.

"Look. A clam. And there's a snail shell," Dad said as he picked up each rock from my lap, wiping them off in turn. "We used to play on those mounds before, too, and there were tons of these."

"With who? Maxim?"

"Maxim and others. Then we painted them. What do you say we go look one day to see if we can find some, too?"

I wasn't a kid anymore, but I didn't say that out loud. I let my dad have his moment of excitement, dropping the fossils back onto my light-colored skirt. I thought of the dollars he might have given to those boys and not to me.

As we neared our destination, I noticed that Dad began to squeeze the steering wheel tighter and didn't slow down for the potholes. He didn't even seem to notice the bumps that made my petrified creatures jump against my thighs. I would have preferred to drop Dad's precious treasures into the footwell. I didn't dare to, though. The snails were huge.

The car stopped, and Dad looked at me expectantly. I didn't know why—I saw only a normal mining landscape. There had to be something special, though, because Dad wanted me to suggest a name for this mine in particular. All the new stores, kiosks, and shacks that kept sprouting up here and there like mushrooms were named for women, so I suggested some women's names, but Dad just shook his head. We needed something more noble. Dad rotated a matchbox in his hand.

"Heroes of the Cosmos. Good name, right?"

"Sounds Soviet."

Dad didn't think a mine could be Pamela or Sue Ellen. This was Donbas, after all, where they paid the best salaries, and Aleksey Stakhanov, the Hero of Socialist Labor, had practically lived next door to us until his dying day. Dad's voice became somehow tractor-like.

"Someday this will be ours. It won't take long now."

"Maxim's and yours, right?"

Dad laughed and poked me in the side.

"Max is getting his own mine. This is ours, yours and mine. So, what do you say to that, my little sunshine?"

The sun was setting behind the mountains, and Dad turned to bask in the fleeing rays as if sunbathing. I didn't know him anymore. I remembered my mother saying once that when people loved old places, they were loving their former selves. Was Dad fulfilling dreams that Mom and I hadn't known about? Had he looked up to miners as a child? Why hadn't he stayed here then? Or was realizing this ancient dream only possible now? I was sure the boys playing on the mountain would have come up with a name for the mine that my father would have accepted. They admired my dad's accomplishments, that he had first become a man with a car and then a man with a driver.

But I didn't want to become the girl who walked her bicycle past Babushka's house in every weather. She was my age and always carried a coal sack on her bike rack, apparently to warm her home. If my father's plans panned out, nothing like that would ever happen to me, of course. I didn't see things that way, though. Maybe because I couldn't imagine what the life of a mining baron's daughter would be like or what kind of money a girl like that would have at her disposal. I didn't know any girls like that. I didn't understand what that would mean. But I could easily imagine pushing a bike. I could already feel the handles and the weight of the coal, which was heavier than the zinc buckets I used to carry water for Babushka.

The last of the flower sellers were closing up their stalls as Dad pulled into the cemetery, stopping right in front of the gates. The latest visitors were packing up their food, pushing the newspapers they had used as tablecloths into the trash, and preparing to leave. Opening the car door, I stepped out onto a plastic aster that had fallen on the ground and tried to cheer up. I had already visited the graves in the morning with Mom and Babushka Galina, but Dad wanted to spend this commemoration of the dead with me alone. He had fetched me from home for this. That was something.

After we had been walking between the headstones for a moment, I realized we were going in the wrong direction. Dad didn't remember where Grandfather was buried. I didn't say anything, I just started subtly guiding us toward the right path. Now that the bustle of the morning had subsided, I realized that the rainbow of flowers had brought summer to all these dead people and made this the most beautiful place in the city. If Snizhne always looked like this, maybe I could live here. I shook the thought from my head. Sentimentality would make me weak and delay my plan. I needed determination, not anything that would root me here. No infatuations, no pets, no movie theaters I'd hope someone would take me to, not anywhere I wanted to go with anyone, let alone the Ukrainian citizenship Dad intended to get for us. In passing, my father grabbed a pastry from someone's grave and bit off a piece before offering me some, too. I declined.

"Come on, this is part of it. Where do you think all the food disappears to?"

"I'm not hungry."

"As I remember, we also visited the cemetery on Victory Days—me and a couple of friends. We always found something to eat, and I think this was the first place we tried cigarettes."

I knew those friends.

"And we drank booze, too."

Dad snatched a bottle off another grave and after swigging from the mouth extended it to me, until he realized to whom he was offering vodka and pulled back his hand with a cough. I pretended not to notice, instead focusing on finding the grave, and finally I did locate the right place. In Tallinn we didn't celebrate Radonitsa, and my grandfather was only familiar to me from pictures, in which he looked very serious because of the line of medals covering his chest in all of them. The picture on the gravestone was similar. We had washed it in the morning with Babushka, and she'd asked whether they also sold medals in the square in Tallinn as tourist souvenirs. Apparently, they did that in Moscow, and there were heaps of medals. Before Mom could answer, I lied that I had never seen anything like that. The corners of Mom's mouth curved up. I couldn't remember the last time she'd smiled.

Dad looked at Grandfather's grave. The Easter eggs we'd placed in a circle that morning were still there.

"I brought those cosmos flowers."

I glanced at the neighboring graves. In front of the very next headstone stood an enormous wreath. We didn't have anything like that.

"Very good," Dad muttered and set a package of Prima cigarettes on Grandfather's headstone. "This is what he always smoked. Babushka didn't remember to bring cigarettes, did she?"

I felt annoyed. I hadn't known my grandfather well enough to be able to complete the day's traditions in a way that would earn my father's praise. It was useless to hope for any dollars now. Shifting my weight from one foot to the other, I tried to think of a yarn to spin, something that would raise my stock in my father's eyes. What came to me was to ask whether Grandfather had really wanted to be a miner, and to my surprise Dad's expression brightened. I was afraid I'd said something strange. But it was just enthusiasm. Apparently, the benefits that came with the job were good. And Dad didn't stop there. He continued telling stories about Grandfather much longer than I would have expected, longer than he had talked to me in ages. The only thing that bothered Grandfather was that in the mines you never knew what the weather was above. The others got used to it, but he never did. Days at work were hot, and yet when he ascended out of the shaft, it could be winter. I watched a stray dog loping along in the distance. When it noticed an interesting treat, it stopped and shoved its nose into a bouquet of chrysanthemums. I didn't actually want to hear any more about my grandfather. I didn't spend my days hundreds of meters underground, and yet I felt somehow the same: my past life was so far away, the people and the TV shows as inaccessible as the summer nights on the Baltic Sea growing lighter without me.

Suddenly I realized Dad had used the word "finally" when talking about Grandfather's desire to be a miner. "Finally," not "at first."

"So originally he didn't intend to work in the mines?"

"Well, no. Have I told you how your grandfather ended up in Snizhne? He was born in Tver."

"Where?"

"Tver was later renamed Kalinin. But by that time, Grandfather had already left home. He marched all the way to Berlin with the Red Army during the Great Patriotic War and spent an entire year there. Then came the order. The soldiers were sent to Donbas to repair the mines that had been destroyed by the war. My father didn't want to come here. He would have preferred to return home. But no, refusing would have meant the camps."

I remembered how Babusya Vilina had snorted at the idea that she could have moved with us to Snizhne. She thought Donbas was too Russian an area, a place people went only after losing all hope—people who had lost their land and their villages, their roots and their families, their language, their faith, and their very souls. People went to Donbas because anyone could get work in the mines, and people had always fled there when they wanted to disappear from the world, whether they were evading the forces of the tsar or the Reds. Before, its melting pot had devoured serfs who had escaped from their masters, then later starving peasants from the collective farms. Later on, people were forced to come. Just like me. I had something in common with my grandfather. He hadn't wanted to come here either. But he had ended up in the Donbas dirt anyway. I wouldn't, though. I would do anything to prevent that from happening. I had twenty-five dollars saved. I needed more. I decided that by next year's Radonitsa, I would be somewhere else.

"Listen, life can be difficult sometimes. Hard work will always get you ahead, though."

I nearly asked whether this lesson came from Grandfather or Maxim Sokolov. I thought it was wisest to keep my mouth shut, though, and took the bottle of liquor hanging from my father's hand. He didn't resist, though he did mention that there was no need to tell my mother.

"The mine where your grandfather worked is still owned by the state, but who knows . . ."

Suddenly Dad stopped.

"What do you say we name the mine Berlin?"

Dad never picked me up from school. That's why I was so terrified when I saw him on the roadside at the end of the day. The sun made his white sneakers shine, and he was leaning on a strange car. I thought that something must have happened to Mom, and slowed my pace. Then I noticed his smile and the matchbox he was tossing in the air. He didn't tell me why he was there. He just hugged me tight. That was strange, too, and had to mean something. Maybe he wanted to talk to me about something that wasn't meant for everyone at home to hear. Maybe it had to do with the woman. The new woman. For a while I'd been picking up the scent of a woman under his stench of old liquor. I could smell her on his leather jacket and the collar of his shirt.

"Let's go for a ride," he said as he started the engine. "I did promise, after all."

As I jumped in, I felt my classmates' eyes on my back. Dad was expecting me to say something. I didn't understand what he was talking about.

"We could get another if you don't like this one. Maybe red. Whatever color you want."

I hadn't realized that this was my father's car. I thought he'd been driving someone. A Western car. The mystery of Dad's sudden appearance was solved. He wanted to share his happy day with me.

"It's beautiful."

"Look at this."

Then he demonstrated all of the dashboard functions. I was afraid he would sense my lack of enthusiasm and was prepared to defend myself by claiming that technology wasn't a girls' thing. But he didn't notice.

"Where are you taking it for the night?"

Dad stepped on the gas. I didn't get an answer. After seeing the Volga, Grandmother had said that nothing bigger than a bicycle was spending the night in her yard. She didn't want to attract thieves to her door. Dad snorted. The topic didn't come up again, and I assumed Dad had found a spot at a garage. But now I was realizing that maybe the new woman had a house with a brand-new garage of its own. Maybe that woman admired my father's business. Maybe they wanted the same life, the kind that moved forward and had goals. No dreams, just goals. The thought of the new woman's home got me worked up in a way the car didn't. What if Dad preferred to store his things there rather than with us? Had he taken his briefcase full of dollars there? I had to meet the new woman, no matter what Mom thought. If the money existed and there was any left, I would find it, and then Mom and Dad could go ahead and get divorced for all I cared. Dad could keep his mine, his fast talk, and his fast cars, his skinhead Gopnik gang, and I would take Mom to Tallinn and buy us a house with walls that weren't made of coal slag like Babushka's. I would buy us a brick house. I would buy a sturdy house that no one would dig a single hole underneath.

I pictured the new woman looking much like the girl I'd gotten my Walkman from in Tallinn. A babe, who would never let a man see her in a garish coatdress or galoshes. She would only listen to the antenna radio or music from her cassette and record collection, and she would definitely have a VCR. Dad would have gotten her videotaped movies from a bootlegger, and they would watch them together. Maybe Dad had also given her the fossils I'd left in the foot-well of the Volga. I wouldn't wonder if he had. None of his gifts would put the same expression on his new woman's face that they elicited in Babushka Galina's house. I no longer used the Western sneakers Dad had gotten me, because that would have been a betrayal of my mother. I'd hidden them in the same kopanka in the backyard where I stored the box that contained my Walkman.

Dad stopped the car on the side of the road. Before us loomed another mountain of coal spoils. A floppy-eared stray dog made its way up the slope.

"Have you made any friends at school?"

This was the first time he'd ever asked me this.

"Shouldn't we be going home?" I asked. "Mom is waiting."

I was about to add that Babushka had promised to bake *vatrushkas*, but I knew trying to entice him was pointless, so I shut my mouth. Dad had wanted to show his new car to me, not the others. I didn't intend to ruin this special moment. Mom hadn't seen Dad in weeks and wouldn't today either, even though she was waiting for him like a Tallinn retiree pining for the postman to bring her pension. Thieves also knew when the mail carrier brought the money, so pension day was always tense for those old ladies. The association was strange. Mom wasn't old. But in a certain way, my mother and Babushka Galina had begun to resemble each other. They could only feel joy about things that were no longer part of my father's life. Dad would never again return home in the same brown sandals he always used to wear and which showed his brown socks that bunched up around his ankles. He would never start his morning by winding his watch, and he would never come to the dinner table enthusiastic about how many adapters he had sold. He wouldn't smoke Primas, he would smoke Marlboros. And I would never get him on a bus, a trolley car, or a train voluntarily. Before Snizhne, I had never traveled alone with my father in a car. Now apparently that had become the only place I would see him, and I knew that he would never give up having his very own vehicle.

Dad struck a match and lit a cigarette. To my amazement, he offered me one, too, as if I were an adult. I shook my head and grabbed a sticky paper cone poking out of the door compartment. His remaining fondness for sour barberry candies reminded me of the father I had lost.

"What if we went somewhere? Where would you want to travel? You can choose."

"Anywhere? Like on vacation?"

"Yes, like on vacation. It's been too long since our last one."

I tried not to show my excitement. Dad hadn't come to fetch me from school only to show off his car.

"Can we go abroad? To the West? To a country that gives visas easily?"

"That doesn't matter. You can decide later. Think about it."

"Are we running away from something?"

Dad flinched.

"How the hell did you get an idea like that into your head?"

"One of the boys in my class didn't come to school, and everyone said that his dad refused to give up his shares. No one has heard from anyone in their family since."

"Then that was their own fault."

"I would have got them to sell."

Dad picked up a matchbox and twirled it in his fingers for a moment.

"Listen, I need to ask you for a little favor, sunshine."

"Can I tell Mom about it? And what about the vacation? Are we all going together?"

"Yes, of course. But you shouldn't worry your mother with everything."

Dad told me that his friend's daughter was having a birthday soon. The man was the director of a factory or plant, and there would be a lot of bigwigs' kids there. Dad was sure that the share certificate lists would be in the director's home, and I could just go ahead and take any lists of names I found. No one would guess which of the guests had stolen them, and no one would pay attention to a little girl like me. If the office door was locked, I should give a signal, and Dad would get me the keys somehow. And he wouldn't drink a lot, because he would have a busy day ahead while everyone else was hung over. After I found the documents, I should pretend to be sick, and Dad would take me home. The earlier the better, but not before I had found the lists. He would take care of it himself but there were men and dogs on guard at the house, so he couldn't break in. It would be easy for me, though.

As Dad elaborated on the details of my mission, I thought about other things. I was already planning how I would run away during the vacation Dad had promised. Or if we visited my uncle in Tallinn, he might let me stay with him or find me work in Finland. And what if a family vacation fixed everything? Would Dad forget even just for a little while why he had ever wanted to come to Snizhne? Would he remember how nice things had been for us before? Maybe I wouldn't need to disappear. Everything could go back to the way it was.

I agreed to the mission for one hundred dollars.

On the way home, Dad called me his little sun.

I hadn't heard from Dad in a week when a guest showed up at our gate. The dog started to bark, and Mom's hands froze in the aster bed she had finally begun to work. I was in the yard doing my math homework and looked up to see whether anyone intended to greet the man who was calling out Babushka's whole name. My grandmother leaned forward but didn't stand up from her stool at the door.

The man said he was from the militsiya. We stared at each other for a moment. This meant something bad.

Babushka took her cane and laboriously forced herself up. After stopping at the gate for a moment, she took hold of the latch. Mom didn't move. The militsiya officer stopped a suitable distance from the dog, which was uttering a low growl, then looked to either side, at his shoes, and then at his fingernails . . . I waited for him to say my father's name, and when he did, I wasn't surprised.

"A body has been found in the Zasyadko mine," he said. "We suspect that it is . . ."

The officer fell silent. He was young and still had pimples on his forehead, which he tried to cover by pulling his cap down too far. He didn't know how to proceed. I understood from his muttering that Babushka or Mom needed to go identify the remains. None of us asked what had happened or why Dad had been in the Zasyadko mine, why he had gone to Donetsk, or whom he had been meeting with. We didn't even ask where the new car was. I realized immediately that the funeral would cost money. I would have to sell the things I had been hiding in the kopanka. I let go of the pen I was squeezing and realized that I had punched a hole in my schoolbook with it.

Grandmother teetered and groped for the wall of the house. I looked at her arm, which was tanned buckwheat brown and didn't change color anymore, even in the winter. Then I snapped out of it and stood to support her. Her breathing sounded like the creaking of rusty cables, or maybe the sound was coming from me, or from neither of us.

The officer cleared his throat and then began to leave. At the gate he seemed to remember something and kicked his foot in annoyance. When he turned back, his acne scars were glowing red.

"We recovered the remains of two men. One of them was immediately identified as Maxim Sokolov, since he still had a head."

"What do you mean?" Grandmother made the sign of the cross.

"One of the deceased was headless."

Mom pressed a dirt-covered hand to her mouth. The officer closed his lips and his eyes, and then continued speaking as if reciting something he had memorized: "The missing body part has not been recovered."

The wake filled the street with strange cars, including Western ones. I didn't know the mourners who came to pay their respects to Babushka, but that wasn't the source of the feeling of unreality—it was the closed casket. In the church I watched the lid being covered with roses, carnations, lilies of the valley, asparagus ferns, and baby's breath. There seemed to be no end to the bouquets or the weeping. I didn't cry, though. Not yet. The casket was supposed to be open. How else could I know if Dad was even under that mound of flowers? How could anyone know? I had to see him to be sure. I thought about it through the entire funeral service, and as the procession crawled forward, I wanted to push through the crowd, order the musicians to be silent, stop the pallbearers, and demand that the casket be opened. I was still gathering the courage to carry this out when they began lowering the casket into the ground, which took an eternity, as if the hole had no bottom. The priest's recitative pressed down like a cloud heavy with rain, and I kept repeating to myself that this was my last opportunity to put an end to all this foolishness. I couldn't get a word out of my mouth, though. I was an actor who had forgotten her lines, and thus a useless part of the play.

The mood remained the same at the memorial, though the star of the performance, the wooden box, was already under the dirt, and liquor was now lubricating the guests' gestures, liberating deceitful words. I listened to people repeatedly drinking to my father's memory, always respectfully, with no clinking of glasses, but I didn't recognize him in the reminiscences of these men in their stinking tracksuits. I waited for my father to finally give some sign of himself, waited to hear the call of a matchbox maraca from the shade of the bushes, waited to see my dad, who would raise a finger to his lips, and I would slip after him, and he would reveal to me his brilliant plans, calling me his little sun and instructing me to play along, for a dollar or maybe ten, and then everything would make sense.

That didn't happen. Nothing made sense. The air swelled with the weight of muscles, tobacco smoke, and heavy perfumes, and no one mentioned the reason for the closed casket. Leather jackets crunched like too-fresh sauerkraut. Someone sniffed the mouth of a bottle of cognac and then exulted at the authenticity of its contents before filling a glass to the brim. The drinker's expression was genuine, too. Nothing else was, not the flowers placed on the burial mound and not my father's framed picture, which Mom had carried and which was how she wanted to remember him.

Babushka Galina went to live with her sister in Minsk, and we moved in with my father's sister in the country. My aunt was delighted at the company, because the compote business had her sleeping with one eye open, and the move was a relief for me. I didn't believe that my father had told anyone about my involvement in the burglary, but still. How could I know?

Dad's pictures were buried in a drawer of my aunt's bureau, and we never talked about what had happened in Snizhne. Not ever. If someone happened to ask about my father, Mom clamped her mouth shut like a dumpling, and no one dared to continue interrogating a widow. When she considered adopting her maiden name and suggested that I start using it, too, I didn't protest, I rejoiced, and so Dad disappeared from our language. We wiped him out of our lives entirely, and I thought this would be a new start, for Mom and for me.

When Mom began to attend church and waste her money on taper candles, I wasn't worried or surprised. I didn't wonder about the cross that appeared around her neck. On Epiphany, she went to be baptized in a hole hacked into the ice in the shape of a cross, with priests fluttering about like crows, and I had no reason to criticize her zeal for purification. I considered the change temporary. Mom would return to her former self in this environment where nothing would remind her of the past. Recovery would just take time.

I was wrong.

I had lost her, too.

A VILLAGE,
MYKOLAIV OBLAST
1996

The blood drained from my mother's fingertips when the dog went crazy outside, and through the lace curtains we saw a Gopnik frozen next to the flower beds. I wondered whether she would faint. Her eyes went wide, their whites narrowing to fish underbellies. Widowhood had made her fearful in a way that was new to me, and it scared me more than the stranger in the yard. I didn't recognize the woman trembling before me. I wanted my mother back.

"They're coming now," Mom whispered. "I knew it."

"Maybe it's a chicken thief," I said and looked to my aunt.

"Yes, a chicken thief. That's obvious," my aunt said. "They've been around."

The dog forced the Gopnik to stay where he was. I looked at Mom and the fingers clutching the belt of her coatdress. They resembled the trunks of the trees we whitewashed on Easter, and the skin of her hands was like the bark. I thought to myself, I would never let what had happened to my mother happen to me. I would not be her.

"Maybe it will be enough for them if I go," Mom whispered. "Then maybe they'll leave you alone."

"Mom, it's probably just a chicken thief," I said. "There's only one man out there."

I reasoned that if the people who had killed Dad and Maxim Sokolov had come to complete their revenge, there would be more of them.

We evaluated the situation for a moment. The tracksuit-clad idiot outside was straight from the sunflower-seed-chomping and empty-Semki-bag-leaving Gopnik crowd in the village. Or maybe this junior thug was better suited to the gang that hung around my dad. Each boy seemed to move in the same way, at the same relaxed pace, secure in the dominance of their uniformity. But no, this man was further along than that crew. Hardening a gaze to that point required experience with things that I shouldn't have known about yet at that age. Still, he was alone.

My aunt tightened the knot of her scarf under her chin, took one of the men's jackets from its nail, threw it over the back of a kitchen chair, and added plates to the table as if we were expecting more mouths. After crossing herself, she took a deep breath and opened the door. I slipped after her despite my mother's protestations, because I thought I had to be brave, braver than Mom, or at least pretend to be.

"Your dog is pretty intense," the Gopnik said and nodded toward the poppies hidden in the garden. "But will it be enough?"

Now we knew what this was about. My aunt sighed with relief. The Gopnik didn't have anything to do with Snizhne. I relaxed enough that I could go peek out the gate to see what kind of vehicle he was using. A taxi. I remembered my aunt mentioning that taxi drivers handled compote distribution. The boy noticed my spying and grinned. Apparently, the trunk was full of electronics he'd received as payments. We could go look to see if there was anything interesting. My aunt ordered me back to her side, and, dragging my feet, I obeyed.

"So, you're the new man."

The Gopnik nodded and introduced himself as Ivan. It seemed his predecessor had opted to take his well-deserved retirement. My aunt pressed her hand to her chest.

"I haven't heard from him in a while."

"Maybe he's enjoying his freedom. He's probably fishing and grilling shashlik."

I realized we couldn't drive off this Gopnik with an ax and a barking dog. If he had been assigned as our new contact, we had no say in the matter. My aunt told the dog, which was still growling, to shut up and invited our guest in and ushered him to the table. Mom had disappeared into the bedroom, leaving the door open a crack. I guessed that inside she was squeezing an icon and an ax in her hands. The Gopnik praised my aunt's cooking, sniffing the salo fatback and slicing it into the borscht with devotion. He claimed he had been longing for just this sort of meal, complete with a glass of raspberry mors, in such a homey atmosphere with lace curtains and everything. He thought we were lucky and said it in a way that didn't sound like a threat. What popped into my head was that this Gopnik must have just been released from prison. I guessed that no one had sent him care packages. Somehow you could sense it.

"Boris told me about you," he said.

I didn't understand what Boris had to do with this. When my aunt had needed a man to help with the farming, the director of the nearby rest home had agreed to rent out the place's only young man to us as day labor for a reasonable price. Boris had grown up in a psychiatric institution and then was transferred to the rest home when he turned eighteen. Before this Gopnik, no one had come asking after him. I liked Boris. My aunt liked him, too. So did my mom.

"Boba could visit a little more often," Ivan said, using Boris's nickname, and warmth filled his voice. "What if I talked to the director of the rest home and arranged for my brother to come help you every day? Boba would be happy to watch the plantings."

The pieces fell into place, and I understood immediately what this proposal could mean for me. Ivan would pay the director, and I could go to Paris. The modeling competition advertisement I'd cut out of a magazine was burning a hole in my pocket. The deadline hadn't passed yet. I hadn't dared to enter the competition because my mother wasn't in any condition to be left alone. Mom's skittish behavior would just infect my aunt, who would start to sleep with her clothes on, her handbag next to her head, a pitchfork under the bed. But now the situation was changing. If I left, Ivan's obvious love for his brother and concern for his welfare would ensure that he would also look out for my mother and my aunt.

I did go. And I won. Afterward, Ivan found me sulking under the apple trees and asked what was wrong. I told him that Mom wouldn't sign the papers required for a minor to prove she had her guardian's consent. Ivan didn't think my mother's signature was a problem. All I had to do was forge it on the certificate and run away. I would be fine. Ivan had been fine, too. He was a runaway also, and he promised to take me to the railway station in his taxi.

"Listen, I don't know what happened to you or your dad in Donetsk. And I don't want to. But you have your whole life in front of you."

Ivan nudged me in the side, like my dad had done sometimes. Ivan thought I had a chance. There was no reason to waste it because my mom couldn't get over Dad's death.

Ivan's words settled the matter. I sensed that if I stayed, my mother's fear would infect me like a disease.

Now I feel like that happened anyway. The disease was just waiting dormant for the right moment.

Sometimes individual flashes bring me back to Snizhne. If I have a stomachache and I'm being offered buttercream pastries. If I step into a room full of Soviet-era books that hasn't been aired out in a while. If I happen to see an ashtray full of sunflower seed shells. It can happen anywhere—visiting, in a café, in a meeting. When it happens, I'm instantly back in that office, surrounded by the smell of tobacco smoke and Soviet paper and glue, where I was supposed to look for the share certificate list. My insides twist in the same way as then, and my tongue touches the roof of my mouth only to find the same coating of fat from the birthday cake. I had wolfed down a healthy serving to assist with my mission and then secretly downed the dregs of a few champagne glasses. No one noticed when I slipped away to the host's office. The door wasn't even locked. The floor creaked under my feet. There were a lot of shelves. I looked around, holding my breath. The chair had been pushed back from the desk as if the man sitting there had just stood up. He had left a crystal ashtray seething with seed shells, next to which stood an empty wineglass. I knew the director was wrapped up in the party, which I could hear through the floor, but it still felt as if he was just away getting something to refill his glass. After hearing the floorboard creak from downstairs, he would remember that he'd meant to go back up, realize that something was wrong, and rush into the room. But no one came. No one surprised me as I found the briefcase full of documents next to the desk.

When the coast seemed clear, I slipped into the washroom with a stack of papers under my dress and shoved my finger down my throat. The buttercream came out through my nose. The mother of the birthday girl heard my retching and ran in search of my father.

I don't remember what business the stock list was for. Maybe I never even looked that closely at the papers. The Donetsk toy factory? Or was it metal pipes? Oil refining machinery? Metal cutting, space, or weapons manufacturing? Mining equipment? Or had Dad dreamed of being master of a coke plant? What was so important to my father that he took such a risk?

I never told my mother what I had done. Not Daria either. Snizhne was more than a mere blemish on my résumé. My involvement in the theft of the stock certificate list was also complicated by how eager I was to tell you about . . . everything.

When Daria appeared at the agency, I felt as if fate had given me another chance to lift her and her family out of the mire they had sunk into after Maxim Sokolov's death. And that wasn't all. I could do better. I could make Daria's future brilliant. We just had to scrub Snizhne from our mouths, from our minds, and from our memories, erasing it from our map of Ukraine. At that point, my intentions were sincere.

Daria was never supposed to know what kind of people she was giving her children to.

IV

Her Father's Daughter

HELSINKI

2016

My mother took my son's urn to Ukraine on the day I expected to be contacted either by the police or my supervisor. Yet I still did my job as if it were any other Wednesday, moving from one address to the next. I'd stolen the money for Mom's plane ticket the previous morning from a pensioner who kept cash at home. I was sure that if she noticed the theft, she would blame her foreign cleaning lady. However, resigning would make me look even guiltier, so I had to continue carrying my buckets from one apartment to the next, wringing out rags and organizing children's toys, even though the cozy clutter reminded me of things I didn't want to remember. I wondered why I didn't feel relieved. Mom would be saved from finding my body, and she wouldn't become an eyewitness who needed to be eliminated. She and Olezhko were safe. That was what I'd wanted, and I had succeeded. So why did I feel so empty?

At the final address of the evening, weariness overcame me, and I took a carton of Finnish kefir from the refrigerator. The company seemed to be marketing it as a new health food product. The sample representatives at the supermarket had tried to offer me some, too, claiming it came from America. As I listened to the sales pitch, I felt old, wondering whether enough time had passed for a new generation who would believe such garbage. The product demonstrator was young. She couldn't know that kefir had been one of the few products you didn't have to line up for in the Soviet Union. But of course Valio was right: I wouldn't have marketed it in the West as an old Soviet classic either.

I poured myself a glass. It tasted like past summers and the okroshka the old lady next door used to make, which I would never eat again. If I was forced to leave Helsinki, I would probably never return to this seaside city. Everything felt so final, my last glass of kefir and my last swing of a mop. It was the end of an era.

Leaving my cleaning for a moment, I went into the woman's office. No one was home, so I sat down at her desk and imagined that it was mine. I'd done that before, setting my hand on the desktop, inspecting the electrical outlets cleanly mounted in it and dreaming about checking my calendar and setting appointments. I heard a knock at the door and saw my secretary bringing refreshments. Aleksey would carry my bag to the car, and my phone and computer would give alerts for new messages. As the workday approached its close, I would spray perfume on the pulsating insides of my wrists and begin to look forward to dining with you.

I'd been sitting at that same desk when I realized that my life in Helsinki wouldn't have made raising Oleh any less complicated, even though I'd thought so during my escape. I couldn't have told Oleh about the past in the same carefree way as the woman who lived in this home, reminiscing about my son's late grandfather, who had been found in a mine without a head, or about how I had ended up in Helsinki. And what would I have told him about you? How would I have explained that he wouldn't be able to meet his father? Would I have claimed that you died on a worksite in Mykolaiv when some cables failed? Here, accidents are just accidents and poppies are just flowers in a flower bed.

The apartment, all decorated in white, had an echo as pure as a well-tuned instrument. I imagined the dog park family's home being the same, the family portraits arranged in a row so openly that their secrets couldn't be any more serious than a little moonshine cooking during Prohibition or the odd love child born to a maidservant chased into a grove of trees on a Midsummer's Eve. If I'd been born here, my son would be sitting at his desk, his eyes glued to his schoolbooks, and nothing would ever happen in my life that would drive me to a foreign country to mop floors. No one would send my ex-lover to end me.

When my mom called after work, I had to answer. I'd begged her to take the urn away before I changed my mind, and now she wanted to hear my voice as evidence that I was alive and hadn't jumped off a roof.

"I just wanted to tell you we got here," Mom said, and the watchful tone in her voice penetrated my ear like an otoscope. I knew she would evaluate each of my words and study each change in emphasis in the hope that they would reveal what was going on in my head. I couldn't let her that far in. I needed to fill my words with light and spring, to sound the same way I'd sounded long ago when faced with new challenges.

But I don't remember how I felt then.

"Olenka, are you home?"

"Not yet. Soon, though."

I was lying and didn't even sound convincing to myself. After work, I'd headed out walking aimlessly so I could avoid the echoing silence of my apartment. Or Olezhko's crying. What if I heard it again? But the urn was gone, so that couldn't happen. Right?

"I left some borscht in the fridge. Warm it up."

"Thanks. I thought I'd watch a movie later."

Our conversation began to flow, and I was proud of the evening plans I invented, which made my life sound remotely normal. My mother seemed to be walking outside. Of all the Mays in the world, the most beautiful was in Ukraine. Olezhko would have time to experience it. My son would see it because he was no longer here.

"Where is Oleh?" I asked.

The question slipped off my tongue by accident and made my mother sigh. Focusing my gaze on the gate in front of me, I scanned the entire building floor by floor. No bundles of wires. No air conditioner cubes protruding from the outside walls. No bars in the windows of the lower floors, none on the balconies. My son could have become a decent person here.

"The urn is in the bedroom," she replied.

"You haven't contacted the priest yet, have you?"

"Of course not. We won't hold the funeral until you come."

"Where will he be . . ."

I didn't want to say the word.

"We can think about that later. Your father's grave is in Donetsk. We can get there if we want to . . ."

Your cemetery wasn't any better an option. It wasn't the right place for Olezhko. Instinctively I shoved my hand into my pocket to feel my Good Things List. All I found was a cigarette I had wrapped earlier, which I lit and then focused on the cable that crossed the street with a lamp hanging from it and a crow perched on top.

"It wasn't your fault," my mother said. "You know that, don't you?"

"I should have gone to the doctor in time."

"Your life was very difficult then."

"I still should have."

"Stop blaming yourself."

I waited for her to say that six years was long enough to mourn, but she stopped talking, and her silence made it seem as if she was mollified. Perhaps I'd succeeded in fooling her. Maybe she was thinking about how I'd used a hair rat that morning. I'd done it just for her, to convince her that I was doing better than I had for a long time. Women who were planning to take their own lives did not invest in their appearance. I'd even put on some of my old perfume and replaced my backpack with a shoulder bag. From behind, my hairdo was the same as the woman from the dog park's, with the difference that I had more root showing.

Or maybe I'd been thinking less of my mother and more of your watchful gaze, how it would examine me the same way Daria had done, evaluating the state of my decline.

"Boris could have taken Oleh fishing," I said and immediately regretted it. My words made it sound like I imagined Olezhko was still alive. As if I didn't understand what had happened, and I was slipping back into the state that had forced my mother to come here in the first place several years ago. In the background I heard a child scream.

"Do you have guests?"

"Your cousin's children are visiting from London."

"You didn't tell me. They're just visiting?"

"They're very interested in all the military vehicles," she said, avoiding my question. I knew my cousin worked long hours in England, and I wouldn't be surprised if she wanted her little ones to move in permanently with my aunt. My cousin never should have had children. I froze in shock. I didn't think that way. Mom was quiet, waiting for what I would say, and I guessed she was testing my state of mind again. She hadn't mentioned the kids, because she'd thought that I wouldn't want to hear about anything like that, and she was right. If everything had gone differently, I would have been watching my son play with his little cousins. Or would I? I'd heard there was a camp for Donbas war refugees in Zaporizhia. I wasn't sure I would have been able to resist the career opportunities presented by the war. Would I have left my children with my mother, like my cousin? I could have hung around the camps with the international charities and canvased the sugar-cube containers to evaluate the girls who lived in them. Rents had risen. There wouldn't be enough work for everyone. More than a million people had been forced to leave their homes. I would do the math. I would offer work. I would get rich. I would save people.

"Shouldn't the kids be asleep already?"

"They're too wound up. I just told them that if they don't settle down, they'll have to stay home tomorrow. Boris promised to take them to see the checkpoints on the bridges in the morning. The older boy already wants to be a freedom fighter."

"Oleh would have seen guns for the first time in Ukraine," I said, struggling to find the right tense to use.

"The checkpoints are a small concession. Otherwise we're trying to limit the TV and news."

"Does it help?"

"What do you think? Apparently yesterday they invented their very own 'Putin is a dickhead' song and chanted it all day."

We laughed together. I was pleased with my burst of giggling. My mother swallowed it and continued chatting more casually, telling me about the *vatnik* Putin supporter joke she had just heard from my aunt. I realized she wanted to hear me laugh. The more talkative she became, the more difficult it was for me to follow her speech. I could picture home vividly. My familiar bus stop loomed in front of me, along with the familiar stores, the familiar convenience store, the familiar rowan trees, the familiar cars in the parking lot. I glanced at my Helsinki windows as if I could have seen something through them. No one was hanging around in the street or at the gate. The light in the stairwell wasn't broken, and the elevator worked. My mother's murmuring continued in my ear. The door lock opened easily. Inside was quiet. I didn't hear Olezhko crying. I didn't smell you. I made a superficial check of the apartment. Everything seemed as it should be. The water jug sat on the windowsill where my mother had watered the plants as she'd promised before leaving, and next to it stood the aloe grown from the cutting she'd brought, so I would have something for colds. All the junk my mother had hauled here, including the aloe, irritated me, and I hadn't used pieces of it for anything. Mom still trusted it more than what they sold at the local pharmacy. I'd pointed out that medicines in Finland lived up to their promises and were quality-controlled, but Mom had snorted and muttered something about the high prices—her skeptical expression reminded me of how difficult it is to build trust after a betrayal.

After ending the call, I realized that might have been my final conversation with my mother. Things should have turned out differently for her. Now she might not end up a grandmother in her old age like the other women in the village. Whereas when I was pregnant and preparing my escape, I'd considered asking my mother to take the baby. I knew finding work would take time, and the prices in Finland terrified me, not to mention my pursuers. I imagined how life would be better for Olezhko with my mother, how he would see the pelicans on their way to the Danube, how Boris would take him fishing. But I knew those were impossible dreams. Eventually word would fly. People would start to talk about the small child who had appeared in the village out of nowhere, with dark hair just like yours, with your eyes and every other sign of your Buryat blood. You would take him, and he would become his father's son. Olezhko would end up buried in the same cemetery as his uncle and his father's father, probably too young, just like them.

Once, we visited your father's grave on the anniversary of his death. His portrait, captured in granite, was the first picture I'd seen of him. I hadn't guessed that an etcher's handiwork could be so vivid. I half expected your father to step out of the stone and greet us, to ask you whom you'd brought to show off. I may have even blushed as if encountering a love oracle. For a moment I imagined that you'd come to seek your father's blessing on our relationship. After we sat down on the stone, you poured a glass of vodka for him, and I took a healthy swig straight from the bottle. I felt as if he was looking at us, that he saw us, that he was smoking with us, and that the cigarette hanging from his fingers only lacked the smoke.

Your father was dressed in a freshly pressed double-breasted suit, and the background featured a carefully etched Audi logo. In addition to the car, he was surrounded by onion domes, a bridge arching over the Dnieper River, wine bottles, and a table heavily laden with champagne and bowls of fruit. Clusters of grapes trailed onto the tablecloth. The grave was next to the road, part of a row of more imposing stones, and your father looked at us so directly that I had to focus my eyes farther away. A few rows off, immortalized in stone, I saw a portrait of a woman draped in a fur stole. Next to this monument stood a living girl with flowing hair, dressed in a miniskirt and stiletto heels, who clearly resembled the woman. There were a surprising number of young women at the cemetery, or maybe I just felt as if there were. Turning back to you, I began to pull chicken legs out of the bag, along with your dad's favorite, stuffed grape leaves. You poured your father another glass of liquor. I'd seen enough to know what kind of company your father rested in. He was with the group of men my father had been groping his way toward and where he would have ended up if he'd been cleverer. Or luckier.

The graves of all of these notable men were well kept, the chrysanthemums plump and not a plastic flower in sight. Someone cared for them or paid for their care. I thought of the mothers, daughters, wives, sisters, daughters-in-law, and mistresses of all of these men who had died before their time, who came to remember their dead in this city of identical rows of gravestones. I had now joined that sisterhood, even if I didn't understand the taste of the people who had commissioned these portraits. Many of the images were precise down to each muscle and wrinkle, and pictured everything significant to the deceased: Mercedes, heavy glass ashtrays, vodka and champagne bottles, gold chains, chunky wristwatches, Nokia phones on the desk or at their ears. Some of the dearly departed were dressed in stylish suits, some in leather jackets and jeans, and a few in Adidas track outfits. The t-shirts featured Nike logos or phrases such as "Two things every American should know—neither of which are taught at school," next to a gun and a Bible. In the backgrounds were bulbous domes, helmets, and motorcycles. Many of the long-since decomposed men had separate gravestones for their cars, with license plate numbers carefully recorded. The rocks dedicated to these vehicles were small, but their owners' stones seemed to match their heights in life, and that made the pictures even more uncanny.

I lifted a chicken leg toward my mouth and nibbled it, trying to fill the silence. I didn't dare ask anything about your father's fate, let alone who had chosen the picture immortalized on the headstone. I thought you would tell me more when the time was right. Finally, you poured one last round and prepared to continue to the next grave. We weren't here just for your father, which surprised me.

Without asking questions, I followed you, seeing more portraits of women along the way. At one girl decked out in tight hip-hugger jeans, I had to stop, pretending to have dropped something. Her spaghetti-strap top left her navel bare, and from her shoulder hung a handbag with a short strap bedecked with rivets. The death years began to jump out at me. Even though I tried not to look at them, they drew my gaze like a magnet, especially if the deceased was a woman. I had to calculate their ages, every one of them. Behind the slender young girl showing off her waist stood a portrait of an older couple, and I was afraid I might burst into tears.

I remembered the withered flowers I'd forgotten next to your father's grave—I said I was going back to put them in the trash and would get more water and then catch up to you. Really, I wanted to get out on the road, into the sun. Once there, I turned my face to the light, fixed my eyeliner, and tried to forget the old couple's grave behind the girl in the tiny top. I didn't understand what moved me so much about them. The man looked like a member of a Communist Party committee. I could imagine the woman stamping important papers, rushing to meetings in a coat with a Persian collar. Despite the stiffness of their expressions, their heads were tilted toward each other, and something in the figures brought to mind New Year's celebrations and birthday parties with the whole family in attendance. This couple probably always had their pictures taken at those gatherings, and it was that festive mood their offspring wanted to convey by choosing this portrait. The size of the tombstone spoke of wealth and love. Still, now the front row places were for other people.

I found you at a grave where a tomcat in a tight t-shirt stood in front of a Khrushchyovka-style apartment block flexing his biceps. The shirt read "This is my peace sign" with a gun sight underneath. Next to him was another dead girl showing off her figure. Her surname was the same as the boy's.

The same as yours.

"My brother," you said. "And his wife."

I didn't know you had a brother or that he had a wife. We sat on a stone bench. I couldn't touch the food. Other women went to meet their beloveds' families at their homes, while I came to the house of the spirits to eat family dinner.

"Was that photograph your favorite?"

"No, I couldn't find any others," you replied. "Although it is a good depiction of my brother."

I took the glass you offered and drained it. Maybe your sister-in-law's fate had been the same and there hadn't been any other pictures of her. I didn't understand how that was possible. How could death surprise someone so thoroughly when we lived in a country where it was present all the time?

"It was an ambush," you said. "They were on their way to the airport. Everyone in the car was shot."

"Everyone" meant your father, your brother, and his wife. After the ambush, you'd inherited your father's place as Veles's right hand. This was when I realized that the couple's death day was the same as your father's. I had a strangely unreal feeling. The details of the tombstones blurred, and I wanted to think it was because of the booze.

"Did you keep the caskets open at the funeral?" I asked

You poured us two more glasses and one for your brother.

"My cousin died in Afghanistan, and my aunt just got a sealed zinc casket," I hurried to add. "That was hard for her."

"They were shot in the chest."

"All of them?"

Despite what you said, all I saw was three headless corpses, and drink didn't chase the image away. I remembered the nightmare that had woken you once—you hadn't given any explanation for the cold sweat that broke out on your skin.

Maybe it had to do with this.

"You don't seem to like cemeteries."

Both your touch and your words startled me, and I rushed to explain that I wasn't used to visiting graves because my family was scattered all over. My hands clenched the edge of the stone bench. Placing them in my lap, I tried to remember how a relaxed pose looked.

"It was a different time," you said.

I knew those times, and I wasn't sure anything had changed.

"Did you find out who did it?"

"Of course."

"What happened then?"

"We responded in kind. There are no half measures for Veles."

"Aleksey retired from that business," I said.

I'd been thinking about Aleksey a lot, about his family and his wife, a perky Georgian woman whose meals Aleksey was always hurrying home for. Their eldest daughter wanted to study psychology, and in the summers the whole brood was taken for language courses in England under the supervision of their parents. That sort of life was possible. Aleksey was proof of that.

"What about Aleksey?"

"After he retired, he came to work for us. Easy stuff, nine-to-five. The pay is good, enough to support a family and have a little left over. His children and wife are content."

You took me by the hand.

"Let's talk about this later."

As we left the cemetery, you pushed a folder into my lap and asked my opinion about the artist whose work was in it.

"What do you think? Is this the right guy to do the boss's portrait? Veles wants a new painting of himself with the metropolitan bishop, and one of his dog," you said.

I turned the pages of the portfolio. Toward the end I found examples of the artist's way of handling animal themes. You told me about Veles's dog, which wasn't any old mutt but a cross between a husky and a Turkmeni jackal. It was the best bomb- and drug-sniffing dog ever.

I couldn't concentrate. I hummed as I wondered whether your boss had become acquainted with this artist while ordering tombstones for his men, since there were plenty of those examples in the folder. What kind of person engraved clothing-brand logos on gravestones? The sample stone used Angelina Jolie's and Brad Pitt's pictures, and the dates were from the eighteenth century, as if the artist wanted to make his clients forget their approaching deaths. All the pictures had begun to look like copies of one another in my eyes. I realized that if I lost you suddenly, your grave would look exactly like this. I didn't have a picture of you that would say anything I could recognize you by.

You almost never talked about your family, but once Maria Kirillovna whispered in my ear that you still hadn't recovered from the tragedy, and that was why you didn't have a wife and a brood of children. You didn't want any vulnerabilities in your life. I took your boss's wife's words as a message that I shouldn't waste my time imagining the impossible. For a moment, I didn't even want to. Nevertheless, I quickly forgot your brother's wife's face on the tombstone, and soon I didn't think about her at all. Maybe I'd never really been in love before, so I didn't know that it could be so sweet, that it would feel like I would live forever, like my heart was immortal. That was why I was only afraid sometimes, only afraid when I was alone, never when I was with you.

I took out the soup my mother had left in the refrigerator. Before leaving for the airport, she had managed to fill the pantry; there would be syrnyky and pierogi for weeks, far too much for one. On the table I found a note in which she defended her cooking zeal: I would have forgotten to use the quark cheese she had already strained so carefully. Mom always cursed the Finnish version, which was useless without additional preparation, and still produced weak results. The constant griping had irritated me when she was here. As if I was responsible for her impossible kitchen conditions. Despite that, I found that I was already missing her instructions, her complaints that she couldn't increase the fat content of the mess they called quark here, her moaning about Finnish salted butter and the unusable cucumbers. I missed her constant whining, because it was my mother's voice. Home.

I crumpled up the message, at the end of which my mother told me to freeze everything that I hadn't eaten within a couple of days. I didn't know whether I would be alive then. My hunger disappeared. Shoving the soup pot back into the refrigerator, I pulled out my phone. I listened to Daria's message again. She'd tried to call several times, but I hadn't answered. I didn't want to continue the argument I'd walked out on, about our fathers' funerals. I was shocked to realize that had happened only yesterday, Tuesday morning, not a lifetime ago. Daria's voice in my ear was cajoling. She said she wanted to talk about our plans for the next few days and to ask my advice about an important matter. She seemed to have forgotten our squabble, so I didn't bother dwelling on it either, and her conciliatory words reminded me of the Daria I had known. Would she finally explain the reason for her appearance if I went to the park with her tomorrow as she wished?

I tried my jacket pocket. Daria's hotel-room key card was still there. I'd kept it just in case, trusting that Daria would think she'd lost it while she was drunk. If the situation warranted, I could easily surprise her. That would be my last resort. I had to keep the hotel security cameras in mind.

My sniff came unexpectedly. Daria sounded like a friend.

"We have time to talk. The family won't be here for a little while."

Daria didn't look like she used to, but something familiar flickered in her cheeks. I felt a warmth in my breast. Maybe it was the smile, the way she directed it at me like in the good old days and patted the park bench in invitation. I sat down next to her and unzipped my coat. I remembered how our friendship had felt and hoped that Daria remembered, too, even a part of it, even a pinch of it. We could solve all of this together, Daria and I, just like before.

"The Mongol has aged, hasn't he?"

I was wrong. Daria had tricked me. Her conciliatory message had been a ruse, and her smile was an act. The bench wasn't warm, after all. It was cold, with chewing gum stuck to it, trash underneath, and peeling paint. Licking a drop of blood from her cracked lips, Daria leaned in closer, took hold of my scarf, and wrapped it around her wrist before pulling.

"Of course, for a man, age only increases his charisma. Aren't you going to ask me anything about your Mongol?"

Daria had caught me entirely off guard by bringing you up and using the name you'd been known by in your world. I didn't understand what was going on. You and I weren't a part of my conversations with Daria. I'd never talked about you to her, and I wouldn't do so now. I had no intention of revealing my longing to her, even if I was dying for word of you.

"Don't try to tell me you haven't wondered whether he has a new woman, children, or a family," Daria said. "You didn't find any pictures of him on my phone because I'm not interested in him. That doesn't mean he's spent all these years alone, though. Or did you think I wouldn't notice you'd been looking at my photos?"

I did think that, but I didn't say anything, instead pulling myself farther from Daria and putting on my fingerless gloves. The family would be here in a moment, and this painful conversation would end. I wanted to check the time subtly, so I pulled up my sleeve, but my wrist was empty. I remembered slipping the watch into my pocket before meeting Daria. I couldn't handle the smirk that had appeared on her face when she saw the ancient object, which said Сделано в CCCP on the back and needed the wristband replaced. At work it was handy, though. I guessed at how much time had passed. Not much. Daria tugged on my scarf again. Still, I kept quiet, counting the seconds and trying to forget that Daria knew more about you than I did, that Daria had stayed when I left and that she possessed information that was precious to me. The fact that she was able to torture me this way required experience with longing. I still remembered how it had grated on my nerves when women droned on about their men, and that was why I'd let Daria think I didn't have anyone. From the agency's perspective, it was best that our little birds didn't have any beaus hanging on, and Daria had always seemed content with her freedom. Or had she just been trying to please me? Maybe I wasn't the only one who had been bothered by the newlyweds constantly driving around Dnipro. There was no escaping them, and nothing stopped them. Not the revolution, not the swine flu pandemic. They just took their wedding photos on the barricades or put on masks. What if Daria had also hated all that sickly-sweet flirting and posing? As she continued her needling, I began to think I was right.

"Your Mongol has money and power," she said. "Women can't resist a man like that."

Daria lowered her voice and leaned toward me again. Apparently flocks of women eager to comfort you had appeared almost immediately. An unmarried, childless man was a magnet, especially when soon all that would be left of his former lover would be a wet smear on the pavement. Everyone had been sure of it. I had killed your boss's son in cold blood, so what else could have followed?

"There were rumors that you were in love with Viktor. That you couldn't stand that he wouldn't leave his wife. Lada helped spread this theory. Everyone knew how close you and Viktor were. Of course, I told your Mongol the truth."

"The truth?"

"That you had been making eyes at each other."

That there could be gossip like this had never occurred to me. I'd searched for news of Viktor's death after my escape, but the press had kept silent about it for a strangely long time, as if no one could decide what to say or how. To my surprise, eventually they reported the incident as a sudden illness at the family's dacha. The funeral had been stately, and on the next Radonitsa, journalists had followed the grieving widow and the newest Kravets to Viktor's grave. The cemetery was packed as always on that day. It was the same place where your father was laid to rest, and I'd expected to see you on the newscast or in the press photos pouring a glass of vodka for your brother or setting a pack of cigarettes on his tombstone. But I didn't see you. You were somewhere nearby, though, somewhere near the widow, of that I was sure, and I was jealous.

Daria wouldn't let go of my scarf. I had purchased it at Munich Airport years ago, and I knew full well that it didn't go with my work jacket, which Daria couldn't seem to get enough of fingering. With a shake of her head, she passed judgment on my outfit, and then began analyzing the qualities of the various women you'd had. Many had style. Brunettes, redheads, and even one with jet-black hair. No blondes, apparently. No one who resembled me in any way. A slant-eyed girl from Moscow, a Pole with long legs, a couple of Azeris with dark eyebrows, and a stunningly fashionable Armenian. Even that Miss Russia who made the Russians so mad because of her ethnic background, since she was half Tatar.

"I'm not making them up," Daria said. "I saw her with my own eyes. She was phenomenal. I ran into their crowd all the time after the agency moved into the new offices across from the Kravetses' headquarters. Once I heard your Mongol arranging dinner with Miss Russia at Mimino. That must have been his favorite restaurant in Dnipro, yeah?"

Daria gave my hair a suggestive tug and shoved a finger into my stomach as if testing the girth of my waist. Even without Daria's pok-

ing, I realized that the Armani blouse I'd pulled out of my old suitcase was a mistake, even though I'd felt confident in my wardrobe
choice at home. I'd conducted countless successful negotiations and
seen you for the first time at Veles's office in this shirt. I hoped that
something about those moments would carry forward to this day.

"You should have heard the words the Mongol used for you."
Daria laughed. "What else could you expect if the person you were
closest to and cared the most about in all the world betrayed you."

I bit my cigarette's brutally thick filter until I tore it off. Not
even the thin cigarettes my mother had brought from Ukraine had
improved how I looked, and they were already gone. I held the smoke
in my lungs for a long time, feeling the nicotine sting my tongue.
Daria would grow bored soon. The family would come. I only had to
endure for a moment longer. What did I care how many brunettes
you had?

"Your breathing doesn't sound good," Daria said.

"It's pollen time. That's what does it."

"You sound like Ladka when she was taking that medication."

I didn't remember any Ladka. Or was Daria talking about Lada
Kravets? Did she use a nickname even for that woman? Had they
truly become friends during the second process? The side effects of
any drugs Lada Kravets was taking shouldn't have been any of Daria's
business. I swallowed for a moment and shifted my tingling feet.
Daria lowered her voice again, and the confidential tone brought a
bad taste to my mouth as if I had drunk milk left out in the sun.

"Ladka and your Mongol became very close. You could almost
have thought they were lovers. It wasn't like that, though. It was
friendship. True friendship. Without your Mongol, Ladka would have
collapsed after Viktor's death. A young widow and a little boy. Did
you hear that your Mongol became the second child's godfather? Oh,
but where would you have heard?"

"You seem to have a lot of faith in your Ladka's affection," I said.
"How far do you think that will get you if she finds out that you've
been secretly taking pictures of her sons? I saw the pictures. I saw
the pictures of your clients. You realize that one of them has already
called the agency, don't you? You realize that they're looking for you?
One of them must have noticed you."

"What would the agency dare to do?" Daria asked. "Are you completely stupid? Where do you think I got all of my clients' addresses? How do you think I was able to track down my children?"

"They made you a coordinator."

Of course that was what had happened. This realization illuminated my thoughts like a miner's headlamp in the darkness. Her talk of daily lunches near your offices hadn't been made up. Daria knew her old clients' names and addresses because she had gained access to the database, and that was why she had the authority to break the anonymity of every person in it. Including mine.

Daria watched as this idea sank into my consciousness, and it was clearly manna to her soul.

"Anyone could have figured it out. Except you." She laughed. "I have to say I was surprised to find your name among the donors. You always pretended to be so much better than the rest of us. I never would have believed that our children were siblings."

"They're not our children."

"Please. Why do you come to this park, then?"

Daria let go of my scarf, spread her arms along the back of the bench, and turned her face toward the setting sun. She purred.

"What would your precious Ladka say if she heard you calling your clients' children your own? Do you think she still worships you?"

"Who would tell her? You?"

This idea amused Daria. She was right. No one would trust my word. I pulled out my cigarette packet and pushed my worn-out boots under the bench. I'd just bought this pack, because of Daria. Roll-ups would have been one more sign of my poverty. With stiff fingers, I pulled the filter off. I did it automatically despite the trapped-mouse sound coming from my lungs. Might Daria do something to the dog park boy? Would she try to take revenge on me through my child?

"Not even your Mongol would listen to you. Not even if you called him and spilled everything."

"I'm not going to do that."

"Don't lie. Of course you've thought about it. You won't be able to explain your actions away, though, believe me. The stories they tell about you . . ." Daria shook her head. "Ladka wanted to lead the investigations personally. She demanded it. She said that was the only way to overcome the tragedy, and no one dared to defy her, since she was in such a rage. Sometimes I heard what they said about you, about what they would do to you when they caught you. It was clear the end would not be quick. It would have to last. Nail by nail, hair by hair, eye by eye. No clean hole through the forehead."

I checked my pocket for my list of the good things that gave me a reason to preserve the life I had built here. The old lady I'd stolen the money from for my mother's plane ticket hadn't called my manager. I still had work and a roof over my head. I still had the opportunity to watch the dog park boy grow up.

"I got the feeling that the Mongol hates you more than anyone else in the world."

I sucked the cherry of my cigarette toward my fingers, letting it slowly burn my skin as I closed my eyes and thought of Odesa and the plane trees, of their bark shining oily from the rain and your breath on my neck. I thought of the branches that scratched at the window that night and of the shadows of the candles on the walls as I picked flecks of paint from the park bench. It was full of initials carved by lovers over the years, surrounded by weatherproof hearts. Once we had sat on a similar bench, although it was under an enormous oak tree and there were more carvings on its trunk than on the bench, and when we looked up, we saw more. That might be the right place for our son's grave. As the tree had grown, the letters had spread, but they still stood out clearly. You carved the first letters of our names in the base of the trunk and a heart around them. The heart would last, for centuries, like oak trees, and we would buy a house with an oak in the yard. With those words, you made that moment the happiest of my life, even though I knew that lightning could strike that tree at any moment.

You can't have forgotten about that oak tree or Odesa or all the moments we had. And I haven't either.

ODESA
2008

I went to Odesa on my boss's orders. Two coordinators had lost their tempers with an American couple arriving in the city, and my boss didn't trust anyone else but me to handle them. Daria's move to the Silverleaf villa was still in the future, so I couldn't turn down the assignment. It wasn't the best time of year for a visit. The fishing season was over, but Turks were still all over chasing Ukrainian women, and cameras were snapping on the Potemkin Steps regardless of the fog and rain. The weather didn't bother the couple I was hosting. Their plan was to build a large family at a fast pace, and the fee was commensurate.

By evening, I was exhausted. After escorting the Americans to their room, I wanted to be alone and crept toward the kitchen. My boss had come up with the idea of setting up a firm that operated like a romance travel agency: we would escort clients on a tour of the companies working in our industry and then take a cut from whichever of our competitors they settled on. The couple was one of the first customers for this new product, and they were the type of people who acted the same way whether they were buying shoes, cars, or children. They didn't just touch the surrogates, they also went for the nurses, and the only thing missing was that they didn't actually look for a price tag hanging from each woman's skirt. Reassuring all parties and acting as an interpreter had kept me so busy that at dinner I hadn't had time to eat.

Opening the fridge, I took out a plate of sliced salo fatback and went to the table. I didn't take a bottle. The couple might wake up in the night and need me, either to verify some trivial detail or to calm their nerves. I couldn't smell like liquor if they did. We'd renovated one floor of a tsarist-era palace for girls and clients to use, and it was cared for by an energetic housekeeper who had done an admirable job filling the cupboards. As I pushed a can opener into the lid of a tin of caviar, I heard the couple's exclamations of delight. They must have just entered the bathroom with its ancient Grecian decor, rose petals, essential oils, and whirlpool bath. It had been installed in the apartment when it was still being used by bachelor travelers.

I didn't hear the doorbell in the kitchen or the housekeeper going to answer it. I didn't notice you until you were standing on the threshold and wiping the rain from your hair, and in an instant my fatigue was gone. I hadn't prepared for surprise guests. My hands smelled like caviar, and I felt my naked skin, my unshaven legs, the film on my teeth, and how thin my kimono was. Too thin. Droplets of water fell on the oak parquet from your jacket. With greasy fingers, I pulled my belt tighter.

"I didn't mean to startle you."

Just then the lights went out without warning, and I think I squealed. I couldn't see anything, and all I could hear were your words saying that it was just a power outage, and they were delivered in the voice of a man accustomed to unexpected situations, in a calming way like evening tea, and nothing in it allowed for the possibility that it was anything else. But still my heart pounded, and my eyes took a moment to adjust to the darkness, until I gradually made out your silhouette as you opened cupboard doors searching for candles. Taking out a saucer and producing a lighter from your pocket, you said that it must have hit the whole block. I didn't see your face until you brought the plates, which you had melted wax onto and used that to affix the candles in place. I couldn't interpret your expression. The flames made the high walls of the room a church. The weather had silenced the hum of the traffic and now the refrigerator. The branches of a tree split by lightning scraped at the backyard window and made me remember my guests. Hopping up, I held one of the edges of my kimono as if not trusting the belt.

"We have American clients," I said.

You laughed, but I didn't. I remembered how the couple had suspiciously eyed the labyrinth of electrical wires winding around the gate. Every wrinkle of a nose had made me somehow smaller, lowlier, and I didn't understand why the local genome was good enough for them if they despised everything else. They would be talking about the blackout at breakfast.

"I'll go tell the housekeeper to take them candles."

But the capable woman was already on her way to rescue the Americans and waved me away from the corridor. Sitting back down, I curled my toes, which were protruding from the ends of my slippers. I hadn't been for a pedicure in ages. I would have liked to care for our clients, so I could also put on more clothing, or at least brush my teeth. I tried to think of a suitable excuse to get me out of the kitchen. I couldn't think of anything.

"Has something happened?" I managed to ask. "Why are you in Odesa?"

"The boss has a meeting here. We're returning to Dnipro tomorrow."

Behind me I heard clinking. You'd found the bottle of Sarajishvili. I wiped my fingers on the hem of my kimono before I took the glass you offered. Your leisurely manner didn't suggest any emergency. If the Kravets princess had a problem, you would have told me already, and we wouldn't be drinking, let alone snacking on slices of salo. It couldn't be about Snizhne, could it? Had you somehow found out and wanted to see for yourself how the rat would try to wriggle out of the trap? In my mind I recited the Lord's Prayer a few times, hoping not now, not today, not this night. Looking at the salo sweating on the table, I felt sick. The mound of lard that the housekeeper had so skillfully arranged on the plate had begun to collapse.

The draft blew out the candle. You relit it and closed the kitchen door. In the silence, my swallowing was clearly audible. And my breathing. Your breathing. The wind. And rain. The Sarajishvili pouring into two glasses again. The squeaking of the oak parquet. The expression I saw on your face was the oldest in the world. It was the expression with which men have always looked at women.

.　.　.

In the morning, I escorted you out. Traffic signs blown down by the wind lay on the sidewalk, and the trunks of the plane trees still shone from the rain. The electrical lines hanging above the gateway had turned into wreaths bedecked with raindrop pearls, and the mat of autumn foliage covering the street was so bright that it could have been taken to a circus. The city was as silent as if it existed just for us. I went back up and out onto the balcony to watch you, not knowing it would become a habit. Whenever you left me, I would have to stop to watch your receding back, because it could always be the last time I would see you.

I'd imagined I would be able to escape Lada Kravets and her world by ushering the process to its desired conclusion. The new mother would keep to the nursery, and I would only ever run into her at Kravets Foundation functions, and gradually I could also distance myself from the responsibilities that came along with them. But after Odesa, I realized that would never work if I wanted to keep you.

You were part of the family, and through you, the world they represented became my world with all its by-products, the greatest of which was a constant, gnawing worry. If I didn't hear from you for a day, I began to think something had happened. If you forgot to call despite your promises, I remembered how Daria's mother had beaten her son who had forgotten to tell her about working a double shift in the mine. I thought about your girlfriends, your wives, your mother, and your lovers, and my own mother, the sound of her slippers pacing in a circle at night. I wondered how any of them slept and how they didn't all become alcoholics. I started to suspect that I was an exception. That there was something wrong with me that would prevent me from being a soldier's wife like Maria Kirillovna, who had been married to Veles for decades. They were still alive. Not everyone became a young widow, or a widow at all. Maybe it would be possible for me, too. I didn't hope for anything more than that, because a star had fallen from the sky into my heart just when I least expected it.

DNIPROPETROVSK
2009

After Daria's egg retrieval went off perfectly, I set out to Lada Kravets's dacha to give a report on the situation. Fifteen eggs had been collected. I expected most of the mature cells to fertilize normally, but we wouldn't know for a few days whether we could celebrate the success of this milestone in the project. You looked tired, too, when you met me on the porch, even though the hand that you placed on my waist was steady, and the nip at my lip familiar.

"Where's the girl?" you asked.

"I left her to rest at the villa."

"It was a good idea to plan that trip to Nice. Will she be able to travel?"

"Yes. Daria is fine."

I checked the time on my phone. In five hours, Daria would be on her way to France with her mother. I'd pitched the trip to her as a well-deserved vacation. This precaution was clearly necessary. You rubbed your forehead as if it ached.

"Is the situation here that bad?"

"It's tolerable."

I pressed my fingers to the sullen groove at the side of your nose and whispered that soon this would all be over, that I could handle everything, that I was good at this. Somehow, I felt as if you needed reassurance, too. I hadn't seen Lada Kravets for a while and didn't know what to expect. I took a few deep, slow breaths, and you followed suit as I held your arm all the way to the library door. I'll never forget the sight we encountered there. Despite the freezing weather lurking outside, the room was full of whirring fans, and every horizontal surface and shelf was full of half-empty water glasses, I even spotted ice cubes that had slipped from tongs and now lay melting here and there on the floor. Lada Kravets had opened the top buttons of her shirt and rolled her sleeves all the way up, and dark bows of dried blood were visible under her fingernails. Her neck and arms looked mangled.

"Don't tell the doctor anything about this," she whispered after seeing us. "It's so itchy. Water from the monastery is the only thing that helps."

Lada Kravets shoved a sloshing glass into my hand. She wasn't the only one of my clients who had rashes or weak nerves. However, she was the first one whom a doctor had declared healthy because he didn't dare mention either condition. I considered it wisest not to interfere either, and I didn't dare think what would happen if none of the eggs transferred from the tissue culture fluid to the petri dishes successfully fertilized.

On the coffee table was a stack of magazines, which I noticed you glancing at. Our eyes met, and you picked up the topmost example, a horoscope magazine, and browsed it for a moment until you gave me a surreptitious nod. I breathed a sigh of relief, but at the same time I was irritated. The stars were favorable for Lada Kravets this month, but how did you put up with it all? I was there only for the first time, and yet I was already imagining uncomfortable situations Lada Kravets might end up in. I amused myself with the thought of what would happen if she got an old-fashioned rural doctor for her birth who would throw cold water on her or hit her. Visions of such a situation helped me tolerate the humiliation. Hand on your heart, didn't you ever feel like screaming that enough was enough?

"Last time only one prime-quality embryo transferred. The others were too weak."

Lada Kravets pulled her blouse away from her skin as if the dampness of the fabric was too much for her. Apparently once a doctor had told her that weaker embryos should be transferred directly and stronger ones should be frozen.

"Maybe we should do something different now," she said. "Let's

just use the strong ones. The strong always survive. There's no reason to hold them back."

As Lada Kravets recalled her failed embryo transfers, the fingers
picking at her shirt began to move violently like the needle of a sew-
ing machine. Forming words became difficult for her, and she had
to chew them thoroughly before being able to spit them out. She'd
blamed herself for the previous failure, until the security cameras
revealed that the problem had been the bad life the donor was leading. She should have been monitored more closely during the process. I looked at Lada's hand. I could easily imagine her attacking
anyone who caused her disappointment on this topic.

"This time nothing like that will happen. We've been keeping an
eye on the donor twenty-four hours a day."

"Are you sure?" she demanded.

"Roman can give you the details."

At which you began to review once more the steps that had been
taken, as Lada Kravets asked clarifying questions. I responded to
those that were in my area of responsibility. I heard my voice, its doc-
umentary conviction, though we didn't know yet how the embryos
would do, how well the fresh transfer would go, or whether the damn
bitch would even get pregnant or just have another series of miscar-
riages. And if Lada Kravets succeeded in giving birth to a living child,
would the couple want siblings for the little thing? Then I would be
standing in this same room again explaining these same things. And
what if Lada beat another donor? Or what if she was left childless but
our relationship continued, and you and I wanted a baby? Would the
prima donna be able to cope with the belly of someone else in her
inner circle swelling when hers wasn't? Would our future be eter-
nally dependent on Kravets whims?

The floor under me had turned to quicksand, and my eyes
blurred as I found myself wondering whether the crystal chandelier
in this room had ever collapsed. It had to be heavy enough that if it
fell, it could kill.

Excusing myself, I left to look for the bathroom. After removing my tight boots, I lay down on the marble floor in the pool area,
pressing my forehead against it as if it were the glass protecting an
icon and took slow, deep breaths. After I got home, I would have
to accelerate my plans for Daria. I hadn't been reading the fashion

magazines lately, and I hadn't been thinking about Daria's modeling portfolio, let alone presenting my intentions to her. Any thought of the photographers I knew had felt somehow exasperating and making contact too laborious. In my free time, I preferred to focus on us and to try to forget everything else. But Lada Kravets tantrumming in the library was a good reminder of why I needed to get my act together. Our relationship was new enough that I couldn't count on your help if the Kravetses were disappointed again. I would have to secure my future elsewhere, and for that I needed Daria.

She still had a couple of years left. After that, she would be too old for modeling.

In my bag, I found an old barberry candy, which covered the taste of bile in my mouth as I pulled my boots back onto my feet. I was ready to continue. This time we wouldn't use Viktor's worthless sperm. This time nothing would go wrong.

As I returned to the library, I stopped for a moment to listen to the chirping coming from the birdcages. I imagined that exotic avians were part of the elite lifestyle, and for Lada Kravets maybe they were a substitute for children. The parrot was eating a peanut. Cracking the hard outer shell with its beak, it deftly removed the brown seed coat, which floated in a spiral to the bottom of the cage.

Later I learned that President Yanukovych had also filled his dacha with birds. He was afraid of gas. The twittering would stop if the ventilation system was sabotaged. The president was so afraid of poisoning that he only ate meat from his own animals, only drank milk from the cows in his own barn. He had an entire zoo on his property.

When the revolution rolled through the gates of his palace a couple of years later, I thought about how pointless all of the precautions had been. Birds could sound the alarm about foreign substances in the air produced by a complex air filtration system, but they couldn't predict the people's rage, even though the signs had been palpable in the atmosphere for a very long time.

I didn't want Maria Kirillovna as a friend. However, I soon found myself in that position thanks to the excellent progress of her daughter-in-law's pregnancy. Keeping my distance was difficult, because I had to answer your boss's wife's phone calls, and I had to attend any event she invited me to, no matter how trivial. Usually there were other women present, and I could get by with talking about my work and the foundation, until once in the dacha's spa I was faced with only the lady herself and the mute Thai women who were doing our treatments.

"There are two new cosmetologists here," Maria Kirillovna said as she led me into the room where our chairs awaited. "These girls are miracle workers."

I'd told you about Maria Kirillovna's familiarity, and you hadn't thought it was anything alarming. If the pregnancy went well and the baby was healthy, I would be like a daughter to her. However, I had no illusions. Had I been called here for this one-on-one meeting because something had happened? Had Maria Kirillovna heard something concerning? My hands stung as if I'd fallen into a dog rose bush.

"My husband's good friend owns this dacha. Aluminum is his business, and politics, but I'm sure that doesn't interest you."

"Too complicated, at least for me."

Maria Kirillovna checked the skin of her cheeks in the mirror, and I looked at the blood draining from my fingertips. Shoving my hands in my pockets, I secretly curled my fingers. Maria Kirillovna turned toward me.

"What do you think about the air-conditioning system in this house?" The change of subject took me off guard. I didn't understand what she was getting at.

"The air is in a class of its own, don't you think?" she added.

"Absolutely. I spent the morning in Kyiv on business, and I couldn't see the horizon from the top floor of the hotel, the smog was so thick."

"You must be feeling better now." She laughed. "I'll tell you at once when I get the contact information for the HVAC company. I promise to get you a good discount."

I glanced at Maria Kirillovna. What was this about? Or was she confusing me with one of your previous lovers? I didn't have a house. She must have known that.

"Don't forget to buy a backup generator. It's always good to have one."

One of the cosmetologists came to the door to see if we were ready, and Maria Kirillovna raised a hand to indicate that we would be another moment. I couldn't imagine any explanation for this line of conversation other than that she'd given advice to the previous woman who had warmed your bed and was just continuing in a similar vein out of habit. Maybe you had been planning a log home with my predecessor, with plans all drawn up and everything arranged with a prestigious foreign builder, as Maria Kirillovna was encouraging me to do now and reminding me that it was always best to hire foreign builders because then the price and other details remained where they should be, in secret. Maria Kirillovna didn't trust nondisclosure agreements signed by local businesses. They were only paper.

"Are you all right?" she asked. "Are you having cold feet? Don't you love him?"

In distress, I began inspecting the stack of fashion magazines on the table. The pages seemed to stick together, and my hands were flushed. I glowed as if I had a sunburn, and as I felt the way she was looking at me, I realized that she hadn't made a mistake.

"I don't think I understand what we're talking about."

"About your future home."

I didn't know what to say. I hadn't prepared for this. I hadn't talked with your boss's wife about my private affairs, and now she was quizzing me about us—about you and me—and the home we would share, even though we hadn't even discussed that ourselves. Did that mean that you were sharing such personal dreams with her? Was this a test I needed to pass before this woman would decide whether to allow me into the family? I couldn't guess what our relationship looked like to them. Maybe I was just a random companion, or maybe I was something more. But a house?

"Yes, you love him," Maria Kirillovna said. "That's good. I've never seen Roman so happy."

With this, she sat down in the chair and motioned for the girls lurking on the threshold to come begin their work. Fumbling, I followed her example, breathing through my mouth and hoping that they would soon put something on my face to soothe the sunstroke feeling, something that would calm the heat better than smetana.

"You have to let me help with the wedding arrangements. Romka is like a son to us."

Swinging my arm, I accidentally hit the worker, who squeaked and ducked.

I apologized profusely, but the girl didn't understand a word.

"I didn't just ruin a secret, did I?"

Maria Kirillovna chuckled and climbed down from her chair. Her fragrant hand touched the fingers I had raised to my face, as gently as a blue fox.

"Don't tell him I revealed his secret, my dear. I thought Romka had already proposed."

Maria Kirillovna's torrent of words continued, and I couldn't tell her to be quiet, not about interior decorating or about the New Year's Eve Ball in Vienna. This year she had missed the season for all intents and purposes, because Lada hadn't dared to travel, and Maria Kirillovna had preferred to support her daughter-in-law. Next time we would travel to Vienna together, and I could have her seamstress make me a dress. Or maybe she was just trying to fill the uncomfortable silence that otherwise would have fallen over the room, because her mention of marriage had struck me dumb. In an instant, all of my old plans had become irrelevant, because nothing was more important to me than what we had. I didn't want to go back to Paris anymore. Settling my accounts with the people who had fired me felt pointless. I didn't want to see them. Why would I if I had something else available?

However, I made one mistake: I lost interest in Daria, who became just another girl among many, and I let one of my colleagues handle her next donations. Around Lada Kravets's due date, I sent Daria and her mother to Spain and then notified them of the healthy baby's birth, but I celebrated the glad tidings with you and the Kravetses. Daria was no longer my gateway to a bright future. My gateway was you.

A VILLAGE,
MYKOLAIV OBLAST
2009

Only Boris came to meet me in the yard, and for a moment I wondered where the others were. However, I assumed that dinner preparations were keeping my mother busy, and I didn't give the matter any more thought, because Boris couldn't hide his curiosity about the gifts I'd brought. I gave him a new winter coat straight from the trunk of the car, and after he ran inside to show off his present, I stayed to pet the dog and smoke a cigarette. I was already starting to regret that I hadn't gone with you to Vienna, since the agency had been forced to shut down because of the swine flu pandemic. The countryside was depressing at this time of year, the trees bony without their leaves, and the stork nest looked like a black hole in the darkening sky.

When I stepped onto the porch, I realized that something was wrong. No one greeted me, and the quick nods were like pecks. My aunt's and mother's gazes swept past me coldly like alcohol evaporating from my skin, and the house didn't smell like fresh rolls, it smelled of valerian root. Setting my bag on the floor, I glanced at the cold stove. I tried to ask how they were, but no one replied, and I left the rest of my gifts packed. The atmosphere was dismal, as if there were a dead body in the house. Boris perched at the table in his new coat, inspecting the hand-painted flowers on the side of a drinking glass. Not even he looked at me, instead just gazing at each brushstroke in turn, and then moved on to a teacup and its flowers, its gilded patterns, the brushstrokes, following it with his fingers, until he slipped out after my aunt as she went to feed the chickens, the porcelain cup still firmly gripped in his hand while the other clutched his coat as if someone had threatened to take it from him.

The mood was tense when my mother and I were left alone, and I expected I would now receive an explanation for her behavior. It had to be something serious. One of them must have a fatal disease. Or someone we knew had died suddenly. I couldn't imagine that it had something to do with the newspaper protruding from her pocket, which she now spread out on the table, still without a word. I recognized the picture printed on the page from an orphanage opening. I remembered the event well—the ceremonial cutting of the ribbon had fallen to Viktor. And there I stood smiling next to the Kravetses, the picture framed by girls with hair ribbons tied in bows. The caption listed all of our names. Veles had come to lend his support to his son, who was taking his first steps into politics, which was why he had agreed to the rare father-son photo op.

"Do you know who that man is?"

My mother pointed at Veles. Turning my head toward the window, I picked the matches up off the table. My mother sounded strange, as if speaking was difficult because she was chewing on barley grits. Then I dropped the matchbox. I had been shaking it, unconsciously. My mother's finger was still pointing at Veles, and it was the finger of a prophet standing in judgment, calling down destruction.

"How can you work for the Man from Donetsk?"

I didn't understand what she was talking about. I knew the Man from Donetsk, but only from old rumors. He had been my father and Maxim Sokolov's business partner before things went bad. Someone had been feeding my mother some very strange nonsense.

"Are you claiming that Vitali Kravets is the Man from Donetsk? What kind of joke is this supposed to be?" I asked with perfect self-assurance. "Vitali Kravets is from Dnipro."

I was laughing, but my mother wasn't. Picking up a glass, she poured in some Korvalol and then splashed some water on top. After draining the glass, she crossed her arms, and her dirt-stained fingernails seemed to dig into the fabric of her coatdress as if she had to restrain herself. In my stomach I felt an unpleasant twinge. As if she hadn't made a mistake. As if I had.

"I never saw the Man from Donetsk, not even a glimpse of him. And as far as I know, you didn't meet him either. Or did you?" I asked. I had to make her understand how insane this claim was. "And did Dad talk about him to you? Did he mention his name? Did we have photographs of him? Do you know what he looked like?"

"Valentina Sokolova knew him and recognized him from that picture."

"Daria's mother? Is she who you've been talking to?"

"Valentina could never forget that braggart even if he's traded in his running shoes for hand-stitched Italian leather."

Instinctively I felt for the phone in my pocket. Daria had tried to call me a dozen times, and I had assumed she just wanted medicine for herself or her friends. The flu raging in the country had emptied the pharmacy shelves and all the bins of lemons and garlic in the stores. I hadn't answered. Pointing fingers wasn't enough for my mother anymore. Now she struck the newspaper with her fist. The Man from Donetsk. Vitali Kravets. Veles. Your boss.

"This man learned of your father's and Max's intentions. This man found out who they were trying to cheat. That they were trying to cheat him. That was why your father and Max were killed."

"Wait a minute. When did Dad tell you about his plans? You two barely saw each other during those years. How can you believe everything you're being fed? Is this newspaper supposed to be proof?"

"Valentina knew everything. Max was always running at the mouth. He could never keep a secret, unlike your father," my mother said. "Unlike you."

As I lit a cigarette, I noticed that my hand was shaking. This must be a misunderstanding. It had to be. Valentina Sokolova was lying. I couldn't think of a reason, though. Had someone paid her? Or was age playing tricks on her memory? My father. Daria's father. Your boss. There are no half measures for Veles. That's what you said. My thoughts were still a big tangled dog rose bush, but in the middle of it something loomed that I couldn't quite formulate. Something I had forgotten. Something I should remember. Something that would help me grasp what had happened. I couldn't put my finger on the phrase, though. On your phrase. Instead, I latched onto your voice, which was winding its way somewhere through the thicket of my mind, and I reached toward it until it was as bright as the whistle of a train at night in Dnipro, and the words were clear, and they included the name Donetsk, and they were from a conversation when you were talking about your boss's wedding. Now I remembered everything.

We both had a full day off, and you took me to Bartolomeo, where I'd never been before. The hotel's private beach was wonderful. I hadn't known it was possible to find a Caribbean experience on the shores of the Dnieper, or to get such unbelievably good coffee in the city. If I hadn't seen the high-priced escorts in the club, I'd have thought it was a perfect place for client meetings. You apologized: you would have brought me to Bartolomeo earlier if you'd known its pirate ship milieu would appeal to me so much. So I stopped my gushing. I didn't want to ruin an exceptionally talkative moment for you, and I was thinking the whole time about what Maria Kirillovna had said. Maybe she'd been mistaken. I didn't want to be the woman who spent her days waiting to be proposed to, and yet I found myself doing precisely that. It was embarrassing. You sighed and said that if you were going to arrange a wedding celebration for yourself and your betrothed, you would choose something simpler, and I smiled, because just then you took my hand and kissed it, and because I was interpreting your words through the conversation I'd had with Maria Kirillovna, even though what you were saying was right in line with the purpose of the day: as we were enjoying ourselves, we were also seeing if this place would be suitable for celebrating your boss and Maria Kirillovna's wedding anniversary. After we ordered our food, you told me more specifically about your assignment. Your father had served as the master of ceremonies when Veles married Maria Kirillovna, a member of the Dnipro elite, and you were to continue the tradition by organizing this party, the details of which you wanted my opinion on. Maria Kirillovna would want nothing less than a confetti drop, the fireworks of the century, and acrobat girls walking on wooden stilts. When I began asking follow-up questions, I referred to the party as a silver wedding anniversary, and you corrected me. This would be their steel anniversary—the eleventh. Maria Kirillovna wouldn't be happy about my mistake and could take it as an insult to her age, so I had best remember it correctly. I muttered something vague, asking whether celebrating steel anniversaries on this scale was some new fad. It wasn't. Maria Kirillovna had read a list of different anniversaries and got excited. She thought it was best to celebrate when you still had the energy, and a steel wedding anniversary party sounded good to her. It was just like them. I'd imagined they had been married for decades, and I held up Maria Kirillovna as an example of a woman who would never become a widow. Only eleven years together shook my faith in that. The revelation confused me, but I didn't have a chance to wonder about Viktor's birth year before you clarified that Viktor was from Veles's first marriage, which had ended so badly that the woman's name had become taboo. Not even Viktor had any contact with his biological mother anymore. The divorce was likely the result of an indiscretion with one of Veles's old friends, though that was only your own interpretation. Once, a childhood acquaintance of Veles had run into you while drunk, and he'd referred to this woman in vulgar terms: the bitch should have picked someone else to screw. I wasn't paying any attention to the details of the divorce, since I was still perplexed by Maria Kirillovna's steel anniversary party, the guest list for which the Kravetses were currently pondering. Every big shot in Dnipro would be there, you said, and there would likely be a dustup about whether to invite anyone from Donetsk or not. The mention of Donetsk made me perk up and focus on the conversation, and I threw a scarf over my shoulders. I asked what Donetsk had to do with it, and you reminded me that the Donetsk and Dnipro clans were competitors. Veles still had financial interests in his old home region, but otherwise he had shaken the dust of the entire oblast from his feet after marrying one of Dnipro's finest. He had no desire to return to Donetsk even by association, which doubtless also had to do with his ex-wife. The sophisticated Maria Kirillovna had done Veles good, you said. Veles had become as elegant as any businessman in Dnipro, who used cunning more than brute force to advance his business interests. Some had probably hoped that the alliance would improve relations between the Dnipro and Donetsk factions. That hadn't happened, though, and you didn't believe there would ever be perfect agreement about who should be invited. Drawing up a guest list would definitely be much easier for us, you said, and I instantly forgot everything else I had just heard.

. . .

Daria's mother's memory had not failed her. Mine had. Veles had left Donetsk in the late nineties, and Valentina had recognized him. There was sufficient evidence of his identity, and I could no longer believe it was all a coincidence, which sapped my desire to crush my mother's claims. Your boss was the Man from Donetsk with whom our stupid fathers had done their stupid business. The man my father had always gone to and whom our industrious fathers had cheated. The man from under whose nose I'd stolen a stock certificate list, which I gave to my father for a hundred dollars, even though it belonged to the three of them, the three friends, who were friends no longer once my father and Maxim Sokolov decided to take over that ridiculous factory on their own.

I stared at the dry breadcrumbs lying on the wax cloth and then slowly stood and walked out. After gaining the shelter of the apple trees, I shoved my scarf as far down my throat as I could and screamed into it until I nearly fainted, and then, retching, I tugged the fabric out of my mouth. The instant I'd escaped my mother's gaze, my determined hauteur shattered like glass that couldn't stand up to heat. My father had made his choice. He'd chosen business and fraud as his guiding star. Not me. Not my mother. Not us. We were never a priority, so why should I mourn what my heart had chosen? What did it matter that my choice fell on someone who was like a family member to the man who had severed my father's head?

I kicked a rotting apple that lay on the ground and made my decision. I would think about this now. I would think about it for this allotted time, and then I would swat it away like a mosquito and never trouble myself with it again, ever. I would not let my father ruin what we had. I wouldn't agree to that. And I couldn't let my nerve fail if I intended to clear up this mess.

Wiping my nose with a towel drying on the clothesline, I tried to regain my ability to function. I would start by listening to the messages Daria had left on my answering machine. There were dozens of missed calls, and I cursed my indifference to her. As I stared at the phone screen, it began to flash. You were trying to call. My gaze rose to scan the dark, silent garden, where the ringtone was as lurid as the cry of a peacock. For a moment, I imagined I could see you deep in the orchard. It was as if you'd heard what my mother and I had been discussing in the kitchen and were waiting, curious to hear what explanations I thought I could use to get out of this fix. Dropping the phone in my pocket, I crouched next to the dog, which had been watching my strange behavior. Its tail wagged, and it didn't growl. Still, the feeling of being watched remained. It was so bad that I had to circle the garden, each shadow making me sweat and every gooseberry or caramel bush that caught on my clothing making me jump. I was surrounded by thorns. But there was no one in the garden. Finally, I ran to the gate with the dog following. I had to see the other side of the fence. The road was empty. You didn't know. I had to remember that. You had reviewed Daria's papers, and you'd seen her father's name. If you hadn't recognized it or the man himself from the old pictures included in her donor folder, Veles had buried his past in Donetsk so deeply that you didn't have a clue about the incident, and that gave me hope. Veles hadn't wanted any daylight shone on it, not even for his closest men. If I made sure that the Sokolovs kept their mouths shut, the whole thing would be forgotten again.

In the messages Daria had left on my phone, she was panting and saying something about strangers coming into her home. We had to talk about what the men had said. I could tell from her voice that something was wrong. She didn't accuse me of working for the enemy, she didn't spit sulfurous vituperations at me, and she didn't specify what was going on. All through the night, she'd left messages with the same basic content. In the meantime, I'd been dreaming zephyr-sweet dreams, and after waking up, I'd thought how lovely it would be to have my wedding photos taken in a park full of fall colors with the Potemkin Palace in the background. I was an idiot. My mother would never come to my wedding. The Man from Donetsk would come with his wife. And there would be no marriage if I didn't find a way to keep my house of cards intact. Leaning my back against an apple tree, I looked at the windows with light flooding out of them from inside. No one was calling for me as I might have hoped. Not my mother. Not my aunt. Not even Boris. The only one treating me with sympathy was the dog at my feet, who nuzzled me attentively and licked the scratches on my fingers. Taking a deep breath, I called Daria. She didn't answer. I selected Valentina Sokolova's number. The phone rang and rang. Then I sent Daria a gentle encouragement to contact me as soon as possible and listened to the messages again in case I had overlooked something. I couldn't deduce from them what Daria knew. However, I assumed that the men who had barged into Daria's home were responsible for this whole unraveling. Confused by the news, Daria had wanted an explanation from me. Instead of making up a story about a misunderstanding and silencing her, I had ignored her calls. She'd spoken to her mother, who had confirmed at least the part of the intruders' report about Maxim and my father, as well as the identity of the Man from Donetsk. In shock, Valentina had blabbed everything to my mother as well. Of course, this was all just guesswork. I couldn't know what had really happened in Daria's home, what the visitors had told her or why. I stood up. I had to return to Dnipro as soon as possible. I would find Daria and fix this. But before that, I would have to ask my mother some questions.

Mom was still sitting at the kitchen table staring straight ahead. Her mottled hands rested motionless on that damn newspaper like an old Eternit fiber cement roof, and there was something final about her pose. I couldn't stand to look at her.

"You can't believe all of that based solely on the Sokolovs' rubbish," I said. "Seriously."

"Daria sent her mother evidence from your work."

"Sent? What do you mean 'sent'? Have you seen what she supposedly sent?"

"Don't start with me. Why would the Sokolovs lie about such a thing?"

Our agency's documents revealed to whom Daria gave her child. That was the only record of Viktor's name and the name of his father, who had acted as his donor. I was guessing Daria had received this information from those uninvited guests, who had also probably brought evidence of the business dealings between Maxim, my father, and Veles Kravets, or at least the connection between them. Daria still should have kept quiet, though, because we'd concealed the true nature of her work from her family. No one should know to whom she'd donated eggs. She had made a different choice, though, shamelessly blabbing everything to her mother.

"Didn't I ask you to get Daria work as a model? What happened? What's wrong with you?"

I didn't understand the finality of my mother's words, because instead of going to my car, I went to the bedroom as if I was still staying the night. All of my pictures had disappeared. In their place, rugs had been hung to cover the bareness of the walls. My cousin's framed face stared back at me as if I no longer existed.

DNIPROPETROVSK

2009

I stopped at the front door, which was covered in dark brown faux leather resembling the back of a tufted couch, and collected my courage for a moment before entering Daria's apartment. I hadn't visited since giving her the keys. The familiar scent of lily of the valley clung to the walls of the entryway around the mirror, and on the shelf in front of it was a half bottle of the same perfume. I gazed around. I couldn't say whether Daria had left in a hurry or whether the one-bedroom apartment was in the same condition as usual. I recognized some of the dresses and blouses hanging in the closet, but I didn't remember everything I'd bought for her. I couldn't say what was missing, whether some of the creams she used daily were gone from the dressing table, or whether the perfume she'd left behind indicated how panicked she had been when she packed. I didn't find any signs that could help me interpret Daria's state of mind or guess at her destination or the anticipated duration of her trip. Still, I went through every room hoping I might find some clue. The wall calendar stopped at October's picture of a guelder rose in autumn colors with red berry clusters. The houseplants hadn't been watered in ages, and the jade plant was dying. On the stove was a long-handled Turkish coffeepot that seemed to still be in use, but the espresso machine I'd purchased was gone, perhaps sold. In addition to the half-full jars of jam and pickles in the refrigerator, there were only a couple of quark bars, as if Daria were still a child. On a plate, a half-eaten *chebureki* turnover sat drying out, and music was echoing from the apartment next door, Svetlana Loboda's "Black Angel," which Daria had also listened to. I went back out into the stairwell. Maybe the neighbor had heard something, noticed Daria's departure or the men barging into her apartment. However, I pressed the doorbell in vain. No one on the floor reacted to my knocking or the buzzers. Returning to Daria's living room, I confined Loboda's voice to the kitchen by closing the door and began to study Daria's lecture notes, the bookshelves, the stacks of magazines, the mail, and the postcards affixed to the entryway mirror. Between the pages of a book of poetry by Lesya Ukrainka, I found dried lilies of the valley. I had given the book to Daria, because reading had been listed as one of her hobbies in her folder, and I'd come up with the idea of having her memorize a few poems in case anyone ever asked. Daria had obeyed, and we discovered that she had an untapped talent for recitation. Throwing the book on the table, I sat down on the couch—one I'd chosen for her—to think. The office had arranged the apartment, and I had furnished it. I'd stashed heaters in the closet in case of gas crises and even scheduled a man to change the silver wires in the water purification system before the new occupant arrived. When she saw all of it, Daria had been overjoyed, immediately trying out the bed, which was entirely different from the bunk bed in her dorm room. Thanks to me, she'd said goodbye to washing everything by hand, acquired her own bathroom, and found something other than fried potatoes on her plate every day. I'd given her brother back his health and found him a legal job. It was because of me that the family had a future. But my judgment failed me in the extreme when it came to what degree of gratitude all of that earned.

I went for some fresh air on the balcony, which I had also furnished despite the exposed and rusted reinforcement of the concrete. Daria had moved the chairs inside and made the balcony into a storage area like her neighbors. In the boxes, I found jars of tomatoes and a sack of potatoes wrapped in a blanket. Next to them was a stack of winter tires. She had a car. I hadn't known that. Had she driven to Snizhne or somewhere else? Was she even in the country anymore? It was only now dawning on me that I didn't have a clue what she'd done with her pay or who had her passport. I hadn't inquired after her or talked with her since I'd sent her to Spain while the Kravet- ses were having their baby. I couldn't believe that Daria would disap- pear completely, though: she wanted to graduate. She would have to return to the university to keep her place. That hadn't lost its mean- ing to her, had it?

I realized that I didn't actually know anything about her, even though I had her chromosome map, her health information, and a list of her hobbies that looked nice to clients. She was a complete stranger to me.

SNIZHNE

2009

I hadn't visited Snizhne since my father's death, and I didn't want to drive there now. However, I had to find one of the Sokolovs. None of them had answered my calls. I wasn't surprised—they had to hate me, and wouldn't swallow my claims that I hadn't known who the Man from Donetsk was—so I didn't believe that making contact over the phone would restore our relationship to what it had been. What I was hoping for was to negotiate a sum that would keep their mouths shut and get Daria back to work. I could find the money later. Not for a moment did I doubt that it would work. In this country, it always worked. You just had to know how to negotiate. If Daria wouldn't agree, I would focus on persuading her mother and brothers.

I saw the familiar towers and mountains, then drove around aimlessly for a while, passing my old school, school number one, and turning the air-conditioning on high, as if it could make the feeling of the compass pricks disappear from the tips of my fingers. I had stabbed my fingers with that compass day after day, closing my eyes and imagining that the snow-covered mounds of coal were really mountains somewhere far away and that I was also somewhere else. I sped past overgrown statues, crumbling monuments, and deteriorating silica brick walls until I realized that I was driving along Lenina and Gagarin for perhaps the third or fourth time. I didn't remember the city being this small.

I parked in front of Daria's childhood home. I'd expected to find a
clutch of old women gathered around the front door, whom I could
ask which apartment the Sokolovs lived in. However, the weather
was too cold for sitting outside, and the yard was empty. Circling the
building, I peered up at the windows, but all I could see were sheer
curtains and the toothlike shadows of snake plants and aloe. I had to
struggle to remember. Daria's little brother had gone to the grocery
store for his mother and the other older residents of the building
when the elevator broke down. The fifth floor. That's what it was. On
the wall of the elevator hung an icon of the Holy Mother of God, and
I asked her guidance as I pressed the button. It didn't help, though.
All of the neighbors disregarded my stubborn buzzer ringing. I went
up to the top landing. I could smell cabbage soup, and someone was
listening to the news. I bet that the central radio was still working
here. At my aunt's house, the only memory of that claptrap-spewing
cowbell was the radio jack in the wall. I squeezed the railing. Someone in this rathole had to know something. I knocked on the door of
every apartment in the stairwell, rang every doorbell, and finally, in
frustration over all the wasted work, I climbed onto the roof of the
building to let the wind dry the sweat I had worked up on the stairs.
The stench of cabbage and cooking oil made my stomach snarl. I
hadn't eaten, let alone slept, since yesterday, so I sat down on the
cement surface. Dish antennas dotted the landscape in other places,
too, but here they reminded me of toadstools. This toxic city had
poisoned my life and was continuing to pollute it, and I couldn't do
anything to stop it. But I had no reason to throw myself off the roof.
Making a whole family disappear was expensive. Before long they
would have to come up for air, and I couldn't believe that I wouldn't
be able to find them.

Returning to my car, I turned the radio on to stay awake until I
could get to a gas station for some coffee, but the familiar song that
came on surprised me, since it was so wrong for the moment. As I
tried to change the channel, a passing truck honked. Pulling over to
the side of the road, I checked what condition my eyeliner was in. Not
good. I rested my head on the wheel and let Plach Yeremiyi continue

on the airwaves. After escaping to Paris, I'd shared a bunk bed with a girl from Lviv who listened to the band constantly. I could hear their music at night from her headphones. She was especially fond of a song about white asters and returning to Russified cities after the summer, and I thought to myself, at least I'd gotten away from those places and would never go back. Still, something in the song made me secretly break the girl's tape player and the cassette. She didn't have money for a new one, so that was the end of the aster song.

She never guessed who was to blame for the vandalism. She cried when she saw the magnetic tape glittering in a tangle on the floor, and I felt bad for maybe a second but no more. I comforted her, and somehow we ended up comforting each other. She didn't have a clue what I was capable of. Despite the fact that we slept so close to each other, I was as alien to her as Daria was to me. I'd investigated Daria so thoroughly that I'd thought I knew who she was. But now I couldn't imagine what she might do or where she might go.

Was I any better? If someone had asked me before, what would I be prepared to do to hear more about my father's fate, I would have responded with a laugh: the past was the past. I didn't even visit my father's grave. Still, I'd acted completely differently two weeks earlier when Ivan had suggested a trade for news related to my dad.

That deal had brought the intruders to Daria's home. That deal had driven the Sokolovs underground.

That deal was something you wouldn't be able to forgive.

A VILLAGE,
MYKOLAIV OBLAST
2009

"I hear you have something of value," Ivan said. "Someone is prepared to pay for it."

My neck tensed immediately. I'd come to get him to eat, but Ivan was dawdling, arranging jars and bottles of compote in his trunk as if he was building a pyramid of crystal glasses. The open trunk lid concealed him completely, so I couldn't see his expression. Finally, he straightened up and, putting his thumb, pointer, and middle finger together, made a kissing sound to express what good compote Boris made.

"It's like selling freshly baked sweet rolls. They're already lining up for this around the corner from the detox facility."

Ivan clearly didn't know how to present his case, and that was new. This couldn't be about poppies then. And I didn't have anything of value. Unless he was talking about what I had access to at the agency. Eggs, sperm, embryos, fetuses. Client lists. Our database contained everything about our clients' health, their genes, their preferences, and their donors. Someone would be happy to shell out a pretty penny for that. There were many options: competitors in the same field, someone's jealous lover, our clients' enemies, or why not a state security service?

Ivan slammed the trunk lid shut with a force that made the icon taped to the dashboard fall into the footwell, so he bent into the car to search for it. I waited. Ivan wasn't a man who minced words, and this topic was clearly difficult for him. I decided to misunderstand in order to move the conversation forward.

"I can't give discounts for infertility treatments without getting caught. My boss is a precise woman."

"Don't worry, it isn't about that. And the arrangement doesn't actually require anything of you."

St. Kuksha of Odesa had been found, and Ivan straightened up. The same holy father had adorned the taxi he'd driven when he was selling compote. Those times were in the past now, though, and Ivan wasn't a small dealer. He had moved up, and he wanted to move up more. Ivan kissed St. Kuksha—whom he'd chosen because Kuksha had also suffered imprisonment, in the Ural concentration camps—and returned the icon to its place. Instead of finally getting to the point, he began to dig in the glove compartment until he found a bottle and then went to the trunk for the three-liter pickle jar my aunt had given him. The trunk lid slammed shut again with unnecessary force, and the bottle of holy oil tied to the rearview mirror swung. The vodka bottle opened with a pop. Ivan took a long swig and then offered it to me. I did not refuse.

"The deal concerns your client."

"Which one of them?"

Ivan glanced toward the house as if wanting to make sure that no one would bother us. It was my mother's birthday, and she would soon begin to wonder where we'd gotten to.

"You're supposed to know. A big fish. Ukrainian, not a foreigner."

Viktor. Whom else could this be about? Instinctively I crossed myself. I didn't want to get any more involved in Ivan's hustles than I had to—and not in this one at all. This conversation alone was a betrayal.

"Who sent you?"

"You don't need to know that."

"I can't."

"It's an easy job."

"There's no such thing."

Ivan munched a pickle and then wiped his fingers on his trousers before pulling out a pack of cigarettes and tapping the head of one on the box for so long that I had to interrupt him to ask him to offer me one, too. We smoked in silence for a moment. I realized that I would have to tell Viktor or my boss about this proposal immediately. Or tell you. You would know how best to act, but Ivan would be in trouble, as would I. The fact that Ivan had been sent as the errand boy wasn't an accident, and my friendship with Viktor wasn't a secret. Speeches, opening ceremonies, galas. Viktor had avoided photographers until his father had decided to push him into politics. There were any number of pictures of us together. I knew more about Viktor than anyone, or so I thought, and that made me interesting.

"I don't know if we have any alternative," Ivan said.

"We?"

"No one can ever know I got this information from you."

"Is that the job? You want my client's patient information?"

"All you have to do is copy it all down to the smallest detail. Totally safe and harmless."

"I can't. There's no way."

"Aren't you even interested in what you would get in return?" Ivan asked and then paused. "You would get your father's head."

A second passed before I understood what Ivan had said. When I did, I had to sit down on the ground, where I felt the moisture seeping through my clothing onto my skin. I no longer wondered why Ivan was so uncomfortable. He offered me the bottle again along with the pickles. I only took the liquor. My father's head. I hadn't thought about it in ages. There wasn't anything to think about. I'd always assumed that kind of score settling just happened in those circles. Desecrating an enemy's earthly remains was a powerful warning. I couldn't imagine anyone wanting to store a part of my father's body for this many years or even remembering where it was buried. But what did I know about how these things were handled? Maybe a freezer full of hands, feet, and heads was like a bank where you could make a withdrawal if the victim's family started talking to reporters. Or if you needed a favor. Desperate relatives are always ready to do anything to lay their loved ones to rest, whole and complete. What was important was that for some reason someone had my father's head in their possession, and that was all I needed to know. You didn't fool around with people like this. The offer these men had made to me was a gesture intended to make clear what would happen if I refused. These men wanted to hurt Viktor and his wife. I didn't care about them. I cared about my own head, which I intended to keep on my shoulders.

"Think of your mother and your aunt. And Boris."

Ivan didn't need to say anything more.

DNIPROPETROVSK
2009

Mom called to tell me the news. The militsiya had come looking for her, but because having the authorities show up at the door usually meant trouble or unexpected expenses—usually both—they'd kept the gate locked. When the man returned the next morning, my aunt was so startled that she dropped the water bucket. Persistence like that meant hell to pay. The militsiya wouldn't leave them in peace unless he was able to complete his business, so they thought it best to let the man into the yard. He gave them and the growling dog some time to get used to his presence before explaining the reason for his visit: during the construction of a certain apartment building, a body part had been recovered that most likely belonged to my father. My mother needed to visit the morgue.

I was sitting at my desk and tried to sound amazed as I pressed the tip of my pen into an empty page of my calendar. The office was still closed due to the flu pandemic. No one had noticed when I'd used my boss's username to increase all of the employees' database rights, on our blundering secretary's computer, of course, where I also printed the information. After delivering the Kravets files to Ivan, I made a mental list of everyone I could blame for the leak if necessary. The secretary was at the top of the list. My mother cleared her throat on the other end of the phone.

"I never told you how much that bothered me," she said.

"How do they know whose head it was?"

"Dental records."

"Is it certain that it's Dad?"

"I already said it was."

My mother sounded younger, and her sentences were complete, not trailing off, and she talked about what she intended to do, instead of just asking me about what I was doing or gossiping about other people's business. Tomorrow she would visit the priest about a new funeral service, and she would thank the saints and light candles.

"You should handle everything quietly," I said. I didn't want any extra attention on what had happened, let alone some enterprising investigative journalist showing up.

"Of course. No guests other than us. And there's no need to tell anyone."

I'd been afraid of this call and expected incessant weeping. But Mom's reaction was the complete opposite. She wasn't lost in her memories, she wasn't cursing herself for not opposing Dad's big plans more forcefully or insisting that we leave Snizhne earlier. In fact, she didn't mention my father at all after revealing the news. I listened in disbelief to my mother's vitality. She was even planning a vacation. If I could arrange the visas, she and my aunt would go to London to visit my cousin. I said yes, agreeing to everything. My mother never would have left the house before with only the dog and Boris watching it. I felt as if I was having a conversation with a stranger until I realized that she sounded exactly how she had in Tallinn when she was younger. I thought I'd lost that mother forever. My deal with Ivan had brought her back. After the call ended, I opened the window to smoke a cigarette and thought about whether the change in my mom would be permanent. A familiar old woman was sweeping the street wearing a floral scarf. A new air conditioner had appeared on the outside wall of the building she was passing, making the rest of the similar machines on the wall look just as ready to collapse as some of the balconies. The building was still standing, though, and old enough that its foundation had to be solid. I wasn't as sure whether my precautions were enough to steady the tremors I had caused.

. . .

After the discovery that Veles Kravets was to blame for my father's death, and after Daria's disappearance, I realized I needed something concrete to keep me safe, something that no one could buy away, something that would weigh more than a command from Veles and force you onto my side if I got caught, and my betrayal was found out.

The child wasn't just my life insurance policy. Still, when I was forced to admit that Daria wasn't coming back, I threw away my pills on purpose at the end of the day. I didn't even dare to start my own car after taking one of the girls to the train in the early evening. Trying to calm down, I watched all the other people who climbed behind the wheels of their cars without hesitation and drove away, sliding like silver-bellied fish into their schools. Daria wouldn't know how to install a car bomb, but I wasn't sure about her brothers. I couldn't negotiate with them, because I couldn't contact them. The whole family had disappeared a week ago. If they didn't want money, I didn't know what they wanted. Probably my life.

Standing up, I started walking to the parking lot and lit a cigarette as I tried to think about something else. Students dragged checkered bags from the railway station, presumably full of food sent from home. They staggered under the weight of their burdens, and watching them reminded me that Daria hadn't shown up at the university. Turning away, I realized that I was accidentally smoking a heartache cigarette. This was a nickname we'd invented at the agency. Sobranie Cocktail cigarettes were so beautiful that they even healed wounds of the heart, so women always chose them in moments of despair. I threw the gold-filtered cigarette on the ground and quickly got back in my car. I'd been telling myself that this silly goose would come to her senses if only for the bonus we were supposed to pay her for the Kravets baby being born healthy. I managed to block the money transfer at the last minute. I'd never met anyone who would turn down cash.

I tried to make myself start the engine. I couldn't do it, though, and my eyes drifted to the rear bumpers of the cars in front of me. Each of them was decorated with a sticker indicating that the car had been blessed. My car didn't have one.

Placing my keys in my bag, I headed for the tram stop. I felt as if I was moving in slow motion compared to the surrounding world, and the tram filled before I could reach it. I decided to wait for the next one, and as it stopped, I focused my gaze on the ticket inspector's seat visible through the window, which was indicated by a teddy bear tied to the seatback. That would be my focal point to hold the world in place. I didn't understand how climbing two steps into a perfectly ordinary vehicle had become so difficult. The thought of strangers' bodies against mine felt impossible. Should I call Aleksey for help and lie that my car had broken down? Was the man who had crowded in next to me watching me? I didn't dare take out my phone.

I jumped down onto the tracks and hurried to the Petrovsky statue, where I stopped. I glanced back. The yellow and red sides of the trams crackled in my eyes like a broken television, but the man was gone. I tried to collect my thoughts, to think of what to do and how you did it, how you dared to start your car even though you set bombs in other people's. At least you had. What was that like? To get behind the wheel right after someone else had been blown to pieces? Was it like a high followed by a hangover or like a birth whose pains you soon forgot? Or was it like the adrenaline rush of a fight? Did it bring you joy that you were alive and someone else was not? Did it make you feel second only to God? Could you get hooked on the feeling, like I was addicted to the respect and admiration that followed me in my work as a giver of life?

A couple of men with cleaning tools were bustling around the base of Petrovsky's statue. Someone had spray-painted the monument again, writing "The Butcher" on it in bloodred letters. The Petrovsky statue in Kyiv had been knocked down. Here it still stood. I remembered Babusya Vilina's mother. They said she had eaten her own child's corpse during the Holodomor, which the Butcher had actively promoted. Babusya's mother had gone mad. Her surviving descendants had continued their lives, though. One of her great grandchildren even drove by the Butcher's bronze statue calmly every day but took fright from insignificant setbacks like some crybaby. I turned back to climb onto the next tram. My behavior was stupid. Babusya had survived much worse. She'd seen that spring in the camps meant bodies being exposed by the melting snow. And my grandfather? He had plunged into the depths of the collapsed mine shafts of Donbas to repair the destruction of the war with only an oil lamp and an ax. I was so weak that I couldn't even approach a random tram stop that would be buzzing with people again after a moment's pause. If the Sokolovs wanted to take revenge on me, this would be the ideal place. Daria could get close to me unnoticed. Or her brother. Or her uncle, since she had those, too. I turned my head this way and that to find somewhere else to go. The metro station. I blinked. The crumbling of the Eastern Bloc had slowed the underground construction plans that had been so grandiose in the beginning, and there were only a few stations. That was why hardly anyone used it, and so it felt safe.

On the deserted platform, I would see any signs of danger more easily, and at that moment it felt important to get farther away from the train station, anywhere farther away. I needed protection from the hostile stares of the strangers I faced wherever I turned my gaze.

By the time I reached the metro station, I was trembling so violently that my token fell out of my hand and started rapidly rolling away. Squinting in the dim light, I chased it on the muddy floor until I caught it in front of the booth of the guard who was watching me. I felt the woman's suspicious gaze follow me to the escalator, which was dizzyingly long. Anyone could run past me and shove me headlong. Anyone could push me onto the tracks, even the guard herself. The station platform was like a tomb whose yellow light made my skin appear embalmed. Its marble echoed death, and its emptiness was a threat. I pulled out my phone and decided to call Aleksey for help. My fingers were shaking so badly that I accidentally took a photo. The flash fired. An elderly person nearby began to gripe that pictures weren't allowed here and waved his cane. I stood frozen in place and listened like a child receiving a lecture for a mistake she had committed. The Soviet-era ban on photography of strategic locations was still in force. I could smell his unwashed skin and the stench of onion, cabbage, and dried fish that clung to his clothing. Spit spattered on me from his mouth. I didn't respond to his curses. I didn't leave either, and I didn't even move away. I just stared at the wall across the tracks. There were no advertisements on it, so it reminded me of Moscow, where I had ridden on a subway for the first time. The light and colors were the same, and I could almost hear my father saying to hold on tight to his hand. I'd been afraid of the jostling people and the endless-seeming escalators and their wooden steps. Metal would make sparks, Dad had taught me, so wood was a safer option. This made me more nervous, because then I started thinking of fire, not the walls of the metro station. I couldn't imagine advertisements on them. I hadn't seen anything like that in trams or at stops, not before Paris, so I couldn't understand what an ad covering an entire station network would mean for my face. I'd just jumped for joy when my agent told me the news: I'd been invited to a test shoot for a chestnut puree. It was a big outdoor advertising campaign, and for once I saw the chance for a job that would pay actual money. My agent had seen further, though. She thought I should have refused. But I went anyway, and I was selected.

I never told you the real reason I left modeling. I said I was tired of the superficiality of the industry and longed for home. In actuality, I didn't dare to admit how my career had been tripped up by my own stupidity. I didn't understand the value hierarchies of my new environment. All of the Western girls had known what Chanel was and what Louis Vuitton was, since they had grown up in a world where brand consciousness came in at mothers' milk. I hadn't comprehended what an earth-shattering difference there was between a Dior ad and a chestnut puree company ad, simply waving it off when my agent warned me that gigs like this were best avoided if I wanted to attract the interest of major designers and get ahead in my career. If I became someone's muse, my slightly too short body wouldn't matter. Catwalks were for muses, not catalog girls, let alone chestnut puree mademoiselles. At the beginning of my career, I'd done reasonably well in the Asian market, where now I was already too old and too fat. Unless I changed my trajectory, my final years would be near at hand elsewhere, too.

However, hunger had stopped up my ears. Our compensation came too often in clothes from shoots, and I needed real money. That was what the chestnut puree advertisement was offering. But when the metro platforms were plastered with my face and people began to recognize me on the street, my purse was no fatter than before. Instead, my calendar emptied. I couldn't get any more shoots, not even for catalogs. I scraped along for a while, thinking that everyone would forget the ad. But that didn't happen. I was always just that chestnut girl, which turned me into a worthless investment, so my agent dropped me. A couple of hundred euros was all I received from the job, even though the same brand is still printing my image in the advertising that used up my face and sent me down the road that led to this Dnipro metro platform. I deserved this old man's rebukes, his saliva, and his cane waving. It was perfectly justified.

Eventually I managed to drive my car home to the safety of the parking garage, and as soon as I arrived, I called you. I assumed that something in your voice would betray you if my panic attack, heartbreak cigarettes, and feeling of being watched were signs that my shaky house of cards had collapsed. I didn't know what I would do if you didn't answer other than not get out of the car and not go inside. The phone rang for a long time, and every beep sounded like the bells of doom. Sitting still, I prayed to the Holy Mother of God until you came on the line. I strained my ears, but I couldn't hear anything except affection in your voice, and that gave me the courage to leave the car and walk to the elevators. Under your words I could make out the London traffic and hurried steps, and I drew out the call so I could reach the right floor, search my apartment, including the closets and under the bed, and pour myself fifty grams of cognac. After tossing that back, I was ready to hang up. I didn't dare drink any more for fear of dulling my alertness. For a moment I leaned against my front door. I remembered the time when people started replacing their wooden doors with more secure ones. Nothing in my apartment in this new high-rise needed remodeling. The previous resident had still upgraded the door, though, which was steel, and for a moment I wondered what had happened to that person. Shaking the vague thought from my head, I was pleased that at least one thing was right, if only one, and soon I'd be able to try to gain more security by the oldest method in the world. The decision to throw my pills in the trash was easy. You would have to protect the mother of your child if someone from that disturbed clan wanted to do me in, and I didn't just mean the Kravetses, I also meant Daria's family. I'd kept her disappearance quiet for too long to report it now. I'd also lied at the office in a moment of panic, saying that Daria wanted to focus on her studies for a while, but that explanation wouldn't hold water for long. If Viktor and his wife wanted more children, they wouldn't want any other donor, not after she had turned out to be a true angel for them.

I didn't dare to use my own car, which didn't have bulletproof glass, unlike Aleksey's SUV, so I traveled as much as possible with him, avoiding being out alone. I didn't go into the parking garage at my building anymore, I didn't go shopping, and I didn't visit public places—not cafés, not restaurants, not nightclubs—and I began to long for your return while you were still only on your way to the Dnipro airport. You didn't notice my strange routines, because I thought nothing could happen when I was with you. But you did notice when a motorcycle that passed close to us startled me, and when a car tire burst on the street, and that I pushed my food around on my plate at restaurants like an anorexic who wanted to make it look like she was eating. Your favorite spot on the terrace at Mimino made me break out in a cold sweat, and eating was difficult because the food caught in my throat. I even carried my own water bottles, like Garry Kasparov. I kept an icon Babusya had given me in my purse, and I looked up the symptoms of poisoning online. In the middle of our weekly meeting, I wondered why the KGB had killed Stepan Bandera by shooting him with a cyanide capsule instead of a regular bullet. And why had the reporter Georgiy Gongadze been pumped full of dioxin before he was decapitated? What sense was there in that? And how big a rug did you need to wrap a person in? How many meters of plastic?

I began to avoid standing in front of windows, and I slept behind the couch with my clothes on. If we were in the city at the same time, I came to your place for the night. It was like drinking bootleg liquor every day: at any moment I could lose my sight or my life.

A while later we were in Zaporizhia, and I was going to see a potential girl in the Leninsky neighborhood before the evening's New Year's gala. The Buryat girl was a local, so she was only valuable to us in our search for other Asian-looking donors, which were in short supply in America. They paid well for them there. You offered to give me a ride, and I explained the situation to you on the way.

"Why didn't you tell me earlier?" you asked. "I know a couple of up-and-coming lawyers in Moscow whose job search has been difficult because of the shape of their eyes. They're saving money for surgery."

"Is the situation really that bad?"

"On Victory Day and other national holidays, they stay home, or they get beat up."

"Maybe they should go to America."

I took out a water bottle and washed the tightness out of my throat. I didn't know whether I felt worse for these Buryat girls or myself. Beat up. I couldn't get the words out of my head. When I met with the girl and explained her assignment, those words were throbbing inside of me. When I returned to your car, where you'd been waiting for me, the words still wouldn't leave me alone, instead pounding on the back of my skull like a train running me down.

I'd booked a facial for that evening at a beauty salon, where I'd intended to go on our return trip. The closer we got to the salon, though, the less I wanted to go. Accidents were constantly happening in the saunas in this country, and the prosecutors always called them suicides. I found no comfort in the low probability that Daria could afford to bribe the judiciary, because how did I know what kind of connections her father had?

"I think I'll cancel my appointment. I'd rather be with you," I said and placed my hand on your thigh and tried to smile, all the while thinking about whether the Sokolovs could scrape together twenty thousand euros. Ordering a murder was cheaper than having a baby via a surrogate, and lying in a strange place alone with a mask on my face would make me an easy target. For a slightly higher amount, they could have me shot in front of witnesses in broad daylight with no fear of prison time. A beating wouldn't be enough for the Sokolovs; of that I was sure.

"What's the matter?" you asked and switched off the engine.

We were there. I didn't budge. I couldn't get out of the car. I couldn't walk the few meters to the salon. I couldn't open the door. I pinched myself. I was becoming paranoid. But Daria hadn't returned to the university. She had abandoned her former life.

"I thought you would be relieved. Lada Pavlovna has a healthy child, and everyone is crazy about you," you said.

"I am relieved."

"No, you aren't. You don't sleep, you're skittish, and you change appointments at the last minute. Or is it because of me? Do you have someone—"

"No, never," I said in shock.

"So, what, then?"

"It can take time for tension to wear off. Maybe it's hard for me to believe that everything is finally okay. I might need a vacation."

"A vacation?"

You turned to look at me. The idea brightened me up. Everything might look better if I could get away for a while. I still didn't want to go to the salon, though, so I needed to deflect your attention from my strange behavior.

"Yes, a vacation. And today we could take a tour of Zap."

"Do you really want to go sightseeing, here? Wasn't the tallest Lenin statue in the country enough?"

"I meant places that are important to you."

Your fingers drummed the wheel. You never spoke about your past with much enthusiasm, but there was nothing strange about a woman wanting to know something about her lover's early years. For a moment I was proud of my tactical move.

"All right. Do you see that kiosk?"

Pointing to the small newsstand on the other side of the street, you talked about getting into the first real fight of your life in front of it. In those days there were older boys lurking nearby who would either steal the chewing gum you'd just bought or take littler kids' money. Then came the time when you decided you'd had enough, and after the fight you became the one who took what you wanted from others, not the one who was taken from.

"Is someone stealing from you?" you asked at the end of your story. "Is that why you've been so nervous? Or did you kill someone by accident? One of the girls?"

"No, for God's sake."

My explanations hadn't worked, and now who knew what you were imagining?

"If you did, it isn't a problem, but you have to tell me what's going on. No matter what it is, I'll help."

That would have been the right time to reveal everything. But I chickened out.

"It's nothing like that. Really. A vacation will help. Or maybe I need to find another job, switch industries."

"You have subordinates. Let them handle the dirty work."

A couple of days earlier, my boss had told me about the future of the company. We were set to expand, and I would become responsible for all operations in Ukraine while she spent time in other countries setting up offices to serve local clients. Even though my boss didn't object to my desire to stay in Dnipro for you—I could handle my additional responsibilities from there—I no longer wanted what I'd been aiming for. I didn't want to be the one who does the dirty work or the one who puts it on others.

"Still. Maybe it would be nice to live somewhere else. What do you think? At least for a little while."

"Why not? Although Veles might have other ideas."

If I'd admitted everything then, you might have understood my mistake. Maybe you would have remembered how Veles helped you avenge your family's murder and would have seen the connection between the two situations. You understood payback, and so you could have helped me solve my problem, find Daria, and force her back to work. But I didn't seize the moment, because as a side effect of my actions, I had betrayed you, and by remaining silent, I was following my family's tradition and my mother's lessons.

You met her once. Early in the summer, I'd built up the courage to take you to Mykolaiv to meet my family, without a clue that in the autumn of that same year I would ruin everything by agreeing to Ivan's proposal. During our excursion, everything was still good. Snow blossomed on the acacia, poplar, and snowball trees like a cotton wool dream, and after we arrived, I saw immediately that you would get along with everyone. I'd been worried for nothing. You may remember that at the end of dinner, my aunt turned on the antenna radio, and the news just happened to be doing a story about some people on trial for causing a famine, which prompted you to mention that most of your extended family had been executed after the Buryat revolt and then the rest were shipped off to the camps. Even though those incidents weren't directly related to the Holodomor, hunger had been familiar in all the camps. Mom nodded and said she was born in Irkutsk, where her parents had been deported, her father from Estonia and her mother from Ukraine. There had been a lot of Buryats in Irkutsk. Friendly people, she said. I didn't express my amazement out loud, but I was shocked at her confession. Never before had I witnessed my mother reveal her origins to any stranger. Even when she'd met my father, my mother told him she was from Tallinn—as she'd become accustomed to telling everyone on Babusya Vilina's advice, for good reason.

My family's tradition of embellishing birthplaces began after Stalin's death, when my mother's father was given permission to return from deportation to his birthplace. The reception at home in Estonia was frosty. People looked askance at the young bride he'd brought back from Irkutsk—Vilina—and no one wanted to hold a daughter who had been born in such a place. My grandfather's family saw his Ukrainian wife as nothing more than a Russian-speaking woman who had taken advantage of a poor man to get ahead and gain access to the Estonian smorgasbord. In their minds, Vilina had Russified our family, and that wasn't just about the tin teeth in my grandparents' mouths.

These tensions bothered my grandfather, but he reasoned that it was all because he had been deported, and his relatives feared the label would attach to them. Irkutsk had that kind of effect. However, things eventually became so bitter that my grandfather broke with his Estonian family.

As time passed, my mother came to understand that my father—the man she was going dancing with—didn't covet a career in the Communist Party or want to gain entry to anyplace that required an impeccable background, as she had feared. He was not inspired by the medals her father had earned in the fight against fascism. Even so, she didn't dare reveal where she was born. At first, she decided to wait until he proposed. Then she decided to wait until they had their marriage license and she could go shop at the specialty store only for those who had one. As she looked at herself in the mirror in her white dress, she thought it would be a shame if she couldn't use it. As the wedding day approached, the right moment never came—a restaurant had even been reserved for the reception, as well as a time at the Palace of Happiness to register the union. What if the groom got angry and canceled the wedding? How would she explain that to everyone? The invitations had already been sent.

Ultimately it was the Estonian apple trees that forced my mother to tell her family's story. My dad began to wonder why we never went to help with the harvest in the fall. My mother's paternal relatives—the ones who looked down their noses at my grandparents—lived on a collective farm, but they had a kitchen garden and more, and that fall the harvest was good. My mother always avoided the topic with a new excuse. Finally, Dad lost his temper, and then Mom told him.

He wasn't even angry. He thought Estonian apples were worse than Ukrainian ones anyway.

Mom avoided telling my father about her background for the same reason I didn't tell you about Snizhne. She worried that doing so would label her as a liar in his eyes. If she had deceived him in one thing, why wouldn't she in others? I thought the same way when I met you, and the more time went by, the more difficult it became. So the right moment never came.

When my mother talked about these events with Babusya Vilina, neither of them ever said she should have acted differently. Instead, once I heard my mom say she couldn't be sure my dad wouldn't have left her if she'd revealed the truth before I was born. Trust is so hard to rebuild after a betrayal. That's why I can't think of a single reason you should believe me if I ever have the time to tell you who killed Viktor.

DNIPROPETROVSK
2010

After returning from our London vacation, there was a surprise waiting for me at the office, a package from my mother. I hadn't heard anything from her on New Year's, at Christmas, or at all since our rift, and I assumed the package was a gesture of reconciliation, a belated gift. As I opened it on the kitchen table, I was imagining calling her in a few moments to say thank you, and that made me smile.

The secretary grabbed one of the magazines revealed under the packing paper to read while she drank her coffee. But I swallowed when I saw them.

"Are you planning to remodel or build a house?" she asked. "Any sound of wedding bells yet?"

I muttered something as she continued to gab about her boyfriend, and I found myself swaying like a lonely poplar in the wind. I didn't remember how many building supply brochures and interior design magazines I had taken my mother, but it looked like every one of them was in this stack. From between the magazines fell a card with a bouquet of asters on the front. Inside I had written a date. That was when the men from the construction company that had been recommended to me would come to inspect my aunt's lot, and building would commence on the new house. The pile of magazines and the card with the date had been a birthday present to my mother.

I left the secretary and the magazines in the kitchen and locked myself in my office. I remembered well all the troubles we had encountered when we tried to get gas at my aunt's house. I remembered the head office my mother and I had finally gone to and the map the official had spread out on the big table. I remembered the red lines drawn on it, which encompassed my aunt's house and the whole village. I remembered my mother's expression when she'd realized that the area had been connected to the gas grid ages ago, and the official's voice when he explained that we couldn't pay to have pipe laid that was already there. That was why our petitions had been rejected. Mom didn't have the energy to argue. I'd pointed out that in reality only half of the village had been connected to the network, so the real question was who had stolen the rest of the building materials. Mom shushed me and apologized to the official for the disturbance and my bad manners. We left the office in humiliation, and after I got to Paris, I thought I would be able to send money to solve the problem. That didn't happen, though, and I decided that when I built a new house, not even the stove would run on gas. Over the years, I had kept notes about everything it would have—running water and an indoor shower for starters—and when I presented my plans, my mother and my aunt were tickled pink. They'd begun looking forward to the foundation being laid the same way they used to anticipate an upcoming dance when they were girls. I'd even mentioned it to you, and you'd promised to set the government officials straight if they caused any problems or I received any excessive bribe demands. Fines wouldn't be a problem.

The package from my mother brought me down to earth. The relief from our vacation was gone, even though during that time I'd managed to allay your suspicions; I'd been able to simply avoid thinking about Daria, which had made a difference. On the bolsters of our hotel bed, we'd begun planning my aunt's new house and also begun speaking of things Maria Kirillovna had been giving me advice about. Our own home. Maria Kirillovna had been right. You were thinking about it.

Surely you can't believe I would have risked that to take revenge for an old grudge. I'm not that kind of person. I wanted a home for everyone. More than anything else.

The following week, I received another package from my mother. I immediately took it into my office. I didn't want to know what it contained, and yet I kept alive the hope that I would find a white flag, some hint of my mother's desire for peace. My hope was futile. Under the packing paper, I found my chestnut puree ads, my cleaning product smiles, my playful winks in the latest fall fashions. I remembered how years ago I'd been shocked to see this photo cavalcade on the wall of the bedroom for the first time, and how I'd taken down all the clippings and hidden them in the closet. Then my mother had put them back.

I couldn't understand the severity of my mother's reaction. She knew how business worked in this country. She was growing poppies for junkies and didn't ask how I paid for my apartment, my shoes, or my credit card bill. She'd met you and seen your SUV, the kind people called refrigerators because of their shape and color. She knew what kind of people drove cars like that and had still welcomed you warmly into her home. She knew you worked for a mining business group, and that hadn't evoked anything from her other than contented nods. Or it hadn't until Veles Kravets had turned out to be the Man from Donetsk. That had changed everything, as I was now being constantly reminded. Mom even canceled the drinking water delivery contract I'd arranged for her, which came to light when the company contacted me to offer a cheaper renewal. I'd been paying the bill. Mom preferred to drink the nasty well water instead of accepting my even more tainted water. She preferred to live in my aunt's house, which was built out of coal clinker, free from the heaps at the nearby factories. The building had held up for decades, but I'd imagined giving my mother a brick house. Instead, apparently I'd been offering a shaky foundation for a straw shack.

After our falling-out, I only kept in contact with Mykolaiv through Ivan. From him I heard how my family was doing, and he answered my questions about my mother's state of mind. There was no sign of the forgiveness I was waiting for.

I didn't visit the countryside again a single time before I left Ukraine.

Ivan hugged me awkwardly like the sister he didn't have and remained standing in the entryway. I guessed that the news would be bad. But still I asked how things were going. Ivan shifted his weight from one foot to the other, zipping and unzipping his tracksuit jacket. I turned to the kitchen to conceal my disappointment. I wouldn't be getting a new passport today.

"Champagne, vodka, or cognac?"

"Boba's birch horilka, if you have any."

After collecting what I had in the cupboard, I carried a platter of food into the living room, keeping my bad mood at bay. I found Ivan admiring the sunset from my window. He commented that this had been the tallest building in the country when it was built and started looking for some suitable music on my record shelf.

"We haven't had time to talk about the price," he said.

I nodded. The situation embarrassed Ivan. I could tell from his body language, how he ran his hand along the stubble on his head, fiddled with his zipper, and focused on the records as if the issue of money were secondary. I'd imagined that Ivan would just give me the papers. Because of the transaction he had arranged, I was preparing to leave everything. I poured two glasses of Boris's horilka and hoped that the amount would be reasonable. Ivan raised his glass.

"To new roads and new opportunities?"

"Why not," I said.

I moistened the edge of the glass with my lips and then set it back on the table. I felt like asking what had gone wrong with the passport and how long I would still have to wait. However, I couldn't reveal anything to Ivan that didn't concern him. Maybe I didn't trust that he would help if he knew the seriousness of my situation. I didn't want to force him to weigh what would be most profitable for him and expose him to temptation.

"Have you heard of Tatiana Fedorova? The businesswoman?"

I shook my head. The passport. I wanted the passport. Not to jabber about some superfluous bitch.

"She helps social orphans like Boris and tries to use legal action to remove declarations of incompetence for people who are able to live on their own without a guardian."

Fedorova wasn't superfluous after all. Nervously I stretched the hem of my shirt and looked at Ivan with suspicion. I remembered what you said once. Philanthropy is always a façade. There had to be a reason for Fedorova's activities: expanding a business, networking, or whitewashing her reputation and wealth. But did that matter if she got results? No one was interested in improving the status of wards of the state. If the institutions lost their free labor, who would handle the work they did, and who would pay the wages?

"You don't believe in Fedorova's good deeds," Ivan said. "But maybe someone from her family was institutionalized or maybe she gave up her own child and regretted it later. Is that impossible?"

Ivan poured us two more glasses.

"To Boba," he said.

I raised my glass. I'd emptied the previous one into a flowerpot while Ivan was looking for suitable music. Hady's "Junkies in the Garden" began to play. Ivan had often hummed this song. He did so now, too, and that made me smile. Maybe he wouldn't want anything impossible in exchange for the passport.

"Our Boba is talented," Ivan said. "No one can make horilka like him."

"Or take as good care of a compote kitchen."

"He's the best cook ever," Ivan said, tapping his glass and inspecting its surface as if it were a poppy pod, putting his eye right up to it as Boris did when assessing a pod's ripeness. "He deserves a better future."

"Absolutely."

"If Tatiana Fedorova takes up his case, she'll need help."

"What kind of help?"

"Your aunt could teach Boba how to read and take him out in public to show him how to ride on a tram car and how to pay for things in a store. The authorities must be convinced that my brother can take care of himself. If your aunt or mother were made his guardian, Boba could move in with them."

"Is that the price of the passport?" I asked in surprise. "Of course they'll agree. All you have to do is ask. What do you need me for?"

Ivan paused as he pulled the lid from a tin of caviar. I settled for a pickle. You hadn't noticed the change in my diet yet, and maybe you thought that I'd cut down on smoking to prevent signs of aging in my skin. I allowed myself a few glasses of bubbly from time to time, so refusing cognac didn't draw attention. I realized I'd placed my hand on my stomach. I moved it away.

"Just in case," Ivan finally said. "So this is a trade, not a gift. No one owes anyone."

I laughed. Ivan was right. This was the fairest way to handle things. As long as I was with you, my family wouldn't need to worry. And what if you and I didn't exist? What then? After the Orange Revolution, the civil service had been revamped, but many of them were in debt after paying hundreds of thousands of euros for their posts; they were as hungry for additional income as the politicians were for voters' favor. You'd told me that poppy cultivation had been slated for enhanced monitoring as expected and that big operations were already being organized. I'd expected the newly opened drug hotline to be jammed with calls from jealous neighbors. The denunciations would send my mother, my aunt, and Boris to jail if they didn't have a support network. Even without the authorities, competitors and ordinary addicts would be a threat. Because of this plan for Boris, my mother and my aunt would be like family to Ivan.

"Are you ready?" Ivan asked.

"For what?"

"To be a Finnish citizen."

At which Ivan removed a stack of passports from his inside breast pocket.

"I think Ruslana Toivonen fits you. And one of these is her mother. Or someone who could be Ruslana's mother."

Instinctively I fumbled for a pack of cigarettes and managed to get one lit before I realized what I was doing. Once again, Ivan was one step ahead. When I'd agreed to our arrangement, I hadn't realized my betrayal could put my mother at risk. I only grasped that later. Now I wouldn't have to think about how to arrange travel documents that couldn't be traced. What I didn't know was whether she would come away. At least she would have the possibility, though. Wiping my nose with a napkin, I remembered the package I'd left on the side table, which contained a burner phone. I gave it to Ivan and asked him to hide it with the passport in my mother's chest of drawers.

"No need to tell my mother."

"Of course not," Ivan said with a nod. "My brother misses you, by the way. He's always asking about you."

"My mother still isn't talking about me?"

"She'll calm down. The Mongol may not be her ideal choice of son-in-law, but mothers always relent."

I said nothing. Ivan had accepted my panicked explanation for my mother's silent treatment without complaint, or at least he kept quiet out of tact.

"And that isn't all," Ivan said. "Three of these are for Ruslana Toivonen's children. You can use them as currency if you run short, and one of these could pass as Toivonen's husband."

I froze, taken aback.

"Even though your Mongol no doubt has his own collection, passports are like cars for men or shoes for women. You can never have too many. Especially ones that weren't purchased through a regular dealer."

For a moment I stared into Ivan's eyes, loving him more than any other member of my family ever. My hand touched my stomach again. Again, I moved it away. A person could dream.

"Well, aren't you going to say anything? As I'm sure you can guess, Ruslana Toivonen's husband was the most difficult. I think he's Korean." Ivan laughed and pushed the stack in front of me. Six passports. Six lives. Six possibilities.

I'd forgotten to stub out the cigarette I'd lit and decided to smoke the rest of it. One couldn't hurt. The nicotine had gone to my head like liquor for a first-time drinker. Ivan spooned more caviar into his mouth.

"I wanted to call you as soon as I got them, but I held off. No sense ruining a good surprise. Don't be shy. Pick them up. Try them out."

So I leafed through the passports, bending the pages and finding that they felt genuine. The stamps suggested active traveling. As a citizen of a member state of the European Union, Ruslana enjoyed all the benefits of a Finn, as did her children; the Toivonen family had visited Ruslana's homeland without visas every time. Despite the fact that she was younger than me, there were enough similarities in our appearances that I could handle the differences with a makeup brush. To my surprise, I found myself smiling, not because of the opportunities offered by these personal documents but because of Finland and the Finnish television I'd watched as a child. Even though that ancient magic had faded, and my Finnish skills had dwindled, the language would come back to me, unlike one that I didn't know at all. A new life as a new person was even taking on a certain attraction. I was tired of constantly having to develop contingency plans. Finland was a good option: clean nature and good schools, a safe environment for a child to grow up in.

But you wouldn't leave without Veles's permission. Unless you had to. Or would you leave if I asked, if no one knew where you were going or under what name, or who had bought the passports? Would you have left?

I'd imagined that knowing I was pregnant would bring a sense of relief—I had the insurance I'd wanted. But the opposite happened. I began to fret more, worrying for two now, and I realized that when the child was born, I would spend the rest of my life worrying about him. I wasn't sure whether I could stand that, so I sped up getting the passports. I only decided to keep the baby after receiving Ruslana Toivonen's family's papers, because they didn't just offer me the chance for a quick escape: they were full of good omens.

Ruslana had two daughters and a baby boy, and I was suddenly sure that I was expecting a son. Ruslana's baby was named Oleh. Olezhko. My Olezhko. That was a sign as well. I'd been browsing baby name generators and looked at all the derivations of my Christian name, even though I warned clients against doing that. Oleh traced back to the same Viking name—Helga—as my own name. Didn't that sound like the north was calling us? As if all of this had been written in the stars ages ago.

I remembered that, at this stage, a mother's emotional states were already being transmitted to the child, which was little more than an enormous heart. It beat between one hundred thirty and one hundred fifty beats per minute. There was something so miraculous about the heart always coming first, before the senses, before the mind, before the limbs, even before the ability to breathe. Everything else may have just begun to develop, but there was a heart beating beneath my own. Our son already had a name, and he already had a heart. I just didn't know whether it pulsed with fear, love, or hope.

Now I know that fear was eating away everything in its path, and that perhaps something toxic seeped into my amniotic fluid as I stared at Viktor's body lying in the back courtyard of our office.

V

The Fairy Godmother

HELSINKI
2016

A realization penetrated my dream, and I got up. I had to talk to Ivan. I hadn't in six years, and I knew it wasn't wise. But you were already on my trail. What did secrecy matter anymore? I had to know whether Ivan had heard anything. If anyone had, or if anyone could give me advice, it would be Ivan.

After running to buy a new burner phone from the convenience store down the street, I called the restaurant in Mykolaiv where Ivan often arranged meetings. The sleepy-sounding girl on the other end of the line repeated Ivan's name after me quickly and then stopped talking. I claimed I was Boris's botany teacher, left the new phone number, and began to make a list of the questions I needed to ask. I hoped that Ivan would remember me giving Boris a botanical encyclopedia. He did, and he called.

"I didn't think I'd ever hear from you again. Is that really you, Alyonka?"

Pausing to take a breath, I squeezed the receiver. Six years was an eternity, and no one had spoken my name in Russian with love in all that time. I sat down on the windowsill in the sunshine and tried to draw out the feeling of happiness.

"Your mom never had that look. That's why I knew you were okay."

"What look?"

"Broken," Ivan said. "But guess what I'm looking at right now. Tram line schedules accurate down to the minute. Just like in the West."

"We really have that now?" I asked in amazement. I didn't remember ever having seen a proper timetable anywhere in the country.

Ivan laughed. He'd been so shocked by the news himself that he'd driven to the stop to see it with his own eyes. Apparently, there were even route maps. In the background, I could hear the screeching of the rails and the hustle and bustle of everyday life. Children's laughter and the sweet sounds of spring in every noise made me press my fingers to the corners of my eyes.

"If you don't believe me, I'll send you a picture."

I looked at my paper. I wanted to continue the call as if this were any normal conversation between two old friends. For six years, I'd helped my friends best by not calling them, and I only picked up the phone to talk to my mother or the people whose floors I cleaned and who didn't know who I was. I remembered that Babusya Vilina had considered exile without the right to correspondence to be a death sentence. She'd been lucky and received letters and packages. She'd survived the camps. I'd survived six years without friends with the help of my mother's visits. Otherwise, I would have exposed myself, because I would have had to talk to someone, someone I knew and who knew me, someone who reminded me of who I used to be sometime long ago, someone with whom I could have had exactly this kind of conversation, and I realized that this might be my only phone call to a friend for years to come as well. Or my last call. That was why I had to keep asking Ivan questions. I wanted to know what it was like there and what the old man I could hear talking in the background was worried about, why he was talking about drivers and saying that they were afraid again. Ivan replied that the old man was concerned because he'd seen a few trams come in close succession. Ivan had showed him the schedule. There wasn't anything strange about it: two trams running on different routes had to come through this section of track.

"The old man didn't believe you, did he?" I said. "Despite the schedules."

"You're right."

I remembered the bus troikas, too. If one bus broke down and thieves or hooligans attacked it, the driver could get help from the other nearby buses. Ivan had gone to prison after being involved in just such a gang. The scheme wasn't particularly lucrative, and after becoming acquainted with some poppy experts behind bars, he'd taken a fall for an assault for some dealer. That was how he earned his place in the network, and after getting out, he had a job waiting for him. Ivan knew how to make a deal.

"But you didn't call to hear what's going on in the new Ukraine, am I right?"

"I'm sorry," I said. "I was never supposed to contact you. I promised myself."

A lighter clinked. Ivan drew smoke into his lungs, and the clamor of the tram stop receded. I knew that he was my friend, but I still doubted whether he would have called me back if it hadn't been for Boris. I banished the thought. I didn't want to sound desperate, so behind the tram stop I imagined a park with white acacia and poplar blooms. I thought of the chestnuts, the plane trees, the maples, the oaks, and all the other deciduous trees that were less common here than in Ukraine. I thought of the carefree feeling I'd once had. I thought about how I'd driven through Kyiv in my own car and sung along to Vopli Vidopliassova. I thought of your hand in mine and happy days, so that was what Ivan would hear in my voice. And I thought of the boy in the dog park.

"I think I'm in trouble again, my friend," I said, emphasizing the final word to touch Ivan's heart. "My identity has been blown, and they're on my trail again. But I have a tolerable life, given the circumstances. I can't leave. I can't run anymore."

"What options do you have?"

"That's why I called."

"Do you have anything to trade?"

"Someone is planning to kidnap Lada Kravets's children."

"You mean the widow? Do you have any evidence?"

"Maybe. Yes."

"Like what?"

"The person planning the kidnapping has secretly been taking pictures of Lada Kravets's kids and tracking their daily routines. I have the pictures, and I know who she is and where she can be found."

Ivan had returned to his car. I imagined him kissing St. Kuksha of Odesa and thinking. His tone had expressed cautious interest, but the silence continued for too long, and then he started the engine. The radio began playing in the background, and Ivan adjusted the air-conditioning. I could almost hear his decision taking shape, but not to my advantage. Maybe he didn't want anyone to realize how close our relationship was. That certainly wouldn't win him anything. And I didn't know whether he would gain anything by acting as a messenger.

"You don't need an intermediary," Ivan finally said. "You could call the Mongol yourself."

"He won't listen. Not after all of this."

"He understands deal making."

I squeezed the handset. I didn't want to end the call. I didn't want to resort to words I couldn't take back. I didn't want to remind Ivan that if I got caught, in my desperation I might also reveal his part in how Viktor's and his wife's information had fallen into the wrong hands and how their anonymity had been violated. Ivan had arranged it, not me.

"For old times' sake," I whispered as I scraped paint from the window frame. A beetle was trapped between the windowpanes. I had to forge ahead. Looking at my list, I asked, "Did you go see the pelicans return with Boris? And the cranes, did they come back to the same field?"

Ivan coughed and stopped the engine. The radio went quiet. In the background I heard a rustling; Ivan had removed something from his jacket pocket and told me what he was holding in his hand. It was a club card, which he kept as a memento in his wallet. It had allowed the cardholder to enjoy the services of President Yanukovych's residence even when the master of the house was not at home. I hadn't known that Ivan had made it so far.

"I met the Mongol there a couple of times."

I fumbled for my half-full cup of coffee and took some sips. My mouth was still dry, though. You and Ivan had drunk together, bowled together, fished together, and shot the president's deer together. And yet Ivan had not given me up. I had to remember that. We were in the same boat. I had no reason to panic. I asked Ivan to tell me everything, and he began by describing your meeting after Viktor's death.

You had gone to Ivan in Mykolaiv and asked who could have hidden me or helped me, and whether I had any relatives in Donetsk or Tallinn. Ivan was surprised. The connection to Donetsk was news to him. He had only known about my uncle in Tallinn.

"Did he buy that?" I asked dubiously.

"Did you ever talk to anyone about any relatives other than the ones in Tallinn? Why would I have heard anything else?"

"It isn't the same thing. You're family. Things went badly for us in Donetsk and you knew it."

"So badly that none of you ever breathed a word about the place afterward. I thought that was a strong enough hint. Or how stupid do you think I am?"

I said that Ivan must have given something up. It would be strange if a friend of mine pretended not to know anything about me. But Ivan claimed that he'd gotten off just that easily, which was a surprise to him as well. He didn't lose any fingers, not even a single nail, and according to him, your interrogation seemed more out of obligation than any real desire to dig up information. I realized I was sweating. Suddenly the sunshine flooding in from outside felt scorching. Still I remained on the windowsill, wondering whether you had really let everything go. I thought I understood what was going on. You could have prevented everything so easily if you had checked whether my father had really worked at a construction company in Mykolaiv and whether I had gone to Paris directly from Tallinn. You could have dug up my old schoolmates, who would have told you about our family's move to a backwater village in eastern Ukraine. If you had shone daylight on my first lie, my career as a coordinator would have been at an end. You hadn't gone to the trouble, though, because you had already done too many background checks during the Kravetses' obsessive child project, and your carelessness meant you bore a share of the blame. You were my unwitting co-conspirator, and no one who was guilty of something like that would be eager to rehash his mistakes. It was probably easier to claim I had been so clever, my murder plot so flawless, that I had even managed to fool you. I swallowed. You would never want to let me tell anyone how helpful you had been. Just as vulnerable to love as me. Just as seducible.

"By the way, you've developed quite a reputation. Conning the

Mongol isn't easy," Ivan said. "Maybe he didn't bother pressing me harder because it would have been embarrassing. His indifference made it seem like you didn't really matter."

Vanity. I hadn't known that you were so vain about your reputation.

"The others wondered why you didn't kill the whole lot of them while you were visiting their house like a proper daughter-in-law. No one would have been left to take revenge on you."

When you met Ivan later at the presidential villa, you acted like you were new acquaintances. There was no reference to me.

"I assume you understand you can never come back here," Ivan said. "There's no trade that could get you that. But I'll deliver your message."

We'd been sitting for more than an hour in a café located in front of the dog park children's school. While we'd been searching for a table on the patio, Daria had said something that wouldn't leave me alone. The way she remarked on the fact that children walked to school by themselves here was suspiciously enthusiastic.

"Get more coffee," Daria demanded.

Even though an hour remained until the bell that would end the school day, the approach of that moment made Daria tap the chair with her foot, and she gave no indication of tiring. As I went to the counter to order, I checked the people on the street for acquaintances or enemies. I placed the coffees on a tray, carried them back to Daria, and sat back down in my wall seat. My legs ached. I'd spent the morning showing Daria places from Aino's life. I'd suggested the tour myself, lying and saying that I had the day off. Some of the places were made up, and some were real, like the parents' offices and the pet store. And the school.

"I've started to learn Finnish, by the way," she said and pulled a grammar book out of her handbag. "Should we practice?"

I took the book, which looked new. Daria leaned in and started reciting sample phrases, too smoothly for a beginner. Occasionally she looked at me, seeking approval of her pronunciation.

"Are you intending to stay here long enough that this is really necessary?"

"We have to have a common language."

"We?"

"Aino and me, of course. Who else?"

Daria looked at me as if I were stupid. Maybe I was. My vague presentiments were proving true. The previous evening, I'd done some searching online related to children in the areas where I remembered Daria's former clients living. One incident had caught my attention: an unknown woman had tried to kidnap a child from a playground in a town in Germany. The assailant had been identified as a foreigner, and the newspaper had published a picture of her taken on the phone of a passerby. Anyone who could identify the woman was asked to contact the police. It was obviously Daria. She intended to abduct one of her old client's children and play house. Why couldn't she have chosen someone other than Aino? Or did she think it was easier to kidnap a child here than in other countries? I stared at the asphalt under our feet. It was as flat as the surface of a cake in a confectioner's window, but the ground under my feet was moving as if I were on a train.

"Are you listening?" Daria asked. "You were supposed to correct my mistakes."

So I began repeating the words from the textbook and occasionally made up my own examples. The message I had sent through Ivan was a bid for time. A bullet to my forehead wouldn't be an option if you wanted to hear all the details of the secret photography of Lada Kravets's children. You would have to talk to me. To sit with me for a moment. To look me in the eyes. As I thought of your gaze, I was no longer sure whether the pictures of the Kravets kids would be enough evidence of the danger Daria posed, let alone the news article from Germany, or whether you would grant me a visit based on them. However, if they were enough and you began to suspect Daria, I would have a little more time. Maybe enough to be able to tell you what happened on the day Viktor died. Still, my word had little value. I needed more proof, fast. I had to get Daria to confess. I took a breath.

"How long were you planning Viktor's murder?"

I presented the question in Finnish, gaining confidence from the mere fact of having succeeded in saying it out loud. Daria didn't understand or played stupid. I repeated the words in Russian. The foot tapping on the chair stopped. Then she laughed.

"Was that supposed to be a joke?"

"Or was it an accident?" I asked. "Accidents happen. Can't we finally talk straight?"

"We're supposed to be practicing," Daria said and waved the textbook. "I don't have the energy for your stupid crap."

"Would you have preferred to take my life instead of Viktor's? If I were you, I would have," I said and for a moment was satisfied with my idea. Empathizing with a client's emotional state. But it didn't work.

"Have you gone nuts? What are you on about?"

Daria set the book down and looked at me as if she didn't understand a word I was saying. I hadn't been able to get her to shoot off her mouth the whole day despite all my coaxing. I'd turned on my recorder again at the counter, and it was still in my pocket documenting our pointless conversation. I wasn't going to get her to confess. She wouldn't admit to anything. She was made of sterner stuff than I'd hoped. She was a smooth enamel surface I couldn't get a grip on. I watched as she sampled her latte as if considering what it was missing, until she seemed to realize something.

"Wait . . . are you trying to pin the blame for your sins on me?"

"Don't start with me. I saw what you did."

Taking her by the wrist, I squeezed hard.

"What if I sent Ladka the pictures you took of her kid?" Daria asked. "Or Veles. Maybe even to him. Wouldn't the Man from Donetsk be the right address?"

"I didn't take them."

"Who will believe that?"

My grip on Daria broke. I shouldn't have called Ivan. I realized immediately what a mistake I had made. I was blamed for Viktor's death. Ivan had wondered why I hadn't killed all of the Kravetses. No one would have come after me then. The logic was flawless. I had a motive. If Daria carried out her threat, you would instantly think that my quest for vengeance was still ongoing, that I hadn't had my fill. I didn't have anything to prove that it was Daria who had taken the pictures, and if Daria got a chance to talk, she would claim that I was trying to set her up.

"Veles would send a whole army after you and your family," Daria said, her voice rising.

My hand looked like plaster frozen on the table. I searched for my fingerless gloves in my bag without finding them and ultimately shoved my hands between my thighs to warm them up. I couldn't get the conversation back in the right lane anymore.

"And guess what? It would serve you right."

Daria's phone rested next to her coffee cup. Our argument had made her forget the seraphic curls visible on the display. During our coffee, Daria had repeatedly looked at Aino's face, kissing the glass like an icon. But now the screen went dark, and she didn't notice as the anger took over and she began to recount the reasons why I should be hunted to the ends of the earth. Daria listed the names. The girls I had forgotten and the girls I had never met. The girls who had been injected with more hormones than they would have been in, say, London. Girls who got sick. Girls whose ovaries had been removed. Girls who had suffered complications or whose uteruses had been punctured accidentally. Girls who had returned to the infertility clinics, but not as donors, as clients. Girls whose well-being no one tracked once they had fallen out of the agency's catalogs. Daria had obviously been reading American propaganda sites. There were activists there for everything, and as if on cue she began to tell me about participating in a meeting for anonymous donors in New York. The number of her fellow victims had surprised Daria, as had how many of them came from Ukraine, Russia, Poland, Romania, the rest of Eastern Europe. Most had begun as donors in their home countries, and then after doing jobs abroad had stayed in America because the pay was better. Not everyone was doing well, and no one had health insurance. Some of the girls had only donated once but still got breast cancer that wasn't present in their families. That was a coincidence, I said. Daria snorted. There were too many cases for chance.

The students at the table next to us cast us long glances—you didn't need to speak the language to interpret Daria's tone. We were attracting the wrong kind of attention. I smiled at them apologetically. Startled, the group turned away. In my head, I thanked the Finns for their courtesy. The preaching began to dry out Daria's throat, so she finished her coffee and checked the time on her phone.

"I didn't understand why the hell you chose me for Viktor, until I realized that you simply didn't care. The Kravetses chose the prettiest face, and that happened to be me, and you didn't dare to tell them no."

"That's not what happened."

"That's enough of this nonsense. Aino is getting out of school soon," Daria said and stood up, knocking over the chair. "You aren't going to spoil this moment."

The other customers turned to look at us, and a passing woman stopped. My neighbor. Her face looked swollen, and her jacket was loose. Pregnant. Definitely pregnant. She raised her hand in greeting. I nodded and picked up Daria's chair. I'd gone too far. My phone was still recording, for nothing. I would try again later. I looked at Daria, whose lower lip was trembling. Taking her by the sleeve, I asked whether she wanted to hear something about Finnish primary education, about the subjects Aino was studying.

Daria sat back down.

"What are you supposed to know about that?"

"I know that Finland has the best school system in the world."

The children rushing from school to celebrate the weekend made Daria perk up. She seemed to forget our quarrel and trembled when she spotted Aino's blond head. Aino started running toward the dog park woman, who looked so athletic in her sand-colored spring jacket. So fit and healthy.

"What is that woman doing here?" Daria asked. "Isn't Aino supposed to walk home from school alone?"

"Maybe she got off work early."

Unconsciously I had taken Daria by the hand, and we watched Aino and her mother disappear into the crowd on the street like it was a dramatic thriller. I didn't like that Daria was referring to the dog park family's children by their first names. We were never supposed to call children by their real names too soon. Even so, Daria's habit began to wear off on me. I caught myself thinking of the girl as Aino and the boy as Väinö.

"I don't hate you. I've never hated you," Daria said. "And right now, I don't hate anyone but that woman."

And I hated her, too. I hated everything that she could give her children. I hated that she had a fat paycheck, new spring jackets, money for a hairdresser, and a father for her kids. I hated how she left empty bottles by the trash cans for people like me to pick up for the deposit, because she didn't need those pennies, and I hated how friends called her constantly and how she and her husband walked hand in hand. Anger united me with Daria for a moment, and Daria felt it.

"Did I sell my child? Did I really sell her?" she suddenly asked. "To that bitch?"

"Aino isn't your child."

Daria pulled her hand away.

"I thought you understood me. I can handle my business without you."

I didn't ask what she was talking about. I didn't need to. The family traditionally started their summer cottage season in the spring. I hadn't told Daria about that and wondered whether she knew where the family had spent the last few weekends. Abducting a child in the middle of the forest would be nothing. But she didn't know. Otherwise she would already be renting a car.

"I think the trip to school is the best option," Daria said. "We'll take Aino first thing in the morning, and you'll notify the teacher that she's sick. That way no one will notice her disappearance until the afternoon."

Daria stood up. She wanted to buy Aino some clothes, and she thought we could get the shopping done before it was time to go to the dog park. I pointed out that we should take a break from the park visits or we would attract too much attention. My objections didn't interest Daria. She simply didn't seem to be able to get enough of watching the family, and I wasn't sure whether that was a result of yearning or whether she was building up her anger against the parents whose happiness she intended to steal. Or maybe her certainty of their impending ruin gave her pleasure, and she was trying to get as much out of it as she could.

"Come on," she said and turned to look at me with the same smile on her face that she had given me after strangling Viktor. When she realized that I would be blamed for everything, there had been no limit to her triumph. Now the reason for the grin was different, though. I was on her leash, and she knew it.

All I could do was follow, and as I did, I connected what Ivan had said to what Daria was telling me now, and what was between the lines. Daria had threatened me with the idea that Veles's men would hunt me and my family to the ends of the earth. But why hadn't Veles done that after his son's death? Why hadn't the SUVs watched my aunt's house for longer? Why had Ivan only been interrogated for appearances, not in more detail or more than once? I had imagined that was because of you, but what if I had misinterpreted everything? Lada had personally supervised the investigation into Viktor's death. So Daria claimed. And what if Lada was the one who approved your careless inquiries? And what if she had even encouraged that approach? Did I have her to thank for everything? Lada Kravets didn't want anyone to do much digging. She had her reasons.

Maybe I just wanted to believe that you had let me go out of pity or mercy. Or love.

A group of teenagers had gathered in the park, and our usual bench was taken. That didn't bother Daria—she chose the stone steps next to the dog enclosure as our new lookout spot. I took off my jacket and sat on it. Personally, I avoided the place on Friday nights, when reading while everyone else was imbibing in the shade of the trees would seem odd. Daria's company didn't help us blend in. We didn't look like friends who had come here to have fun. We should have at least had a bottle of wine and a few beers, some credible reason for hanging around outdoors. Or a dog.

"I'd assumed you would be a little more helpful," Daria said as she sat down beside me. "I'm disappointed in you."

Deliberately misunderstanding, I apologized for not knowing the city's children's clothing stores better. The charity thrift store I'd suggested hadn't been good enough for her, so we'd been forced to go downtown in search of clothes for Aino. Amazingly, Daria had paid for them herself. She had money. Credit cards. Cash.

"Knock it off. How are these for motivation?"

Daria searched in her pocket for her phone. I averted my eyes from the pictures she brought up. I wondered whether she'd taken these photographs of your boss's grandchildren just in order to be able to tell the story she had threatened me with. That I was stalking them. Holy Mother of God, this bitch couldn't be that cunning.

"Ladka looks good, doesn't she? That bungling secretary doesn't look quite as lively, though. Did you hear what happened to her? I doubt they'll give you such a quick end."

Daria searched for a news report about an accident in a deserted building and shoved it in front of me. I saw the headline before looking away. A young woman had fallen through a hole in the floor of the Parus Hotel. I focused my gaze on Daria's finger and thought about you and me on the riverside promenade, about how the smell of halva wafting from the Oleina factory tempted my nose and a bouquet of flowers left on the balustrade was withering, but the roses in my hand were alive. The proud profile of the Parus had been to our left. The collapse of the Eastern Bloc and the end of the ruble had interrupted construction of what was meant to be an icon of Soviet glory, and despite many attempts, the hotel had never been completed. Since then, it had become a favorite of drunks and lovers. The views from the upper floors were undeniably stunning, and the façade was still beautiful. I had breathed in the scent of April rising from the ground. The warm weather attracted the same urban climbers to the hotel who also scaled the bridge cables. Spring along the Dnieper. That's what I missed.

For a moment I held my breath and then breathed in deeply and slowly.

"After your escape, they went through everything with a magnifying glass, and all sorts of things came out. For example, that the secretary had been gossiping about confidential customer information in her emails."

I shrugged. She had been an unskilled career climber. I didn't care about the secretary or that I had contributed to the events that had led to her death. Daria's voice dropped, her gaze remaining fixed on the road that led to the park as her grip on the paper bags containing Aino's outfits tightened. They would be coming soon.

"What happened to the secretary could happen to you. Do you really want your mother to read a news story like this about you? Haven't you already caused her enough pain?"

The cold of the stone steps was beginning to penetrate my bones, and I felt my legs going numb. I'd forced my mom to go back home so she wouldn't have to find my body. Obviously, that wasn't a sufficient precaution. She might still see things that were unfit for any mother's eyes. The tingling that had started with my fingers was spreading to my arms, and I looked for my fingerless gloves, again to no avail. I must have dropped them somewhere. Mom had knit asters into them, and I could have used those right now.

"But I won't tell anyone about you if you help. What do you say? Monday?"

For a moment, I pressed my hands to my face. The flight from Kyiv to Helsinki only took a couple of hours. Ivan must have called you already. Off the top of a tall building. Off a balcony. Wrapped in plastic in a landfill. Unless I had something of value. Something that Lada Kravets couldn't beat. Something that your boss couldn't overlook. Evidence. A confession.

Daria poked me.

"Hey, what do you say about Monday?"

"All right. And then what about after that? Where will you take her?"

"Home."

"To Ukraine? You don't have her passport."

"We could steal it."

"By breaking into their apartment? We can't do that."

"Aino is small. She'll fit in a car trunk. First, we can drive to Estonia and then through Latvia and Lithuania to the Polish border and home. Donbas has become a popular area for anyone who wants to avoid the authorities."

Daria was right. The arm of Finnish law enforcement would not extend to the Donetsk People's Republic. The plan wasn't bad. Crazy is what it was.

"Do you have enough money for all of that? Where are you going to get a car?"

Daria stared at a couple approaching the dog enclosure teaching a puppy to walk on a leash.

"Hey, should we get Aino a dachshund like that? Or the same kind they already have? Would that help Aino feel at home?"

The couple was exactly the kind that would have caught my attention in the past. They had a future, and it radiated from them. Instinctively, I extended my hand toward the puppy but then immediately drew it back. I'd considered getting a pet once I'd ascertained that Väinö and Aino's parents didn't recognize me. Getting to know the boy would have been easier with a dog. However, I knew that if the ground started to burn under my feet, I would have to leave, and I couldn't go on the run with an animal. Besides, I'd had a nightmare that reminded me why it was best not to have a dog, and now I was happy with my decision. You liked animals. You might not shoot a dog who was protecting his mistress. Someone else would. Or it would be put out on the street. Or would starve to death next to my body. Or would start nibbling on my cheeks.

But then Daria forgot her puppy dreams and straightened up. The family was approaching the park. Mother and father walked hand in hand. They were laughing at something, the boy shuffling along a couple of meters behind. The girl was carrying a May Day pinwheel. She was trying to spin it, without success. The boy snorted and said something. The girl waved the pinwheel a few more times, and the boy laughed. The girl began to cry. I didn't realize it until the bawling intensified.

"What happened?" Daria asked in alarm.

As the father comforted the girl, the mother turned irritably to the boy, who blushed and then got angry. Daria had stood up. The boy started marching along the street. The mother ran after him and began dragging him back. Mistake. The boy was too old for that. I tugged Daria by the arm. The family's internal friction was none of our concern. We couldn't show that we were interested in the bickering of strangers' children, but soon it attracted other people's attention as well, when the boy picked up a handful of sand and threw it in the girl's face. Daria gasped and took a step forward. The girl cried out and dropped the pinwheel, and the boy took off running. The mother wrapped her arms around the girl, but it didn't silence her. I didn't have time to do anything. Daria was faster. Rushing to the woman, she grabbed the girl away from her. The woman shrieked. The girl screamed. The dog began to bark. I stood up and began to creep toward the street. Now or never. The boy was skulking at the edge of the grass with his back to the park, prodding the asphalt with his toe.

"Sisters can be annoying sometimes," I whispered to him.

He heard and gave a sniff. My first and last conversation with him was completely different from what I'd imagined.

"Yeah. She is. Everything always revolves around her."

"That can't be true," I said, amazed that I could speak at all and how natural I sounded. "It's just that she's younger. You're as important as she is."

And even more important to me, but I didn't say that out loud.

"Look, it's always better to take your revenge quietly. Otherwise you get in trouble." The dog was still barking in the park, the girl was crying, and the father had raised his voice. I heard whispering as passersby turned their heads toward the sound and took out their phones. I pulled my sunglasses out of my pocket. An older woman who stopped on the street was sure that the mongrel had bitten the girl and asked if she should call the police. I nodded. That's exactly what had happened.

"Although I think the girl hit the dog first," I said. "Probably not the first time."

The boy glanced at me in astonishment. I smiled at him and started down the stairs to the street. I would have to walk normally. I could never return here again.

I found myself trudging along my home street toward my familiar building, not remembering how I had made it there from the park. I remembered the boy, my conversation with him, and how the few steps down to the road had felt as if I'd been pushed down from somewhere high. The stones of the steps had shifted, the asphalt had broken, the ground had disappeared from below me, and I had fallen. I had felt the same when I saw, through my office curtains, Viktor lying lifeless in the back courtyard of the agency. The seconds were endless, and the floor didn't materialize under my feet again until I understood that I had to flee without delay. At first, I didn't know how I would get out of the building. My office had only one door, which led into the corridor and the reception room. I heard people rushing around out there. My solution was the street-side window, and this plan got my blood circulating again. I tossed out my fur coat, my handbag, and my shoes before climbing after them, protecting my belly. After I hit the ground, I looked up. I saw the angel wings of the drapes flying in the draft but none of my pursuers. Ignoring the ankle I'd sprained in the jump, I walked into the middle of the road and stopped a battered oncoming car. I'd been so resourceful then. Of course, I had money and the backbone money imparted, along with the prestige of my position. But still. I didn't even ask the driver if he would take me to the airport. I just ordered him to do so and tossed a wad of cash onto the front seat. The vehicle took off immediately, and I wrapped my scarf around my ankle. Before I threw my phone away, I sent a short message to my mother and looked at the mute screen for a moment. I remember thinking that no one would dare to call a dead woman, and that's what I was now. I didn't understand what had happened at the office. Viktor had died, that much I realized, but that was all. Despite everything, I acted logically, finding that I'd prepared surprisingly well: in case of a sudden departure, I'd hidden a bag at the apartment of one of my little birds, and I ordered the driver to make a detour there.

The girl may have realized that something was wrong. Still she didn't ask any questions and left me to root through my suitcase, from which I retrieved boots to replace my high heels, and a new burner. I let it charge for a moment while I went to tell the driver that he would have to throw away the spare tire in the back seat. Because of the natural gas tank, my luggage wouldn't fit in the trunk. The man refused and seemed to be starting to doubt the profitability of the whole gig. I didn't give up. My ankle ached, my head hurt, and my escape was seeming like it might get bogged down by a spare tire. Something in it made me laugh, the absurdity of it all. However, I noticed the driver eyeing my wolf fur, and I whispered to him that his wife would look like a queen in it. He must have been thinking the same thing. That settled the matter, and the man tried harder to get everything to fit in the car, eventually managing it. During the delay, I had time to think about my flight in more detail and decided to head to Kyiv. You could close the Dnipro airport if you wanted. Maybe you had already done so. I promised the driver more dollars, and he didn't complain about the change of destination, even though he would have to drive through the night.

On the way, we stopped at a gas station, the same one you and I had visited together before my first meeting with Lada Kravets. Now I was there but in a car I wouldn't have touched before, which ran on natural gas and was saving my life. I listened to the tank fill, which sounded like the rumblings of hungry intestines, or no, it was a wheezing, and I covered my ears as I watched my surroundings. I saw the driver give the man filling the tank a reasonable tip, not in dollars, and after the driver left to get a bite to eat, I climbed out to stretch my legs. I saw that the car had been blessed, which I took as a good omen, and bent down to open my bag so I could change my wolf coat for my fox vest. I remembered that I had to eat because of Olezhko and followed the driver into the convenience store. There I found him waiting for his order at the counter, apparently calling his wife. His voice purred with satisfaction, and I guessed the wife was on the verge of learning about the gift he would be returning home with.

On the way back to the car, a pack of stray dogs loped toward me, after some food. I was about to throw a sandwich to them when one grabbed it right out of my hand. Startled, I jumped back, dropping the rest of my meal, and hid in the back seat. I didn't belong at this service station, not surrounded by mangy mutts and not in this natural gas–powered car. But no one seemed to pay any attention to me, nor to the car or the driver, and that was the main thing. I didn't cry. We were alive, Olezhko and I, and we still had a chance at a future. Everything wasn't over yet. Even so, that journey led to the loss of my son. My final journey home from the dog park would have the same result, even though the situation and the country were different.

But you don't care to hear about my escape. It doesn't interest you. You and Veles want Viktor's killer, and the only currency I have left is the identity of the perpetrator.

I've been considering for years how to tell you about the day Viktor died. You've heard lies from his widow and from Daria: neither of their stories is the truth. What is true is that all three of us were there. Before he drew his final breath, Viktor met with his wife, Daria, and me.

Everything was still fine at the point when Lada Kravets booked a time to discuss her next round of treatment. She made the appointment directly with me, announcing in a voice brimming with pride that she and her husband would be coming together. I immediately cleared my calendar and told the remodeling crew to keep away to ensure that the atmosphere in the office would be peaceful, because the new mother needed to be confident that the embryos stored in our nitrogen tank were safe, even though she wanted to do a fresh transfer again. I couldn't tell her I had no idea where the donor she worshiped was.

As the agreed time approached, my anxiety grew. I set out fruit, Swiss chocolate, napoleon pastries, and Lomonosov china. I did everything myself, because I needed small, simple tasks that didn't require concentration, and I was thinking about the heartbeat of the fetus growing inside of me. I rearranged the napkins again, straightened the saucers, mixed myself sugar water in a teacup, and cursed the fact that because of my condition I couldn't calm my nerves with anything stronger. However, I felt emboldened by the cobalt blue tea set my mother had given me. It was the only truly personal thing in my office, and the forget-me-not patterns on it reminded me of something I couldn't precisely describe. Maybe it was the time they came from, when acquiring each translucent piece of the set had required work at building and maintaining relationships. The lightness of the bone china in my hand made me stand up straighter: I'd made it far after all. I had a car, an apartment, a job, and my own credit cards. I had a man, and I had this heartbeat. I had a full place setting of life and a lot to lose. I didn't intend to lose any of it, though.

A few hours before the Kravetses arrived, you sent a message confirming that you would be returning to the city the following evening. You missed me, and I missed you. I still do. Mixing more sugar water, I considered what to wear when I went to meet you, and I absentmindedly browsed our list of clients, from which I intended to choose a couple of limited means. Many of our clients were short on money after having pumped their savings into our services, and I chose one of the most desperate examples to deliver to my boss the story I'd invented. They would claim that Daria had offered to donate to them for a reduced rate, and I would reward them with a few free rounds of treatment. To my boss I would lie that Daria had obtained the couple's contact information through my own carelessness. Admitting this small mistake would make my fabrication more believable. Aleksey would be dispatched to find Daria wherever she was hiding, and no one would believe her no matter how she tried to defend herself. It would be straight off the balcony. Off the top of a tall building. My worries would be over.

At precisely four o'clock, the secretary escorted the Kravetses into my office. Viktor and Lada could have been mistaken for newlyweds, sitting side by side with their thighs touching. The new mother had a glow in her cheeks. She was more feminine, her breasts full and her shirt open, her previous garden sorrel delicacy now gone. The scarf around her shoulders slipped repeatedly, and she didn't seem like she was trying to hide beneath it anymore. She carried her larger body with dignity, and the strength in her was something new.

Viktor complimented the remodel of my office. Soon the entire premises would be ready for sale.

"By the way, I paid a visit to our new space in the Menorah Center," I said. "It definitely leaves this place in the dust."

"Nice, isn't it?"

"Dazzling."

I felt lively movements in my womb. I forced a smile onto my face. Sometimes I got the impression that Olezhko wanted to run away. Maybe he did. I still hadn't told you about our son, but the risky months were behind me now, and I was just waiting for you to return to the city. I intended to reveal the news when we saw each other the next night.

In the middle of the meeting, the secretary knocked on the door, even though I'd forbidden her from interrupting. Irritated, I marched over to her, and she whispered in my ear that I had a visitor who had been trying to force her way into my office. Even the obvious anger on my face didn't make the secretary slink away.

"Go ahead and straighten it out," Viktor called. "We're not in any hurry."

As I followed the secretary into the kitchen, she finally whispered to me who it was. The news made me lean on the door frame for support. As I held on to it firmly, I looked at my hands, which momentarily reminded me of my mother, because the tips of my fingers had gone white.

"Does she know who's in my office right now?"

"I doubt it. At least I didn't tell her," said the secretary. "She probably came for her bonus. We haven't paid it yet."

Of course. That was it. Daria was finally broke. My fright turned to relief. I wouldn't have to set her up. Contrary to what I'd imagined, she wasn't above taking money. That could still work. The winter sun sprinkled holy oil into the room, and I felt like gathering it in my palm. I would forgive her for her stunt. I would be merciful because I could afford it now. I was going to survive this. We were really going to survive.

"Bring Daria into the kitchen. Ask the guard to help you and tell Daria that she has to wait or she won't get any money. Is that clear?"

As the secretary repeated my orders back, I watched her expression. She seemed to understand the instructions, so I sent her to the reception room. I didn't dare imagine what would happen if Daria caught even a glimpse of Viktor Kravets and recognized him as the son of the Man from Donetsk. But that wouldn't happen.

I returned to my office as if to a kingdom I had just recaptured, now able to return Lada Kravets's smile with an effortlessness I haven't felt since that day. She was waiting for me alone, because Viktor had gone out to smoke after receiving an important call. I nodded in approval of Lada's attempt to teach the new father to smoke outside for their child's sake, and I sat down on the chair that had transformed into my victor's podium. I felt as if I could bend fate with my fingers like an aluminum spoon.

Even though the back courtyard was fenced, sometimes a dog or a cat would get in, so I immediately thought of a stray dog when our tea was interrupted by a scream from outside followed by a clatter. I pinpointed the sound as coming from behind the building.

"What was that?"

Lada Kravets looked at me. Suddenly I shivered, and my legs felt like they were being filled with cement. I couldn't stop Lada from rushing to the window. After glancing out, she sprinted for the reception room, and a strange wailing came from her mouth, intensifying after she reached the back door. I heard her try to wrench it open. It was locked. Who would have locked it?

Slowly I stood. Before I could see what was happening outside, Lada Kravets crashed back into my room, shoving me out of the way and ripping the window open. I looked down. Tea had spilled on my dress. A cup with a forget-me-not motif was in shards on the floor. My hand was still in the same position as before, holding the cup that had fallen from it. My fingertips looked dead, like marble. Forcing them into a fist, I pushed aside the curtains wafting in the breeze and saw Lada Kravets, who had climbed out, slipping toward her husband where he lay on the ground. Daria was holding one of the electric cords that was usually hanging over the back door. There was blood on the snow. The concrete trash bin had fallen. If I was seeing right, there were stains on it as well. It seemed as if Viktor's head had been bashed against it. But it didn't just seem that way. It had happened.

Viktor wasn't moving.

Lada made her decision in an instant and grabbed Daria's shoulders, wrapping her arms around her. At first, I thought she was attacking Daria, until I heard her words ring out clearly—"catch the killer, catch the killer"—and the howl that followed. Lada Kravets pointed at me, and her howling seemed to increase her height. There was a steely quality to her voice. She looked like the Motherland Monument in Kyiv, her sword in one hand and her shield—Daria's head—in the other. The back door was finally open, and the guard rushed out from wherever he had been loafing as the people crowding into the courtyard tried to understand what had happened. All of them turned to stare in the same direction as Lada: at me. I was still leaning against the window frame, and my blood had stopped circulating. No one looked at Daria, who now seemed to wake up and smile. She was smiling at me, and that was what made me move.

Locking my office door, I kicked off my shoes. I had a few seconds. Someone would have to call an ambulance, examine Viktor, and then check on the condition of the women wailing outside. Only then would someone think to come after me. Opening the street-side window, I prepared to jump.

I remember every detail from that day, even the list of departing flights glowing on the screen of my new phone, the destination of each flight, and that all of them seemed impossible: all of the Ukrainian airlines that operated out of Kyiv were owned by Vekselberg, who was close to Viktor. Finally, I noticed the other airlines, but

I remember the despair when it felt like every road I turned onto seemed to be rising to block my way. After Daria arrived in Helsinki, I felt that again.

I should have realized earlier. Maybe my realization took time, because in Ukraine I'd become lulled into complacency by a life in which money grew on trees. In the natural gas–powered car, I grasped that my assets would melt away in an instant. So how had Daria and her whole family been able to hide for so long? They must have had help.

Suddenly I was certain what had happened.

That was why I hadn't found the Sokolovs.

That was why they had money to get away.

I had never been their target, Viktor had.

I recognized the genius of the plan. The men who had invaded Daria's home had turned her into a projectile that had slowly and surely flown toward Viktor. No one would question Daria's motives. She had reason to be angry based solely on her family background. But above all, she was a donor, and there were plenty of mentally disturbed donors. No one would suspect there was anything behind Viktor's death other than the emotional collapse of one woman who had lost her mind.

Without Lada, Daria would be in prison.

If you wait long enough to let me tell you who killed Viktor, you could look for the people who received the Kravetses' information. You could force Daria to describe the intruders. The Sokolovs must know something about them, because the family went underground with their help. You could track down the real enemy, the one who has been more cunning than all of us. Wouldn't your boss like that more than anything else? Wouldn't that be enough to buy my freedom?

I knocked on the door of Daria's hotel room. No answer. As I took from my pocket the key card I'd stolen, I couldn't guess what condition I would find her in, if she was even in her room. A couple of hours earlier I'd received an angry message from her wondering where I'd disappeared to after the park. She didn't mention the incident with Aino's parents or how it had ended. What if Daria had taken her own life? What if my problems were already solved? With my hand on the door handle, the possibility also flashed through my mind that you would be waiting for me surrounded by her musty towels and despair-stained wineglasses, and my chest ached as if the oak stake that had been pounded into it had shifted.

Daria had passed out in the wrinkled, twisted sheets and didn't stir when I poked her in the ribs. She was still alive, though. Restraining myself, I left the bag of clothing I'd brought her next to the bed and started collecting the empty bottles in the trash. They were the only clue to how she had taken the incident, and I decided to use the opportunity to my advantage. I was instantly as alert as a soldier. Even though I'd searched Daria's belongings before, I would do it again with fresh eyes, because now I knew more, and the time to find evidence was running out. At home I'd checked the passport Ivan had given me for you. It was still valid.

I began by counting the contents of Daria's purse and going

through her credit cards. I would steal all of it at the appropriate moment, which would help, but the suitcase lying open on the floor didn't offer anything interesting. The stickers from previous flights showed that Daria had been an active traveler on the budget airlines, and her international passport was full of stamps. At the bottom of the suitcase was a little sand, as if she'd carried shoes in it without protection, some bits of loose tobacco, and a battered bag of Semki sunflower seeds. Shaking a handful of them out, I crunched the seeds between my teeth as I moved to the desk. It was covered in new papers. A map of Helsinki had our morning route marked on it: the dog park, the family's home, the husband's and wife's offices, the children's school, the market hall, the corner store. The family's schedules were written on sheets of hotel notepaper, which also included the phone numbers of the school and teachers, as well as a series of numbers that looked like a door code. Maybe Daria had chosen Aino out of all those children because here she had an accomplice, one who knew the language. That might be the only reason she hadn't exposed me to the agency or the Kravetses. Daria's resentment toward me had been no secret.

Despite my hopes, I didn't find any maps of the Kravetses' daily routes, no handwritten notes, nothing that would prove that Daria had been stalking Lada Kravets's kids. Taking Daria's phone, I opened it with her thumb. The camera roll had been cleared except for pictures of Aino. I decided not to give up. Throwing the bag of sunflower seeds on the floor, I moved on to searching the bathroom. At the door, I held my breath. I wasn't used to the helter-skelter of odors Daria had created there. Everything was somehow sticky. Dust and hair were stuck to the threads of bottlecaps. From the cosmetics bag, which was stippled with dots of toothpaste and stank of valerian, protruded a brush that smelled of dust and whose bristles were covered in blond hair. Toothpaste had dried around the handle of the toothbrush, and its head was splayed into a fan. Next to the washbasin were plastic bags turned opaque from use, which based on the smell contained chaga tea. Strong painkillers, including Pentalgin. Maybe back problems? Some donors developed those. However, given her physical condition, Daria's movement seemed effortless. Cancer? Maybe. That happened, too.

As I searched the cosmetics bag, my fingers hit something sticky. I pulled my hand back. A ball of bee glue rolled out and fell onto the floor. I washed one of the glasses with soap and drank some tap water. The ball was still staring at me from the floor. My family believed in the power of bee glue, too—my mother and my aunt ground it up and prescribed it for every ailment—but here it just looked like excrement. It was in the wrong place. I was in the wrong place. So was my life. None of Daria's things were helping me forward.

Picking up the waxy ball with a paper tissue, I dropped it in the trash but managed to knock the brush onto the floor. I picked blond hairs out of it. Short hairs. Very short. Daria's hair was dark now. Returning to the room, I tugged on Daria's bob. It didn't move, but I still saw the mesh of her wig cap. I didn't dare tug anymore. The wig was genuine, and it was good quality, Indian. Maybe she really was taking the Pentalgin for cancer. If that was the case, she only had herself to blame. For not stopping in time. For continuing. Stupid girls kept donating. Stupid and greedy girls. Daria's possible health problems didn't bother me. Something just didn't add up, though. If she had the money to spend thousands of euros on a wig to disguise herself, why was she dressing practically like a bag lady? Then I realized. She didn't care what she squandered her money on. She didn't care about her sale value. She didn't have anyone she needed to look good for. She was alone, like me. I felt this realization for a moment, like the pinch of a pair of tweezers, no more than that.

As I shoved the brush back in the bag, I noticed another bottle buried in the corner. Prenatal vitamins. I glanced at the expiration date. Despite the worn look of the bottle, it was quite fresh. Half of the pills had been taken. I pulled out a thermometer I also saw in the bag and then finally dumped all the contents onto the table. In the middle of the pile of junk, I saw the corner of a ripped cardboard box. I would have recognized the logo on it anywhere. Had Daria been pregnant? Had she wanted a baby and not been able to have one? Had that driven her to start chasing her clients?

"How did you get in?"

Daria had woken up and was stretching on the bed.

"You dropped one of your key cards on the steps in the park," I said and started cleaning the floor with the cleaning rags I'd brought from home. She swallowed my lie or at least didn't have time to think about it properly, because it reminded her of Aino's clothes. She'd forgotten them in the park because of the incident. Tomorrow we would have to go shopping again.

"I'm really glad you came." Daria sighed and watched me work for a while. "Isn't that a job for the staff?"

"We can't leave any trace of ourselves here."

"That's wise," Daria admitted and then started chattering about Aino as if they had a common future.

The "Do Not Disturb" sign was still hanging on the door, and for a moment I was annoyed. There were few people in the world I wanted to be cleaning up after less than Daria. The faucet dripped in the bathroom like a clock. I tried to shut my ears and thought about the dog park boy's life as I cleaned. Finally, I sat down on the edge of the bed and looked at Daria for a few seconds. She seemed to be sober enough now. I would have to take the clothes she'd been wearing during the scuffle and throw them away. I pulled at Daria's blouse until she agreed to turn over and wriggle out of the sleeves. There was a clinking sound. From the shirt pocket a ring rolled onto the floor, narrow and gold. I grabbed it before Daria. The epiphany cleared my head. The vitamins, the thermometer, the pregnancy test box. Had I guessed right? If she couldn't have children, it wasn't our fault. It was her own fault, at that weight, with that lifestyle. She knew the factors that affected fertility just as well as the rest of us.

"When did he leave you?" I asked.

"Did you know that in England there are a lot of couples who fund their own treatment by donating? They give other people baby after baby, but their own nurseries stay empty."

Daria held out her hand. She wanted the ring. I dropped it into her palm. Why the hell had I called Ivan? I could have handled this situation without anyone's help. Couples who split up because of infertility were a familiar problem to me, and I knew better than anyone what strings to pull. I no longer wondered at Daria's state. Maybe it was endometriosis, maybe a burned-out ovary, maybe something else. Or maybe the problem was with the guy. If I could figure out the background, I could nurse Daria back into shape. Then she would leave Aino and Väinö alone to focus on her own family. Then I remembered that I could never return to the dog park.

"Haven't you ever wondered what your life would be like with your son?" Daria asked.

"Excuse me?"

"We can take him, too, and run away together, the four of us. What do you say?"

I wanted to say yes. Oh, how I wanted to do that, and for a moment I considered it. But I knew how Donbas would look in the eyes of a boy who had grown up in Finland.

I checked on social media whether the dog park woman had written anything about the incident. There were no new updates. Instead, a picture from a couple of days earlier caught my eye. I showed it on my phone to Daria, who was huddled next to the hotel bed. The woman had shared with her followers some memories from the previous summer as an aperitif for the upcoming vacation season. A typical shot of vacation toes: sugar-waxed legs, pedicured nails, heels rasped soft, and nearby a book to signal intellectualism.

"Look," I said. "This is what we have to shoot for. You have to pull yourself together and set an example for Aino."

Daria turned her gaze away. I zoomed in on the heel in the picture. No cracks, no dry skin, not the slightest sign of hardening, no rubbing from the wrong size shoes. The wrinkles in the soles were so shallow that sand wouldn't even stick in them.

I took hold of Daria's head and forcefully turned it toward the mirror. It was the only object in her room Daria hadn't managed to dirty, and it was merciless. Her eyelids were swollen to overripe fruit, and discharge leaked from the corners of her eyes to dry in her lashes. I saw from her expression that she understood what I meant: she looked like a vagrant.

"You're attracting attention, too much attention. Your behavior in the park only made carrying out your plan more difficult. How do you think you're going to get Aino to go with you after this? She'll be afraid of you."

The mockery that had played across Daria's face ever since our meeting disappeared. I understood. Aino wasn't sitting in her lap, she was with that woman.

"You knew what kind of a bitch she is, and you still made me believe she would be a wonderful mother."

"Isn't she? The children have a dog, hobbies, and expensive clothes. Their parents make good money. What more do you want? A spaceship to the moon?"

Daria wrinkled her nose. I didn't want to think about how she must have looked walking through the hotel lobby to the elevators. The scene caused by a confused Slavic woman in the dog park would be in the tabloid headlines within hours, and someone might recognize Daria from pictures readers sent in. The obscenities she'd shouted would be enough to tell the family that their attacker wasn't a local, and by now the parents must have figured out who Daria was. Recovering from the shock would take a while, and it would take time to straighten things out with the police, defend the dog, comfort the children, and cry. But eventually they would realize what the incident in the park meant.

"We have to get out of here," I said. "That woman is going to press charges against you for assault."

"She doesn't know who I am."

"Of course she does."

Daria snorted. Nothing seemed to shake her belief in her own invisibility. Then she thought of something and perked up.

"Should we take Aino to your place first?"

To my place. Of course. At home I could squeeze a confession out of Daria and record it. And after that? What then? You said once that a human skull is like an eggshell that can be cracked with anything that fits in the hand. I'll make everything easy for you.

I told Daria to make a shopping list while I finished the cleaning. This idea seemed to excite her, and she started looking on social media for hints about Aino's favorite foods. After finding a picture of the father shopping for groceries, she showed it to me. The man was a good dad, just as I had assured Daria, and progressive in many ways. He handled most of the shopping, enjoyed cooking, and did laundry. This didn't affect Daria's plans.

"Should we get something for your son, too?"

Daria had repeatedly pulled this same trick, and every time I felt like hitting her. I didn't, though. A pillow. That would be quick. But not yet, not here.

"Have you ever seen them fighting?" she asked, still browsing pictures of the parents.

"Never."

"Good actors," she quipped.

I didn't argue. Although the air-conditioning tried its best, I could still smell vomit, bile, and liquor, partying without the party. But things were beginning to look reasonable. There were people banging around in the neighboring room. Closet hangers hit the wall. They had a child, who started running around, and a baby, who would be crying soon. I didn't know how Daria would react to that. Probably not well.

"Why the hell did you keep donating?" I burst out.

"For money. Why else?" Daria asked in confusion. "I stopped when I had enough for a good life. Aino won't have to worry about anything with me."

I raised my hands in a declaration of truce. I couldn't argue. I had to seem like a sympathetic helper, with whom Daria would leave the hotel chatting cheerfully. Telling her to change into clean clothes, I pulled out the shirts and skirts I'd brought for her. They weren't anything special, but they were fine.

"Find something that fits. So Aino won't be embarrassed."

That worked, and Daria dragged herself into the bathroom carrying the bundle of clothes. Obediently she climbed into the shower. That was something. The baby in the next room burst out crying, and I glanced at my watch. My wrist was empty. I patted my pocket. My mother's watch wasn't there either. I shoved my hand down into the pocket and found a hole at the bottom. It could have fallen out anywhere. Hopefully just not in this room. I felt around the floor with my hands and checked the spaces between the pillows, with no luck. Maybe it was gone forever. I would never wind it again, and for some reason that thought made my determination falter for a moment.

"What do you think?"

Daria had sneaked in from the bathroom without me noticing. She was holding her hands in front of her as if she were naked and trying to cover herself. I looked her up and down, taking my time. This was my moment to give back some small part of the agony she had caused me. But I held back.

"Well?"

"Good."

A smile lit up Daria's face, and she ventured a look in the mirror.

"Shall we go?"

Reaching out, I took the packet of biscuits and dropped it in the shopping basket. It was surprisingly easy and felt good. Next to me another immigrant was bent down, inspecting the selection on the bottom shelf, but I stood tall and straight like the dog park woman. For a fleeting moment, I was almost a local, a person who didn't have to crouch in front of the cheaper products on the lower shelf. I calculated it in my head: the price of that feeling was about a euro. That was how much I was willing to pay for a few seconds of feeling like I was Väinö's mother. I left the package in my basket. Next to it a bag of semolina thudded down.

"I want to make Aino semolina pudding," Daria said.

"She may not like it."

"We'll try. It was one of my favorites when I was little, and children like to make food with their parents. What else might Aino want?"

I smiled indulgently at Daria's silly plans.

"Ice cream?"

Daria headed toward the freezers.

"What do you think? Will these do?"

A proper meal had done Daria good, as had the new clothes. She had accepted the vitamins I'd purchased her. She still wouldn't talk about the man who had left her, but even so, this was a promising start, and Daria was following my directions. If my plan succeeded, the dog park family would be able to keep everything they had, their life in which they didn't have to kowtow to anyone even when they were grocery shopping. Next week Väinö would come to this same supermarket with his parents. His father would push the loaded cart, and his mother would select a snack cracker packet from this same shelf. None of them would have any inkling of the disaster they had just avoided because I had saved their paradise and their son's childhood. I would be his secret fairy godmother.

"One of our doctors moved to Finland to work," I said. "He could examine you. We can go to him together. Right now."

"I've had enough of white coats."

"That's what clients always say when they come to us, and some of them were genuinely desperate cases, some over sixty years old. Just think, you're only—"

"Chocolate, or something else?" Daria asked, marching toward the candy aisle.

I would have taken the offer immediately, if I had been Daria. But I wasn't. Still I intended to try my best. Sometimes the tiniest crack was enough. If she became convinced that I could get her pregnant, she would do anything for that, and then she'd be ready to pay the price I asked in return: a confession. I just had to ignite the spark and blow on it.

I followed Daria, who was assembling a new selection of delicacies. She didn't even glance at the cheaper stacks of chocolate bars on the bottom shelf. At the checkout counters, the workers were reading bar codes at Friday evening speeds. The constant beeping hurt my head. On the other side of a shelf, a toddler, who should have been asleep already, was crying. But I let Daria do what she wanted and didn't rush her.

"You're going to be a great mother," I said.

Daria smiled a smile that people would have been willing to pay to see. After I got the confession out of her, I would do what I had to, taking her money and her credit cards, and leaving her to rot in my apartment. She would never threaten my child's life again. That was all I would ever be able to give my son.

I smelled you as soon as I opened the door. I sensed you from the air, which was electrified like the night before a big party, and I knew before I even stepped into the kitchen that there would be a cup on the counter that I hadn't left. Sometimes you used old KGB tricks. You thought they were more effective and cheaper than gunmetal. Apparently, the message always hit home.

I was too late.

"It's smaller than I imagined," Daria said, walking straight into the bedroom. "Don't you have a living room?"

The view from my window made her click her tongue, and her palm left a greasy mark on the glass. I thought the view was passable. Daria clearly disagreed. Her judgmental gaze picked at my furniture, my drapes, and my rugs, and every gesture as she poked at my belongings like trash communicated how well she remembered what I had once had. On any other day I would have been embarrassed.

"We need to figure out how we're going to make Aino feel at home here. Or should we get a car tomorrow and start driving right away on Monday? Aino won't be able to sleep in a place like this."

"I'll make tea," I said and left Daria to criticize my home. I closed my eyes when I stepped over the kitchen threshold. I was afraid of making a mistake, as I had done so many times. So many times I had thought a passing stranger was you. I searched for you in crowds, packed buses, and train stations. A familiar scent of aftershave could instantly carry me back in time, and I took fright whenever I thought I recognized your back. I was always disappointed when I realized I was mistaken. Now I wasn't. The cup was on the counter. I pressed my lips to its side. The inside smelled of weak brewed coffee. I touched the coffee maker, which still felt warm. I breathed in deeply and glanced out the window, where the glow of the setting sun was just disappearing. Nothing out of the ordinary was visible. You weren't standing on the street. There weren't any strange men hanging around. The cars in the parking lot all belonged to building residents. But you had been in my home. You were close. You were already here. With the cup in my hand, I sat on the sill and opened the window. I looked at my fingers. No tingling. The tips were rosy. I was breathing calmly. I was not afraid. I would not run. I would not scream. I would just take deep, slow breaths.

Glossary

BABUSYA, BABUSHKA: A grandmother or an old woman in Ukrainian and Russian, respectively.

BOLONKA: A Russian dog breed of the bichon family.

BUKHANKA: The UAZ-452 off-road van produced by Ulyanovsk Automobile Plant (UAZ) in the USSR.

BURATINO: The main character of *The Golden Key; or, The Adventures of Buratino* (1936), by Aleksey Tolstoy, a derivative of Pinocchio.

BURYAT: The largest indigenous group in Siberia, closely related to other Mongol peoples. Many Buryats were forced to migrate to Ukraine during the Stalinist period.

COMPOTE: Also *kompot* or "Polish" heroin. A low-grade heroin prepared from poppy straw, the leftover parts of the opium poppy after the higher-grade opium latex has been removed from the seedpods.

DACHA: A country house or cottage used as a vacation home.

DNIPRO: Previously Dnipropetrovsk, the fourth-largest city in Ukraine, located in the central-eastern part of the country along the Dnieper River. Formerly a key industrial area for the Soviet nuclear and space industries, which resulted in the city being closed off from the rest of Ukraine. Dnipro remains a power center in Ukraine and home to many oligarchs.

DONBAS: The easternmost region of Ukraine and location of the ongoing Donbas War between Ukraine and Russia-backed separatists. Consists of the Donetsk and Luhansk Oblasts.

DONETSK: An industrial city in eastern Ukraine and center of the breakaway Donetsk People's Republic. Also within the Donetsk Oblast.

GOPNIK: An urban youth gang member in a Slavic former Soviet Republic. Stereotypically associated with wearing track suits and squatting in groups.

HELSINKI: The capital of Finland, an EU member country. A major hub for Western access to the Soviet Union during the Cold War and popular destination for tourists and expatriates from post-Soviet states like Ukraine.

HOLODOMOR: The "Terror Famine" of 1932–1933 in which the Soviet Union starved to death millions of Ukrainians. Despite Ukraine being the "breadbasket" of the country, Soviet collective farming practices resulted in severe crop shortages. Less desirable ethnic groups were assigned insufficient rations, resulting in widespread disease and even cannibalism. These events are now recognized as an intentional, politically motivated genocide intended to quell Ukrainian resistance to collectivization and erase Ukrainian culture. As Ukrainian speakers were dying of famine in the countryside, Stalin was exporting Ukrainian grain to the West.

HORILKA: A Ukrainian term for a wide variety of distilled alcoholic beverages, including home-distilled moonshine.

KHRUSHCHYOVKA: A three-to-five-storied block of flats built of concrete panels or bricks. This style of building originated during the Khrushchev era of the 1960s. Because many were intended as temporary housing with a building lifespan of only twenty-five years, they are notorious for their poor construction.

KOMSOMOL: The All-Union Leninist Young Communist League was the political youth organization in the Soviet Union. Younger children would first join the Little Octobrists before graduating to the Young Pioneers and then Komsomol before being old enough to join the Communist Party of the Soviet Union.

KOPANKA: An illegal coal mine.

KRAVCHUCHKA: A light, two-wheeled, collapsible handcart.

KYIV: The capital and most populous city of Ukraine, located on the Dnieper River in north-central Ukraine. Often also spelled Kiev, although since this derives from Russian rather than Ukrainian, the choice has become political.

LUHANSK: A city in eastern Ukraine and administrative center of the Luhansk Oblast.

MAIDAN REVOLUTION: Also known as the Revolution of Dignity or Euromaidan Revolution (2013–2014). A series of protests and violent clashes with riot police focused in the central square of Kyiv (Maidan Nezalezhnosti, literally "Independence Square") after President Viktor Yanukovych refused to enter into an agreement that would have deepened ties with Europe. Clashes with police resulted in more than one hundred deaths, which led to parliament relieving Yanukovych of the presidency and his flight to Russia. Subsequent events led to the Russian annexation of Crimea and the secession of the Donetsk People's Republic.

MARSHRUTKA: A shared taxi that follows a set route. Usually a minibus.

MORS: An uncarbonated fruit drink made from berries. Often jam reconstituted with hot water.

MYKOLAIV OBLAST: An area in south-central Ukraine bordering the Black Sea.

NOMENKLATURA: Influential posts reserved for Communist Party appointees in the Soviet Union; also, the people who filled them.

OBLAST: A geographic administrative subdivision of Ukraine. Similar to a province or county.

ODESA: A port city and center of tourism on the Black Sea. The third-largest city in Ukraine.

OKROSHKA: A cold soup consisting of raw vegetables such as cucumbers, plus boiled potatoes, eggs, meat, and kvass or sour cream.

ORANGE REVOLUTION: A series of nationwide protests in 2004–2005 following a rigged presidential run-off election. The win by Russian-backed candidate Viktor Yanukovych was ultimately invalidated by the Ukrainian Supreme Court. A second runoff, which international monitors declared free and fair, was won by the more democratically minded Viktor Yushchenko. Orange was the color of Yushchenko's campaign.

PARTY OF REGIONS: The pro-Russia party of Viktor Yanukovych. Although it was the largest party in Ukraine from 2006 to 2014, involvement of key party members on the losing side of the 2014 Revolution of Dignity and their subsequent flight to Russia, as well as separatist activity in the eastern part of Ukraine, have led to its gradual disintegration.

PATRIARCH OF MOSCOW: The Patriarch of Moscow and All Rus' is the official title of the Russian Orthodox bishop of Moscow.

PETROVSKY: Grigory Ivanovich Petrovsky was a Ukrainian Soviet politician who participated in many of the founding events of the USSR. He has been identified as one of the main administrative perpetrators of the Holodomor.

PROPISKA: An internal passport in the Soviet Union. One's "papers."

QUARK: A soured-milk dairy product common in Europe. Similar to fromage blanc, paneer, queso fresco, or labneh.

RADONITSA: A Russian Orthodox commemoration of the dead observed on the second Tuesday or second Monday of Easter.

SALO: Cured slabs of pork fatback similar to pork belly but with little or no meat. Unrendered lard.

SARAJISHVILI: A Georgian producer of brandy, cognac, and vodka.

SMETANA: An Eastern European soured-cream dairy product similar to crème fraîche.

SNIZHNE: A minor city and coal mining center to the east of Donetsk near the Russian border. The likely site for the launching of the missile that downed Malaysia Airlines Flight 17 in 2014.

STAKHANOV, ALEKSEY: Aleksey Grigoryevich Stakhanov was a Russian Soviet miner used by the regime as a poster boy in a campaign to increase worker output in the Soviet Union. In 1970, he was awarded the honorary title of Hero of Socialist Labor.

SYRNYKY: Fried quark (cheese) pancakes.

TALLINN: The capital of Estonia, located on the Baltic Sea approximately eighty kilometers due south of Helsinki. While Estonia is now a member of the European Union and NATO, it was occupied from 1940 to 1991, first by the Soviets (1940–41), then the Nazis (1941–44), and then the Soviets again (1944–91) as a Soviet Socialist Republic. During the Soviet period, Moscow carried out a campaign of mass deportation and murder against ethnic Estonians.

UKRAINKA, LESYA: A Ukrainian author, poet, and translator born in

1871, who is widely credited with dismantling prejudices imposed by Russian narratives of Ukrainian culture as provincial and backward.

VATNIK: A political slur for someone who follows Kremlin propaganda. Based on an Internet meme introduced in 2001 by Anton Chadskiy.

VATRUSHKA: An Eastern European ring pastry often filled with quark and raisins.

VYSHYVANKA: An embroidered shirt common in Ukrainian national costumes.

A NOTE ABOUT THE AUTHOR

Sofi Oksanen is a Finnish-Estonian novelist and playwright.
She has received numerous prizes for her work, including the
Swedish Academy Nordic Prize, the Prix Femina, the Budapest
Grand Prize, the European Book Prize, and the Nordic Council
Literature Prize. She lives in Helsinki.

Translated from the Finnish by Owen F. Witesman

A NOTE ON THE TYPE

This book was set in Scala, a typeface designed by the Dutch designer Martin Majoor (b. 1960) in 1988 and released by the FontFont foundry in 1990. While designed as a fully modern family of fonts containing both a serif and a sans serif alphabet, Scala retains many refinements normally associated with traditional fonts.

Typeset by Scribe,
Philadelphia, Pennsylvania

Printed and bound by Sheridan Minnesota,
a CJK Group Company,
Brainerd, Minnesota

Designed by Soonyoung Kwon